LYLE CHRISTIE

This book is dedicated to all who have faced

adversity in terms of health, work, relationships,

or even a really disgusting public restroom, and

now desperately need a FUCKING literary, if not

FUCKING literal, break from this crazy thing we call

life.

•Please excuse the use of profanity and be warned
that there will be more to follow, as well as some
traditional humor, bathroom humor, and a goodly
amount of spirited sexual encounters, though it
will all be delivered tastefully and with the intent of
conveying a deep, rewarding, and soulful catharsis.

BOOK SIX IN THE

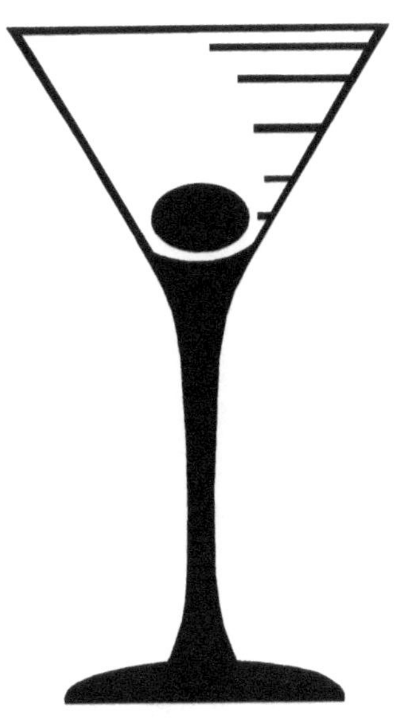

MANTASY SERIES

CHAPTER ONE: PROLOGUE
Prelude to a Kiss of Death

The man looking at himself in the bathroom mirror was named Rudy Mahelona, and he was feeling a bit apprehensive as he got ready to work a private party at the Kuilimi Bay Resort on Oahu. Normally, he would be excited, as these kinds of events tended to be packed with an abundance of beautiful young female tourists, and, more often than not, Rudy would end up in one of their beds. He was the kind of guy that the young women traveling to the islands dreamed of meeting, as he was charming and, more importantly, particularly good looking with his tan skin, square jaw, and tall athletic frame. Unfortunately for Rudy, he had a second job tonight, and, while it paid a lot more than his primary job, it came with some consequences. Rudy, while being a typical young college student and part-time model, also had a criminal record and had served six months in Halawa Prison for burglary. It could have been a lot worse, for the original charges included second degree assault for drugging his victims with rohypnol, which came with the potential of serving up to ten years in prison. Rudy was lucky, however, in that he had been a starving student with no criminal record, and, because he didn't rape or physically assault the people he robbed, his charges were plea bargained down to felony burglary.

Rudy, however, didn't actually see himself as a criminal, and having grown up particularly poor in Waianae, he saw himself more as a Hawaiian version of Robin Hood. His victims had been wealthy tourists with more money than they could ever spend, and he thought that taking their cash and a few of their trinkets was fair payment for them being able to enjoy his island home. Needless to say, the authorities felt differently, and, while they cut Rudy a break with the plea deal, he still had a felony on his record, which all but ended any serious job prospects, regardless of the fact he was about to graduate from college.

So, when the man in the business suit came knocking on his door a week ago with an unusual offer, Rudy couldn't help but take the job. He didn't learn the man's name or his actual profession, but he suspected he was some kind of lawyer or government bureaucrat, because he had serious money, and, more importantly, serious connections. He was willing to pay Rudy fifty thousand dollars and have his felony expunged from his record, but, ironically, Rudy needed to revert to his old ways for one night. Rudy agreed, though, now that the actual day was here, he couldn't help but wonder if he was making a huge mistake. It had been hard to get the job at the resort, and he didn't want to jeopardize his only income, but fifty grand and a clean slate was just too good to pass up. Still, the man was pretty intimidating, and there was something about him that scared the shit out of Rudy.

He finished up by brushing his teeth then headed down to his white Ford Fiesta and plugged in his phone and brought up a playlist. Listening to music always relaxed him, and, now, with the music blasting, he headed off to the resort, which resided up on the northern end of the island. From the H1 he turned onto the H2, and it eventually became a smaller two lane highway that wound along the shore and led to the entrance of the resort. Instead of going out to the main hotel, he made a left and pulled into the parking lot of the golf course. There, he waited until a white Chevy Malibu pulled up and parked alongside him, at which point, Rudy got out of his car and took a seat in the other vehicle.

The man in the drivers seat slid on a pair of rubber gloves then reached down and pulled a manilla envelope out from under the seat.

"Aren't you being a little overly cautious?" Rudy asked.

The man smiled.

"You can never be overly cautious, nor should you ever take advice from the guy who got caught and went to prison," he responded.

Rudy shrugged in response.

The man reached into the envelope and brought out the contents. First was the fifty thousand dollars in cash, which the man showed to Rudy before placing it back in the envelope. Next, he pulled out two vials filled with clear liquid.

"As you can see, this vial has a *P* written on the side of it because it's for the party. The other vial has a *B* on it, because it's for the bar," he said, before placing them back in the envelope.

"Now, here is your target for the bar," the man said, as he pulled out his phone and brought up a picture.

Rudy scrutinized the picture.

"She will be there shortly after the party, which should be around nine."

"Are you going to text it to me?"

"No, put it to memory."

Rudy continued looking for a bit longer then nodded.

"OK, I've got it."

"Good, now, considering your past, I'm pretty sure you should be able to get this done properly."

"Yeah, I can get it done no problem, but how soon will my record be cleared?"

"If you don't fuck up this job tonight, then by the middle of this coming week, you'll no longer be a convicted felon, and you'll be fifty thousand dollars richer."

Rudy couldn't help but smile as he pondered that thought.

"All right then, assuming everything goes to plan, we'll never be seeing each other again, and you can go live happily ever after. If there is a problem, we'll definitely be seeing each other again—and you won't be living happily ever after. Got it?"

The man hadn't used this kind of language on their first meeting, and it wasn't doing much to quell Rudy's nagging unease. Still, this was his shot to get his life back, so he tried to appear confident.

"Don't worry, I've got this," Rudy said.

"Good."

There was a moment of awkward silence, then Rudy climbed out and took a seat in his own vehicle and nodded before starting his engine and driving off to the resort. The man in the Malibu waited for a moment before pulling out and following him at a safe distance. After Rudy parked, the man in the Malibu watched him as he put the contents of the envelope in his backpack then walked into the resort's employee entrance. At that point the man in the Malibu smiled and pulled out his phone and dialed a number. Two rings later, his call was answered.

"Well?" the other person asked.

"Rudy's a little nervous, but I put the fear of God into him, so I'm confident he'll get the job done."

"Good, then everything is in motion, and, by tomorrow morning, it will be clear that John Matheson will never be the president of the United States."

CHAPTER TWO
Rehearsal Disaster

The Eskimos had a hundred words for snow while I had only about eleven for diarrhea. Beyond its official medical name, were a number of more colorful euphemisms such as the scudders, the runs, the squirts, Montezuma's revenge, the green apple splatters, rocket ass, the Havana omelet, liquid fire, the trots, or quite simply—the shits, and any one of these colorful descriptions could have accurately described the building pressure I was feeling in my abdomen at this particular moment in time. I wiped the sweat from my forehead then gazed at my watch. It was currently seven thirty-six p.m. local time on a beautiful Saturday evening on the island of Oahu, and I was attending a luau to celebrate the engagement of two very close friends. One of the people in question just happened to be John Matheson, the current vice president of the United States, while the other was Jessica Thurman—a friend and former client of sorts. Coincidentally, I was also the reason that these two found each other, and I was at last seeing the fruits of my labors rewarded with holy matrimony. Love was in the air, but so too were the tepid odors of a public restroom, which, for the moment, was thankfully empty.

My stomach grumbled, and I looked down at the toilet before me and felt a great deal of trepidation, which was basically pointless, because I was only moments away from painting a masterpiece in my pants. I desperately needed to spill my innards but feared and abhorred public restrooms, so this was my only salvation—my only hope of containing the situation. Mind you, I was in a fine hotel, and the bathroom was relatively clean, though other problems were now plaguing my mind—namely the infrared sensor that automatically flushed the toilet. While it made sure that all manner of waste was sent on its way in a timely manner, its sensitivity often caused it to flush prematurely. That might occur when someone leaned to one side to wipe his or her ass, and it would bring about an accidental flush, with the unfortunate result being a fine toilet water mist spraying all over the dumper's backside, cock, and balls—assuming that the person was, like me, a male of the species. So, right now, I needed to think rationally and call upon my unique expertise forged by a lifetime in special operations, clandestine services, and, more recently, my work as a private investigator.

The sensor was infrared and therefore triggered by a heat signature, and it would activate the moment it sensed a warm body then wait until that person left before flushing. That was the theory, anyway. The reality was very different, however, but I refused to be beaten by my little porcelain and chrome nemesis. Looking around the stall, I realized that my only tools were my wits, some seat covers, and a roll of toilet paper. Bingo! I had an idea. I needed to defeat the sensor, which could be achieved by simply blocking it with a swath of toilet paper. Simple, stupid, and effective. I tore off a good sized piece, folded it in half, and laid it over the sensor, thereby placating the mechanical monster. I grabbed a sanitary toilet seat cover, placed it on the seat, and dropped down, ready to do battle with my most fearsome of enemies—the public toilet. I wasn't happy, but I would survive.

I tried to relax by taking a minute to reflect on my current situation, and my thoughts turned to trying to figure out what in the hell I had eaten to end up in this particular predicament. I was also fairly buzzed, but the alcohol was at least giving me the temporary bravado I needed to endure this indignity. I needed to keep my eye on the prize, which meant shitting and getting the hell out of here before someone else came in. It seemed like a good plan until the door opened, and in walked a number of strangers. Worse still, they were obviously drunk and talking incessantly. The only thing worse than a public restroom was a crowded public restroom, and now I had to contend with both. Wait a minute—the voices were female. What in the hell were these women doing in the men's room Goddammit?

Two of the offenders walked into the adjoining stalls and literally trapped me in the middle, though their conversation was almost worse than their proximity. The woman to my right was complaining that her husband was a little light in the foreplay department, and that he considered taking off his pants to be more than enough to get her in the mood. The woman on my left, however, was more concerned with the odor emanating from her husband's balls, and if he truly wanted that blowjob, then he might try showering before bed. What in the hell did I do to deserve this? At least I could take a small amount of solace in knowing that it couldn't possibly get any worse. Wrong again. The woman to my right started peeing then let loose a long, terrible fart followed by a massive movement which, judging by the sound, was mostly liquid fire.

"Jesus, Sharon! I guess you had the poi as well," the woman to my left said.

"I did. You think that's what upset our stomachs?"

"I think so. I got a funny feeling after I finished mine."

"Well, it's a luau, so I figured I should try a little of everything."

Wait a minute. There was only one luau going on at the hotel, and it was a private affair, which meant these women were guests at the same party. Wonderful—there would be witnesses to my indignity. Suddenly the woman to my left started peeing and, like her friend, let loose a fart, though the gas soon turned into solid, or, more accurately, liquid, though it was hard to tell from the sound alone. A sharp pain in my stomach made me remember the fact that I too had a similar feeling after finishing my poi—the feeling in fact, which led me in here.

"Nice one, Liz! I see the poi is having an effect."

"Wow, it is, and it doesn't smell good."

She was, of course, correct in her assessment. It did not smell good, and in fact it smelled like shit—if you could make shit smell even worse than shit. Sharon, the woman to my right, let loose another salvo, and her odors started heading my way and mixing with Liz's to create a vortex of unpleasantness so vile that I was on the verge of retching. Stifling the tiniest of gags, I accidentally let loose a pretty good sized fart that quickly turned to liquid and rocketed from my ass and hit the waters of my toilet with the intensity of a fire hose. Sweet mother of God, I had unleashed the Kraken, and soon another wave of waste was leaving my body in an expeditious and noisy manner.

"I guess someone else had the poi as well," Liz, the woman to my left, said, with a small chuckle.

Here it was—the entirety of my life's nightmares all rolled into one horrific moment. I looked around my small cell of torment and wondered how I might get free of this particular predicament—this veritable poi predicament, but nothing came to mind. I was trapped, and the only actual way out would probably entail suicide, though there would be no dignity in that either. I had to soldier on, hold true to myself, and muster through this time of great despair.

Another explosion rocked my backside, and I prayed the toilet could endure this much punishment and not crumble and send me and my waste spilling onto the floor. Sharon responded in kind, as did Liz, and the air grew so thick with fecal scent that my eyes were beginning to water. The door to the bathroom opened yet again, and more people filed in, probably because of the very same food item that Liz, Sharon, and I had eaten. By their voices, I realized that they too were women, and I had to wonder why in the hell they kept coming into the men's room. Perhaps the women's was out of order, or the universe had just randomly decided it was time to decimate any sense of self-esteem that remained after high school.

A great pain came to my lower abdomen, and I let out what was easily the largest fart thus far, and the entire bathroom became deathly quiet.

"Are you still alive in there?" Liz asked.

"Yeah, are you OK?" Sharon added.

I stayed quiet, hoping to hide the fact that I was a rooster in the presence of so many hens.

"Hello? You OK?"

Fuck. They weren't going to give up, so I needed to say something—anything, just to get them to leave me alone. I mustered my best female voice and spoke.

"Oh, I'm fine, thank you. My tummy is just a little upset from the poi."

A familiar voice came from over by the sink.

"Wait a minute. I know that voice. Excuse me. What is your name?" the woman asked as she walked closer.

"Um, Natalie," I said, now fully recognizing the woman's voice.

The woman in question was Lux Vonde, a close friend, former lover, and the woman I recently rescued from a place called Soft Taco Island.

"Oh my God, Finn! What in the hell are you doing in the ladies room?" Lux asked.

"I'm Natalie."

"No you're not. I know damn well who you are. Now, what the hell are you doing in here?"

"Oh for fuck's sake. What the hell are you doing in here?" I asked in my normal voice, only to receive a round of gasps from the other ladies.

"It's the women's room, jackass."

"No it's not. I looked very carefully at the outside sign before coming in here."

"The one on the actual door or the one on the outer wall?"

"The one on the outer wall."

"There's your problem. The outer one is wrong. I know because I almost walked into the men's room by mistake."

Lux was obviously fucking with me, though it was odd that there were so many women in here. Either way, I was mortified beyond belief and would very likely go take a flyer off the nearest cliff when this was over. That would have to wait, however, as I had one final salvo to deliver unto the bowl, and this one might actually take me airborne. I waited until I could hold it no longer, then released what felt like the mother lode. It was probably ten percent solid, ten percent liquid, and eighty percent pure rocket fuel, and it came out so quickly that it actually hurt. When it finally came to an end, my butthole slammed closed the way an angry woman slammed a door after a particularly heated argument, and now I was sitting in the stillness of the moment, with the room utterly quiet and everyone waiting to see if I had somehow survived.

"Finn? Are you OK?"

I stayed quiet, as I was still in shock at the violence of my anus.

"Finn, speak to me goddammit!"

"I'm OK," I said, somberly.

"Oh, thank God. I thought that last one might have killed you," Lux said.

"Only my self-esteem."

My body was completely empty, and I was suddenly feeling a lot better, though I desperately craved a shower. I reached down and grabbed the end of the toilet paper, and the roller clattered as I unfurled an adequate amount then wiped my ass. I repeated the procedure, and, after four good passes, stood and pulled up my pants. The last step was to remove the small piece of toilet paper from the sensor and watch as the toilet drained the muddy mess, which thankfully left the bowl without a clog. I made sure my fly was up, then I exited the stall, only to have the women around me erupt with applause. I walked to the sinks, pumped out four dollops of soap, then placed my hands under the faucet and washed them vigorously—all the while trying my best to remain stoic in the face of such adversity. The applause died down, and I dried my hands and moved towards the door but paused and turned back around to face the curious group of onlookers, as I felt that I should deliver some parting words.

"Ladies, it's at times like this that you really reflect and feel thankful for everything and everyone in your life, and if there's one thing we all learned this evening, it's that shit happens, and, more importantly, diarrhea happens even faster, so to that end, I have two simple parting words—moist towelettes," I said, as I exited the bathroom and felt the beginning of tears forming in my eyes.

I checked the sign directly outside the door and saw that Lux had been correct, and I was indeed in the wrong bathroom. I continued farther and discovered that the outer sign was reversed—probably just a minor oversight from when they built the hotel. Fuck, I really needed to be a lot more careful in the future. Of course, I wasn't exactly bringing my A game after all the fucking rum drinks at the luau. Lux appeared a minute later and smiled and tried to hold back her laughter.

"No need to say it. I see now that you were correct about the signs," I said.

Lux leaned forward and looked closely at my face.

"Are you crying?" she asked.

"No."

"You are! Oh, my God—I'm sorry. I forget how sensitive you are about going potty," she said, reaching out and hugging me, which pressed her large breasts against me and almost made me forget the last, and perhaps worst, ten minutes of my life.

"I'm going to go kill myself now."

"Oh, don't be such a pussy. That was actually pretty funny."

"Yeah, to everyone else."

"Relax, no one gives a shit that you just took a shit."

"That shit was biblical."

"True, but you have to come to terms with the fact that everyone and everything on earth shits. It's perfectly natural."

Several women exited the bathroom, and all of them giggled as they passed by me. The tall, pretty brunette at the back of the pack paused and reached over and patted me on the back.

"Epic shit, my friend. I'll never forget you," she said.

When they were gone, I turned back to Lux.

"You were saying," I said.

"Just forget about it. What's done is done. Let's get back to the party—and, I think it's a good idea to abstain from any more poi."

"Very funny. I take it that you didn't have any?"

"Hell no, too starchy, and it has the consistency of semen."

"You don't like semen?"

She smiled.

"Oh, I like it well enough—just not on my plate at a luau."

"Good to know."

CHAPTER THREE

Dante's Eleventh Ring of Hell: the Luau

Lux and I returned to the luau just as John was just wrapping up his speech, and I segued to the bar in hopes of grabbing a cocktail to dull the mental anguish left over from my nightmarish bathroom experience. Just ahead, and standing between two barstools, I spied Jessica, the bride to be. She was facing away from me, but there was no mistaking her red dress and fine figure, and I was guessing she had been driven to drink by her soon to be husband's smug speech. As I arrived, I reached out and gently slapped her backside. This would have been a gross social faux pas and a veritable assault in the age of the Me Too movement, but for us it had become a wacky way to scare the shit out of each other—especially in her case, as she tended to deliver her blows with a lot more force and surprise. I kept it fun and light, and, as my hand met her butt cheek through the thin fabric, she abruptly turned around and looked rather shocked, which made perfect sense—as it wasn't Jessica. Instead it was a complete stranger, and now I was the one looking shocked.

"Oh my God. I'm so sorry! I thought you were someone else."

"Really? And who might that be?" she asked, smiling.

The woman before me, like Jessica, was very beautiful and in truth, very similar in appearance. Both had green eyes, brown hair, lovely smooth skin, and annoyingly were both wearing body hugging red dresses this evening.

"The bride. You look identical from behind."

"I take that as a compliment. She has a nice ass."

"Indeed, and so too do you."

"Well thank you. I suppose that since you've already had your hand on my ass, we should properly introduce ourselves. I'm Melissa Williams—and you are?"

"Tag Finn," I said, holding out my hand.

"Ah, of course, the best man. I've heard a lot about you. It's very nice to finally meet you."

"So, do you know the bride or the groom?"

"The groom. My father is Frank Williams."

"Oh shit. Please don't tell him I smacked your ass."

Now, I recognized Melissa, although I was pretty sure she used to have blond, rather than light brown, hair. We'd never met in person, but I'd seen her in pictures with her famous father Frank Williams. He was a big time power player in Washington as well as a close friend of the Matheson family, and it was a commonly held belief that no one became president of the United States unless he personally approved them.

"Oh, my dad is actually a big teddy bear," Melissa said.

"Well, I can't help but imagine he's the kind of teddy bear that would use his claws to remove the testicles of the idiot who accidentally smacked his daughter's ass."

"Don't worry, this exchange will be our little secret."

"Thanks, I appreciate keeping my testicles firmly attached to my body. Well, it was nice meeting you, but I had better get back to John, as he can be very needy at major social events," I said.

"Don't I know it."

"I take it you two are good friends."

"Hello! Our parents have been best friends since before we were born, so we pretty much grew up together."

"Oh yeah—duh—sorry, I'm just a little slow at the moment—probably from all the booze," I said, leaving out the fact that my diminished capacity was actually due to my bathroom nightmare.

"Hey, no need to be sorry, as you're the guy who saved John's ass in Afghanistan."

"As well as the rest of his body."

"No doubt, so thanks for doing that. We were all very grateful to get him back."

"It was my pleasure."

"Well, it was nice meeting you, Tag. Perhaps we could get a drink later, and if all goes well, you could grab my ass on purpose."

"Sounds good," I said, slightly shocked, but definitely interested.

I reached the main table at the exact same time as John, though he was welcomed with a kiss from Jessica as he took a seat beside his lovely bride to be. I too took a seat then found myself inadvertently having a look around the party. Weddings were a fascinating affair, and, as a social psychology major, I found the whole seating arrangement to be an interesting phenomena—one which told a very accurate tale of the guest's importance to the bride and groom. The closer you were to the main table, the more important you were. Get an outer fringe table and it was likely that you were probably there to help pad the gift registry or were a semi-forgotten relative that the parents included out of guilt. Such wasn't the case for me, however, as I was sitting at ground zero directly beside his majesty the vice president while around me sat his father Senator Matheson, Daniel Vandenberg, and of course the infamous Frank Williams. His daughter Melissa was obviously at another table, where her ass was currently safe from any more unwarranted assaults from me. Also at our table were some more friends—namely, Lux and her husband Cornelius Wallace, or, as I called him, Corn. Corn also happened to be the Deputy Director of the CIA and a man capable of consuming vast amounts of alcohol and food. John, who had just finished speaking with Jessica, looked over at me and scowled.

"Goddammit, Finn! You missed my speech!"

"Was it any good?"

"Yeah, it was fucking good! In fact, it was a fucking tear jerker, and I even mentioned how you saved my life in Afghanistan."

"Sorry, but I had a little poi predicament."

"Dude, you seriously ate the poi? Nobody eats the poi! It tastes like semen."

"And how would you know what semen tastes like?"

"Blowback."

"The force is obviously strong in your balls."

A voice came through the PA system and brought everyone's attention back to the stage, where our luau hostess was standing. She was a lovely Asian woman wearing the obligatory flower print dress, and she was informing us that it was finally time for the show. First on the stage were a number of scantily dressed men who performed with flaming spears and did a number of cool tricks that involved spinning and tossing them into the air. Next, were the beautiful female hula dancers, and they performed an exquisite synchronized dance that entailed rapidly shaking their hips, though, unfortunately, any residual shaking of their breasts was covered up by their coconut bikini tops. The war drums eventually came to an end, and all but two of the dancers exited the stage. They were soon joined by two of the male fire dancers as well as the hostess, who stepped up to her microphone and smiled at the crowd as she spoke.

"Let's have a round of applause for our dancers!" she said, excitedly.

Everyone in the crowd clapped enthusiastically, and the hostess had to wait few seconds for the noise to die down.

"All right, everyone. It's officially time for a little audience participation. Do we have any volunteers out there who would like to come up and learn how to do the Hula?" she asked, as she looked out at the audience.

I was starting to get a bad feeling, as I always seemed to get singled out during events like this, and as I'd already had more than enough public shaming tonight, I decided it might be a good time to make a run for the bar. The four dancers left the stage and started moving through the audience to find their victims, so I stood up and started moving quickly through the tables. Only a few steps into my swift retreat, a spot light shined on me, and I froze in terror. Survival came down to action, so I set off at a brisk walking pace, though the fucking spot light stayed right on me. Still, I kept moving in the hopes they'd give up, but those hopes were dashed when I heard the hostess. Fuck.

"Excuse me, sir, but you can't leave now. We're just getting started!"

I smiled, waved, then decided to try and keep moving, but, before I could get out of range, one of the dancers was on me. She was a lovely young twentysomething island girl, and she had quite a pair of coconuts on her chest. She wrapped her arm through mine and, despite my protestations, started dragging me towards the stage. Sweet mother of God—let this just be a bad dream. A second later we were passing the main table, and John smiled smugly at me.

"Oh, look who was lucky enough to get picked," he said.

"Yeah, and guess who else is coming with me," I responded, as I grabbed hold of his arm.

John tried to resist, but I made enough of a scene that the other hula dancer was on him! Ha! Fuck that fucker! If I had to do it then so did he! It was his party after all. She managed to drag him out of his chair, then all four of us climbed onto the stage to join the two other victims. There were now four of us, and we were all staring out into the audience, and not a single one of us looked too happy. These kinds of public events were always humiliating—kind of like when your friends sang happy birthday at a restaurant. Nobody enjoyed it, but we continued to do it to each other year after year, thereby perpetuating an endless cycle of misery. I looked over at John and saw that he was putting on a pretty good fake smile, though I suppose it wasn't too grand a feat when you took into account that he was a politician and made that kind of face for a living.

"All right now, everyone, our dancers are going to show you what to do, so just follow along and give it your best shot!" the hostess said.

The music started, and the four dancers began showing us the moves, but, just as I was starting to get into the swing of things, a woman sitting at a nearby table called out to me.

"You go, shitter! Shake those hips!"

Oh my God. It was the tall pretty brunette from my bathroom escapade, and, annoyingly, her entire table full of women started clapping and cheering me on. I looked more closely at the group and realized that I recognized pretty much all of them as having been witnesses to my embarrassing little incident. Lovely. When it rained, it poured. Had fate been merciful, I would have never seen any of them again, but now I had been offered up to them like a sacrificial lamb.

"What's with that table full of fans?" John asked.

"Oh, they're just my bathroom buddies."

"Excuse me?"

"Long story."

"I bet it has a funny ending."

"Yeah, like the Titanic."

The hostess was speaking again, and all attention turned to her, which also included my dance partner, and I thought about using the moment to make a bold break for freedom. Before I could act, however, the hostess pointed towards us, and my opportunity was gone. I therefore soldiered on and continued to move my hips and hands in sync with my lovely partner. The music eventually changed, and our partners turned to face us in what appeared to be the beginning a Hawaiian hula version of dirty dancing. I was all for a little grinding but not on a stage for all to see, least of all in front of my bathroom buddies, who were still yelling and cheering. My attractive dance partner was directly in front of me, and her coconuts were dancing before my eyes. She could certainly move her body and especially her hips, which were now rubbing up against my man parts and causing an unwanted stirring. The girl smiled and winked as she brought her hands up over my shoulders then down my sides where she reached around and took firm hold of my backside. At that point, she increased the intensity of her grinding, and sure enough I was in the opening stages of a boner. What the hell did I do wrong in life to reach this moment of karmic backlash? The music thankfully came to an end, and my partner leaned in and kissed me on the lips, before glancing down at my groin and smiling as she moved beside me. Everyone formed into a line facing the audience, except for John, who was staring at me with a stupid smile on his face.

"What?" I asked.

"Strange—my dance partner didn't kiss me."

"Yeah, because your filthy lips have been on every ass in Washington."

"Oh that's an exaggeration. It's no more than ninety-eight percent at best."

"Well, that's still plenty of ass."

The hostess led us in a group bow, then everyone was thankfully free to return to their seats. I adjusted my man parts to conceal my budding erection as best as possible then departed the stage and unfortunately had to pass my table full of fans.

"Nice boner, shitter. Why don't you swing by my room after you take a shower," the tall pretty brunette from earlier said.

My self-esteem was officially at an all time low as I trudged over and sat back down at the main table and chugged the remainder of my cocktail in hopes of dulling the pain of the combined horror of the evening's events. John was also back, and he was looking at me with a wicked smile on his face.

"You ready for the bachelor party?" he asked.

"Maybe—as long as we aren't doing the whole stripper thing."

"Oh, does it bring up sad memories of Fiona?"

John was referring to a woman that I had dated a couple months back. She was a sociology major turned Playboy Playmate, who I met when I rescued her from a sinking boat just off of Alcatraz Island in the San Francisco Bay. Technically she wasn't a stripper, but she had been doing a one time stripping gig at a sea-born bachelor party to raise money for her brother's legal defense fund, as he had been unjustly accused of sedition for providing international aid relief to an impoverished population. Unfortunately for Fiona and everyone else on the boat, the drunk shitbag of a host accidentally ran his father's yacht onto some rocks, and then he and his bachelor boys climbed into the only lifeboat and headed off to finish the party ashore. My friend and I rescued the girls, and Fiona ended up becoming a pro bono client as well as my next serious love interest. After helping her with her brother, we managed to have a rather nice, though short, relationship that lasted until she set off to save the world with her brother's international relief agency Globo-Care.

"Maybe a little—but I'm just not a fan of the whole stripper thing. I think it's ridiculous to pay a woman to wiggle her boobs in your face."

"You don't like having boobs in your face?"

"I love having boobs in my face. I just don't like to pay for the privilege."

"Fucking communist. Strippers need to earn a living too."

"I have nothing against them earning a living. I just don't want to be a part of it."

CHAPTER FOUR
Bachelor Party

At least that's what I believed until I was at the bachelor party two hours later, where I was sitting off to the side of the festivities and drinking another cocktail as I tried to mind my own business. I had thus far done my best to avoid the debauchery, but my efforts were thwarted when a beautiful woman appeared before my eyes. She was probably in her late twenties or even early thirties, though it was hard to be sure, as she was of mixed ethnicity, probably European and some kind of Pacific Islander—perhaps Hawaiian. She had the requisite lovely tan skin, but her hair was long and blond, and her figure was awe inspiring with her nicely toned muscular legs and arms and flat stomach that all hinted she might be some kind of fitness model. Of course, I was able to discern all these details, as she was dressed in a revealing sparkly blue police officer costume that consisted of handcuffs, a short skirt, and a matching bikini style top that was barely able to contain her rather full breasts.

"How about a lap dance?" she asked.

"No thanks, but you might want to ask the groom over there," I said.

"Seriously? You're not interested?" she said, as she grabbed her breasts and wiggled them enticingly together.

"You're certainly interesting—it's just that I'm not really the stripper type."

"Which is?"

"I don't know—lonely or desperate?"

"True. I don't imagine that you're either lonely or desperate, but it doesn't mean you can't have a little fun."

"Honestly, this hotel convention center room is about as close as I've ever gotten to a strip club."

"You've never been to a strip club?"

"Nope."

She eyed me curiously.

"I thought all guys went to strip clubs," she said.

"All guys except me, apparently."

"Well, good for you. I actually respect that."

"Doesn't that go against your job philosophy?"

"This isn't my main job. It's more of a sideline to help make the house payment."

"Really? Well, I imagine you could easily make a hell of a living at it."

"Thank you," she said.

"So, what's your name?" I asked.

"Viola."

"Is that your stripper name?"

"It sure is. What's your name?"

"Well, if we're using faux names, you can call me Bartholomew."

"Funny, you don't look like a Bartholomew."

"Why do you say that?"

"You're too attractive."

"I officially feel sorry for anyone named Bartholomew now, but, seriously—you really won't tell me your actual name?" I asked.

"Sorry, that's confidential."

"And I suppose you can't tell me your other job either?"

"Nope. I like to keep that life separate. So, Bartholomew, how about a lap dance?"

"I would love one, but, honestly, I don't have any cash on me, so you'd do much better with one of the other groomsmen."

"Don't worry, this one's on the house."

She straddled me then unsnapped her top and dropped it on the floor, and I gazed in wonder at her full un-augmented breasts, which were a testament to the female form. They were firm and round, and her large pokey nipples seemed particularly hard in spite of the lack of cold or stimulation.

"Sweet Aphrodite's yabbos! You're not going to poke out one of my eyes are you?"

"I'll be careful."

She pulled out a pair of handcuffs, and I felt a brief moment of nostalgia. Wonderful—yet another reminder of my ex Fiona. We'd had a particularly wild night with a pair of handcuffs, though ours had been lined with pink fur. Viola's cuffs, however, were all business and looked every bit the real deal.

"Hands behind your back," she said.

"Isn't that scenario only for the groom?" I asked.

"Not tonight. We need to make your first lap dance special, so hands behind your back," she said, guiding my hands behind the chair, where she expertly cuffed me.

"So, is there any point to the cuffs, besides the whole cop thing?" I asked.

"Keeps your hands off the merchandise."

Clearly Viola had done this routine plenty of times, and, because of her keen proficiency with the props, I thought about suggesting she consider an actual job in law enforcement. Those thoughts were interrupted, however, when she smiled and shoved her breasts into my face then began moving her hips against mine. Her erogenous zone was now conspicuously rubbing over Tag Junior, who I desperately hoped would stay put in my pants. She continued to grind, and her entire body was undulating seductively before my eyes and giving me some real time to study her exquisitely beautiful face. She was obviously part Asian, or, as I suspected earlier, perhaps Hawaiian, but she had large intensely light blue eyes that glowed with a discerning intelligence, and just below them, resided her cute little aquiline nose and the fullest, most sensuous, lips I had ever seen.

The song playing in the background came to an end, and Viola leaned her head forward until her lips were hovering only inches away from mine, and it looked as though she was about to kiss me. I'd never gotten a lap dance before, but I was fairly certain that they didn't kiss or exchange any bodily fluids, so it was particularly surprising when she inexplicably closed the distance and planted her lips on mine. Caught unaware, it took me a moment to realize that her tongue was literally knocking at the door. I opened my mouth to find a slippery new friend, and I exchanged the second most unexpected kiss of my life—the first being delivered by Lux on an airfield in Afghanistan. At least I had known Lux, but Viola was a complete stranger, which, of course, made it all the more exciting, and soon I was feeling the obligatory rush of blood to my nether regions. Fuck. I really hoped that I could keep Tag Junior firmly in my pants, but every second of tongue action was bringing on some very serious wood. At long last, Viola pulled back and smiled deviously.

"Someone apparently is enjoying his first lap dance," she said, as she looked down and gazed at my boner, which was currently straining against my pants with all its might.

"I thought strippers liked to maintain an emotional disconnect—no kissing because it was too intimate."

"We do—usually. Somehow I just got carried away. Might be all the alcohol—or perhaps I just wanted to kiss you."

"Well, you won't get any complaints from me."

"Yeah, I can see that," she said, as she regarded my man parts yet again.

I saw movement to my left and turned to see John approaching, and, as expected, he was carrying yet another cocktail. The two of us had been drinking Mai Tai's pretty religiously for the last two hours, so if my state of inebriation was any indication, then he too was fully hammered. He sauntered up a bit wobbly and stopped a few steps away and shook his head from side to side as he smiled at me.

"Oh, look at Mr. Righteous getting his first lap dance! What a fucking hypocrite!"

"Get lost, Sasquatch. We were just talking."

"Yeah, with your genitals."

"He's got a lot to say," Viola said.

"Apparently. Well, I'm going to rejoin the rest of the party, because I would rather not spend any more time with your erect penis."

"Obviously, because it's way too much temptation."

"Obviously," he responded as he left us alone.

Viola watched him go then turned to me and looked particularly confused.

"Was that John Matheson the vice president of the United States?"

"Yeah, I take it you didn't know that this was his bachelor party?"

"No, this entire affair was organized under an incredible amount of secrecy. No one was told the name of the groom or his groomsmen. I figured it was a VIP, but I didn't realize just how important."

"Oh, he's just a lackey."

"Who could end up being our next president."

"Yeah, hopefully, as he's actually a good guy in spite of being a politician."

"Good, as I'd like to think there's at least one."

"No doubt."

We had a quiet moment, then Viola looked at me with a devious twinkle in her eyes.

"Wanna get out of here?" she asked.

"Sure, and go where? The beach perhaps?"

"Well, either there or up to your room."

Gulp. I was suddenly feeling a little hypocritical, as I had always detested the idea of strip clubs, and one of my reasons had been that I had known a number of men who went to them with the belief that they would be the one guy to win their stripper's heart. Of course, none of those guys managed that task, but they did manage to reach their ATM daily disbursement limit and then proceed to use about twenty percent of it to buy alcohol while the other sixty percent was stuffed into a G-string.

"Um, sure."

She reached behind me and un-cuffed one of my wrists, and I pulled my hands back around and held them before Viola's eyes.

"You forgot one," I said.

"I didn't forget. I plan to re-attach it when we get to your room."

"Oh."

"Let's go."

We walked past the other groomsmen to find the majority of them were engaged in all manner of lecherous activity with the scantily clad female entertainment, though Corn, and, even more surprisingly, John were actually watching casually from the sidelines. I could see Corn being a good boy, as he was still ironing out some difficulties in his marriage, but John always made himself out to be such a player that I was a little surprised. I should have known that when that fucker finally fell in love, he would fall hard enough that petty temptations of the flesh would no longer hold sway over his flesh sword. I purposefully gave him a shocked look as we passed, and he smiled and shrugged. Meanwhile, Viola led me to the little improvised dressing area in the corner, and she grabbed a small bag and her purse, and we headed out and walked along a corridor inhabited solely by a number of Secret Service agents. We reached the elevator, hit the button, and the door dinged, and, when it opened, there stood Lux, and she immediately noticed the handcuffs dangling off of my right wrist.

"I see the groomsmen are having a good time," she said, as we stepped in and joined her.

"Yeah, how's the bridal shower? It's not over already is it?"

"No, it's still going. I just needed to pop back into my room for something."

"Well, have fun, and don't do anything I wouldn't do," I

said.

"I would say the same, but it appears that you already have."

We arrived at my floor then said good night to Lux as we headed off to my room. We reached the door, and I slid in my key card and, upon entering, Viola went to the minibar and made herself a vodka on the rocks.

"Do you mind if I jump in the shower?" I asked.

"Not at all, I'm just happy to enjoy a drink and a little quiet time."

I went into the bathroom, took a monumental piss, then stepped into the massive shower and was thrilled to be bathing after the earlier events of the evening—namely my emergency dump in the ladies room. Feeling refreshed and clean, I exited the shower, dried off, and wrapped a towel around my waste before exiting the bathroom. I joined Viola at the minibar and made myself yet another cocktail, and, like my beautiful guest, also went with a vodka on the rocks. Before taking a sip, I held my glass up to hers.

"What shall we toast to?" I asked.

"Viola and Bartholomew," she said.

We each took a sip of our drink then I motioned towards the couch.

"Shall we have a seat and get to know each other?" I asked.

"No, in fact you should go lie down on the bed and put your hands over your head."

"Seriously? No chit chat? I mean—we hardly even know

each other."

"Yeah, I know, but I have a good feeling about you, Bartholomew," she said, as she took off her top and dropped it onto the floor.

I gazed in wonder at her beautiful body, for now that she was under proper lighting, I could see the full extent of her figure. She was truly in amazing shape, and beneath her pert full breasts was a six pack of sexy abs that formed an enticing trail to her lady region. She apparently saw where I was looking, because she reached down and slid off her short skirt and thong then proceeded to give me a look that implied I should also get naked.

"Oh, was that a hint to lose the towel?" I asked.

"I would say it was more than a hint."

I dropped my towel onto the floor and stood there feeling a tad bit intimidated.

"That's better. Now get on the bed," she said.

I did as instructed, then Viola straddled me and lifted my hands up over my head and cuffed me to one of the vertical stays of the headboard.

"I think you should know that you don't need handcuffs to keep me in this bed," I said.

"Maybe not, but I'm not sure you understand how hard I'm about to fuck you."

"Oh, meow! Kitten has claws."

"Oh yeah, and they're sharp as fuck," she said, as she hovered over me and smiled.

She began stroking my mantool with one hand and used

the other to take hold of the stepchildren, and, while it felt pretty damn good, the predatory look in her eyes was starting to make me wonder if I had made a mistake in getting cuffed to the bed. Then, without warning, she abruptly leaned down and kissed me just as she had back at the party, but this time it was more gentle and exploratory. The longer it went on, however, the more it grew in intensity until our tongues were toe to toe and entwined in a ticklish tangle. It was always strange and sometimes awkward kissing someone for the first time, but, with this officially being our second meeting of the lips, I was surprised that we seemed to have an unusually intuitive sense of each other's desires. This, in turn, seemed to escalate the underlying passion, but, just as quickly as it began, it ended, and she suddenly pulled her head back and took a second to think as she eyed me curiously.

"Um—did you decide that kissing was too intimate for a first date?" I asked.

"No, I—um—well, I just want you to know that I've never gone home with my work before."

"Well, then I'm honored to be your first."

She leaned down and kissed me, but, after a time, moved to my neck before continuing down to give each of my nipples a playful nibble. She set off again on her southerly journey and paused just below my stomach then looked up at me and smiled wickedly. I couldn't help but smile back, but it quickly turned into a visage of shock when, without warning, she took Tag Junior into her mouth and set upon him with unbridled tongue action. Sweet fires of felatio! The pleasure of her efforts was so powerful that I gasped out loud and felt my entire body grow tense. She had an unusually strong tongue, and I wondered if she worked it out as mush as she did the rest of her lithe body, and if so—how? Vegetables, fruits, or perhaps even ice cream cones? God only knew, but of course none of that mattered, because, at the moment, I was floating gleefully through heaven, and every second was making me want to reciprocate the great pleasure I was feeling.

"I think it's time you un-cuff me and let me return the favor," I said.

"Sorry, no can do. You're a stranger, after all."

"As are you, and I let you cuff me to my bed."

"It's not my fault you're easy."

"OK, fine—if Muhammad can't go to the mountain, then the mountain can come to Muhammad, and if the mountain manages to make it up here to my mouth, then Muhammad is going to make that mountain cum pretty fucking hard."

She thought for a moment then smiled.

"OK, fine, I guess I can allow you the one little favor," she said, as she made one last pass at my manhood before moving forward and pressing her lady parts against my face.

I knew she might retreat at any moment, so I needed to be swift if I were to be successful. To that end, I pressed my tongue deep into her essence then dragged it up to her clitoris and set about making very deliberate and intense circles. She started to writhe and moan, and, when I took it to the next level by sucking her clitoris up into my mouth, she threw back her head and arched her back.

"Oh, fuck me!" she cried out.

Her breasts were pressed up towards the heavens, and her taught nipples were begging for my touch, but these damned cuffs had me locked in a sexual purgatory. My tongue was therefore my only vehicle to delver pleasure, and I used it with all my might to bring necessary stimulation to Viola's clitoris. It wasn't long before her hips were shaking, and she was calling out and grinding on my face. Her hands went to her breasts, and, as she caressed her nipples, she abruptly climaxed, and her entire body shook violently until she finally came to rest and moved back down so that my penis was resting firmly against the opening of her vagina.

"OK, Bartholomew, you were right. That was officially an excellent idea."

"Does that mean you're going to un-cuff me now?"

"No, because, now, more than ever, I don't want you leaving my sight until I've fucked the living shit out of you."

"Fine, then I guess I'll just have to continue enduring this abominable torture."

She lifted her hips, and, with precipitous amount of lubrication already in abundance, she took in my entire length in one fell swoop. She felt hot, warm, and wonderful, and a lustful euphoria clouded the entirety of my awareness as she started to rock up and down. Her breasts were moving about before my eyes, and I wanted desperately to reach up and hold them, but I was thwarted by the damn handcuffs.

"Oh, did you want something?" she asked.

"I did."

"Would it be this?" she said, as she leaned forward until her nipple was only a tongue length away from my mouth.

I reached for it hungrily and tickled it's tip with my tongue before sucking on it and making Viola utter a moan of pleasure. She then pulled back and steered her other nipple into my mouth, and she again moaned. Viola apparently had very sensitive nipples, and the additional stimulation inspired her to begin grinding against me with a harried urgency. Soon, loud cries of passion began to erupt from her lips, and suddenly she leaned back and took hold of her breasts and began caressing her nipples until she went headlong into a great and violent climax. Her entire body shook, and she writhed in ecstasy until she could endure no more and finally came to rest with her chest still heaving.

"Sorry about that. I feel a little selfish," she said, once she had recovered enough to speak.

"It's OK. Normally I would have been right there with you, but I've had a lot of alcohol tonight."

"I think I know how to deal with that," she said, as she pulled free and dropped her mouth down onto Tag Junior yet again.

"Um—you really don't have to..."

"Shhh," she said, placing a finger to my lips.

Again, I was lost to her presence of tongue, and the pleasure was almost maddening, for I desperately wanted to take her in my arms. Instead, I lay there bound and helpless as she continued to perform tortuous oral action with her mouth, and I was starting to wonder if she might play a musical instrument—perhaps the flute considering her unique ability to correlate the movements of her mouth and fingers. It was therefore only a matter of minutes before I was rapidly approaching sweet release, and the great numbing effect of the alcohol was now utterly defenseless against Viola's oral onslaught.

"Um, you might want to be careful. I'm really, really, really close and..."

That only seemed to spur her on, and her efforts became even more persistent until I at last crossed the great orgasmic divide, and my seed exploded from my manhood. Viola never wavered, however, and instead continued to deliver the pleasure of a lifetime, all the while drawing out every last drop of my seed before stopping and gazing down at me with a satisfied smile.

"Shit, sorry, I tried to warn you."

"It's fine, I found it exciting, though you really did have a lot of..."

"Pent up energy?" I suggested.

"Semen," she corrected.

"Yeah, it's been awhile."

"I can tell."

"I can't say that I wasn't a little surprised when you um..."

"Swallowed?"

"Yeah."

"I don't do it too often, but I was having too much fun watching you writhe in ecstasy, and I didn't want to interrupt your flow—so to speak."

I laughed.

"Good one, and, for the record, I definitely appreciated it."

She smiled.

"Yeah, but tonight is also kind of a special occasion," she said, as she reached up and un-cuffed my left hand, but forgot the right.

"Well it was certainly special for me, but why was it special for you?"

"Tonight would have been the three year anniversary of my ex and I if we hadn't had an extremely painful break up four months ago."

"That sucks, and I pretty much know exactly how you feel, as I'm about two and a half months out of my last relationship, so if you'd like to talk about it, I'm a good listener."

She looked at me a moment, then reached over and finished the remainder of her vodka.

"We worked together," she said.

"He's a stripper?"

"No, I'm talking about at my main job, obviously."

"Oh, so he had a problem with you stripping on the side?"

"No, and while he wasn't too happy about it, our problem was related to our shared profession. It's a fairly high stress atmosphere, so it finally got too hard to do both, and it basically came down to one of two options."

"Let me guess. One of you quits, or you break up."

"Yep, and neither of us were quitters—except when it came to our relationship, apparently."

"Yeah, unfortunately work was ultimately the reason for my breakup as well."

"Oh, did you work together?"

"No, but she ended up working far away, so the end result was the same."

"That sucks."

"It does, but at least the two of us are here together right now. That's a pretty excellent consolation prize."

"I'd have to agree."

I walked over to the bar, grabbed the vodka bottle, and poured a splash in each of our glasses, before holding mine up to toast.

"To relationships. The one thing in the world capable of making a person equally happy or miserable," I said.

We toasted then threw back the final drink of the night, and I turned off the light and lay beside Viola. She pulled my arm over her body then placed my hand on her breast, and we spooned like two people in love, in spite of the fact we were practically strangers. Sweet Lord, it had been a hell of a day followed by a hell of a night, and I was ready to take refuge in sleep. I closed my eyes and enjoyed the calming sound of the ocean in my ears and the quiet comfort of a beautiful woman in my arms.

CHAPTER FIVE
Wedding Blues

I awoke at nine thirty-five feeling hungover as fuck as I dragged myself out of bed and stumbled into the bathroom feeling unsure if I needed to puke, piss, or shit. My head was throbbing as I looked down at my porcelain mistress, and I was curious what substance I would put down her elegant throat. I did some quick calculations and realized that I wouldn't be able to reach the sink if I were sitting on the toilet and therefore decided to put off a number two in favor of pissing—the idea being that I could easily transition into vomiting if the need arose. Pulling out Mr. Happy, I realized that I had a pair of handcuffs hanging from my right wrist, and I couldn't remember where in the hell they had originated. Then, it came to me, and I smiled to myself as I recalled the wild events of the previous night. It wasn't often that I ended up handcuffed to a bed by a beautiful woman—at least not since my ex Fiona left for Malkarta.

Careful not to pee on the dangling cuff, I let loose a nice

long, deeply yellow piss, which was yet another sign that I was grossly dehydrated. I finished and suddenly felt the urge to vomit but only managed a terribly acidic belch. I went to the sink, brushed my teeth, then looked in the mirror and took a moment to gaze at my haphazard appearance. All things considered, I didn't look that bad when you took into account that I had survived John's epic bachelor party the night before, though God only knew how he and the others were feeling. I grabbed a washcloth, soaked it in cold water, and retreated to the bed, where I laid it over my face and closed my eyes. I felt a stirring and lifted the corner of the washcloth just enough so that I could look over at Viola, and I saw that she was awake though cringing as she shaded her eyes from the bright Hawaiian sunlight that was flooding into the room.

"Morning, Sunshine," I said.

"Morning," she said, the sound of sleep still in her voice.

"How are you feeling?"

"Like shit. I really have to pee, but I'm afraid to stand up."

"I know the feeling. Do you think you could call the front desk and tell them to send someone up here to stop the room from spinning?" I asked.

"Yeah, if I could only open my eyes."

"Still, you have to admit that was pretty fun last night."

"It was."

We both lay there unmoving for another half an hour, before Viola finally got up and headed to the bathroom to take an equally long piss, during which she let out a long, dry, and distinctly girly sounding fart.

"Nice fart," I yelled from the bed.

"Oops—sorry. I'm so hungover, I kind of forgot you were here and just kind of let it slip out."

"I would say that was a lot more than kind of let it slip out. Sweet Lord! Isn't it a little too early in our relationship to cross the fart barrier?" I asked.

"Apparently not."

"Oh, well in that case, how's it smell?"

"Why don't you come in here and find out. It'll give you a really good sense of what I ate last night."

"My semen?"

"Yeah, if your semen smells like barbecued pork."

"I've been told it generally smells of fresh flowers and tastes like sunshine."

"At the moment, it's neither flowery nor sunny."

"Then it's a good thing I don't need to use the bathroom."

It had only been about fourteen hours, yet she had accidentally broken the fart barrier, which was something I would have never done with less than a month of relationship time under my belt. I suppose it shouldn't have been a surprise, however, as our relationship had thus far been mostly impulsive and completely spur of the moment. Viola returned from the bathroom and saw the little washcloth on my head and asked if she could borrow it. I said no, but she took it anyway and let out a long sigh as she lay back on the bed and placed it over her eyes.

"I'm never drinking again," she said.

"Agreed—well—not until the wedding reception tonight, anyway."

"I think I'm ready for coffee, but I can't face actually getting up to make any."

"Me neither, I'll call room service."

I reached over, grabbed the handset, then pressed zero and waited until someone picked up at the front desk. A woman answered, and I asked to be transferred to room service, and, after two painful minutes of talking, finally had coffee on the way. Ten minutes after that, there was a knock on the door, and I threw on my hotel robe and went to let in our liquid breakfast. The room service person turned out to be a slightly nerdish young man in his middle to late twenties, and he was wearing the obligatory khaki dress shorts and Hawaiian shirt common to all the hotel staff in the islands.

"Good morning. How are you folks today?"

"So fucking hungover," I said, as I tried to read his name tag.

His name started with a J, but the rest was unintelligible in my hungover state, so I gave up and just patiently waited for coffee.

"I've got just what you need here," he said.

He smiled and wheeled in the cart, but abruptly paused when his gaze fell on Viola. She was now buck naked and sprawled out on top of the bed in the next room, and her only feature hidden from view was her face, as it was still under the washcloth. The Poor guy was utterly speechless, with his mouth agape and his eyes the size of billiard balls.

"Um, Viola, we have company," I said.

She pulled the washcloth off of her face and smiled.

"Sorry, too hungover to care. I hope you don't mind," she said, to him.

"Not at all," he responded.

"Hey, you don't happen to have any toast or pastries on that tray do you?" I asked.

He was still gazing at Viola but momentarily turned his attention back to me.

"You're in luck, I've got croissants right here. It's standard with any morning coffee orders."

"Well sweet fucking titties. I'm gonna kiss you all over," I said.

He laughed a little uncomfortably as he lifted the lid off of a silver tray and set the plate of croissants on the dining table. Next, he poured two cups of coffee.

"Cream?"

"Yes please, you sweet angel of mercy," I said.

"Me too, please," Viola mumbled from the bed.

He added cream to each cup then looked up at me.

"Will you be needing anything else?" he asked.

"No thanks, we'll be fine now," I said.

"You sure?"

"Yeah."

"Well, anything you need—just give me a call."

"I will."

I signed the bill, and the guy smiled as he noticed the handcuffs hanging off my right wrist.

"I take you had an interesting night," he said.

"Yeah, though I'm not sure I can even remember it all at the moment," I said.

"I'll take your word for it, though I imagine it at least had a happy ending."

"Oh yeah, and then some," Violet mumbled.

I gave him a substantial tip then said goodbye to our soon to be stalker, so that I could now focus on coffee. I grabbed both cups and brought them over to the bed, and Viola sat up and looked eager for her first cup.

"You just made someone's day," I said.

"It's kind of sad that my naked body could affect someone like that."

"We men are simple creatures, and I can tell you that right now, he's telling every dude he works with what he just saw."

"Are you serious?"

"Yeah, either that or he's jacking off, and will tell all his friends after he's done."

"I'm not sure if I should be flattered or disgusted."

"Flattered. Trust me."

I took a seat beside her and sipped my coffee, though I took it slow to make sure that my stomach was actually capable of holding it down. On too many occasions, I had underestimated a hangover and ended up running into the bathroom five minutes later to puke up a half a cup of java. Not today, however. The god's of alcohol had been merciful, and, soon, my headache was dissipating and order was slowly being restored to my personal universe. Suddenly, there was a knock at the door, and I imagined that our waiter had probably returned in the hope of getting another look at Viola. I closed the doors to the bedroom, then walked over to my suite's entrance.

"Who is it?" I called out.

"Finn, it's Sandra. I need to talk to you."

Sandra was the head of Vice President John Matheson's Secret Service contingent, and I had absolutely no comprehension what in the hell she might be doing at my door the night after his Bachelor Party—except to perhaps relay that his majesty had died of alcohol poisoning. I opened the door to see a very unhappy looking Sandra.

"Is he dead?" I asked.

"Not exactly, but someone else is."

"Jessica?" I asked, starting to worry.

"No, but you'll hear the rest when you come to Sasquatch's room."

"Fifteen minutes to shit, shower, and shave?" I asked.

"No problem. I can wait."

"Here?"

"Yeah."

"Really?"

"Yeah, is that a problem? It's not like I'm going to come in there with you. I remember how sensitive you are when you go potty."

"Fine—feel free to wait. There's more coffee on the table, and if you see a woman come out of the bedroom, her name is Viola."

I refilled my cup and noticed Sandra staring at the handcuffs dangling off my wrist.

"I imagine there's quite a story there," she said.

"Not really—it's just another night in the life of an underpaid private investigator. Oh, hey—you wouldn't happen to have a handcuff key would you?" I asked.

"Right here," she said, pulling it out of her pocket and unlocking the cuff for me.

"Thanks."

"No problem."

I grabbed some fresh clothes and my iPhone then headed into the bathroom and, most important of all, locked the door behind me. I dropped onto the seat, adjusted until I found that perfect amount of anal opening, then took a sip of coffee, grabbed my phone, and set about berthing my calf. With the waste migrating gently from my body, I opened my internet browser, and pulled up the local news, curious to see if I could find out anything about recent deaths on Oahu. Finding nothing, I instead clicked on a story summing up several studies done on the health benefits of coffee, and I learned something I already believed whole heartedly—namely that coffee was beneficial to your health. The article summarized numerous studies conducted over many years, and it found that coffee improved mood, reduced depression, and even healed the liver and reduced the chances for developing cirrhosis. As if that weren't enough, coffee also lowered the possibility of skin cancer, type II Diabetes, Alzheimer's, and Parkinson's. Combine all that with the fact that it improves cognitive functioning and you have the world's cheapest and most affordable super drug. I finished the article then immediately reached over and finished my cup of coffee and instantly felt the healing. Just as I set down my cup and pulled off a swath of toilet paper, there was a knock on the outer door to my room, and I heard Sandra's voice.

"Come on, Finn, pinch it off," she said.

"Goddammit, Sandra, don't you know that it's a harbinger of doom to interrupt one of my dumps?" I yelled back.

"Sorry, somehow, I didn't know that your digestive process was linked to the fate of the universe, so I'll just keep patiently fucking off in your living room."

I wiped, flushed, and entered the shower and wondered if Sandra's intrusion might bring some kind of misfortune in the coming hours. Perhaps the spirit of aloha would somehow shield me from the evils of my fate, though only time would tell. I lathered up my hair with a flowery shampoo, then started with the soap, and every moment under the rush of hot water brought me ever farther out of my hangover. By the time I turned off the taps, I was up to about seventy five percent of normal operating power, and I dried off, slid on some fresh shorts and a T-shirt, then exited to find Viola up and dressed in standard street clothes—namely some short knee length black exercise pants and a stretchy short sleeve shirt. She was also looking at her phone and appeared to be a little stressed.

"Shit, I have to go," she said.

"So soon?"

"Work beckons."

"A stripper gig this early in the day?"

"My other work," she said, moving through the double doors and out into the main part of the suite to where Sandra was waiting for me.

I quickly introduced them, and they exchanged the usual pleasantries, before Viola moved towards the door. I followed and caught up to her before she could leave.

"Wait, I don't even know your number or your real name," I said.

"It's probably better that way."

"Seriously? I really enjoyed hanging out with you last night."

"I enjoyed it too, but my life is a little complicated at the moment."

"Then sadly, I guess it's goodbye."

"You never know. If it's meant to be—then perhaps fate will bring us back together."

"In my experience, fate can be kind of an asshole at times."

"Well, I guess we'll find out. Goodbye, Bartholomew," she said, kissing me a final time on the lips before leaving my suite.

"Well then—I guess that officially makes it a one night stand," I said, to myself as I closed the door and turned to find Sandra frowning as she regarded me.

"What?" I asked.

"And you give John shit about being a dick swinging bachelor."

"I can't help it if I'm a people person," I said.

"Nice try. Let's go, man-whore," she said.

How in the hell did she know about that recent nickname? Fucking Secret Service. We left my room and walked down the hall and over to the other side of the hotel to where the presidential suite resided. Sandra knocked then ushered me in, and I found Jessica and John both looking grave as they sat together on one of the living room couches.

"Isn't it a little weird that you should have this room?" I asked.

"How so?" John responded.

"Don't you you ever find it a little annoying that hotels don't have vice presidential suites?"

"I do—though I think I should point out that they don't have dirtbag private investigator suites either."

"Yeah, so I guess we're both out in the cold."

"Not really—I still get this room."

"True. Well, Sasquatch, what the hell is going on? Who died?"

"No one died per say, but someone was murdered, so

you might want to get some coffee and take a seat. If you woke up feeling as bad as I did, I'm sure you'll need it."

I filled a cup and added cream, then took a seat, feeling ever curious to find out what all the fuss was about.

"OK, enough theatrics—who in the hell was killed last night?"

Jessica looked at John, then back to me before speaking.

"Steven," she said.

"Steven?"

"Steven Green. You know—my ex and—and your favorite former client."

Jessica and I had originally met when her former, or should I say dearly departed, husband hired me to follow her and collect evidence that she was having an affair. She had been, as had he, but he wanted the upper hand, as he was about to serve her with divorce papers. I decided I liked Jessica more than Steven and divulged all of this news to her then officially relieved myself from Steven's employ.

"Jesus," I said, taking a seat on the opposite couch.

Jessica wiped a tear from her eye, obviously upset at the death of her ex. He wasn't a very nice guy, but he didn't deserve to be murdered.

"What happened?" I asked.

"He was shot in his hotel room last night—right here in this very hotel."

"Steven was staying in this hotel?"

"Yeah, and the preliminary pathology believes he was shot with a 9mm Pistol, though they don't have a complete ballistics report yet," John said.

"What in the flying fuck was he doing here?"

"That's a little complicated—and part of the reason we're talking to you."

"Meaning?"

"The Police believe they already have a primary suspect."

"Who? Angry hooker or disgruntled client?"

"Me," Jessica said.

"That's ridiculous!"

"I know, but I just spent the better part of the morning getting questioned, fingerprinted, and everything else you can imagine," Jessica said.

"How in the hell could they have possibly come up with a suspect in so little time—let alone you?"

"Well, first of all, I have no alibi for the time of the murder."

"Doesn't a bachelorette party count?"

"It happened later—after I got back to my room."

"And you didn't stay here with John?"

"No, I had my own suite, as the bride and groom are supposed to sleep separately the night before the ceremony."

"Speaking of—is it still on for today?"

"No," John said, somberly.

"Well that sucks."

"It does."

I thought for a moment.

"Well, aside from opportunity, what motive could you

possibly have? You're happily moving on with your life, engaged to the future president of the United States, and you have no kids or alimony to fight over. It doesn't make sense."

Jessica looked to John yet again, then back to me.

"He was blackmailing me," she said.

CHAPTER SIX
The Proof is in the Pudding

It was too bad that it was mid morning and I was still hung over, or I might have thought about making myself a cocktail to soothe my nerves. I never imagined waking up to the daunting news that two of my dearest friends had a massive monkey wrench thrown into the machinery of their upcoming nuptials.

"Blackmail? Seriously?"

"Yeah, and right now the Honolulu Police are compiling all manner of evidence in hopes of pinning this on her," John said.

I rubbed my temples and tried to clear my head and process all the information.

"So, why are you talking to me? Shouldn't you be talking to an attorney?"

"Definitely, but we also need our own investigator on

this. Someone we can trust to try and figure out what the hell is going on here," John said.

"No doubt, and I assume you've already surmised that this may very well be related to your upcoming run for the presidency?"

"Absolutely."

"Do you mind if I ask what he was blackmailing you about?" I asked Jessica.

She stewed for a moment and gathered her thoughts before speaking.

"Back in college, I got pregnant and had an abortion."

"And Steven knew about it obviously."

"Yeah, he was the one who got me pregnant, and needless to say, neither of us were ready for a child, so we decided it was best to have it taken care of."

"Shitloads of people get abortions."

"Yeah, but not future first ladies."

"Did you know about this already?" I asked John.

"Yeah, she told me on our second date. Knowing my job, she thought that I should know about any skeletons before things got serious."

"Well, I must admit that I admire a couple who can communicate."

"Yeah, and I had no problem with it. I firmly believe that it's a woman's right to choose."

"And what about your supporters? I imagine some might feel differently."

"Some do."

"So, when did the blackmail start?"

"A month ago, after John announced that we were engaged and rumors started surfacing that he might run for president, I received an email from Steven that said he wanted ten million dollars to keep quiet."

"But you don't have ten million."

"No, but I do," John said.

"Jesus, I knew Steven was an asshole, but this takes it to an all time high. He had more than enough money, so it almost makes me glad he's dead."

Jessica was quiet as she dabbed her eyes with a tissue.

"Any idea what Steven was doing on Oahu? He could have easily blackmailed you from home. Why come all the way here?"

"No idea."

"Well, I'm obviously going to help in whatever way I can."

"Good, as we need someone to investigate this who knows that Jessica is one hundred percent innocent."

Sandra, who was standing off in the corner of the room, said something into her radio mic then came over and joined us.

"The file from the Honolulu Police is on its way up," she said.

A minute later, there was a knock at the door, and another Secret Service agent handed an envelope to Sandra, and she brought it over and set it down on the coffee table. Everyone looked at it, but no one actually wanted to pick it up, so I relented and grabbed it and set it on my lap. I took a calming breath then opened the file to find a standard police report detailing Steven Green's murder. It turned out that a hotel maid found him lying dead on his bed at seven forty a.m. and called the police. They arrived soon thereafter, and determined that the cause of death was a single gunshot wound to the chest, which occurred some time between midnight and three a.m., and the murder weapon was a Beretta 92F pistol that was found in the reef about twenty yards off the shore of the hotel by a spear fisherman named Danny Keahi. Ballistics tests showed that it matched the bullet found in Steven's chest, though the next line was so ridiculous I had to go back and read it again.

"No fucking way," I said.

"What is it?" Jessica and John both asked at the same time.

"The weapon in question is registered to you."

"How can that be?"

"Well, I know from personal experience that you own a Beretta 92F pistol," I said.

I was familiar with the weapon, because I had actually fired it on several occasions when Jessica and I had gotten together to go shooting at our local range.

"Yeah, but it's back home in California. How the hell could it have ended up here?"

"Good question, and there's more. Your prints were all over the gun."

"Well, of course—it's my gun, but what idiot would use their own gun to kill someone, let alone leave all of their fingerprints?"

"Very good point. I think you would be a lot smarter if you really had wanted to kill Steven. Speaking of which—did you happen to have gotten a silencer made for it?"

"No, nor would I have even known where to get that done."

I read on, and my heart started to pound, as each page relayed yet another air tight clue relating to Jessica's supposed guilt.

"So, they did a GSR test, I see."

"A what?"

"Gunshot residue test."

"Oh, yeah, they did—can you fucking believe it?"

"Yeah, and guess what?"

"I tested positive?"

"Yep."

"For Christ's sake. I didn't kill Steven."

"I know, but it get's worse. A woman matching your general description and wearing a navy blue hooded sweatshirt was seen on security footage leaving your hallway around one fifty a.m. this morning."

"And let me guess—entering the hallway leading to Steven's room a moment later," Jessica said.

"Correct, and the same footage also shows you returning via the same route forty minutes later"

"Ridiculous. I was passed out asleep."

I read on and couldn't help but sigh before I detailed the next bit of info.

"Lovely—your prints were found in several locations in his room, which also happened to include his bathroom."

"Well, yeah, I met with him in his room earlier in the day to discuss his little blackmail scheme. I had to pee, so I used his bathroom."

I returned my attention to the report, and the next bit of evidence to be detailed was the sweatshirt.

"The navy blue sweatshirt seen in the security footage was found in your room, and it was, of course, stained with the victims blood."

"I haven't even worn that sweatshirt since I got to Hawaii, because it's too fucking hot."

"Not hot enough if this report is accurate."

I thumbed through to the next page and found a picture of a shoe print as well as a picture of the sole of one of Jessica's tennis shoes.

"Fuck, they were somehow able to pull a print from the lobby, and they claim it's a perfect match to the sole of a pair of running shoes found in your room."

"That's ridiculous. Hundred's of people walk through there every day. How could they have possibly singled out one of mine, let alone have any idea when it was made?"

"Cops are sneaky fuckers."

"It just get's better and better."

"Indeed, as it seems they also found a copy of Steven's ransom letter on his laptop, where he had it cleverly hidden in his documents folder as well as in his email outbox. He wasn't exactly the world's smartest blackmailer, but his incompetence proves that he emailed it to you, which, in turn, provided the police with a very lovely motive."

I closed the file, took a sip of coffee, and looked at the unhappy bride and groom to be.

"So, to recap—we have your gun as the murder weapon, footage of a person believed to be you walking to his room at the time of the murder, a shoe print from said walking trip, gun powder residue on your hands, his blood on your sweatshirt, and fingerprints proving you were in his room. Add all that to the fact that you have an excellent motive, and we suddenly have one of the most air tight murder cases of all time."

John shrugged and leaned back on the couch and groaned as he closed his eyes and rubbed his temples.

"Why now?" he muttered.

"No shit. I keep thinking I'm going to wake up and it will all be a bad dream," Jessica said.

"I know the feeling, but I have to tell you. The most puzzling aspect of this whole case is that it's just too convincing. No murder case ever has this much evidence, nor do the police manage to put this much together in such a short time. Speaking of which—when did the Police arrive at your door?"

"Nine thirty."

"They found Steven at seven forty-five, and it's now twelve thirty. That's four hours and forty-five minutes, and only three of those hours were even spent with you. How in the hell did they perform and complete all these tests in that small amount of time?"

"Finn has a point," Sandra interjected.

"Yeah, and, Sandra—where were the Secret Service last night?"

"Guarding John. Until he and Jessica are married, she doesn't fall under our purview."

"Shit monkeys. We're not getting many breaks here so far."

"Apparently not," Sandra said.

I had another sip of coffee then asked my next question.

"So, when were you going to announce that you're running for President?"

"End of the week."

"Well, that at least explains why everything happened last night. I'm guessing whoever engineered this whole thing is very intelligent, has a lot of resources, and, more importantly, is on a very specific timeline."

"Fuck—everything was going perfectly to plan. We would have gotten married today then had a week to honeymoon and relax before all the campaign hoopla started."

"Life—she is a motherfucker at times."

"No doubt, and you know what the shitty part about all this is?" John asked.

"What?"

"Whoever is doing this is obviously using Jessica to get to me."

"Yeah, so do you have any thoughts on who in the hell would be fucking with you like this?"

"Not off hand."

"You must have plenty of enemies."

"Being in politics means it's inevitable, but, without trying to sound vain, I'm pretty well liked—even across party lines."

"Well, I'm going to do my best to get your lovely bride-to-be cleared, but in the meanwhile I'd like you to think about all the people who you might have pissed off."

"Deal, and we're going to have a damage control meeting this evening around six o' clock with my father and Frank Williams as well as the rest of my team. I'd like it if you could be there, so you can get everyone up to speed."

"Will there be food and drink?"

"Yeah."

"Then I'm there."

"Good, what's your first move?"

"I want to talk to Jessica. Are you feeling up to it right now?" I asked her.

"I suppose."

"OK, good. Now, the murder apparently took place between midnight and three a.m., so what time did you leave your bachelorette party?"

"A little before midnight."

"That seems a little early."

"I was super tired and a bit groggy, as it had been a long night."

"Well, I can say with confidence that the bachelor party was just getting started at that point."

Jessica looked at John and delivered a look of scorn.

"Don't worry, as Sasquatch, aside from the excessive drinking, was actually a very good boy last night."

"Good to know, though who knows if it will even matter with all that's going on."

"Don't worry, I'm going to fix this. Now, did you have a lot to drink?" I asked.

"No, in fact I only had a couple glasses of wine."

"That's it?"

"Yeah."

"How did you feel this morning?"

"Shitty—as though I'd had a lot to drink. In fact, I was still a little groggy when the police showed up at my door. I can't tell you how embarrassing it was to be standing there in my pajamas."

"I can imagine. No one wants to wake up to the police banging on their door. So, to recap—you left the bachelorette party a little before midnight, returned to your room, and remember nothing until the police woke you up this morning."

"Correct."

"Well, I think I'll go to the Police station and talk to the detectives and forensics people who are actually working on the case, as you can only learn so much from a Police report," I said.

"Oh, and I almost forgot to mention that you'll be working with a local FBI special agent," John said.

"Seriously? Why? I don't need some asshole in a suit telling me what to do and where to go."

"It was the only way to guarantee you any official kind of authority."

"So, the vice president of the United States doesn't have the pull to get me any authority? Like I always say—you're just a glorified lackey."

"Well, that might be the case for a long time if you don't find out what the hell is going on here."

"I'll do my best. I don't want one of my dearest friends to always be an underachiever."

Jessica stood up and came over and hugged me.

"Thanks, Finn. I'm glad you're on this," she said.

"It'll all work out. I promise."

I said goodbye and headed back to my room to brush my teeth and put on some more official looking clothing. I kept the black board shorts but threw on a short sleeve button up shirt and some light weight breathable Saucony Jazz sneakers. Of course, I would have preferred thongs, or, as the locals called them, *rubba slippas*, but I was an official representative of the vice president and decided I should dress in accordance with the position—mostly, anyway. Fresh and ready for the day ahead, I left my room and headed down to the resort's parking lot and slid behind the wheel of my metallic blue Subaru Impreza rental car. It wasn't even close to the three hundred horsepower monster I had at home, but it was at least all wheel drive and would be nice if I ventured onto any of the many back-country dirt roads.

I left the resort and headed south towards Honolulu, and it took about forty minutes before I was finally pulling in front of the Honolulu Police department, which just happened to reside about a half mile west of the iconic Waikiki Beach. I parked on the street and entered the air-conditioned building and stopped at the front desk to figure out where I needed to go first. After a brief conversation, I showed my ID and was sent upstairs to meet with the lead detective on the case. His name was Alan Kamakana, and his desk was the third from the door, and he just happened to be eating a plate of Korean Barbecue consisting of pork, rice, macaroni salad, and cole slaw.

"Is that from Helena's?" I asked, as I looked at the plate of food.

"Of course. You know about Helena's?"

"Oh yeah, I like to eat where the locals eat when I'm in the Islands."

"Smart move. How can I help you?"

"The name's Finn, and I'm here to talk to you about the Steven Green murder case."

"Ah, yeah. They said there would be some kind of VIP coming in on this one."

"I wouldn't exactly say VIP. More like helpful friend."

"Well, friend. How can I help you?"

"I just wanted to talk to you about the evidence you have against Jessica Thurman."

"It's a slam dunk—pretty much everything but a signed confession."

"Seems that way, but my problem is that it's just a little too perfect. Body is found at 7:40 a.m., and by noon you have the murderer and at least five major pieces of evidence."

"Sometimes we get lucky."

"Have you ever been this lucky on any other murder case?"

"Honestly—no."

"And don't you think it's a little odd that the maid went into his room that early?"

"Apparently he called the night before and requested an early maid service."

"I can't help but think that it all sounds a little too perfect."

"Granted—me too, but it doesn't take away from the fact that all the other evidence is air tight, and she has a pretty substantial motive. I mean, let's face it—she's very likely about to become the next first lady of the United States. People have killed for a lot less."

"Indeed they have, but not Jessica Thurman. I know her."

"Everyday, I meet people that you would never think could commit murder—right up until the moment they confess."

"Trust me, I'm absolutely sure on this one."

"I'm sorry, but it is what it is. We're just doing our job

and going wherever the evidence leads us."

"Or going wherever you're being led."

Ed shrugged.

"So, where is the evidence lab?" I asked.

"Downstairs in the basement. Your liaison from the FBI just went down there to go over the evidence."

"Lovely."

I left Alan and boarded the elevator and hit the button for the basement, where I would enter the geek center of the Honolulu Police Department. I exited into a plain white lobby and walked through a double door to find a large open room with offices situated at its perimeter. In the middle, there were a number of people in white coats fretting over various pieces of forensic evidence, and one of them, a tall gangly man about thirty years old and wearing the obligatory horn rim glasses of a tech nerd, saw me looking lost and came over.

"Hello, can I help you?" he asked.

"Yeah, I was hoping to talk to the techs working on the Steven Green murder."

"You're looking at them."

"Can I speak with the ballistics person?"

"That's me," he said.

"Oh, perfect! Do you mind if I ask you some questions?"

"Not at all. They told me someone might be coming, so why don't you follow me to my office. The Chief and the Fed are already in there. My name's Bert, by the way."

"I'm Finn."

"Nice to meet you," he said.

"You too," I said, before following Bert across the room and into his office.

It was fairly large and filled with a lot of equipment and had microscopes, a computer setup with several large flat screen monitors, and on the far end, behind a wall of glass was a small firing range. Standing beside his desk was an older man as well as a woman in a suit, and both were turned away from me and looking at one of the monitors.

"Excuse me, sir, I have a Mr. Finn here."

The man turned first.

"I'm Chief O'Hara, nice to meet you," he said, holding out his hand.

I laughed to myself as I thought about his name—Chief O' Hara. That was the name of the Chief in Batman, which made me wonder if there might also be a Commissioner Gordon down at City Hall.

"Nice to meet you, Chief."

"And this is FBI Special Agent Violet Kalili."

The woman turned from the monitor, and our eyes locked in surprise, with neither of us able to speak. The beautiful brown haired Violet was in fact Viola—the stripper I had hooked up with the previous night. Apparently, her true hair color was brown, not blond, so she must have been wearing a wig or managed to visit the fastest hair salon on the island after leaving my room this morning. Oddly, the unexpected moment also suddenly made me try to remember what color her pubic hair had been and whether or not the carpet matched the drapes. Seeing her now, I preferred her real color rather than the brash blond, as it gave her a much softer and more exotic beauty. As I recovered from my surprised stupor, I smiled and looked into her lovely blue eyes.

"Nice to meet you, Special Agent Kalili," I said.

"It's nice to meet you too, Mr. Finn. I assume you have been told that I've been assigned to assist you in your investigation."

"I have, and please call me Tag, though my good friends call me Bartholomew."

Chief O'Hara watched our exchange curiously.

"Do you two know each other?" he asked.

"No," Violet and I said, at the exact same time.

"Oh, because I kind of got the impression that you two had met before."

Clearly, Chief O'Hara was a career policeman and could read people, though I hoped he believed our little ruse.

"I was hoping to talk to Bert about the ballistics report," I said.

"Be my guest. I have to get back upstairs. Feel free to come see me if either of you have any questions," Chief O'Hara said.

"Thanks," I responded.

The Chief left, and Violet gave me an uncomfortable smile. I smiled back then turned my attention to Bert.

"So, Bert, this may sound a little silly, but I have to ask—are you a hundred percent certain that the ballistics test conclusively matched the bullet to Jessica Thurman's gun?"

"I am, and, if you take a seat, I'll show you."

I sat down, and Bert opened two pictures on the screen then placed them side by side. One was the test-fire from Jessica's gun, and the other was from Steven's heart.

"As you can see, the bullet recovered from Steven was mostly intact, which made it a lot easier to discern the marks created when it left the barrel."

I nodded.

"And now look at the same spot on the test-fire bullet," Bert said, as he pointed at the picture on the right.

I did as instructed and looked at the picture.

"Now, as you can see here, they are absolutely identical."

"Absolutely, and is it unusual that the bullet is in such good condition?"

Bert thought a moment.

"Actually, yeah, as most gunshots to the heart pass through the rib cage and become greatly deformed. This bullet entered his abdomen at an upward angle, just below the ribs."

"That seems like a lot of unnecessary work. I know from my experience that if I want someone dead, I'd just pop two in the chest, and one in the head."

Violet and Bert stared at me with a legitimate surprise in their expressions.

"What? I play a lot of first person shooters. Don't I look like the type to pown a noob?"

Apparently they didn't understand gaming lingo, but it

seemed to placate them for the moment and allow us to turn our attention back to the screen.

"So, my next question is—when were you able to perform the ballistics test?"

"This morning at nine thirty, when it was all dumped on my desk with orders to drop all other cases and complete this one. Why do you ask?"

"Honestly, I find the timeline of this entire investigation a little improbable."

"How so?" he asked.

"What is the usual turn around time on an investigation like this?"

He thought for a moment before answering.

"Weeks, I guess."

"So, a two hour turn around is unusual."

"I suppose you're right."

"And who made this case a priority?"

"I'm not actually sure. You'd have to ask the Chief."

"Oh, one final question. How did you confirm that the weapon belonged to Jessica?"

"Serial number."

"Can I see the gun?"

"I suppose it's OK."

He went to an evidence drawer and pulled out the Beretta 92. It did indeed have a silencer and was currently being stored in a plastic evidence bag. Burt opened it up and handed it over.

"It's OK to handle it?"

"Yeah, it's already been fingerprinted and cleared. I assume you know what you're doing?"

"We'll see."

I took hold of the Beretta, dropped the clip, then pulled back the slide to check the chamber to verify that it was indeed empty. More gun owners shot themselves or family members during cleaning or routine handling than any other time, so I always made a point of clearing a weapon—even after it had been taken into Police custody. Satisfied, I set my attention to the silencer and noticed the expert mill work that had gone into its creation. I unscrewed it from the barrel and freed it from the end of the gun, so that I could look at it more closely. In the movies, they always showed the assassin screwing on the silencer, but no one ever thought about the mechanics and craftsmanship involved. The end of the barrel had to have threading machined into it, and it had to be absolutely perfect so that the bullet's trajectory wouldn't be affected. A good silencer was therefore a hybrid of art and engineering, and this one was as good as any I'd seen before. I set it down and began disassembling the pistol by thumbing the release and taking the upper slide off, so that I could inspect its inner workings. I had installed a modified spring on Jessica's pistol to reduce recoil, and I found it cozily nestled just below the barrel. Next, I checked the bottom of the grip and saw the tiny mark I had made at its base. We had gotten our Berettas mixed up at the firing range one time, so I had made a small mark on hers, so we could tell them apart. This was indeed Jessica's pistol.

"This is Jessica's Beretta, but I find the silencer a little troubling."

"How so?" Bert asked.

"It's incredibly well made. The person who fashioned it is seriously world class. Do you know of any master gunsmiths on the island?"

"Not offhand, but you could talk to one of the local gun stores. There's a good one on Queen Street, and their gunsmith is top notch."

"Any chance of me taking the weapon and silencer with me?"

"No, but as a Federal Officer, she could—as long as she fills out a temporary transfer of evidence form."

"Do you mind doing that, Special Agent Kalili?"

"Not at all."

Bert rustled through a drawer and came up with a piece of paper, which would officially transfer temporary custody of the pistol and silencer to Violet. She filled it out, then Bert made copies and handed one to us.

"We will need it back if and when this case goes to trial."

"No problem. It should only be a couple days at most. Alrighty then, I suppose we're done here. Can you point us to the person who did the gun powder residue test on Jessica?"

"That would be Andrea."

"Is she here?"

He looked at his watch.

"No, but she'll be back from her lunch break in another fifteen minutes."

"Excellent. Any place to get coffee nearby?"

"Starbucks is around the corner."

I reattached the silencer then slipped the pistol into its bag before handing it over to Violet, who stuck it in her purse.

"Perfect. Agent Kalili, what say we go for coffee and get to know each other a little better."

"That would be nice, Bart," she said.

CHAPTER SEVEN
My So Called Secret Life

Special Agent Violet Kalili and I exited the building, and waited until we were on the street and well away from the Honolulu Police Department before speaking. We were obviously going to have an interesting conversation, and it would best be done far from prying eyes or ears.

"Well now, Special Agent Kalili, it would appear that fate did indeed bring us back together, and now that we're alone, is there anything you'd like to tell me?"

"Not really, but I guess I have to."

We reached the Starbucks and ordered a couple of large coffees before taking a seat at one of their outdoor tables. I had a sip of coffee and eyed Violet, as I was anxiously waiting to hear how it was that she happened to be an FBI Special Agent and part-time stripper. She took a sip of her coffee then set it on the table and looked at me and let out a long sigh before speaking.

"Obviously you now know my official profession and should at least understand why I keep my other one on the down low."

"Obviously, but at least it explains your proficiency with the handcuffs and the whole sexy cop thing," I said, stifling a laugh.

"This might seem funny to you now, but for me it isn't a joke. It's my life."

"I understand, but I'm a little surprised you haven't thought to do the whole sexy special agent routine. You could wear a tear away suit with nothing but a tie on underneath. I'm telling you right now that it would be in my top three stripper fantasies."

"You done?" she asked, seriously.

"Yeah, sorry. It's just that you are the first FBI Agent and part-time stripper I've ever met."

"OK, jackass. If I agree to tell you the whole story, will you stop with the comments?"

I smiled and nodded.

"Yes. I promise."

"OK. Two years ago, I did an undercover assignment at a strip club down on Waikiki. It was believed that the owners were involved in human trafficking. As it turned out, they were importing their strippers illegally then making them work off the cost of their passage."

"Lovely business model. So, let me guess—no one ever actually managed to work it off?"

"Of course not. Anyway, while on assignment at the club, I found myself taking home about four grand a night."

"Well, you clearly have the requisite assets for that kind of haul."

"Thank you, Mr. Finn," she said, looking a little uncomfortable.

"You can stop with the whole Mr. Finn horse shit. After last night, I think it's more than appropriate to call me Tag or Finn, or even Bart of you prefer."

"Fine, as long as you call me Violet."

"Deal, so what's the rest of the story?"

She shrugged.

"After the assignment was over, I decided that I would be crazy not to find a decent club and continue for awhile and do a few gigs a month until I paid off my house. It's not illegal or anything."

"You don't have to justify it to me. I've been there."

"You were a stripper? Do tell."

"Afraid not, as what I mean to say is that I've been in a place where it's hard to pay the bills, and I would have been more than willing to use some rather creative means to get by."

"I find that hard to believe."

"Why?"

"You were at the vice presidents bachelor party for fuck's sake."

"Doesn't mean I haven't had to scrape by."

"Really? So what is it you do for a living?"

"Private investigator."

"Seriously?"

"Yeah, why?"

"You look more like the government type."

"Well, actually I used to be."

"Oh, are we talking Secret Service? That would explain how you know the vice president."

"No, it was a different entity."

"Interesting—that would leave the CIA or NSA. You don't look like a computer nerd, so I'm guessing you were Agency."

"Can't officially say."

"So, that's a yes—and I suppose it explains your whole two to the chest, one to the head thing."

I nodded.

"Well, don't worry about maintaining your secrecy, as I have top secret security clearance."

"Is that how you got the assignment as my babysitter?"

"Not exactly. As it turns out, the vice president is good friends with the director of the Bureau, and I just happen to be good friends with the director. Obviously this is a very sensitive affair, and your friend the vice president wanted someone he could trust."

"Interesting. How is it you're so close to the Director, when you're five thousand miles from Washington? It's not a romantic entanglement gone bad is it?"

"Hardly—he and my dad were best friends, and they came up through the ranks of the Bureau together."

"Where is your dad now?"

"Retired. He and my mom live just past Diamond Head."

"Must be nice having your family nearby."

"Sometimes, except he get's kind of protective of me when I'm on a big case."

"Nothing wrong with caring."

"Until he shows up at a stakeout and makes me feel like an eight year old child around my fellow agents."

"That could be awkward."

"So, how is the private investigation field? Lot's of intrigue and excitement?"

"Ha! Up until recently, the majority of my cases were adultery and lost pets."

"Bullshit."

"I'm serious. That's why I can understand you pursuing an alternative income, though I doubt I could get by as a part-time stripper."

"Don't sell yourself short. I know plenty of women who would pay to get a look at that body of yours."

"Would that include you as well?"

"No, I'm not the stripper type."

"Touché."

"So, I take it that you don't have a problem keeping my little secret to yourself."

"None whatsoever."

"And about last night—I assume you also understand that because of the nature of our working relationship that what happened, however enjoyable it may have been, cannot happen again."

"I don't officially agree with that last statement, but I'll do whatever makes you happy. Besides, I was just drunk and vulnerable."

"Indeed, so was I."

"I guess it's settled then. We are officially just partners," I said, holding out my hand to shake.

We shook hands and looked at each other a moment, and I could see something behind Violet's eyes that I secretly hoped was a tinge of regret at the terms of our unusual relationship.

"So, partner, I guess you're officially my babysitter."

"I'm not exactly your babysitter. My orders were to assist you in any way necessary to complete your investigation."

"Any way? What if sexual gratification becomes necessary?"

"That's why God gave you two hands."

"And women."

"Not this one."

"What do you call last night?"

"Poor judgement in a moment of weakness."

"Strange—I saw it as two people finding comfort in the emptiness of existence."

"You would, Bart."

We finished our coffee and headed back to the Police Station and entered the building with a number of other employees. A man and woman branched off from the bunch and entered the elevator, and Violet and I followed them inside. Both looked like nerds, though the woman was kind of reminiscent of a sexy Velma from the *Scooby Doo* cartoon. She had a lovely figure as well as a very pretty face that was framed by short brown hair cut in a bob. To complete the look, she also had the obligatory tortoise shell glasses. She happened to turn in my direction just long enough for me to get a look at her name tag, and I saw that she was Andrea. Talk about perfect timing!

"You did the GSR test on Jessica Thurman today," I said.

"Yeah, as well as the finger and shoe prints. How did you know?" she asked, looking at me curiously.

"We already talked to Bert."

"Oh, so you are?"

"Tag Finn. I'm here as an independent investigator for the vice president."

"Well hello, Mr. Fancy Pants."

I had to laugh at her sassiness.

"More like Mr. Old Navy outlet guy."

She laughed then looked to Violet.

"And you are?"

"Oh, forgive my rudeness. This is Special Agent Violet Kalili of the FBI. She's my babysitter," I said.

She shook Violet's hand then turned her attention back to me.

"Well, how can I help you—Mr. Un-Fancy Pants?"

"I'm curious about the GSR test."

"Follow me, and I'll show you my results."

We followed Andrea to her section of the lab, and she

brought up a series of pictures as well as some kind of color coded chart with a number of chemicals listed on the left hand side of the screen.

"You familiar with GSR?" Andrea asked.

"A little, but feel free to speak to me as though I'm a rookie biatch, as I'd love to better understand the nature of the evidence."

"Well, it's pretty basic. I use adhesive dabs to scour the potential suspect's hands and clothing then bring them back here and look at them under an electron microscope, which of course has an energy-dispersive X-ray spectroscopy detector."

"Well, of course. And all that means?"

"It means it can tell me all of the trace elements of gun powder residue—namely lead, antimony, barium, and in some cases, copper from the shell casing."

"So, you used these adhesive dabs on Jessica?"

"Yeah—her hands and her clothes."

"The clothes she was wearing?"

"Yeah, as well as another article of clothing in her room."

"And?"

"Her hands were positively covered in GSR, though her immediate clothing was not. I did however find some extremely minute traces of GSR on the right sleeve of the bloody sweatshirt found in Jessica's closet."

"Shouldn't it have more residue if she were supposedly wearing it when she shot Steven Green?"

"It should. Usually anything within three to five feet will

have particles, but the elements can rub off fairly easily on furniture or any number of items a person comes into contact with, which would explain the lesser amounts."

"So, in your professional opinion—did Jessica fire the weapon in question?"

"Absolutely."

"And what about the prints?"

"Well, I found a fair amount actually—some on the gun, obviously, as well as a number in the bathroom and around the room, though primarily on the door handles."

"Don't you find that unusual?"

"Not really, as those are the places people usually touch the most."

"Exactly, but wouldn't a good killer try and leave as little evidence of herself behind as possible?"

"Yeah, but maybe Jessica isn't a good killer."

"Or perhaps she's not a killer at all."

"Perhaps, but ultimately it backs up the assumption that she is our killer."

I thought for a moment.

"Can you explain the shoe print?"

"Yeah, after I was done with fingerprints, I moved on to the lobby to see if I could find any shoe prints that matched the shoes in Jessica Thurman's closet."

"And you obviously did."

"Yeah, several, though only one was clear enough for an attempt at a match."

"And how is it you found a clear print in an area where so

many people have obviously walked."

"Excellent question, and the answer is timing. The Janitor does the floors around midnight and usually finishes around one a.m., so the floor was still wet when Jessica, or I should say our alleged killer, walked through. By the time we were on scene, the prints were dried and clear as could be—almost as though they had been painted on the floor."

"And you believe it's a match to the shoes found in Jessica's room?"

"I'm about 99% certain."

"Can you explain why?"

"Firstly, the print is identical to the shoe's tread pattern. It's a size eight Nike Women's Air Pegasus, but the real clincher is the wear pattern. The person in question has the tendency to Supinate

"Or wear out the outer edge first."

"Exactly, and I directly compared the sole and the print and found them to be a perfect match."

"So, you have no doubt that the shoe print belongs to Jessica Thurman?"

"None whatsoever."

"Fuckinzee."

"Well—you might want to talk to the blood spatter specialist. He had some interesting conclusions of his own."

"I guess we're off to talk to Dexter."

"Funny. That's what we nicknamed him."

"Really?"

"Well, I think he bought the cargo pants and grew the

five o'clock shadow after we gave him the nickname."

"What's his real first name?"

"Princeton."

"Kind of pompous. I think I'd prefer the nickname too. Anyway, thanks for your time, and on the subject of nicknames, might I say that you look quite a bit like a very sexy Velma from *Scooby Doo*."

"You might, and it wouldn't be the first time."

We left Velma and moved across the lab to see a man that did indeed resemble the television character Dexter. He had brown scruffy hair, five o' clock shadow, and was wearing the obligatory cargo pants but had opted for an untucked button up shirt, probably to better conform with police dress code.

"Hello, Dexter, I'm Finn, and this is Special Agent Kalili of the FBI," I said, holding out my hand.

He smiled as we shook hands, though his gaze quickly moved on to Violet, whom he appraised for some time before looking back to me.

"Nice to meet you. What can I help you with?"

"Velma said that I should talk to you about the blood spatter on the Steven Green murder."

He thought for a second then laughed out loud.

"Funny! I've often thought that Andrea totally looks like Velma!"

"Yeah, though a sexier version."

"Without doubt. Well, follow me, and I'll show you what I have."

We followed Dexter to his desk, and he brought up the Green Murder Investigation on one of his two monitors.

"So, first, we have a blood spatter pattern that clearly shows that the weapon was placed at about a forty five degree angle and fired, point blank, up into the chest cavity, penetrating the heart and causing the death of Mr. Green."

He showed us the crime scene pictures of Steven, and strangely, it was the first time I had seen him since he hired me six months previously to spy on his then wife, Jessica. He was lying on his back, his skin was pale white, and there was a large stain of blood on his abdomen that trailed off his body and down onto the bed. I'd seen plenty of dead bodies over the years, but Steven was an acquaintance, so it really brought the impact of the experience into my awareness.

"So, Velma said you had some interesting conclusions."

"Well, they are to me."

"I'd love to hear them."

"In cases such as this, it would be common to find that the perpetrator too would have some blood splatter on their clothes. The sweatshirt found in Jessica Thurman's room does indeed have blood on it, but it's more than it should in my opinion—almost as if someone made a point of dousing it with the victim's blood. I also checked the rest of her clothes, and none had even the slightest trace of blood. The amount on the sweatshirt would have easily soaked through into any undergarments, but it didn't, which leads me to believe that it wasn't worn over any of the clothes found in Jessica's room."

"Meaning she might have gotten rid of those clothes," Violet said.

"Yeah, but, if so, why keep the blood soaked sweatshirt?"

"Very interesting," I said.

"I think so."

"Did you tell this to the Ed Kamakana or any of the other detectives upstairs?"

"I did, but they have a different take on this. In their minds, it's incontrovertible proof to link Jessica Thurman to the murder."

"Cops will be cops. Oh well, I guess it's time to move on to the surveillance tape. Do you know who that might be?"

"Ernie, next office over."

"Wait a minute. You seriously have someone named Ernie and someone named Bert working here?"

"Yeah, and Dexter and Velma. Quite a crew."

"Indeed. Well, thanks for your time."

"You're welcome, and please feel free to come back if you have any more questions," Dexter said, though I think he was mainly referring to Violet.

We left Dexter's office and moved one over to find Ernie sitting at his desk, where he was watching a YouTube video. Unlike his Sesame Street counterpart, he was not orange, but he was wearing a striped shirt. I knocked on the doorframe, and he turned to greet us, though his eyes quickly left me and moved over to Violet.

"Hello, I'm Tag Finn, and this is Special Agent Violet Kalili of the FBI. I hope we aren't interrupting anything," I said, gesturing at the YouTube video.

"Oh no, not at all. I was just going over some footage of a local vandalism case. The dumbass posted a video of himself spray painting a store window, and I managed to find a reflection of his face. We'll have him in less than twenty four hours."

"Not bad," I said.

"It's easier to find people on an island, as there are fewer places to hide."

"And it apparently helps if they're stupid."

"No doubt."

"So, do you have a minute to talk about the Steven Green murder?"

"Absolutely. What do you want to know?"

"Well you're the video guy, so I wanted to know your opinion about the footage. Can you say conclusively that the woman in question is Jessica Thurman?"

"Well not one hundred percent, but it's highly likely after having compared the woman in the footage to pictures of Miss Thurman. I can show you the footage if you want."

"That would be great," I said.

He opened a folder and scrolled down and double clicked on an icon, and a new window opened up. He clicked the play button, then hit a key on the keyboard, and it started playing in full screen on his other monitor.

"The first shot is from the camera in the hallway. The second is from the lobby, and it's where we managed to get a good look at her face."

A few seconds passed, and there came a woman that for all intents and purposes was similar looking to Jessica, though she had the hood up on the incriminating sweatshirt, and it was concealing the majority of her face. The time on the screen's counter said it was one fifty two a.m., and she disappeared from the screen, and up came the footage of the lobby, where she reappeared and pressed the button for the elevator. All of a sudden, she looked straight up into the camera, and my heart skipped a beat, as it did indeed look like Jessica. She disappeared from view as she entered the elevator then reappeared in what I assume was the security camera footage from Steven's hallway. She continued down the hall and out of camera view—presumably to Steven's room. The time on the counter was one fifty three am..

"The next shots are from forty-five minutes later," Ernie said.

The video jumped, and the time now read two thirty-five a.m. and showed what appeared to be Jessica walking back from the direction of Steven's room. It jumped to the lobby, and again she paused and looked up into the camera. She was, of course, wearing the supposedly blood stained sweatshirt, though it was impossible to tell whether or not it was indeed soaked with blood because of its dark color. She entered the elevator, and, a moment later, appeared in the hallway and walked until she left the frame, and the video stopped playing.

"Have you done any frame grabs and gotten better images of the woman?"

"Yeah, just a second."

He grabbed the mouse and brought up a series of still frames then zoomed in on the image and cleaned them up to show greater detail of the person in question. The image was a little grainy, but it sure as hell appeared to be Jessica.

"Is it possible any of this footage might have been altered?"

"Not that I can tell. Of course, the timeline is such that it would take a person with extremely good editing skills to pull it off."

"Fuckinzee."

"I take it you don't believe that Jessica Thurman is our killer."

"I know for a fact she isn't."

"The evidence tells a pretty conclusive story," Ernie said.

"I'm afraid he's correct," Violet added.

"Any idea why she might have paused and looked deliberately into the camera?"

"I wondered about that as well and checked out the lobby. There's a clock right next to the camera, so I'm assuming that's what she was looking at."

"Can I get a copy of the video and the still frame?"

"Sure. You want all of it, or just the highlights?"

"All of it—in case there's anything else of use."

Ernie grabbed a flash drive and placed it in the USB slot, then dragged over the files onto its icon, and a minute or so later it was done, and he ejected it and handed it to me."

"Thanks."

"No problem."

We left Ernie and headed for the exit, but I had a quick thought and detoured back around towards Velma, as I had another question. We arrived to find her gazing intently at her computer screen, but she brought her attention up to us upon hearing our approach.

"Let me guess—you have positive proof Jessica Thurman is innocent?" she asked.

"No such luck, but I do have a final question now that I've seen the security footage from the hotel."

"Fire away—no pun untended," she said.

"Well, I noticed that our supposed killer touched the elevator button. Did you fingerprint those as well as the internal buttons as well?"

"I did, but they were almost completely devoid of any discernible prints."

"So, someone, possibly our killer, wiped them down but conveniently forgot to wipe down the room. Seems a little suspicious to me," I said.

Velma thought for a moment as she considered my words.

"You might have a point, though it's entirely possible the janitor cleaned those areas as they resided in the public domain."

"Possible though unlikely in my opinion. Alrighty then, Velma, Agent Kalili and I will be leaving you in peace now."

Violet and I left the forensics lab and ventured back upstairs to meet with Chief O'Hara one last time. He was sitting at his desk and talking on the phone, so he nodded for us to come in and take a seat. A moment later, he hung up.

"How can I help you?"

"Just one final question, Chief."

"Sure, fire away."

"Who gave the order to have this case fast-tracked?"

"No idea, though I got the email from the Police Commissioner about ten to eight, so you might want to ask him."

"Thanks, I'll be in touch."

We left the air-conditioned Honolulu Police station and walked out into the always pleasant Hawaiian sunshine.

"What now, Bart?"

"Lunch?"

"Sounds good, I've hardly eaten, and that coffee is making me a little twitchy."

"How about Helena's?"

"You know about Helena's?"

"Doesn't everybody?"

"Not *hoales*. I'm impressed—you're apparently a regular local *moke*. I assume you have a car here?"

"Yeah, why?"

"No reason to take two cars. Why don't we drop mine off at the Bureau. It's not that far away."

"Good thinking."

I got in the Subaru and followed Violet in her white Ford Fusion west past Pearl Harbor and out to the FBI's local office. It was a nice, modern looking building that sat next to the Barber's Point Naval Air Station, and Violet pulled in and grabbed an end space before walking over to the door of my car.

"I have to pee. Do you want to wait or come inside?" Violet asked.

"I wouldn't mind a quick bathroom stop as well. That coffee has brought on the need for a proper horse piss."

I exited the Subaru and followed Violet inside, and the air was suddenly cool and dry, as the building was fully air-conditioned. We went past a reception desk, and a young woman of Asian descent said hello to Violet and me. Violet exchanged some pleasantries then led me upstairs to the restrooms, and we parted ways. I entered the men's and discovered a thirtysomething guy standing at one of the urinals. He was tall, good looking, and his physique hinted that he was a devout workout junkie. He was also wearing dress pants and a button up shirt, and his clean shaven appearance and nicely quaffed hair made me assume he was an agent.

He immediately turned and eyed me suspiciously, so I smiled and continued on past him and into one of the proper stalls. A moment later, he flushed, and I heard the sink turn on, and I used that brief bit of inspiration to start emptying my swollen bladder. Only moments into my piss, I felt the rumblings of a fart simmering on the periphery, but I managed to keep it buttoned up until the guy left. At that point, I let her rip, and the sound was far louder than I had anticipated. This brought on a brief bout of giggles, but they eventually subsided by the time I was done peeing. I used my foot to flush the toilet then washed my hands and exited to find Violet standing directly outside. She was talking to the same nicely quaffed hair guy who had been in the bath-room, and they both turned to me, but Violet was smiling and eying at me with a raised eyebrow.

"Nice fart," she said.

"Oh, you heard it?"

"The people on the north shore heard it."

"Then I guess we're even," I said, recounting her fart from this morning.

She smiled.

"Touché."

"What's that supposed to mean?" the guy asked, looking annoyed.

"Oh nothing. Tag, this is Special Agent Dave Moore, and, Dave, this is Tag Finn, independent advisor to the vice president on the Steven Green Homicide."

"He doesn't look like an independent advisor to the vice president."

"I take that as a compliment, actually."

I held out my hand, and he took it, though he had an odd smile playing on his face that I'd seen a more times than I cared to remember. It was smug with a touch of pride and suggested that it was apparently time to establish who was the alpha male. He started to clench down on my hand, as he was hoping to crush it with his vice-like grip. As a guy, I'd had this treatment more times than I could remember and al-ways responded in the same way. Instead of delivering force, I rolled the other guys knuckles together into the shape of a C then added pressure on the median nerve. It was excruciating, and soon Dave's face changed to a nice shade of red as his smile became pained, and he at last relented and released his grip on my hand.

"Very nice to meet you. Do you guys ever feel less special when you realize that almost all of you have the word special in front of your name?" I asked.

"No, it's just a fancy way of stating that we enforce over three hundred different federal statutes," Violet said.

"Three hundred? That'll keep you busy."

"Indeed. Anyway, we better get going," Violet said.

"Where?" Dave asked.

"The evidence desk," Violet said.

"Then lunch," I added.

Dave didn't look very happy as we left him and headed deeper into the building and passed various cubicles and agents before reaching the records room. It looked a like a vault with its armored door and small service window at its center, and on the other side of the it sat a middle aged fellow, who immediately smiled the minute he saw Violet.

"How are you, Harry?" Violet asked.

"Good, and you?"

"Excellent."

"How can I help you?"

"Just filing this form to document that I have temporary possession of some HPD evidence."

Harry took the paper, made a computer entry, then stuck the file in a bin on the counter.

"That all?" he asked.

"That's it. I'll see you later."

We left Harry and walked downstairs and out to my car.

"I guess we're off to Helena's, *brudda*," I said, as I slipped behind the wheel.

We headed to the parking lot and pulled out of our space only to find Dave had come outside to see us off. His expression looked rather unfriendly, so I waved then gave him the 'hang loose' hand gesture, but he remained unfazed as he glowered. Oh well, you can't please everybody all the time.

CHAPTER EIGHT
Lunch Date

We headed east on H1 and passed the infamous Pearl Harbor before reaching Helena's Kitchen in a little over ten minutes. It was after lunch, but it was still crowded with locals as we walked in and managed to get a table for two. A young woman of Asian descent brought us water and asked if we were ready to order. We both went with the Barbecued Pork rice plate as well as a side of Korean style pickled vegetables, and the girl left to put in our order. Meanwhile, Violet and I quietly sat until I broke the silence.

"So, I'm assuming the guy you told me about last night is Special Agent Dave Moore."

"How'd you guess? Was it his overwhelming charm or the handshake?"

"The handshake."

"Yeah, that was awkward."

"I think he still might hold a torch."

"If he would have cared that much before, we might not

have broken up."

"So, it was mutual?"

"Yeah, but it doesn't look like it now does it?"

"Nope, and he definitely did not like me."

"Maybe he was jealous of your fart."

"It was pretty amazing."

"It put mine to shame."

"Only in volume—not in smell."

I took a moment to look around at our fellow diners and saw a perfect demographic sampling of the Aloha State's population. Hawaii, like the rest of the United States, had experienced a large influx of immigrants over the years, and sitting around us were a myriad of races and ethnicities— everything from Europeans to Hawaiians, Asians, African Americans, Samoans, and hispanics. It was truly a melting pot and proof positive that this was the place to eat. Our waitress came by with two waters, and I lifted mine up to Violet for a toast.

"To exes," I said.

"To exes," she added, as we touched glasses.

Violet took a sip then set down her glass.

"So, you know about my ex, but I don't know much about yours?"

"Well, like you and Dave, our breakup was work related, but, as I said, before, it was mainly because she moved re- ally fucking far away."

"Like to a different state?"

"Like to a different part of the world. She started working for the international aid relief organization Globo-Care, and our three lovely months together came to an abrupt end."

"At least your breakup was for a good cause."

"True, though it didn't make it any easier."

"Yeah, I guess not. So, how did you two meet?"

I had to laugh.

"You wouldn't believe me if I told you."

"Try me."

I went on to explain that we had met when I rescued her as well as three other strippers from a sinking boat out on the San Francisco Bay.

"So, she was a stripper? You're a liar and a fucking hypocrite!" Violet said, testily.

"Not exactly. She was primarily a Playboy Playmate doing a one-time stripping gig."

"Jesus, your last girlfriend was a Playboy Playmate? That's a hard act to follow."

"It's not like it sounds. She only did it to raise money for her brother's legal defense fund."

Violet shook her head in dismay.

"To think I listened to all that bullshit at the party last night about you not being the stripper type."

"It's true, I'm not. Besides, stripping wasn't technically even her part-time occupation."

Violet sat back, crossed her arms over her chest, and scowled at me, but, thankfully, our waitress returned with two delicious looking, steaming hot plates of food, and our conversation was temporarily put on hold as both of us dug in and devoured our lunch in a matter of minutes. Finished, I leaned back in my chair and suddenly felt particularly full as I hazarded a final sip of water.

"So, you were pretty quiet back at the Police Evidence Lab. Do you have any thoughts?" I asked.

"Are you purposefully trying to steer the conversation away from yourself?"

"Not at all. I'm legitimately curious what you think."

"Honestly, it looks pretty bad for your girl."

"It does, but I'm surprised that you don't find the abundance of evidence a little disturbing."

"I admit that it's a little too much of a slam dunk, but sometimes it just happens, so what makes you so sure she didn't do it?"

"I know her pretty well."

"That's what everybody says—right before they learn that their loved one, friend, or next door neighbor is a serial killer."

"This time, I really do."

"How?"

"It's complicated."

"That's not an answer."

"I know but…"

"But what? Did you date her? I need all the facts if I'm going to make an accurate judgement call on this."

"We didn't date. In fact, her dearly departed husband Steven Green hired me to follow her in hopes of proving that she was having an affair."

"Was she?"

"Yeah, but so was he."

"And what happened?"

"I gave him back his money then went and told Jessica the whole story. A couple months later, I sort of hooked up with her and had a one night stand."

"That seems to be your MO."

"It's not what you think, as we didn't have intercourse. We were just too lonely people having a little fun."

"Lovely, does that mean I should feel special or easy that I went all the way?"

"Special, of course. Anyway, Jessica and I became good friends. In fact, I'm the one who introduced her to the vice president."

"Pardon me if I'm overstepping my bounds here, but isn't your involvement in this a gross conflict of interest?"

"My entire life is a gross conflict of interest."

"Jesus Christ, Finn. Do you realize that you were employed by the victim, and, worse still, more or less romantically linked to the murderer."

"Alleged murderer, and technically it would be less romantically linked."

"Fine, but that doesn't even take into account that you also boned one of the special agents currently assigned to the investigation."

"More like got boned by a special agent, and I thought you were assigned more as my babysitter."

"At this point, I'd say it's a little bit of both."

"So, speaking of you—what is the deal with your whole handcuff thing? Fetish or control issue?"

"Control issue. I was just being cautious. If you turned out to be a nut job, it would be a hell of a lot easier to deal with you if I had you cuffed to the bed."

"Oh, do you sleep with a lot of nut jobs?"

"No, it's just that paranoia is a side effect of my job."

"Apparently."

Suddenly my iPhone rang, and I looked down to see that John was calling, so I hit the accept button and held it to my ear.

"What's up, Number Two?" I asked.

"Oh, have you grown tired of calling me Sasquatch?"

"No, I just like to mix it up every now and then. What's up?"

"I was just calling to tell you that we'll be meeting at the Outrigger Canoe Club around six for dinner to discuss damage control. You know where it is?"

"Of course."

"Good, and bring your FBI handler as well."

"Anything else, your majesty?"

"Could you swing by Leonard's Bakery and pick up some more of those malasadas?"

"Sure, if you don't mind being a fat president."

"If only. The way things are going, I'll be lucky if I end up as nothing more than just another fat asshole."

"Don't underestimate yourself—you're already an asshole, so it should be no problem to top it off by getting fat."

"Thanks for another great pep talk, fucker, I'll see you at the Outrigger."

"Not if I see you first."

I hit the end button and saw Violet staring at me.

"What?" I asked.

"Seriously now—what do you have on the vice president that you can talk to him like he's a piece of shit?"

"Nothing— we're just friends."

"Obviously there's more."

"There is, but it's a long story, and the long and short of it is that I saved his life a few years back."

"Assassination attempt?"

"No, it was back in Afghanistan when we were both in the Service. His helicopter was shot down in enemy territory, and I had to go in and rescue him."

"What branch of the service?"

"Air Force Parajumper."

"Is that special operations?"

"Yeah, though our main objective was rescue operations."

"And you rescued the potential future president of the United States."

"Yeah, potentially I did, though it's not looking too good at the moment."

"I can see why you're so invested in this now."

"No shit. Everyone involved is a friend, and, worse still, I have a real stake in making sure that fucker is our next president."

"And the whole special operations background also explains why you went into the CIA."

"I suppose, though it's less common for PJ's unless they have a pretty remarkable military career."

"I'd say that saving the future vice president of the United States seems pretty remarkable."

"Well, more than anything, he was a friend."

"You know my ex Dave was also in the Service."

"Interesting. I'm betting he was probably in the Marines or, more likely, Army."

"Good guess. He was Army. In fact, he was a sniper in the Rangers."

"So, unless I want to be taken out by a bullet at long range, we should probably not tell him about our night of passion."

"Don't worry, he loves being an FBI agent too much to kill you, and if he did do it, he'd want to do it up close and personal."

"Good to know. Well, we have a few hours to kill before the damage control meeting. Want to go to that gun store?"

"You sure know how to treat a lady. First lunch, then the gun store."

"I'm romantic that way."

I paid the check, left a formidable tip, and we got in the Subaru and headed towards Queen street, and made the journey in about ten minutes. The place was called The Honolulu Gun Range, and we managed to find parking on the street a half block away, which wasn't always an easy feat in this part of the city. We left the warm eighty degree weather and were soon in yet another cool air-conditioned building. The first area we entered was basically a showroom with display cases stocked with various pistols while the walls behind were adorned with all manner of rifles. On the right side was the cash register and counter where people checked in before being allowed out onto the range. There were a lot of customers, and it took a good ten minutes before we finally made it to the counter, where we were greeted by a rather pretty and busty, though serious looking, woman who was probably around thirty and dressed in jeans and a tight T-shirt that had the words *You can have my gun when you pry it from my cold dead hands* printed across her chest.

"Howdy, I'm Charlotte. How can I help you?" she asked, in a cute southern drawl.

"Hello, Charlotte, my name's Finn, and this is Special Agent Kalili of the FBI. We were wondering if we could talk to your resident gunsmith."

"Oh yeah, of course. Let me call him."

She picked up the phone and spoke a few words then turned back to us.

"Simon is coming out. Do you mind if I ask why you want to talk to him?"

"Oh, don't worry. We're just doing a little research on silencers and need some technical advice," I said.

"Oh—sounds interesting."

"Hopefully," I responded.

A man around fifty appeared a moment later, and he was wearing shorts and a Hawaiian shirt and had a thick mop of grey hair framing his tan face, and all of it worked together to make him look like a hybrid between a surfer and a gun nerd.

"This is Mr. Finn and Special Agent Kalili of the FBI," Charlotte said.

"I'm Simon Wilson. How can I help you?" he asked.

"They want to know about silencers," Charlotte interjected.

"Specifically this one," Violet said, pulling the pistol and silencer out of her purse and handing it to Simon.

It was still in the evidence bag as he scrutinized it, and he appeared to look more intrigued with each passing second.

"Oh nice! Do you want to come back to my workshop, so we can talk in private?"

"Sure."

We followed Simon behind the counter and down a hallway into a large room full of gun smithing tools and weapons in various stages of assembly. He went to what I assumed was his main work area and took the Beretta out of the bag and immediately checked to see that it was unloaded. Good habits were the hallmark of responsible gun handlers, and Simon obviously didn't take any chances. He unscrewed the silencer then viewed it more closely by holding it under a large magnifying glass with a built-in light.

"This is absolutely top notch craftsmanship," he said.

"My sentiments exactly. Could you craft something like this?"

"Potentially, but it would take time and testing. Speaking of which, do you mind if I test-fire it to measure the decibel rating? That, and not effecting the accuracy are the only true tests of a silencer."

"Indeed."

Simon put on safety glasses, loaded two rounds into the clip, then walked over to a test-fire apparatus in the corner of the room. It stood about three and a half feet tall and looked like an old penny arcade viewer, though its purpose was to test-fire weapons to see that their machinery was in proper working order. What looked like a viewing port was actually the firing chamber and included rubber flaps that minimized peripheral blow back when a weapon was discharged. Beyond that, was the interior, which was filled with ballistic gel that stopped the bullets.

"Fire in the hole," he said, before chambering a round then pointing the pistol into the test bin and firing.

He fired, and the shot was surprising quiet, which was unusual, as silencers weren't actually silent. This one was as close as they got, and Simon was quick to look at his decibel meter.

"Wow, a little over fifteen decibels. This is one hell of a piece of hardware."

"Yeah, and we believe that it was made in about two or

three days."

"So, the person who crafted it knew exactly what he or she was doing."

"Any idea of someone on Oahu who might be able to do this kind of work?"

He thought a moment, then a smile formed on his face.

"There is one guy. He's a bit of an eccentric who only comes out about once a year, and, when he does, it's usually to meet with me to talk about guns."

"Do you have a name, address, or phone number?"

"Not exactly. As I say, he's a bit eccentric and is really protective of his privacy. All I know is that his name is Walter Zeibt, and he lives somewhere up on the north shore."

"German?"

"Maybe his parents, but he sounds as American as apple pie. He's also a Vietnam Vet—former Special Forces, but he apparently took up the family business after returning from the war."

"Which was obviously gunsmithing."

"Correct, and the guy really is a genius."

Simon cleared the weapon by pulling back the slide then handed over the Beretta.

"Did you want to take it out on the range?" he asked.

"Can we?"

"Absolutely."

"Cool, as I'd love to see how it performs."

I looked to Violet for final approval, and she gave me a nod.

"Right this way," Simon said.

We followed him out of his workshop and through the lobby, where Simon grabbed us a fresh target as well as ear protectors and safety glasses—or, as the regulars called them, eyes and ears. We went through a door and entered a sort of anteroom to put on all our gear, and there we came across a man and woman doing the same. He was probably close to thirty and looked like a young professional—probably an attorney or accountant judging by his preppy clothing and well kept appearance. His lady friend was a beautiful twentysomething blond wearing short tight fitting exercise pants and a bikini top that made a grand show of her rather large breasts—not that I'd noticed. On the table between them was a massive gun case, and inside were a number of pistols neatly lined up beside their clips on the black foam lining. Mr. Preppy was currently lecturing his beautiful companion about the subtleties of shooting a pistol, as he was apparently an expert, and, to that end, he took great pains to describe even the most minute of details. He eventually noticed me listening and turned his attention my way.

"First time?" he asked.

"Yeah, but I play a lot of video games," I responded.

"This isn't like any video game you've ever played. This is the real deal, friend, and, if you're not prepared to pull the trigger, that fucker could go flying out of your hands."

The guy seemed to enjoy his expert status and took a moment to look over the entirety of our little group, and his eyes lit up when he noticed Violet.

"If you need any tips, darling, feel free to swing by our stall," he said, to her.

"Oh, thank you. I will," Violet said.

We proceeded out to the range and took up residence in the last lane, which resided along the far wall, and was reserved for employees. Our fellow shooters from the anteroom arrived a moment later and took up residence at the next stall over—probably because Mr. Preppy hoped to impress Violet with his shooting skills. That theory was proved correct when he gave her a smug smiled then proceeded to take a lot of time to lay out his various weapons. It was a nice collection and included a Glock 17, a Sig Sauer 220, and three model 1911 Colt 45's that were all decked out with a shit load of competition mods. It was the collection of either an expert or a douchey wannabe, though my vote was obviously on the latter.

Meanwhile, back in our lane, Simon pulled out a box of 9mm ammunition and proceeded to load a clip then placed it on the little shelf in front of us. I connected the target to the clips on the overhead wire pulley system and hit the button to send it out about twenty-five feet.

"Simon, do you want to shoot first?"

"Sure, if you don't mind."

He picked up the Beretta, slid in the clip, and released the slide to automatically chamber the first round. He got comfortable and squeezed off a shot, and the sound was completely inaudible now that we were wearing ear protection. He hit the target about a quarter inch below the bullseye, so Simon was definitely an accomplished shooter, which wasn't surprising, as most gunsmiths were also marksmen. He put the weapon down and smiled as he turned around.

"That things shoots as smooth as butter."

Mr. Preppy had apparently also been watching and looked puzzled.

"What's with the silencer? I thought they were illegal," he said, raising his voice so that he could be heard over our ear protection.

"They are, but loud noises make me jumpy, so Simon here, as the holder of a federal firearms license, was kind enough to let us use one of his," I said.

"Oh, typical," he said, before retreating back to his stall.

I picked up the gun next and fired off a quick double tap, and the first bullet hit the bullseye dead center while the second was directly beside it.

"You're right. The silencer doesn't diminish accuracy one iota. It's perfect. Care to give it a try, Agent Kalili?"

"Sure," she said, picking up the Beretta.

She aimed and fired, and her shot went right through my bullseye hole, so Violet too was a hell of a shooter. I handed the pistol back to Simon, and he gratefully accepted it and finished off the rest of the clip, which also finished off the rest of the bullseye. Done on the range, we started preparing to leave, and Mr. Preppy popped his head around the corner of his stall.

"Done so soon?" he asked.

"Yeah, afraid so."

"Well, shooting isn't for the feint of heart. I'm sure you'll be much more comfortable back in front of one of your video games," he said, retreating back to his stall yet again.

Simon smiled at me, as he was obviously thinking the same thing I was—that Mr. Preppy needed to be taught a lesson in humility. We therefore all moved to the next stall over and watched as he tried to position his lady friend by adjusting her hips and shoulders and, more annoyingly, shouted erroneous advice. He finally backed away, and she pulled the trigger and jumped when the gun went off, which sent her shot high and right.

"No, no, no! You have to relax! Watch me," Mr. Preppy said.

He nudged her aside and took hold of the gun and fired, and his shot went low and right. He fired again, and the second shot hit about five inches below the bullseye. At that point, he switched places with her, and she fired again, and, just like the first round, her shot went high and right.

"No—you're not listening, Erika!" he complained.

"I'm trying," Erika said, sounding annoyed.

"Perhaps I can be of some help," I said, stepping forward.

"I've got this covered," Mr. Preppy said.

"Apparently not."

"Oh, give him a chance," Erika said.

"Fine," he said, stepping back and smiling smugly.

"By the way, the names Finn, Tag Finn," I said.

"Nice to meet you. I'm Erika."

"OK, Erika, let's get you shooting."

My first move was to get her to change from the isosceles triangle position to the more effective cheek weld.

"See that? Just think of your right arm as the stock of a rifle."

"Cool!" she said.

"Yeah, now, I'd like to adjust your grip, but that'll entail invading your personal space a bit."

She raised an eyebrow and smiled.

"Whatever it takes," she said.

I moved behind her and placed my hands over hers, which inadvertently nestled our bodies together, and, best of all, it made Mr. Preppy look noticeably annoyed. At that point, I adjusted her arms ever so slightly.

"Nice, now move your trigger finger out a tiny fraction. You're holding it too deep, and it's pulling your shots wide and right.

She did as I instructed.

"Perfect! Now, let's take this shot together, but, most important of all, don't anticipate it. So, to accomplish that, we're both going to take a breath, let it out about halfway, and then squeeze the trigger."

We both shared a breath, then gently squeezed the trigger together, and the next shot went dead in the center of the bullseye."

"Oh my God! You're amazing!" she said, before putting

down the gun and hugging me.

"No, that was all you," I said.

"No way! That was awesome!" she said, as she did a little jump that nearly jiggled her boobs free of her top.

"Oh, that was just a lucky shot," Mr. Preppy interjected.

"Hardly, she's a natural," I countered.

"Bullshit. Have her shoot again. This time alone," he said, sounding annoyed.

She took up the stance and repeated all I had just shown her then squeezed the trigger ever so gently, and her next shot hit so close to her first one, that the holes were literally touching. She called out excitedly and jumped up and down yet again, only this time her breasts popped out. She didn't notice, however, so, when she hugged me, I was up against some bare boobage, and, as she stepped back, I felt compelled to warn her.

"You might want to holster those," I said.

She looked down then smiled at me as she adjusted them back into her bikini top.

"Oh, what's the big deal of having a couple of boobs between me and my shooting instructor?"

"Good point."

"Seriously now! You're amazing!" she exclaimed.

"Oh, anyone can get lucky," Mr. Preppy countered.

"Once is lucky. Twice is skill," I countered.

"Well if you're such an expert, then why don't you shoot a few and prove it?" he said.

"Fine, I'll give it a try."

I picked up the Glock she had been firing and slid in a fresh clip before calling out my targets.

"I'm going to do this one like I do my video games — two to the groin, two to the chest, and two to the head. If you care to time me, it should take a little less than a second."

I double tapped and sent two shots directly into the groin, then did two more to the chest, and, last but not least, two to the head, and all six landed perfectly on target in tight groupings. Next, I placed the pistol in my left hand, called out the targets, and repeated the pattern, and all the shots landed within a quarter inch of the first round of shooting.

"Wow, I must be the luckiest guy on the planet. Violet, maybe you should fire a few—as a sort of double blind to test my theory," I said, placing the Glock down on the shelf.

Violet stepped up, slid in a fresh clip, then proceeded to mimic my shot pattern perfectly by placing two bullets at each point on the target. The guy stood there in shock with his ego so bruised that not a single word left his lips. There was nothing wrong about lacking proficiency in something as long as you had the balls to admit it, and Mr. Preppy just learned that lesson the hard way—in front of a potential love interest that I suspect he was trying to impress. Now, there was a lot less chance of him getting his man parts anywhere near his lovely date's lady bits. Live and learn.

"Well, I'm back to my video games."

"Yeah, fuck you, because I know you're not just some video game player!" Mr Preppy protested.

"You're right, and you're not much of a shooter, so I guess we're both full of shit. Now, enjoy the rest of your day, my dear, and believe me when I say that you're a natural."

She smiled and thanked me yet again for the brief lesson, then Simon, Violet, and I left and were soon in the anteroom and laughing as we took off our glasses and ear protection.

"We certainly put that asshole in his place," Violet said.

"No doubt, but he definitely deserved it," Simon said.

"Men will be men."

We exited to the main area, thanked Simon, and left the Honolulu Gun Range, before walking the short distance to the car.

"Five O' Clock. I guess we can head to the Outrigger Canoe Club," I said.

"I thought the meeting was at six."

"It is, but if we're early, we can kill some time by having a drink out by the water and watch the planes coming in from the mainland."

"Lunch, gun range, and now the beach?"

"It's like I said—I'm a romantic."

CHAPTER NINE
Damage Control

We left downtown Honolulu on H1 and headed east towards Waikiki Beach, and, about five minutes later, we made a right onto Kapahulu Ave, then a left just before the water onto Kalakaua Ave. This would take us to the Outrigger Canoe Club, which resided just below the famous landmark Diamond Head—the iconic long dormant crater that was seen in the background of nearly every picture ever taken of Waikiki Beach. We pulled into the parking area and were directed by the attendant to the garage which sat beside the club. After finding a spot on the second story, we walked downstairs and entered the club and were greeted by a lovely hostess in a Hawaiian print dress. I gave her my name and told her we would be meeting Frank Williams at six, but we were going to kill some time with a cocktail, preferably near the water. She steered us outside to the Hau Terrace, and we managed to get a table right on the edge of the beach, where we had a bird's eye view of the incoming flights as well as the club's members as they headed off for late afternoon paddling runs. Our server, a young man around twenty, took our order for two Chi Chi's then returned about five minutes later with two icy white cocktails adorned with a piece of pineapple and an obligatory miniature umbrella.

"To our partnership," I said, as I held up my glass to toast.

"May it continue in platonic bliss," she added.

"Or at least until we break down and have sex again," I said, taking a sip.

The drink was delicious and made for a nice capper to a particularly unusual day. Usually, coming to Hawaii was about relaxing and having fun rather than solving a murder case, but at least we now had a moment to unwind.

"So, I'm curious—have you been told to officially take any kind of active role in the investigation—or just play babysitter?"

"Not sure exactly, but my impression was that it was more about being a good babysitter."

"It can't be very fun getting a shit assignment like this when you're a special agent."

"Normally it wouldn't be, but so far I'm finding this case pretty interesting."

"It can't be everyday that you're dragged into a case involving the vice president of the United States."

"No shit."

We sat in silence a moment and enjoyed the warm Hawaiian evening until I turned my attention back to Violet.

"So, Special Agent Kalili. Why don't you tell me more about yourself."

"Where should I start?"

"Formative years."

She took another sip of her drink and thought for a moment.

"Well, I was born in Hawaii, but we moved around a lot during childhood. When I finally graduated High School, we were living in Washington D.C., but I was a little homesick for the islands and applied to the University of Hawaii. I got my bachelors but stayed on and eventually earned both a law degree and masters in criminology."

"Typical overachiever."

"What can I say? I liked school."

"And then you followed your father's wishes and joined the FBI."

"Pretty much, and, after getting through the Academy, I moved stateside and worked in Washington D.C., California, Arizona, and eventually here, where it was believed my Hawaiian ancestry would give me an advantage in allowing me to blend more easily into the local population."

"A girl with two graduate degrees going undercover as a stripper. What has the world come to?"

"Hey, some of the girls in that profession are incredibly bright."

"True, and they certainly know where the money is."

"And how to get it."

"So, did your dad pull the strings to get you this posting?"

"Officially no. Unofficially, it's very likely."

"So, are you happy here, or would you prefer a different locale?"

"There's nothing wrong with being here, obviously, but sometimes I crave a little more action."

"Not enough action in the aloha state?"

"Not exactly, though it's nice being able to spend time with my family."

We finished our first round of drinks and soon were on to our second when Frank Williams appeared at our table, looking like his usual intimidating self. He had classic movie star good looks, perfectly tan skin, and a tall, athletic frame that belied his sixty plus years of age. He was in excellent shape and worked out daily, and, tonight, he was wearing khaki pants and a Tommy Bahama shirt that showed off his rather beefy arms, whose size made me wonder if he might perhaps be taking some human growth hormone. Violet and I stood up to share a proper greeting, and he smiled at Violet, who he thankfully didn't recognize from the bachelor party the night before.

"Nice to meet you, Agent Kalili," he said.

"Nice to meet you too, sir," she said.

"Oh, please call me Frank.

"Frank, it is."

"So, are you two ready for our damage control meeting?"

"Yeah, and we have a lot of news from the Honolulu

Police department."

"It's good, I hope."

"Not really."

Frank didn't look very happy about our news but soldiered on and told us to grab our drinks and follow him to the formal dining room. Violet said she'd meet us after she made a quick stop at the bathroom, so Frank and I headed off through the bar, only to have a distinguished looking Asian man sitting at one of the nearby tables wave at Frank.

"Oh shit, do you mind if I take a second to talk to my friend?"

"Not at all, I'll go get a fresh drink."

I headed for the bar, ordered another chi chi, and, by the time it arrived, Frank was already back at my side. We set off, and he led me through a hallway that contained a number of pictures on the walls, and he paused to talk.

"Are you familiar with the Outrigger and its history?" Frank asked.

"Not really," I said.

"It's quite an amazing club. It was originally founded in 1908, with the idea being to promote and maintain Hawaii's ancient cultural pastimes—namely surfing and paddling."

"Which do you do?" I asked.

"Both, actually, though I also like to drink while I'm here."

"Well it certainly is an amazing location for any of those pastimes—especially drinking."

"And believe it or not, this club used to be located right

on Waikiki Beach where the famous Royal Hawaiian Hotel now stands."

"When did it move here?" I asked.

"1963."

"Well, I think I prefer this location."

"I agree, though there aren't as many hot wahine running around in bikinis."

"Life is all about sacrifice."

"Indeed."

I gazed at some of the pictures on the wall and managed to recognize several.

"You've had a lot of prestigious members," I said.

"Yes, and that includes some of Hawaii's most esteemed residents—including, of course, the late Duke Kahanamoku."

Duke Kahanamoku was one of Hawaii's most famous natives after having won three gold and two silver medals swimming for the United States in the Olympics. He was also known as the person to have popularized surfing across the world, and there was even a statue of him on Freshwater Beach in Australia.

"I also heard Tom Selleck was a member," I said.

"Oh yeah, and he used to play beach volleyball here all the time and, needless to say, was quite a ladies man."

"It's funny, but whenever I tell people that I'm a private investigator, they all make some kind of comment about *Magnum P.I.*—in spite of the fact it aired over twenty years ago."

"Well, it is enjoying newfound popularity on Netflix, and I must admit that it's my guilty pleasure whenever I'm missing Hawaii."

"Same here!" I said.

"Well then, you'll be interested to know that I own what was called the Robin Masters estate in the show."

"No shit?"

"No shit, and if you ever decide to move to Hawaii, I could rent you the guest house, and you could indeed become the real life version of *Magnum P.I.*."

"I'm tempted."

"And of course you know that the fabled King Kamehameha Club in the show was modeled after the Outrigger."

"I did indeed."

We moved on and entered the Koa Lanai dining area, which was more formal than the rest of the club, and I was relieved that I had not worn thongs, as it had a dress code, and my current outfit was probably only passable due to the presence and occupation of my fellow diners. Everyone was there, and John was at the head of the table, Jessica was to his left, and there were two empty seats immediately to the right of his majesty. Violet appeared at that moment, and the two of us went over and took our seats.

"I knew if I said there would be food and drink that you'd show up on time," John said.

"Just like the bachelor party, minus of course the hookers," I said, as Violet and I took a seat.

Jessica gave John a glare.

"He's kidding, my darling," he said.

"True, they probably weren't all hookers," I said, soon feeling a hard pinch on my thigh from Violet.

Oops. I kept forgetting that she too had been there.

"Everyone, this is Special Agent Kalili. She comes highly recommended from the Director of the FBI himself, and might I say, Violet, that you look very familiar," John said.

"Perhaps we met at some Washington event," Violet responded a wee bit nervously.

Or your bachelor party last night, I said, silently to myself, which made me suddenly realize just how incredibly awkward this dinner must feel for Violet. Here she was dining with the vice president and some of Washington's most respected political minds, when only the day before she had been a stripper at a bachelor party with a fair portion of the very same gentleman. The world certainly could be a small place at times.

"Most of you know each other, but I'll just go around the table and introduce everyone for Finn and Violet's sake. Starting on the right, we have Frank Williams, the veritable heart of Washington."

"Truly an exaggeration. Now, please continue on to the more important people," Frank said.

John went on to introduce his father Senator Douglass Matheson then moved on to Stuart Turnbull, who was his media and publicity strategist. Next was Brent Forbes, his chief political advisor, followed by Jeremy Kline, his attorney and expert on all things legal. Last but not least was Corn, Lux, and John's lovely wife to be Jessica Thurman—soon to be Jessica Matheson—assuming I managed to get her out of this mess.

"All right then, folks, I say we order our food and drinks then get to business," John said.

A waiter appeared and took our drink orders before returning about five minutes later with a bevy of cocktail concoctions filling his tray. He passed out everyone's respective drink, then set about taking our dinner order. When he finally got to me, I ordered a chicken dish that came with mashed potatoes and seasonal vegetables. Violet, last to order, went with the Mahi Mahi special and, soon, the conversation turned to the evening's topic—namely damage control.

"So, Finn, I know that you spoke with the Honolulu Police Department today. Do you want to fill everyone in?" John asked.

I went on to describe all that I had learned from the detectives and various techs, and the people at the table didn't appear to be too pleased with the news.

"And what was your take?" Frank asked.

"Well, pretty much all of them are absolutely confident that the evidence is conclusive, though the blood spatter guy was the only exception. In his opinion, there were some abnormalities."

"Such as?"

"He found it to be a little strange that only the sweatshirt tested positive for the victims blood. As a matter of fact, he said that it had more blood than it should, and he wondered why the blood hadn't penetrated deeper into any of her other clothes."

"So, that's kind of good news," Frank said.

"I suppose, but the detectives just see the blood as more proof of Jessica's guilt."

"And what's your take, Agent Kalili?"

"Please, call me Violet, and I would have to more or less agree with Finn. There is an abundance of conclusive evidence, though it seems a little too perfect. In five very busy years with the Bureau, I've never seen a case this cut and dry, let alone put together in such a short amount of time."

"Stuart, what's your take?" John asked.

Stuart the public relations strategist cleared his throat and looked grave as he leaned forward in his chair and prepared to speak.

"Well, needless to say, it's a PR nightmare of epic proportions. It sounds harsh, but the safest thing to do would be to call off the wedding and get as far away from Jessica as possible," Stuart said.

"Which you understand means not running for president as well," John responded.

"It's better than a scandal that'll end your political career for good," Stuart said.

"That's essentially true, sir," Brent added.

"I don't give a flying fuck. Jessica is innocent, and I'm not going to distance myself from her in any way. If it comes down to it, I'll forget the presidency entirely and retire to a nice normal life far from all of this bullshit."

"You can't do that, son. This country needs a man like you more than ever—someone who can cross party lines and unite the House and Senate, and help heal the divide that's tearing this country apart at the seams."

Jessica took hold of John's hand and gave him a reassuring squeeze.

"Well said, Douglass. It couldn't have come across any better had we all been humming the Star Bangled Banner," I said.

There were a few chuckles, though the majority remained quiet and brooding.

"I didn't intend to be overly dramatic. I'm just telling it how it is," the senior Matheson said.

"When exactly does Sasquatch here have to officially announce that he's running?" I asked.

"Beginning of next week," Frank said.

"So, we have a week to figure this out, and, honestly, I've done a lot more in less time."

"If you're referring to Soft Taco Island, then I would have to say that you spent at least half that time binge drinking and fornicating," Lux said.

"It doesn't matter to me as long as he gets it done," John added.

Lux scowled at us.

"On a serious note—we really are going to need a miracle from you, Finn," Frank said.

"Trust me, I'll do my best, as I don't want to go through life always knowing that my good friend peaked at number two."

Everyone laughed, and it was a good tension breaker.

"Now, how about we discuss an important question—namely, who might actually be behind all this? Who has the big four?" I asked.

"The what?" Frank asked.

"The big four—intent, motive, opportunity, and ability. Targeting the vice president of the United States means that our bad guy or guys, or even girls for that matter, have some serious balls as well as some serious clout. This affair can't have been perpetrated by your average bears. I mean, we have the most perfectly laid out crime, committed in the tiniest of windows, and dependent upon so many outside factors that it's actually a little mesmerizing. And how is that they managed to lure the victim to the very same hotel and got the supposed murder weapon across two thousand miles of ocean. Transporting a firearm is no small task in the age of Homeland Security, so it would have to be brought on a private plane or maybe even smuggled aboard Air Force Two for all we know."

"That seems highly unlikely," Frank said.

"Yeah, though it's possible," I countered.

"But it also implies that someone in our very circle could be complicit in this affair," Frank said.

"Hopefully not, but we can't rule anything out at this point."

"I suppose you're right, and we should at least consider it."

"Indeed, and it's also incredibly alarming that the Police had this entire affair more or less solved in a matter of hours. That leads me to believe that our conspirators have some pull in the local government as well."

"True, though that's not exactly a very comforting thought at the moment," Frank said.

"So, again, who has the balls, desire, and means to try and keep John from being the next president?"

"The Republicans for one," Brent said.

Everyone laughed.

"True, though they see John as a moderate team player and someone they might be able to work with in the event that they didn't get their guy into office, and, let's face it, they wouldn't risk a scandal like this, as the repercussions would absolutely bury the Republican Party."

"True," Matheson Senior said.

"And anyone who would be involved in this would have to have considerable motive and be utterly ruthless. I mean, a man has been murdered for God's sake. This isn't just about hurling political pot shots at the opposing party. This is some serious shit we're dealing with," Forbes said.

"Agreed, and as much as I don't want to admit it, Finn could be right that we need to at least consider the possibility that our enemy might very well have access to our inner circle in some way," Frank said.

"So, how do we proceed?" John asked.

Frank spoke first.

"Finn and Violet continue with their investigation while we put our heads to the grindstone and try to figure out who in the hell has the most to gain, and might therefore be the most likely perpetrators behind all this."

"Which means we hope for the best but plan for the worst," Brent said.

"Yes, I suppose, but at least the authorities have agreed to keep a lid on it for the moment, so we don't have to contend with the media thankfully. I'll personally head up damage control, so, Finn, I want you and Agent Kalili to keep me apprised of every aspect of the investigation. That way, I can confer with Brent and Stuart and keep them up to date should any official statements become necessary."

John let out a long sigh.

"I guess we have a plan of action," he said, looking at Jessica, who tried her best to smile but couldn't hide her underlying anxiety.

It wouldn't be fun to be in her position, and it wasn't just because she was accused of murder. Jessica was very likely the linchpin behind the love of her life's career success or failure. Dinner came to an end, and the conversation petered off as people began leaving, though John, his dad, Frank, Jessica, Corn, Lux, Violet, and me all stayed behind, and we decided to go to the Outrigger's outdoor deck and have an after dinner drink to reflect on the damage control meeting. After we sat down at a table that resided on the very edge of the beach, a waitress appeared and took our order then headed off to the bar. In the meantime, I gazed out towards the setting sun and saw storm clouds gathering on the distant horizon and couldn't help but wonder if it was an omen of things to come. Our drinks arrived soon thereafter, and John picked his up and turned his attention to me.

"So, what do you think of my team?" he asked.

"They seem very competent, though Stuart is kind of a fucker."

"That's to be expected, as he went to Harvard."

John had gone to Yale, so he of course threw in a college jab whenever the rival school was mentioned.

"Apparently, Harvard grads can be a little ruthless."

"Not all of us," Lux said.

"I suppose he has to be," John said.

"So, now that it's just the inner inner circle, do you mind if I ask you a few questions?"

"Of course not. Fire away," John said.

"Who came over aboard Air Force Two?"

"You're looking at them."

"That's it?"

"Yeah, as well as some support staff."

"And who would that be?"

"My assistant Jill and my Secret Service detail. After that, it would be Frank's aide-de-camp and chief of security Rex as well as a few of his important staff. Speaking of which—you'll want to meet Rex. He was stationed in Afghanistan at the same time as us, and you two might have crossed paths," John said.

"What branch?"

"Army. He was part of the Joint Special Operations Command."

"Oh, we may very well have crossed paths. It could be fun to talk to someone from the bad old days."

"He's got some wild stories," Frank said.

"Don't we all," I said, patting John on the back.

"No shit," John said.

"Oh, also, I'm curious if there is any kind of manifest for the flight?"

"I'll check and see if I can get you a copy. I assume you're trying to eliminate Air Force Two as an official conduit," Frank said.

"Yeah, it would be nice to know that the home team is clean."

"Indeed, I'll get on it first thing in the morning, Frank responded"

"Thanks."

"So, where will you start?"

"I think I'll start with the bachelorette party, which means talking to the bartender and wait staff."

"Why there?" Jessica asked.

"You said that you woke up hungover, yet didn't drink very much."

"Yeah, so why talk to the bartender?"

"Sometimes at special events, like a bachelorette party for instance, we drink more than we think. Perhaps we'll get lucky and find out that you were too drunk to have killed anyone—except perhaps your liver."

"I'm not exaggerating when I say that I only had three drinks at the most."

"And how did you feel when you left to go back to your room?"

"Actually, I was extremely tired."

"And that was after your apparent third drink?"

"Yeah."

"Interesting. Well, I'm sure it all happened the way you say, but I just want to verify everything for myself. It might be redundant, but it's a force of habit."

"You're the investigator."

"And I gotta say—I'm very intrigued by the gun."

"How it got here?" John asked.

"Well that's part of it, but I'm also curious to know how it was found. The police say that a local spear fisherman discovered it just off the beach this morning. I can tell you right now that if I had lost something in the ocean, it would have taken me hours, if not days, to find it. In fact, a friend of mine lost his wedding ring while honeymooning in Jamaica, and it took him and most of the resort staff a full day to find it. Mind you, it was smaller, but Jessica's Beretta was found on a craggy reef, which is no easy feat in the dim light of dawn, least of all when you're not even looking for the thing in question."

"That is interesting," Frank said.

"It is, but first things first, so I'll start with the bar and see if I can find out anything of interest then give you an update tomorrow. Oh, and I'm going to need to bring in a friend."

"Who?"

"Justin Beeber."

"The singer?" John asked.

"No, the former Agency tech wiz. I could use his help on some technical stuff."

"I suppose, as he at least has got top secret security clearance," Frank said.

"Great. I'll talk to you about it tomorrow."

"Thanks, Magnum."

"No problem, Robin."

"And feel free to come by the house sometime if you want to see the actual place where your television counterpart supposedly lived."

"I'd love to. Well I suppose we should be going. Good night, everyone."

"Yeah, good night, everyone. It was nice meeting you all," Violet added.

We headed out of the Outrigger and made the short walk to the garage and entered my surrogate Subaru. I fired up the engine, and we exited the parking garage and headed back the way we had come on Kalakaua Ave.

"There's no reason to go all the way back to the office, so why don't you drop me off at my place."

"What about your car?"

"It's my company car. Besides, we'll be working together

tomorrow as well anyway."

"Well OK, but are you sure you want me knowing where you live?"

"I think I can handle it."

Instead of heading west back towards Pearl Harbor, we drove east until H1 became Highway 72. About a mile later, Violet directed me to take a left on Laukahi Street, where we wound up the hill before taking a right onto Ihiloa Loop then another right onto Ohawai Place to reach Violet's house, which was at the very end and separated from the street by a long, narrow driveway.

"Think you'll be able to find your way back out of here?" she asked.

"Well—certainly not by using the street names."

I, of course, wasn't kidding, as all these Hawaiian names could get confusing, which was to be expected when their alphabet only had twelve letters—five vowels and seven consonants along with something called the glottal stop. The glottal stop or quick pause existed to emphasize a vowel sound at the end of a word such as Hawaii, or spoken properly, Hawai with an *e* sound at the end after a tiny pause. So, with very few letters to work with, the early missionaries who translated the Hawaiian language apparently managed this feat by stringing together a shit load of vowels and consonants, and on occasion, adding a glottal stop for good measure.

"Nice view, by the way," I said.

"It's home."

"It's fucking amazing. No wonder you're stripping in your free time to pay for this place."

"I suppose, though I was lucky and bought at the bottom of the market, so I'll have it paid off pretty soon."

She opened her door and stepped out, though she paused just outside and looked at me as though she wanted to say something.

"So, I guess I'll see you in the morning. Do you need me to come pick you up?"

"No, I can drive my own car up there. It's more fun to drive than my company car anyway."

"So, we can talk in the morning, which I suppose means that we have to exchange numbers now."

"Indeed we do," she said, pulling out her iPhone.

I gave her my number, and she quickly dialed it, then we both saved each other's contact info.

"Alrighty then—I'll see you later," I said.

"Good night."

I waited for her to walk inside her house while she waited for me to drive away, though neither of us moved.

"Well?" I said.

"Well what?"

"You going in?"

"Yeah, are you leaving?"

"Yeah."

"Well, you first."

"No, you first. I want to make sure you get safely inside your house before I leave."

"I think you just want another look at my ass."

"Nah, I've been looking at that all day. I've pretty much put it to memory."

"Really?"

"Absolutely. You have quite an incredible ass."

"Well, thank you."

"You're very welcome."

We headed into yet another awkward silence until Violet spoke.

"Look, I really would like to invite you in, but I can't."

"I understand. Our situation is very—complicated."

"That it is."

"You know, this is starting to feel like one of those phone calls you made in high school," I said.

"The kind where neither of you wants to be the first to hang up."

"Exactly."

There was another long moment with neither of us talking or apparently moving, so we were again at a stalemate.

"You should go inside your house now."

"You should drive away."

"How about this. If you're still standing there when I count to five, I'm going to get out of the car and kiss you good night. One, two, three..."

She looked conflicted, and a hint of a smile formed at the corner of her mouth.

"OK, I'm going in, but seriously now, last night was a one time thing, so we really need to keep our relationship all business," she said.

"Too bad."

She smiled, turned, and walked towards her house, and, just as she reached the front door, I called out.

"You were right."

"About what?"

"I did just want another look at your ass."

She smiled.

"Good night, Bart."

"Good night, Viola."

CHAPTER TEN
Partners in Fornication

It took me a good twenty minutes to drive back to the resort and pull into a parking spot, and, instead of going to my room, I decided to swing by the patio bar for a nightcap. There, I discovered a number of the other wedding guests apparently had the same idea, and, sitting at a table beside the pool were Lux, Corn, Lux's little sister Bridgette and her boyfriend Adrien Babineux, and, last but not least, Melissa Williams. They were all talking animatedly and doing what people were supposed to do in Hawaii—namely, enjoying themselves. Corn and Babineux, or Babs as I called him, were of course in shorts and a T-shirt, but Lux, Melissa, and Bridgette were all wearing bikini's and looking particularly lovely in the dancing light of the nearby tiki torches.

"I didn't know you guys all knew each other?"

"Everybody knows everybody in Washington," Melissa said.

"Apparently."

"I take it you've met the best man?" Lux asked Melissa.

"Oh yeah—in fact, he introduced himself by smacking my ass at the luau last night."

"Not too surprising," Lux said, scowling at me.

"Not surprising at all," Babs added.

"I thought she was someone else."

"Really, so whose ass did you think you were smacking?" Lux asked.

"Jessica's."

"The bride to be? Classy guy," Lux said.

"Indeed," Babs added.

"It's just this stupid thing we do. A joke between friends. Now, let's discuss something more important—namely what are we drinking?"

"Mai Tai's. Take a seat," Corn said, as he stood up and went to the bar for another glass.

He returned a moment later and filled my glass from the pitcher on their table then took a seat beside Lux.

"So, this is all looking pretty bad," Lux said.

"Yeah."

"Fuck—John's never going to get married, is he," Corn said.

"God only knows at this point."

I lifted my glass to toast.

"May Sasquatch get to the alter," I said.

"And in turn, the White House," Corn added.

We all clinked glasses then sipped our drinks, and I found the cool beverage to be a decidedly lovely counterpoint to the eighty degree evening.

"Wait—Sasquatch?" Melissa asked.

"You've never heard that nickname for John?"

"No."

"It came from Afghanistan. It's what Finn called him the night he rescued him from his downed helicopter," Corn said.

"Oh, I see, but, in that part of the world, wouldn't it be Yeti?"

"That's exactly what John said at the time."

"It makes sense, as we did grow up together."

"What was his majesty like as a youth?"

"Same."

"He was an asshole?"

"No, he was sweet."

"Well, that's enough about Sasquatch, so why don't you tell me about what you do back in Washington?" I asked Melissa.

"I run a nationwide educational foundation that raises money to provide scholarships for underprivileged children."

"Wow, that sounds very—altruistic."

"Something you perhaps might not understand," Babineux said.

"Says the arms dealer."

Babineux just happened to be an arms dealer as well as a French aristocrat, though he was also a member of a secret powerful secret society and president of the oddly named Caribbean paradise Soft Taco Island. When we first met, we were enemies, but he turned out to be a decent guy—in spite of being incredibly French.

"Well, I've got to raise money for my various charitable causes somehow," he said.

"Indeed."

I finished my drink and saw that the pitcher was empty and went to the bar for another before returning to the table to fill everyone's glasses.

"So, how did you get into your line of work?" I asked Melissa.

"I always wanted to be a teacher, so I taught high school for about a year after grad school then created the foundation so that I could reach more children, and it just sort of grew from there."

"You make my profession as a private investigator seem kind of lame and meaningless by comparison."

"No need to feel bad. Everyone has their calling."

Lux abruptly laughed.

"Face it, Finn, your true calling is obviously being a world class man-whore," Lux said.

"At least I'm world class."

"And don't forget that he's also a world class *trou du cul*," Babs added.

"Which is?" Melissa asked.

"An asshole," Babs answered.

"Well, once again—at least I'm world class."

Everyone had a nice laugh, then the table grew quiet for a brief moment, so I steered the conversation away from me and over to Lux and Corn.

"How have you two been?" I asked, knowing that Lux and Corn had been having a little marital trouble and had recently begun going to couple's counseling.

They exchanged a knowing smile then turned back to me.

"Good," Lux said, placing her hand on Corn's knee.

"And how about you two love bears?" I said, to Babs and Bridgette.

Babs and Bridgette were an interesting couple, as the two love bears had met and fallen in love during Lux's covert mission to thwart Babs's arms deal that was taking place on his oddly named Soft Taco Island. Unfortunately, at that point, Babs was still believed to be the bad guy, so Bridgette's little lapse in judgement was kind of a sore spot—for Lux anyway.

"We're engaged, and you'll be getting another wedding invitation in the mail soon."

"So, Lux, I assume you're her maid of honor?" I asked.

"Correct."

"Have you seen the movie Bridesmaids?"

"Of course, and, if I have my way, I'll make sure Bridgette gets food poisoned and suffers a pretty good case of explosive diarrhea."

"Ahhh—sisters."

Lux obviously still held a grudge against Bridgette for screwing up her operation—in spite of the fact that it all turned out fine in the end. Unfortunately for those close to Lux, myself included, she had a memory like an elephant and held on to grudges the way most women held on to their Coach purses. The conversation thankfully moved on to happier subjects, and the five of us continued to chit chat well into the evening. By eleven, everyone was thoroughly drunk and tired, and Lux, Corn, Babs, and Bridgette excused themselves and left the very lovely Melissa Williams and me alone beside the pool.

"I guess it's just the two of us," I said.

"So, Tag, I've been meaning to ask you if you have any romantic entanglements at the moment?"

I instantly thought about the lovely FBI Special Agent Violet Kalili, but she had made it abundantly clear that our relationship was to remain all business.

"None at the moment, sadly. How about you?"

"I have a part-time boyfriend back in Washington, but we're taking a break at the moment."

"So, you're single-ish?"

"I am," she said, as she placed her hand on my knee.

She started slowly inching it up my leg and towards my manhood, which was in turn growing and gently inching it's way towards her delicate finger tips. Drunk guys almost always hit on women, but drunk women hitting on guys was far less common, so it was more than a little exciting to be the object of Melissa's affection. Perhaps this was turning out to be a proper Hawaiian vacation after all.

"How about a dip in the pool?" she asked.

"I could use a little frolicking at the moment," I said.

We moved to the pool's edge, and I took off my shirt and walked down the steps until my feet were submerged enough to feel the water's cool embrace. Melissa, however, skipped the steps and dove in the deep end then swam over and stood in the shallows and smiled lasciviously as she reached around her neck and pulled off her bikini top to reveal her large wet glistening breasts. Sweet mother of God! They were glorious, but the moment annoyingly brought about thoughts of Violet, and I wondered if I were perhaps on the cusp of doing something stupid. But, why would it be stupid? How could it be wrong to have a little adult fun with another woman, if the original woman made it very clear that we were not going to have any kind of romantic entanglement? Unfortunately, my brain was feeling conflicted, but my penis was practically yelling at me to get my ass into the water. I decided to throw caution to the wind and descended further into the pool but couldn't shake the uncertainty that it might very well be the metaphorical first level of hell.

"I prefer to swim in the nude. I hope you're not offended," she said, as she slipped off her bikini bottom.

"Not at all. I find female nudity soothing."

"I'm glad to hear that, but I hate to be the only naked person in the pool," she said, as she came over and pulled off my shorts.

"Well, you've officially freed Willy," I said.

"He seems a lot happier. Does he do any tricks?"

"Other than spelunking, seminal regurgitation, and getting me into trouble? Not really."

She threw my shorts onto the edge of the pool then swam to the other end and back before surfacing beside me, where the view of her wonderfully wet naked body was making my heart race and my penis surge with enthusiasm.

"You swim like a fish," I said.

"I was a swimmer in college."

"And apparently a good one."

"Yeah, though I suppose I have an unfair advantage because of my large feet."

"So, it's like wearing flippers?"

"Pretty much."

"Well, anatomically it makes perfect sense. You wouldn't be able to stand if you didn't have proper footing to counterbalance your extremely well developed chest."

She smiled as she came forward and unexpectedly kissed me, and her tongue arrived a second later. It was sweet, warm, and slippery as it slid into my mouth, and we engaged in a veritable tongue tug of war until we parted lips.

"Well, hello, my new favorite pool buddy," I said.

"When I see something I want, I don't fuck around. I go for it."

Melissa once again planted her lips on mine, and I had

to admit that there was nothing quite as exciting as being drunk, wet, and frolicking with a woman as attractive as Melissa. It certainly didn't hurt that she apparently had the multi-tasking skills of a juggler, as she was able to maintain proper lip contact while simultaneously reaching down and expertly exploring my manly goodies. She had firm hold of Tag Junior, and she had managed to work him into a raging hard-on that was now precariously perched between her legs. Sweet Poseidon's libidinous daughter! I was falling grossly behind in the foreplay department, so I therefore decided to do a little exploring of my own and set off on a mighty quest. I ran my hands down her shoulders and took hold of her formidable breasts and gently teased her generous nipples until they were as hard if not harder than my manhood. Of course, such delicacies of the flesh required the presence of my mouth, and I parted from her lips and used my tongue to tickle both nipples until Melissa elicited soft gasps of pleasure. I decided to head back up towards her lips, but couldn't help but stop and kiss her neck along the way. This seemed to increase her efforts with my manhood, and that, in turn, inspired me to reach down and gently explore the hot, wet contours of her neatly trimmed garden of sunshine. I started at the bottom, then slid my fingers up and over her clitoris, where I began making slow luxurious circles that made her writhe and moan.

"Shit—maybe we should take this party inside," I said.

"Yeah, inside my vagina—but, first I'd like to have a little fun of my own, so, I'm going to need for you to sit on the edge of the pool."

I slid up onto the edge of the pool, and Melissa smiled devilishly as she took hold of my mantool and ran her tongue its entire length before taking the tip into her mouth. She did a couple of extremely powerful passes then leaned back and smiled.

"I'm not trying to brag, but I'm the queen of blowjobs."

"Then I think you should know that I'm the king of cunnilingus."

"Perhaps we should have a royal contest."

"Here?"

She looked around.

"Why not, we're alone."

"I don't know—kids will be swimming here in the morning."

"True. Can you walk with Willy that hard?"

"I can do a lot more than walk."

"Well, let's go."

"My room or yours?"

"Yours," she said.

We grabbed our things and left the pool area, and I used my shorts and shirt to cover my groin. We were in a popular crowded resort, so it stood to reason we might run into other hotel guests, and I decided to err on the side of modesty. It turned out to be a wise decision, because, as we rounded the final corner before my room, we ran into Sandra, and she paused and crossed her arms over her chest as she regarded me.

"Nice boner, Finn," she said.

"It's not what it looks like."

"So, that's not a boner?"

"No, it's definitely a boner."

"Then it's exactly what it looks like."

"Sorry, but I have to go take care of this."

"Indeed, I think you should."

We left Sandra and entered my room, where I was feeling ever relieved to at last be out of the public forum.

"So, what kind of contest did you have in mind?" I asked.

"Who can make the other person climax faster."

"And what does the winner get—aside from the obvious?"

"They get to choose the next activity."

"Won't it be over at that point?"

"Only for you, so I'll be sure to stop right before you climax. Now, lay back on the bed and keep a close eye on your watch."

I lay back and looked at my watch in order to mark the time that her mouth touched down on my penis. It was twelve ten and ten seconds, and, suddenly, I was awash in pleasure, as her tongue action and secondary use of her hands was exemplary. The seconds flew by, and it was at twelve ten and fifty-five seconds that I called time, barely able to hold back the inevitable.

"Well, how did I do?" she asked.

"Forty-five seconds."

"Not bad."

"Not bad at all—especially considering the amount of alcohol I've had tonight. Now, it's my turn."

We switched places, and I handed her my watch.

"Start counting the minute my tongue touches down."

Now it was my turn, and it was pretty unlikely that I could beat her time of forty-five seconds. The vagina could be a slippery slope, but there was always a chance. I set to work by going straight to the clitoris, and Melissa's hips flexed involuntarily, which I saw as a good sign that I was on the right track. Not all women could climax very easily and some couldn't climax at all. Interestingly, it was a rare known fact that nymphomaniacs, in spite of their sexual addiction, rarely, if ever, achieved climax—so I was therefore hoping that Melissa was not a nympho. About fifteen seconds in, I was hitting my stride and decided to use a little hand stimulation in conjunction with my tongue, and I slipped two of my fingers just inside her opening, and Melissa began to cry out. I had found the apparent sweet spot between vaginal and clitoral stimulation, and I continued quickening my pace in tiny increments until she was in the full throws of an impending climax. Her back arched, and her vagina constricted around my fingers, and she began screaming in ecstasy as her entire body continued to convulse. I finally relented, and she at last came to rest with a satisfied smile on her face.

"Fuck, was that fast!" she said.

"What's my time?"

"Fifty-nine seconds, which is by far the least amount of

time it has taken any man or woman to make me cum."

"I aim to please, though I can't help but think that you're just blowing smoke up my ass."

"I don't lie or fake it when it comes to orgasms."

"Good to know."

"But, I still won."

"Indeed, so what's your preference?"

"Intercourse, of course, but let's take it up a notch. I've been a naughty girl, so why don't you to tie me to the bed and punish me properly."

"Punish you?"

"Yeah, with your cock."

"OK, though I am practically a stranger."

"Hey—you saved my oldest, dearest friend's life, so I imagine I'm in pretty good hands."

"Well, OK then."

She stood up and went to her purse and pulled out a handful of silk scarves before returning a moment later.

"I take it you always come prepared," I said.

"Because I'm always prepared to come."

Gulp. She looked around the room and made some mental calculations before moving to the foot of the bed, where she opened her legs, bent over, and stretched her hands out towards the bedposts.

"I'm waiting," she said, as she looked back at me with a wanting and naughty smile.

I wavered a moment, as I was feeling a sudden pang of apprehension, but lust won out over reason, and I proceeded to use the scarves to tie each of her wrists securely to the bedposts.

"Alrighty then," I said.

"You forgot my feet."

"How thoughtless of me," I said, as I picked up the two remaining scarves and secured her feet, thus leaving her bent over, spread legged, and utterly helpless.

Finished, I took a moment to admire my work and watched as Melissa pulled on her binds to test that I had indeed tied her properly. Unable to get free, she appeared to be satisfied with my work, and she proceeded to wiggle her backside in delightful anticipation. This evening had certainly taken an unexpected turn, and now seeing this naughty side of Melissa instantly brought to mind thoughts of her time as a teacher. I could only imagine what it must have been like for her male students, as she was every school boy's walking-talking-fucking fantasy, and when I say fucking I literally mean fucking.

I stepped forward and ran my hands up her thighs and over her smooth round buttocks then pressed my hips to hers so that my hard member was between her legs and resting against the outside of her lady region.

"Are you going to stand there and admire the view, or are you going to fuck me?" she asked.

"I'm going to do both," I said, as I slid my hand around and gently caressed her nipples.

She purred like a kitten and pressed her hot, wet opening against my straining member, and, after a moment, she turned and looked at me over her shoulder, and there was something a little manic in her expression.

"So, yesterday, you said I had a nice ass."

"I did, and I meant it."

"Good, because now I want you to tap it," she said, as she wiggled her backside.

Did I just hear her correctly? Did she really say tap it? Jesus. Who in the hell was this woman?

"Come on. Get to it! Tap it," she said, again as she continued to wiggle her lovely backside.

"Sorry, but are you inferring anal sex?"

"No, I'm using an expression that means I want your cock in my pussy! Now, tap this ass!"

"Ahhh—got it," I said, though in truth I wasn't entirely sure I did.

I reached down and guided Tag Junior unto her warm wet essence and slid inside until reaching full mount.

"Oh yeah, that's it!" she said.

I took hold of her hips and started thrusting in and out and couldn't help but relish the tantalizing visual aphrodisiac that was Melissa's ass. It was held high in the air, and each meeting of flesh sent a powerful ripple through her glutes. For Melissa, however, it was more than just visual stimulation, for this position also happened to provide an opportune angle for hitting the hotly contested Gräfenberg Spot—the very sensitive area that supposedly resided about an inch or so inside on the upper reaches of the vagina. So, as I reached a steady heart pounding pace, she began calling out so loudly that I was starting to worry about the legitimate possibility that I would receive a noise complaint from the hotel.

"Oh yeah! That's it! Now tap it and slap it!" she bellowed.

"What?"

"Fucking tap it and slap it!"

"Wait, I thought I was tapping it."

"Yeah, but now I want you to slap it, and that means spank me! Spank my ass!" she yelled.

"What?"

"You heard me, tough guy. Spank me! I've been a bad girl, so spank my fucking ass!"

I wasn't sure what she meant by bad, but I was in no position to argue, so I gave her a gentle pat.

"Harder, you pussy!"

I gave her another one that was a bit harder, and there was a decently loud smacking sound at the point of impact.

"Not bad, but the next one better be harder."

I gave her ass another slap, though this one was a little harder.

"Oh yeah, that's it! Again!" she yelled.

I did it again.

"Oh God yes! Now, come on—fuck the shit out of me, you fucker! Slap and tap!"

I did as told, and now our bodies were coming together violently, and my balls were sailing forward and inadvertently colliding with her clitoris and making an additional, though dull, slapping sound. When you combined it with the spanking of her ass, the combination was not unlike a complicated drum beat with her ass serving as the snare drum and her clitoris serving as the hi-hat—and together they were making the noise tap-tap-tap-slap—tap-tap-tap-slap.

"Oh God, yes, fuck me, fuck me, fuck me, you fucker!" she screamed.

Now, it was official. I wasn't just starting to worry—I was full on seriously worried that the noise would bring a visit from hotel security. If only she had another silk scarf, I would have gladly used it to gag her.

"Pull my hair!" she said, excitedly.

"What?"

"I said pull my fucking hair!" she yelled.

Again I did as instructed, though I was starting to wonder if perhaps I had made a grave error in judgement in bringing this hellcat up to my room. I wasn't shy in matters of the bedroom, and it was some damn exciting intercourse, but her unusual sexual appetite and propensity for hollering was a bit disconcerting and making me feel oddly victimized—which was saying a lot considering the fact that she was the one tied to the bed. I mustered my resolve, however, and did as asked and pulled her long mane of hair.

"Now, pull my hair and spank me at the same time you little bitch!" she yelled.

Jesus, now she was becoming openly abusive in her commands. How many fucking hands did she think I had? I wasn't an octopus for God's sake! Fortunately, I was coordinated enough to multitask, and I used my left hand to pull her hair, while I used my right to deliver a series of smacks to her backside—making the entire affair feel as though I were a jockey coaxing a galloping steed. Still, I stayed true to the cause and pounded away until her cries of ecstasy picked up in pace and volume. Her hands pulled against her silken bonds as she started into a climax, but thankfully she dropped her face onto the bed, and her scream was muffled by the comforter, which served as an improvised gag to lower her volume and hopefully keep the neighbors at bay. She stopped moving then popped back up and looked at me over her shoulder.

"OK, untie me, fucker. It's time to finish what I started earlier," she said, with a sinister smile now playing across her lips.

For a split second, I thought about leaving her tied up and making a run for it, but I thought it prudent not to leave Frank Williams's beloved daughter tied to my bed. I therefore undid her hands and feet, and she immediately knelt and took my mantool into her mouth. The pleasure was intensely wonderful, but thoughts of her unusual lovemaking style continued to fill my mind with uneasiness. Still, as haunting as it was, it wasn't enough to stave off her Herculean efforts, and the inevitable occurred no more than seventeen seconds later, when the entire inventory of my balls was pulled from my body as though by a vacuum. Melissa's efficiency bordered on super human, and, like the night before with Violet, I had been blessed with some other worldly oral pleasure, but the craziness of the encounter left me feeling oddly vulnerable and uncomfortable. I couldn't be sure if it was guilt relating to Violet, or just fear of Melissa's cuckoo for Cocoa Puffs lovemaking style, but, either way, I was sure I was going to regret it in the morning.

Melissa stood up then headed for the bathroom, and I was left standing there alone and in shock. I heard the shower turn on, and I waited for her to finish before I went in and did the same. Upon returning, I could see that she was already asleep, and I gingerly slipped into bed and took a moment to quietly ponder the evening. I was already starting to feel a lot of trepidation over my unusual sexual encounter with the hellcat Melissa Williams, and, as I tried to close my eyes and put those thoughts aside, I found myself thinking about the beautiful Violet Kalili. Were we really doomed to only have a business relationship—and if not—did I just somehow fuck that up by having a one night stand with crazy Melissa? Oh well, what was I worrying about? I was a single man at the moment and therefore hadn't done anything wrong. Fuck it! Violet didn't need to know anything about this little indiscretion, and tomorrow it would all become a thing of the past. With those thoughts bolstering my resolve, I relaxed and took refuge in sleep and felt ever optimistic about the day ahead.

CHAPTER ELEVEN
Rudy the Rohypnolist

I awoke the next morning alone and with the hellcat Melissa nowhere to be seen as I slipped out of bed and walked to the bathroom. I found the door closed, so I knocked, and it opened a minute later, and there was Melissa looking fully dressed, showered, and, thankfully, ready to leave.

"Oh, did I wake you? I tried to be as quiet as I could so that you could sleep," she said.

"No, it's OK, I woke upon my own accord."

"Well, I need to get going, as I've got a busy day."

"No problem. I do too."

She began gathering her remaining belongings, and I went over and picked up my iPhone to see if I had any important texts or calls from Violet, John, or even Frank. There wasn't a single notification, and I breathed a sweet sigh of relief, though I nearly shit myself when my iPhone rang, and I looked down to see it was Violet calling. Oh shit—this was where a dumb drunk late night escapade could come under the scrutiny of the harsh light of morning. I mustered my courage and tried to remove any lingering guilt from my mind as I hit the answer button.

"Hello," I said, a little timidly.

"Morning, sunshine. You awake?"

"Of course."

"Good, because I'm on my way over."

"Oh, when should I expect you?"

"Soon, I just arrived at your hotel."

"Oh wait—hold up. I still need to get ready, so perhaps I should just meet you in the lobby," I said.

There was no response, as she'd already hung up, and now I was starting to panic. Fucking Violet was going to arrive just as Melissa was about to leave—but, did it matter? I wasn't exactly sure, though I had a pretty strong feeling that it would be a lot easier if their arrival and departure didn't overlap. I therefore silently prayed for a smooth and easy transition, but, as Melissa opened the door, there stood Violet, and she was looking more than a little surprised to see that I already had a visitor.

"Oh, sorry, I didn't know you had company. I can come back later," Violet said, uncomfortably.

"Oh, no worries. I'm on my way out. See you later, Finn, and thanks for a hell of a night," Melissa said, as she slapped her ass then blew me a kiss and turned and left.

Violet walked in and stood there with her arms crossed

over in front of her chest as she looked at me with deep and unflinching scorn. So much for keeping last night to myself

"You don't waste any time, do you?" she said.

"It's not what it looks like."

"Oh, so you two didn't have sex last night?"

"Um, well—yeah, I suppose we did."

"Well, then it's exactly what it looks like."

Shit—that was the second time in twenty-four hours that I'd been called out for using the phrase it's not what it looks like, so it was probably about time that I stopped using it.

"In my defense, I was extremely drunk and therefore freely admit that it was a grave error in judgement."

"I know the feeling."

"Very funny."

"Yeah, yet still very true."

"You want some coffee or breakfast?" I asked, trying to lighten the mood.

"I already ate, but I'd love some coffee. In the meanwhile, you can tell me all about last night."

I got on the phone and ordered a pot of coffee and a vegetable and bacon omelet with a side of potatoes and wheat toast. After putting down the phone, I noticed Violet was still quietly staring at me, so she was apparently not willing to drop the subject of my unusual female visitor.

"So, you really want to know about last night?" I asked.

"I do, because I think it will make our relationship a lot less complicated."

"Really? How's that?"

"Well, seeing that you're obviously some kind of man-whore, there is no way in hell that I will have any kind of romantic involvement with you now."

"I thought we had already established that fact."

"Not officially."

"But you literally said it to me last night."

"Yeah, but I didn't mean it. It was a test—and one which you failed, obviously."

"It might have been nice if you had told me all this beforehand."

"Then it wouldn't have been a proper test, would it?"

It was yet another Men are From Mars, Women are Just Fucking Crazy moment as I stared at Violet and realized that she was apparently dead serious.

"I honestly thought that we were not going to have any more romantic involvement."

"Good, because now we aren't."

There was a knock at the door, and a moment later the same waiter from the previous morning was wheeling in a cart full of goodies. He glanced at Violet for a second, though he thankfully didn't recognize her now that she was properly clothed and not wearing the blond wig. I signed the bill, poured us each a cup of coffee then took a seat at the little dining table. Violet took a seat across from me and sat there sipping her coffee and watching me eat, all the while still brandishing the very same look of disapproval. I finally finished my extremely awkward breakfast then stood up.

"Well, I'm off to shit, shower, and shave. Will you be OK on your own out here?" I asked.

"Yeah, as long as there aren't any more women in here that I need to worry about," she said.

"Well, if you find any, you know where to send them."

"You do understand that I carry a gun and know how to use it, right?"

I ignored her rather unveiled threat, then refilled my coffee cup, and left Agent Kalili behind as I entered my holy sanctuary. I set my coffee down, turned to make sure I locked the door, and, now feeling safe and sound, I took a minute to breath, relax, and empty my mind of the turmoil of the morning. Feeling better, I sat on the throne, took a sip of coffee, then relaxed my sphincter and let loose a mighty dump that allowed any remaining worry or negativity to flow free of my body. I picked up my iPhone, took another sip of coffee, and brought up my good friend Justin Beeber's number. It was a little after nine local time, so it was about eleven a.m. back home, and that meant Beeber would be wide awake and probably playing a flight simulator video game instead of writing code. He was the boss, however, so it would be his prerogative to fuck off at work. I hit send, and he answered on the forth ring with his usual snarky response.

"What do you want?" Beeber asked.

"Seriously, you can't say hello first?"

"There's no point, so why waste the time?"

"I thought you'd be a little nicer since I helped facilitate you losing your virginity."

"Fuck you. I wasn't a virgin before Lizbeth."

Beeber liked to refer to his girlfriend as Lizbeth, because he loved the Lizbeth Salander character from the Girl With the Dragon Tattoo books. His girlfriend's real name, however, was Rachel, and their budding relationship happened solely because of my ability to bring people together. Sure, they were already attracted to one another, but the fact that Beeber was her boss created an uncomfortable barrier that neither of them were willing to cross—without help, anyway. That help came in the form of me arranging a night of drunken private room karaoke, and, ever since, the two lovebirds have been inseparable, which, of course, justifies my claim that I had indeed helped Beeber lose his virginity.

"Really? So, who was your first?" I asked.

"A girl at MIT."

"What's her name?"

"None of your business."

"I'm serious. Just tell me her name, and I'll drop it."

"A gentleman never kisses and tells. Anyway—what do you want?"

I decided to let it drop, as I needed Beeber's help, and there was no need to bring up the emotional pain of his formative college years.

"How would you like an all expenses paid trip to Hawaii?" I asked.

"Can I bring Lizbeth?"

"Absolutely."

"Which island?"

"Oahu."

"I guess that's OK. What's the catch?"

"I need your technical expertise."

"As usual. When is our flight?"

"I'll text you the details in a few minutes."

"OK, I'll be waiting. This better not be a trick."

"No trick, but it will be the best working vacation you've had in a long time."

"We'll see. OK, I gotta go."

"Yeah, get back to your flight simulator."

"Fuck you. How'd you know?"

"The same way I always know—I'm a detective, and you're a nerd."

I hung up and brought up another number in my iPhone, namely Daniel Vandenberg. He was Lux and Bridgette's father and one of the principle owners of the Vandenberg Corporation. I hit the send button, and two rings later he picked up.

"What's up, Finn?"

"Are you busy?"

"No, just enjoying breakfast out on the lanai."

"I have a little favor to ask."

"I assume this concerns John and Jessica's predicament."

"Yeah, I need to bring in some specialized help from the mainland."

"You need the jet?"

"Is it possible to send it to San Francisco to pick up some people today?"

"Absolutely, as it's already sitting on the tarmac in San Francisco. So, tell your people to be at the private terminal in two hours."

"Thanks, I owe you one."

"Hardly."

I hung up the phone and all but had a heart attack when I looked up to see Violet entering the bathroom.

"What the fuck? That door was locked!" I said.

"It may have been locked, but the bolt wasn't engaged."

"Sweet Lord! Do you mind? I'm trying to take a shit here!"

"Quit your whining. I just need a tissue, then I'll be out of your way."

"I don't think you understand what you're messing with here."

"You mean you're not just a guy taking a shit?"

"Well, yes I am, but what you don't understand is that whenever my shit get's interrupted, something very, very bad happens."

Violet tried her best not to laugh, as she was apparently ignorant to the severity of forces she was dealing with here.

"I'm serious about this," I said.

"I believe you are—and that's what makes it so funny."

"Well, now that you've most certainly brought about some kind of major disaster, do you mind leaving me in peace now?" I asked.

"Not at all," she said, fanning the air around her head.

Violet left and closed the door, and I finished up my dump, though the joy was long gone from the experience. I flushed and entered the shower under a veil of trepidation, as bad things were now on the horizon, and that wasn't good—considering how bad things already were. At least I had the warm invigorating embrace of the shower to console me in this time of great despair. Once I was fully clean and feeling better, I turned off the taps, dried off, and adjourned to the bedroom to get dressed. There, I noticed Violet was watching me through the open door as she sipped her coffee out in the living room.

"It really is too bad that you had to turn out to be such a man-whore. Sexually, I felt we really had a good connection and lots of room to grow."

"Agreed, though we are apparently lacking in communication—on your part, anyway."

"Yeah, so let's change that with some communication right now, starting with you telling me who that skank was."

"Frank Williams's daughter."

"No shit?" she asked, sounding legitimately curious.

"Of course, I don't fornicate with just anyone, and you should also know that she runs an educational scholarship foundation for underprivileged children."

"Well, she's still a skank."

Fucking women. If only she had been even one tiny bit optimistic about our potential relationship, I would have abstained from my reckless evening with the lovely, albeit crazy, Melissa Williams. Now, it was very likely that I would never hear the end of this brief lapse in judgement. After putting on my shoes, I walked into the living room and poured myself the remainder of the coffee and downed it in one gulp before returning to the bathroom to brush my teeth. Minty and fresh, I rejoined Agent Kalili, and we left my room and headed over to the lounge, where I hoped to learn the name of the bartender working the night of Jessica's bachelorette party. The place was mostly deserted this early in the day, and there were only a few die-hard alcoholics inhabiting the bar. Violet and I took a seat and were soon joined by the bartender, who was a pretty twentysomething woman with long sun bleached blond hair, a nice tan, and a curvaceous figure that nicely accentuated by her tight low-cut dress.

"Hello, what can I get you?" she asked.

"Believe it or not—just information concerning a recent event here at the hotel."

"Oh, would that be concerning the murder here two nights ago?"

"It would."

"Oh, so, who do you two work for?"

"My name is Finn, and this is Special Agent Violet Kalili. I'm a special investigator for the vice president, and she's obviously with the FBI," I said.

"Well, I'm Lindsey, and I obviously just work for the hotel—but I'm happy to help in any way I can."

"Excellent, as we need to know who was bartending the

night of the murder."

"That's easy—me."

"So, you also handled the bachelorette party?"

"I did."

"Well, Lindsey, I have a few questions regarding the bride to be. Namely, how much did she have to drink that night?"

She thought for a moment.

"Not much, actually, which is kind of weird. Usually people in her position go a lot more apeshit."

"So, what do you mean by not much?"

"I think she had about three glasses of Pinot Noir."

"That's it?"

"Yeah, why?"

"She woke up feeling fuzzy—as though she'd had a lot more to drink than that."

Lindsey thought for a moment then sighed.

"Goddammit! I might have an answer," she said.

"What is it?" I asked.

"Rudy."

"Rudy?"

"Yeah—Roofie Rudy."

"Excuse me?" Violet asked.

"That's Rudy's nickname, and we had some trouble with him in the past when he got caught slipping rohypnol into our female guest's glasses."

"Was he using it to sexually assault them?"

"No, just rob them. He'd dose them, help them back to

their rooms, and when they woke up, their money and a number of valuables would be missing."

"So, you think Rudy might have slipped something into the bride's drink?"

"I'm not sure exactly, but when I turned around to take her order, he was standing right beside her. He's supposedly left all that behind, but it wouldn't be a stretch to think he might be up to his old tricks and tried to dose her."

"Do you have a full name for Rudy?"

"Yeah, Rudy Rafael."

"Anything else on him?"

"No, that's about it, though sometimes he moonlights here as a waiter at special events."

"Really? Even with his past indiscretions?"

"Yeah, sadly he's a bit of a charmer and convinced one of the female catering managers to give him a break."

"Any other unusual characters hanging around that night?"

"Not that I remember."

"Well, thanks, and here's my card in case you remember anything else."

She looked at the card, and her bright blue eyes came alive as she smiled at me.

"What if I don't remember anything? Can I still call?"

"Absolutely."

"We better be going," Violet said, as she took hold of my arm and led me out of the bar.

Once we were out in the lobby, she pulled out her phone

and called her local FBI office.

"This is Special Agent Kalili, and I'd like for you to run a search. Name is Rudy Rafael, and he likely has a record. Yeah, I can hold."

A moment later, Violet was back on the phone, and she told them to text her the details. A second later, her phone beeped, and she turned the screen towards me, and, there, before my eyes, was all of Rudy's relevant information, and it included his picture, address, telephone number, and make and model of his vehicle. Below that was a detailed listing of the arrest and charges that Lindsey the bartender had told us about.

"I guess we have our next stop," I said.

We left the resort and headed south on the Pali Highway in the direction of Waikiki Beach, as Rudy the rohypnolist lived in an apartment on Lime Street, which resided only a couple of blocks inland of the famous tourist mecca. We reached Rudy's parking lot and saw his white recent model Ford Fiesta, so, assuming our guy wasn't much of a walker, he was very likely at home. We parked on the street then walked through the gate and up the stairs to the second floor, where Rudy's apartment resided. The door was open, but the screen was closed, so Violet knocked on the frame, and a man with wet hair and a towel around his waist appeared a moment later.

"Can I help you?" he asked, looking a little nervous as he peered at us through the screen.

"Yeah, my name is Finn, and this is Special Agent Kalili

of the FBI, and we'd like to ask you a few questions. Can we come in?"

"Do you have some kind of identification?"

Violet pulled out her wallet and flashed her FBI credentials.

"Oh OK, well come on in."

He unlocked the screen door and led us into his living room, and I finally got a good look at the infamous Roofie Rudy. He was in his late twenties, tan, good looking, sporting a large mop of curly Brown hair, and he also had the slender though athletic physique of an Abercrombie and Fitch model, which was probably integral to ingratiating himself to lonely female tourists.

"Do you mind if I get dressed first? I just got out of the shower."

"Not at all."

He exited to his bedroom but left the door partially ajar and continued to talk.

"So, how can I help you?" he asked.

"We're investigating an incident at the Kuhio Resort bar. It seems a witness says you were there the night before last."

"Yeah, I was."

"Do you remember seeing a very pretty woman around thirty with brown hair and blue eyes?"

"That describes a lot of women."

"This one is particularly attractive and was having a bachelorette party."

"Oh yeah, I remember her. What about her?"

"Well, she woke up feeling as though she had a lot more to drink than she actually had."

"So, why are you talking to me?"

"Because you're Roofie Rudy."

"Not anymore. That's all behind me."

"Well, the evidence would say otherwise."

He was suddenly quiet, and Violet and I looked at each other and nodded, as it seemed as though we were on to something. I waited a little longer then spoke again.

"Rudy, if you come clean with us right now, we'll forget about your little indiscretion that night."

No answer.

"It's true, Rudy. You have my word," Violet added.

We looked at each other again, and I could see that Violet was probably thinking the same thing as I — that we had a runner. We jumped up and raced into the bedroom to find it was empty, and the sliding door to the deck was open, and the curtains were billowing in the wind. We stepped out onto the deck and saw Rudy climbing down the fire escape ladder.

"Do you want to grab the car or follow him on foot?" I asked.

"Do these look like running shoes?" she asked.

"Fine," I said, as I tossed her the car keys then stepped onto the ladder and made my way down to the ground level, where I took up the chase.

Rudy was young and fit and had a sizable lead, and, while

I had a couple more years on this planet, I was probably more fit and, more importantly, very very stubborn and therefore wouldn't give up. He ran along to the back of the building and emerged onto the next street, which happened to be Kapiolani Boulevard. It wasn't the brightest move, because it bordered an inland canal and was kind of a dead end. He continued on and headed towards some kind of park that was full of children playing baseball, and I followed at a slightly faster pace, which meant that I was chipping away at his lead. He ran around the outskirts of the baseball diamond and continued on towards the water, where he stopped and turned back to me with a great big shitty smile on his face.

"I was all state at the University of Hawaii in the two hundred meter freestyle, so this is goodbye," he said, before turning and diving into the canal.

When I was a PJ, we trained to operate on sea, air and land, and I was happy in pretty much all three of those environments—especially the sea. Of course, I had also been a swimmer in college, so Roofie Rudy was going to have to do a lot more than jump in a canal to lose me. Without hesitating, I dove in and popped up just off the shore and began a nice steady stroke that allowed me to close in even more quickly on Rudy's lead. He looked back over his shoulder and was shocked to see me gaining on him.

"Hey, Rudy, I forgot to tell you—I was all state at Stanford in the four hundred meter freestyle."

This news didn't appear to make him all that happy, and

he turned back around and put even more effort into his strokes. He was a definitely a good swimmer and may very well have been all state in college, but, judging by his look of exhaustion, I was guessing he had been out of the pool for a while. He finally reached the other side of the canal and clambered up the bank, and his footsteps were looking labored and inefficient. I reached the shore a second later and again took up the chase, which had now reached Ala Wai Boulevard. In a break between traffic, he dashed across the street and headed towards Waikiki Beach, which would be crowded with people and a hell of a lot better place for him to try and disappear.

"Rudy! We just want to talk!"

"Fuck you!" he yelled back, before continuing to run.

"I'm going to catch up to you, you little Abercrombie and Fitch fuck!"

I heard a horn and looked up to see Violet in my Subaru. She saw the direction we were headed and made quick right, obviously to head off Rudy at the end of the next block. He was still going at a decent pace, but his lead was rapidly diminishing, and he was getting tired, apparently never imagining the crazy *haole* might be in better shape. An Asian tour group was coming from the other direction, and Rudy had to slow down as he tried to navigate through the crowd of slow moving people. I used this opportunity to cut out into the street, and I managed to get to within only a few feet of Rudy as we reached a park. He cut left onto the grass, and I put on a quick burst of speed then leapt forward and caught him at the knees. He fell to the ground, and, as he tried to struggle free and stand up, Violet came screeching to a halt a short distance away then exited the Subaru and raced over and pulled out her pistol.

"Freeze, Rudy, or I swear to God I'll blow your fucking balls off!" she said.

He relaxed, and I released my grip so that he could stand up.

"It's OK, no need for the gun, as I'm done running," he said.

"About fucking time," I responded.

He turned to me and shook his head side to side.

"Dude, seriously now! Who the fuck are you?" he said, looking haggard from our little chase.

"Just a very dedicated guy with a few questions."

"Look, I don't do the roofie thing anymore. Last night was a one time thing. I swear."

"Why Jessica?"

"Who?"

"The bride. Why did you pick her?"

"Because they paid me."

"Who are they?"

"I don't know."

"Come on, Rudy—you must have some idea."

"I don't, and even if I did, I wouldn't say anything."

"Why? What have they got on you?"

"Nothing, but, in addition to the money, they also said they would make my criminal record disappear, and let's face it, people like that can just as easily make a guy like me disappear."

"Well, Rudy, if you want to talk about connections, then you should know that I work for the vice president of the United States, and that fucker is just a bit higher up the food chain than your fuckers."

"You don't understand."

"Oh no, I do."

Rudy took a moment to think, and then something in his expression changed, and he abruptly took off again and ran towards the street. I followed, but he had a decent lead as he cleared the sidewalk and headed out into traffic. I suddenly heard the sound of a car's roaring engine, and I turned just in time to see a large black SUV come racing down the street. Rudy was unaware, and never even saw it as it slammed into him and catapulted him through the air. He landed and rolled to a stop on the side of the road while the big SUV continued on up the street before squealing around the corner and disappearing from view. I ran to Rudy and found him still breathing, but his body looked battered, and blood was pouring out of a nasty looking wound on his forehead.

"Did you get the license plate number?" I asked Violet.

"Yeah, how's Rudy?"

"Not good."

Violet pulled out her phone and called in our location to emergency services while I applied direct pressure to the wound on Rudy's head. He opened his eyes and looked up at me.

"What happened?" he asked groggily.

"You had a little trouble with an SUV, but you're going to be OK."

"No, I'm not," he said, as he tried to get up.

I gently held him back.

"It's better if you stay where you are. Now, relax—you're going to be fine."

"Fuck, this is all going to violate my parole."

His heart was pounding, and he was looking disoriented, so I was pretty sure he was starting to go into shock.

"Rudy, who paid you to dose the bride?"

"I—I don't know. I only ever met a guy..."

"What guy? Come on, Rudy. This is important."

"I feel so—cold."

"Come on, Rudy! Help us get these people."

He thought for a moment, then his eyes appeared to momentarily clear up.

"He—he kind of looked like you," he said, before closing his eyes and passing out.

What the hell did that mean? I checked his pulse and realized that Rudy was dead, as the combination of his head injury, shock, and blood loss were too much for his body to bear. I gently laid his head back down and stood up and looked at the young man before me.

"What a waste," I said.

"Yeah," Violet added.

"So, what do you think about all this now, Agent Kalili?

Any chance that you believe me when I say that things are not as they appear?"

"I'm definitely starting to see your point, Bart."

CHAPTER TWELVE
Leave it to Beeber

The ambulance arrived, and the EMTs tried to revive Rudy, but it was obviously too late, and they called in the coroner. In the meantime, the Police arrived, and Violet and I gave our statement, which included our interest in Rudy as well as the make, model, and license plate number of the SUV that ran him down. About forty minutes later, we were finally free to leave, and the mood was a bit somber.

"Well, what now?" Violet asked.

"The airport, I suppose. We have to pick up Justin Beeber."

"So, you seriously have a friend named Justin Beeber?"

"I do, though he's not anything like the Justin Beeber you're probably imagining. This one is actually talented—though not at singing."

"I believe you called him a tech wiz last night?"

"Yeah—anything to do with computers and software. He used to work for the CIA, but now he develops security software for big corporations, the government, and anyone who needs to protect their shit. I figure he can help track down some of our electronic leads and perhaps even take a look at the surveillance footage."

"Can't imagine going through life with that name."

"Well, I suppose it wasn't so bad until the other one arrived."

"Luckily your Beeber is out of school or the other kids would have tortured the shit of him."

"No doubt."

We headed west to Honolulu International Airport's private terminal to find the Vandenberg Jet had already landed, but there was no one on the tarmac except for ground crew, who were securing the jet's wheels with blocks as well as connecting the various ground cables. We exited the car and walked over in time to see an overly tan pilot come strutting down the stairs.

"He's cute. What's his name?" Violet asked.

"Biscuit."

"Seriously?"

"Yeah, and don't even think about trying to make me jealous by dating that fucker."

Biscuit, real name Brett, spotted us and headed our way and immediately started sizing up Violet. It was strange, but I think he actually appeared more tan around attractive women—almost as though he were a human version of a chameleon, though his color change was intended to help him mate rather than hide from danger. Only ten feet away, he smiled, and I found myself unintentionally shielding my eyes from the glare of his brilliantly bright teeth.

"Hey, Finn, who's your friend?"

"Agent Kalili of the American Dental Association, and she's here to cite you for offenses against excessive tooth whitening."

"Very funny."

"It's nice to meet you, Biscuit," Violet said, reaching out her hand to shake.

"It's Brett, actually, and it's nice to meet you too."

Violet gave me a look then hit me in the shoulder.

"So, where are your passengers?" I asked.

"They'll be out in a second."

Just then, Rachel, or Lizbeth in Beeber's sordid little mind, appeared at the door of the plane, and she was looking as pale as ever.

"Hey, Finn! Thanks for the invite!" she said, as she descended the stairs and came over and hugged me.

"How was the flight?"

"Fucking awesome. It was my first time on a private jet—and hopefully won't be my last."

"This is Agent Violet Kalili of the FBI, by the way."

"Nice to meet you," Rachel said.

Beeber suddenly appeared at the top of the stairs, and he was smiling from ear to ear.

"Aloha, bitches!" he said.

"Aloha, my precocious little *menehune*," I responded.

"What the hell is a *menehune*?" he asked.

"It's a Hawaiian version of a leprechaun, but they write code, masturbate nonstop, and steal socks out of the dryer."

"I've never stolen any of your socks."

"Two out of three ain't bad."

"Yeah yeah—whatever, dude. Have you ridden on this fucking jet?"

"Several times."

"Well, I'm going to buy a private jet when I get back home. This is the way to travel."

"Yeah, it's not bad."

"Not bad? Fuck you—it's amazing."

"Yeah, it is amazing, actually, but enough about jets. Are you fuckers hungry?"

"A little. Why?"

"I figure we can have lunch, and I'll get you up to speed and explain why you're here."

We loaded up into my rental car, and I was happy to see that Beeber and Rachel were both light travelers, and their luggage easily fit in the trunk. We then drove to the Gordon Biersch Brewery out on the water in Honolulu and got an outdoor table and were soon ordering drinks, though everyone abstained from any alcohol for the moment.

"I can't believe we just flew two thousand miles to eat at the same place where I eat back home."

"Today you get the view and the weather."

"Same thing back home—except for the weather."

Rachel backhanded Beeber in the arm, and he made a sound not unlike the squeal a guinea pig might make if you stuck your finger up its butt. Beeber's statement, while seemingly innocent, was actually related to the fact that he used to eat at the Gordon Biersch Brewery back home in order to gaze at the many attractive female Gap employees who frequented it at lunchtime. As Beeber was now in a serious relationship with Rachel, he was no longer allowed to let his eyes wander—at least not officially, anyway. Our waitress returned and took our lunch order, and, with that out of the way, I began filling Beeber in on all the exciting events of the last forty-eight hours.

"So, you flew us here just to do a little digital snooping?"

"Yeah, and I want your opinion on some of the evidence, namely the surveillance camera footage."

"I can definitely help you there. We've developed the most sophisticated software for facial recognition in the world, and I'll be able to tell you unequivocally whether or not it's actually Jessica in the footage."

Our food arrived, and the four of us enjoyed a pleasant lunch and conversation during which I learned that Rachel had never been to Hawaii. I therefore made a point of telling her about all the things she had to do while here, with the first and foremost on the list being snorkeling. I of course recommended Hanauma Bay, which, in spite of its touristy nature, still afforded an excellent variety of fish. Next on the list was Shark's Cove up on the north shore, and, unlike its name would suggest, it was not full of sharks. Rather, it had an abundance of native fish species as well as sea turtles, and it was easily my second favorite snorkeling spot.

"That's a lot of sun for a native San Franciscan," Rachel said.

"You can wear a rash guard. That way you only have to put sunblock on your face and legs."

"Are you getting kickbacks from the board of tourism?" Rachel asked.

"Nope, I'm just someone who loves the islands."

We paid our check and drove to the resort, so that Beeber and Rachel could check in to the hotel. They managed to get the suite next door to mine, and then we adjourned to my room, so that Beeber could digitize the security footage and give it a preliminary viewing.

"Shit. Just glancing at the footage, I have to say that it really does look like her," Beeber said.

"I know, but it can't be."

"Well, I guess we'll soon find out. So, what else did you bring me here for?"

"I also want to know who fast-tracked the investigation. It'll entail a little phone work on my part and some electronic snooping on yours, though we might also have to bring Doug in on this as well."

Doug was an old Agency friend and third member of our esteemed CIA super group the Three Amigos, but, while Beeber and I had left that life behind, Doug had remained and slowly worked his way up the ladder at Langley. Now, he was one of their chief technical strategists and had access to pretty much all of the government databases, so whatever Beeber couldn't find out would fall under Doug's purview.

"Oh, are you going to try and get him to fly to Hawaii?" Beeber asked.

"I would love to, but we both know that jackass is way too afraid to fly."

"Yeah, no shit."

"I can't imagine every vacation being a road trip. Pretty fucking boring," I said.

"Do you know he spent last year's vacation sitting in front of his home computer and using Google street view to travel Europe," Beeber said.

"It's just plain sad."

I left Beeber to his laptop and walked out onto my deck and pulled out my iPhone in the hope of letting my fingers do a little of the walking. Using my web browser, I found the number for the Police Commissioner, and I dialed and, three rings later, reached his assistant. She took my name and details before putting me on hold, and I listened to Don Ho singing Tiny Bubbles for nearly a minute before the assistant transferred me to the Commissioner.

"Commissioner O'Brien here," an authoritative voice said.

"Hello, sir. My name is Tag Finn, and I'm a special investigator to the vice president of the United States."

"How can I help you, Mr. Finn?"

"As you probably already know, we have a little problem at the moment with a murder case involving the future

Mrs. Vice President, and I could use your help."

"Of course."

"Well, I'm a little curious about the timing and efficiency of the police in this matter, and I was wondering if you wouldn't mind telling me who fast-tracked the investigation?"

"It's definitely not a secret. I got an email from the governor's office at seven thirty on the morning of the murder, and it stated that we had a potentially very sensitive case and were to proceed as quickly as possible."

"Was it from the Governor himself?"

"I'm not sure. There wasn't a name attached, so all I know is that it came from his office."

"Well, thank you, sir."

"Is that it?"

"I believe so."

"Well, it's not often that I have any direct dealings with the vice president of the United States, so, if you need anything else, please feel free to call."

"Thank you, I will," I said, before hanging up.

I walked back inside to find Violet, Rachel, and Beeber hovering behind Beeber's laptop.

"What did I miss?" I asked.

"You're going to want to see this," Violet said.

I walked over and looked at the screen, and there before my eyes was the frame grab from the security footage. Beeber had plugged it into his software, which now showed it beside another similar image of Jessica with the words

100% match in red letters.

"So, that's definitely Jessica?"

"According to the software—yes."

"Jesus. You did all this while I was on the phone?"

"Of course. I don't fuck around."

"Except when you're at work—in which case you play flight simulators and massively multi player RPG's."

"As well as first person shooters."

"Bullshit."

"No, that's actually true. I know because he usually plays against me, and I always smoke his ass," Rachel interjected.

"In reality, it's generally quite even."

Rachel punched Beeber in the arm, and he let out another little guinea pig squeak.

"OK, she might have won a couple more matches than me."

Rachel prepared to hit him again, but I was quicker to the punch and interrupted their little lovers' shenanigans with a question.

"So, where did you get the second image?" I asked.

"Facebook profile."

"Nice"

"Yeah, so you basically flew us all the way to Hawaii for one minute of work."

"Don't worry, as there's plenty more. In fact, I need to get access to the Governor of Hawaii's email and possibly even the murder victim's as well."

"How wonderful. You want me to hack into the private

account of a victim in a homicide investigation and a highly ranked elected official."

"It's nothing our government isn't already doing, and if you do end up in prison, you probably won't be alone, as Doug might be joining you if he gets caught illegally accessing the phone records I need."

"I don't think that Doug and I would be good cellmates."

"Are you kidding? It would be awesome. During the day, you two could play D&D, and at night you could do Lord of the Rings sexual role play. I'm thinking hobbit on hobbit, ranger on hobbit, or, if you want to take it up a notch, go dwarf on elf."

"How dare you bastardize the holy trilogy in the name of making silly prison sex jokes!"

"Easy there, Bilbo, as you're too good at what you do to get caught and be sent to prison, so, you won't have to do any dwarf on elf unless you really want to."

"Says the troglodyte."

I picked up my phone and dialed Doug, then hit the speaker phone button, because I assumed Beeber would want to chime in and talk with our dear old friend. Oddly, Doug answered after the first ring.

"Hello, Finn. What do you need? Are you stalking an ex-girlfriend and need me to track down her phone number and address?"

"No, because I'm actually on a very important assignment for the vice president."

"Then why are you calling me? I'm sure you're quite capable of picking up coffee and sandwiches all by yourself."

Beeber laughed.

"Hey, I recognize that laugh. Is Beeber with you?"

"He is."

"Hey, Beebs. What's up?"

"I'm in Hawaii helping Finn, if you can believe it."

"You fuckers are in Hawaii?"

"Yep."

"Well, why in the hell does Beeber get to be there?"

"He's not afraid of flying."

"Well neither am I now."

"Are you saying you would actually come if I bought you a ticket?"

"Of course."

"On a plane?"

"Yeah, I know that Hawaii is in the middle of the fucking Pacific, but it's not a problem—I have medication now."

"Bullshit."

"No, I'm serious. I have Lorazepam, and I use it for the dentist, but my doctor also said it would help me deal with my fear of flying."

"Better living through chemistry indeed!"

"The world is my oyster."

"So, seriously now, do you really want to come out?"

"Hell yeah!"

"Can you access all your databases remotely?"

"Of course."

"OK, fine, I'll get you a ticket as soon as we get off the

phone, but you can't chicken out."

"Book it, Dano," he said, quoting the most famous of lines from the television show Hawaii Five-o.

"Ha! I got to fly here on a private jet!" Beeber blurted out.

"Wait, did Beebs just say he got to fly there on a private jet?"

"No, Beeber was just talking about someone's irate pet," I said, as I smacked Beeber's arm to get him to be quiet.

"That doesn't make any sense."

"I know, it's probably just sun stroke. Now, Doug, I'm going to book your flight, then I'll text you in about ten minutes with your info. Pack light, as all you really need are shorts and T-shirts."

"And bring your D&D stuff!" Beeber yelled out.

"Doug is getting on a plane for the first time in years to travel to a beautiful tropical island, and you're telling him to bring his fucking D&D stuff?"

"You bet your ass I am! We haven't played in years."

"Don't worry. I never leave home without it," Doug said.

"Fucking nerds. I'm so sorry that I got you into this, Rachel."

"It's OK. I've actually come to enjoy playing it with Beebsy."

"Wait, Rachel's there too?" Doug asked.

"Yeah, I never leave home without her, and, better still, she'll play D&D with us!"

"Seriously?" I asked.

"Yeah, in fact, I have a fifteenth level Ranger I've been playing."

"Perfect! I've got a fourteenth level Wizard I've been dying to use," Doug said.

"I'm hanging up now, as I'm afraid all this nerd talk is starting to diminish my testosterone production."

I hit the end button and looked over to see Beeber glowing with excitement. I had forgotten how close we had all been back at the Agency, but, sadly, Doug's fear of flying, had kept him isolated from our little social circle, and the only bonding time was via the phone or during his and Beeber's online gaming sessions. Now it was time for our long awaited reunion, and to that end, I called Frank Williams, and, three rings later, heard his voice.

"What's up, Finn? Any news?" he asked.

"Plenty."

"Any of it good?"

"Not really. Our first good lead was hit by a car and killed today."

"Jesus."

"Yeah, it's not exactly a good omen, but I did want to give you a heads up that I'm bringing in another person."

"Who is it?"

"A friend from the CIA."

"Do you think he can help?"

"It certainly can't hurt."

"Well, the more the merrier. Might as well bring him in."

"Thanks, do you want to meet later for an update?"

"Is there any more news?"

"Nothing than what I've already told you."

"Then it can wait until tomorrow."

"OK, talk to you later," I said, hitting the end button.

I went to my laptop and brought up a travel website and managed to book Doug a first class ticket on Virgin Airlines. I texted the details, and Doug came back about a tenth of a second later with the words *FIRST CLASS????* written all upper case and with four question marks. I wrote back *YES* in all caps, and he wrote back to ask who died. I responded by saying it's a long story and that I'd tell him when he arrived. With Doug squared away, it was now time to think about how to proceed, and, given the fact that my first lead in Steven's murder was killed, I couldn't help but wonder if every person that came up on my radar would suddenly become a target. It actually felt a little like a night dive I once did in Thailand. I'd obviously had a dive light with me, and every time I shined it on a fish, a larger predator like a barracuda would use the opportunity to eat my subject, and it made it feel as though I were playing God with my veritable flashlight of destiny. I would therefore prefer that my future meddling not needlessly endanger anyone else, and that meant moving forward with a great deal of caution.

"So, what now?" Beeber asked.

"Agent Kalili, do you happen to have a bathing suit with you?"

"This is Hawaii—of course I do."

"Good, and, as we have nothing left to do today, I say we take this investigation down to the beach, because our recent arrivals have yet to dip their feet in the warm blue Pacific ocean."

"Good idea, Magnum," Beeber said.

"First, we need to get you two sun-a-phobes the rash guards I mentioned."

Everyone went to their respective rooms to change, and Violet, of course, came to mine. Properly dressed, we grabbed sunblock and towels then joined Beebs and Rachel in the hallway before grabbing snorkel gear from the hotel and heading out to my car. We threw everything in the trunk and drove south to one of the two Costcos that resided on the island of Oahu. This particular one was in Hawaii Kai, and, as usual, it was crowded with locals and tourists alike, because everyone was looking for a better price on their basic necessities. In Hawaii, those necessities fortunately also included snorkel gear and rash guards, and, after getting Beeber and Rachel properly outfitted, we went to the front to pay then also grabbed four icy blended coffee drinks on the way out.

Now, we had about a five or so minute drive to Hanauma Bay, which was a long dormant undersea crater that was a haven to all manner of Hawaiian sea life. It was a tourist mecca and even charged admission, but it was worth visiting when you wanted a quick, easy, and safe place to snorkel. We paid then did the obligatory orientation and learned all about Hanauma Bay as well as the history of the islands, and the final parting words were not to touch the delicate coral or hassle any sea turtles, as the result would be a hefty fine and possible jail time. Finished, we at last hiked down the road and arrived at the beach to find the area was full of tourists. At least half were Asian, most likely Japanese, while the other half were, judging by their lighter shade of pale skin, most likely from the American heartland. Strangely, the majority stayed close to the beach, as they were unaware that the best snorkeling was farther out in the vast labyrinth of coral. We put on our fins and waded in, and Rachel looked incredibly surprised.

"Holy shit. It's really warm!"

"Yeah, I keep forgetting it's your first trip to Hawaii." I said.

"Yeah, no shit."

"Well, let me tell you—you're going to shit when you see the fish."

"Anything in there I need to worry about?" she asked.

"Other than Beeber? Not really."

Everyone continued on until the water was deep enough, then we dawned our masks, and I immediately heard Rachel gasp as she realized that we had been walking through a school of yellow and black striped Lemon Butterfly fish or Lau Wiliwili as the Hawaiians called them. She excitedly pointed and tried to speak, but her words were obscured by the snorkel. She was clearly excited and had never seen fish like this outside of a tank or aquarium. I waved for everyone to follow, then led them to the opening in the reef, which resided below a small buoy that marked a channel of sorts. Out here, it got even better, because there was even more sea life moving about the reef, and around us swam blue parrot fish, squirrelfish, boxfish, and pretty much every other fish you could imagine.

We continued on and followed the channels and passed through school after school of fish before rounding a corner and seeing our first sea turtle of the day. Beebs began yelling what sounded like *urtle*, obviously because it was impossible to make a proper T with a snorkel in his mouth, and we all looked over to see the gentle creature swimming slowly along the sea floor. Upon seeing us, it actually swam closer and hovered in front of Rachel and Violet and stayed with them for several minutes before being startled by a bevy of Japanese tourists that suddenly appeared from around the corner. Seeing the crowd, it turned and high tailed it for the deeper open waters of the bay.

With the turtle gone, our attention turned back to the reef, and we set off and followed a school of baby butterfly fish. I was now at the back of our group, and I took a precious moment to gaze at Violet and her otherworldly backside. It was even more glorious from this vantage point, as the magnification of the water made the experience feel a little like iMax 3D. Suddenly, as if she knew I were watching, she turned around and gave me the finger, and I held up my arms and shrugged in an attempt to look innocent. It wasn't easy being a man.

An hour and twenty minutes later, we at last stepped

up onto the warm sand of the beach, and I had a second to admire the lovely wet glistening bodies of our female team members. I, of course, already knew Violet had a spectacular figure, as I had been lucky enough to have seen her naked, but there was just something about the right bikini that made for an enticing visage. I was also pleasantly surprised when Rachel set her gear down and turned around and I had a moment to really see her lovely and toned physique as well as her very hard nipples. Somehow, I had always expected her to have a nipple piercing, but I was happy to see that her double helix tattoo on her forearm was where her alternative tastes stopped. Seeing her in her wet bikini, I could only imagine that poor Beeber had probably ejaculated the very instant he first saw her naked. She was a lovely girl, and even now he still gazed at her with the wonderment of new love, and it made me feel pretty warm and fuzzy inside knowing that I had helped bring them together.

"Finn, this is fucking awesome. I can't believe I've never been here before."

"Yeah, I know, right?"

"Fuck it! This is where we're coming for our honeymoon," Rachel said.

"Honeymoon?" I asked, looking at Beeber.

Beeber shrugged.

"It's not official yet."

"Well, congratulations anyway."

We walked over to the fresh water showers, and Violet

and Rachel went first, and the spectacle of them frolicking in their clingy suits made it look like a calendar photo shoot. Beeber, obviously thinking the same thing, glanced at me, and we shared a knowing smile. Men would be men. The girls stepped aside, and we took their place and felt the welcome relief of washing away the sticky salt water. Feeling fresh and clean, we headed out and found a deserted section of beach beneath a palm tree and sat down to dry off, relax, and do a little people watching. As I gazed out at the water, I could see Hawaii's latest snorkeling trend, which was to use long foam noodles for flotation. It now meant that the bay was awash in color and butts. Saltwater was already incredibly buoyant, and, when combined with a flotation device, it sent the snorkelers butt high in the air, so, while they were looking at fish, we were looking at their butts, and that, depending on the specific snorkeler, could sometimes be a good or bad thing. Beeber, meanwhile, had been deep in thought and broke from his reverie to interrupt my reverie.

"So, you said that a spear fisherman found the gun the very next morning?" he asked.

"Yeah, why?"

"Well, having just spent the last hour and a half out on the reef, I realize that you were correct in your assessment that it would be unlikely that someone could find that gun so easily."

"No shit. In fact, tomorrow, I want to talk to that spear fisherman."

A reflection up on the hill suddenly caught my attention, and I saw a man up near the parking lot looking through binoculars. From this distance, I couldn't tell which direction he was specifically looking, but odds were pretty good that he was checking out one of the many girls that were running around the beach—perhaps even Rachel or Violet. Still, the events of the last few days were feeding my paranoia and making me wonder if he might be watching me.

"Do you guys see that dude with the binoculars standing up on the bluff?"

"Where?" Violet asked.

"Right there," I said, pointing.

"Yeah, what about him?"

"I don't know. My scrot-sense started tingling when I saw him."

"Your what?"

"My *scrot-sense*."

Beeber laughed.

"He's referring to his version of his little voice," he said.

Beeber was again referring to the television show *Magnum P.I.*, and the fact that its lead character often claimed to be following the advice of his little voice or, in layman's terms, intuition. In my case, I preferred the more colorful term *scrot-sense*.

"Care to elaborate on that?" Violet asked.

"I have a pet name for my intuition that alludes to the idea that when danger is near, my balls will sense it first and retract towards my body, and in extreme situations, perhaps even taking refuge in my butthole."

"Did it ever occur to you to just call it your intuition?"

"Sure, but I like to be creative."

"It's kind of more stupid than creative."

"I like it, but then I was there when you came up with it," Beeber said.

"Thanks, Beebs."

"You're welcome, but are we to assume that your balls are currently nesting in your butthole?"

"Not quite, but they're certainly knocking on the back door."

"Why would anyone be following us?" Rachel asked.

"Well, a guy we were trying to talk to was murdered in front of us yesterday."

Everyone got quiet and turned their attention back up to the hill, but the man was nowhere to be seen.

"Looks like he's gone," Violet said.

"But not forgotten."

CHAPTER THIRTEEN
Death Race

We stayed on the beach until everyone was dry then decided it was about time to get going. We began the long walk to the car, but stopped at the beach bathroom for a quick pee. The girls went into the ladies, and Beeber and I headed into the men's side, where Beeber took the urinal and I took the stall. He let a long sigh, started peeing, then let loose a tiny high pitched fart.

"Dude, you not only squeal like a guinea pig—you fart like one."

"Fuck you. That was just the opening act."

I decided to show Beeber how it was done and let loose a massive fart, with the result being so loud and powerful that I feared for the seams of my shorts. Argh! I feared might have had too much sail up for that kind of wind, so I reached back with my free hand and felt that I did indeed still have material covering my bum.

"Do you need an icepack?" Beeber asked.

"No, but my butthole is feeling all tingly, and I'm pretty sure I'm experiencing the onset of postpartum depression."

"Have you picked out a name?"

"I'm thinking something powerful like Odin."

"Wait a minute. Here comes the main attraction. Step back and feast your ears on this!" Beeber said.

He bent over slightly at the waist, clenched his fists, and pushed with all his might.

"Easy there. Don't shit your pants," I said.

"Dude, this is going to be huge."

"Yeah, but I will seriously never stop laughing if you shoot a turd into your shorts."

He pushed even harder, and his face was starting to turn red as another fart came out. It was slightly louder than his first, and he appeared to be fairly proud of his efforts.

"That was a little better, Beebs, but you still sound like a guinea pig."

"Fuck you. That sounded like it came from Hogzilla."

"More like Babe, so that'll do pig. That'll do," I said.

I finished up by making sure Tag Junior was free of any urine then used my foot to flush the toilet before walking over to wash my hands at the sink. Beeber joined me a moment later and did the same, all the while smiling as he was obviously still very proud of his little fart. We finished washing our hands and exited to find the girls waiting directly outside.

"Did you two have fun in there?" Rachel asked.

"Yeah, why do you ask?"

"We heard everything," Violet said.

"Oh, then I guess you know that Beeber farts like a guinea pig."

"That's so funny! I've told him the same thing," Rachel said.

"Oh come on. You can't judge me by the first one. That was the warm up. The second was rich and full of body," he said.

"More like a dog's squeaky toy," Rachel said, as she patted his behind.

"So, the foghorn was obviously you," Violet said, to me.

"No, that one obviously came from some big ass *haole* with diarrhea."

"Nice try, Odin."

"Don't you girls have anything better to do than hang around outside the men's bathroom?" I asked.

"No, not when the god of thunder has the car keys."

"Good point."

We left the bathrooms and joined in the procession of people that were slowly making their way back up the hill to the parking lot, and, upon reaching the car, we climbed in and headed north onto the winding road that would take us on the scenic route back to our resort. The afternoon traffic was mild as we drove along a spectacular section of road that overlooked a treacherous patch of coastline, and everyone was admiring the view. Suddenly, we felt a very purposeful bump from behind, and I looked in the rearview mirror and saw a tricked-out older model Toyota four by four right on our bumper. It was painted matte black and had one of those ridiculous lift kits that made it look like a baby version of a monster truck, and, annoyingly, its windows were all tinted, so its particularly aggressive driver was hidden from view. We came to a sharp turn, and he made yet another attempt to ram us, only this time the fucker sent us off the road and towards the looming cliff. All of my passengers screamed as I steered back over just in time to keep us from plummeting down hundreds of feet to our certain death. We had a short straight up ahead, and I gunned the Subaru, desperately wishing I was in my Silver Hornet, which would have easily left the cumbersome four by four in the dust. Unfortunately, the standard model sedan just wasn't all that quick—least of all with four passengers.

"Goddammit, Finn! Every fucking time I get in a car with you, somebody tries to kill us!"

Sadly, Beeber was mostly correct with that statement, as we had indeed almost been killed one night back home in San Francisco. In that instance however, my nemesis had been a group of deadly Chinese spies, but this time around, I had no idea who I had pissed off. The truck came up and rammed us yet again, but I was able to keep the car in our lane. Shit! I desperately needed some kind of game plan if I hoped to keep all of us alive. I hazarded a quick glance in the rearview mirror in order to size up the truck and thought about how ridiculously high off the ground it sat.

The Subaru may have had lackluster acceleration, but it definitely had the handling advantage with its lower center of gravity. Perfect! I would use physics as my ally. I waited until there was a break in oncoming traffic then turned the wheel and yanked up on the parking brake. It brought the car into a full one hundred and eighty degree spin, and now that we were facing the opposite direction, I gunned it and headed back towards Hanauma Bay with the intention of continuing on to the busy Hawaii Kai shopping center. It stood to reason we'd be safe there, as I was fairly certain that the deranged driver in the truck would give up the chase once we were in a crowd.

The truck was a lot slower to turn around due to its top heavy nature and wide turning radius, and it gave us a decent lead. We passed Hanauma, and the road wound around and onto a long downhill stretch that ended at a traffic light. The light turned red, and I stopped and kept my eyes on the rearview mirror as I desperately hoped that the truck was still far behind. No such luck. It came barreling over the hill at dangerously high speed, and I glanced back at the light and desperately hoped it would change. Beeber, who was entirely focused on the approaching vehicle, started to panic.

"Dude, he's going to ram us. You're going to have to turn or run the light."

I followed Beeber's advice and made a right at the intersection and headed into a local neighborhood. The truck did the same a moment later and was soon on our bumper yet again. It accelerated and hit us, and, as the car lurched, my passengers cried out. I made a left at the next street, and the back end pitched sideways before I corrective steered and brought the car straight again. Up ahead, kids were playing roller hockey in the street, so I hit the horn, and all of them thankfully scattered and ran for cover. Unfortunately, they left their net, and it bounced up and over the car and landed in the path of the truck and managed to get caught in its grill. I turned right at the next block and again sent the car sideways before straightening out in time to see a car suddenly come backing out of a driveway. I managed to swerve around it, and the driver hit the horn and gave me the finger. The truck wasn't as lucky and was forced to swerve up onto the opposite sidewalk, where it took out a mailbox before having to slow down to use the next driveway to return to the street.

We had finally gained a little breathing room, and I made a right on the next street and headed out of the neighborhood and back to the main highway. There was only one car between us and the light, and it was a fucking white Toyota Prius, and, as I raced around it, I again got the horn and an angry hand gesture from its driver, who, not surprisingly, was an older hippie woman wearing a muumuu dress.

"I think I'm going to puke," Beeber said.

"Just hold on a little longer, Beebs."

I reached the light just as it turned green and roared through the turn, again sending the car sideways.

"Not helping," Beeber moaned.

The truck was caught behind the Prius, and it was one of the few times in my life that I was actually happy to see the great beacon of smugness blocking the road. It gave us enough time to safely leave the highway and enter the crowded Hawaii Kai mall, where I parked in a loading zone in front of an ice cream parlor packed with people. Safe at last, we had a moment to catch our breath, and, soon thereafter, the truck appeared and slowed down ominously as it passed by our car. I waved, then it accelerated, and its tires chirped as it roared out of the mall.

"Well, that was fun," I said.

Beeber, who happened to be sitting on the curb side of the car, suddenly opened his door, leaned out, and began puking his guts out all over the sidewalk. The crowd of people all eating their ice cream a short distance away watched in horror until Beeber finished up and leaned back up into the car and closed his door. After such an awkward arrival, I figured I should deliver some parting words.

"Sorry about that, folks, but I'm sure you'll all be fine as long as you didn't get any chocolate sprinkles on your ice cream."

"He's kidding," Violet said, before punching me in the arm.

"Let's get the fuck out of here," Beeber mumbled.

"No problem."

I pulled out, and we left behind a small puddle of Beeber barf as we headed back towards the main highway.

Anyone get the license plate number of that fucking

truck?" Beeber asked, still looking a bit peaked.

"I did," Violet and I both said, at the exact same moment.

"Jinx! You owe me a blowjob!" I said.

"Hmm—blowjob eh? Well, after you plugged that skank, I wouldn't spit on your dick if it were on fire."

"Well, technically smothering it with your vagina would be more effective."

"Anyone ever tell you you're an insufferable optimist?" she asked.

"No, but I can't help thinking that makes me sound like a Jane Austin character."

"Yeah, the one who doesn't get the girl."

"Wouldn't that make me an insufferable pessimist?"

"No, and either way you don't get the girl."

"Ouch," Rachel said, from the back seat.

I headed back the way we had started and took the scenic route north to our resort, and the black four by four never reappeared, thus making the ride mostly uneventful except for a peculiar smell that surfaced, but went unclaimed. My money was on Beeber, but you could never write off the girls, as they tended to use their feminine charms to get away with unclaimed flatulence. Within twenty minutes we were back at the resort, and Beeber and Rachel went to his room while Violet and I went to mine.

"Is it OK if I use your shower?" Violet asked.

"Not at all—but what if I need to pee?"

"You can wait."

"Seriously?"

"Yeah, and if anyone enters that bathroom before I'm done, I'll shoot first and ask questions later."

Again, it was obvious that Violet and I were stuck firmly in the friends zone, although it was probably a good thing, as I had more than enough on my plate without having any romantic entanglements. I took a seat on the couch and looked at my watch and realized that Doug would be landing in about two more hours, and I was starting to get excited. The three of us hadn't been in the same actual place in about five years, so I was really looking forward to our impromptu reunion. We'd been close during our time at the Agency, and this would be our first face to face gathering since Beeber and I left. About ten minutes passed, and Violet emerged from the bathroom looking utterly beautiful. Her long hair was down, and she was wearing some kind of casual dress that made quite a point of emphasizing her spectacular figure.

"Of all the dresses, you had to bring that one?"

"Oh, do you like it?"

"Obviously."

"Well then, I suppose it's too bad that you turned out to be a man-whore. Otherwise you might have been peeling it off of me later tonight."

"You know that you did tell me we'd never have a romantic relationship."

"It's not my fault you were too stupid to know it was test."

"You should have known I was that stupid."

"I guess I'm also just an insufferable optimist."

"Touché, Jane."

Violet pulled out her phone, took a seat on one of the couches, and crossed her long legs, inadvertently, or even purposefully, providing me with a view of her supple upper thighs that bordered on painful. She pressed the send button then gave her name and soon was relaying the details of our little encounter, so she was obviously calling in to her office. The last detail was the license plate number of the truck, then she paused and listened for a moment and said thank you and hung up.

"Truck is stolen."

"Of course."

Violet's phone suddenly rang, and I saw her look at the caller's name then sigh.

"Fuck."

"Who is it?" I asked.

"Dave."

"As in Dave your charming ex?"

"That's the one."

She hit the answer button and said hello then remained quiet for some time. Obviously, Dave had a lot to say before Violet finally managed to interrupt.

"Look, Dave, I'm a trained FBI Agent. Believe me, I can handle myself."

She was quiet for a short while then looked decidedly annoyed as she told him that she had to go and that they could talk later. She hit the end button then let out a long pained groan.

"I get the impression he's concerned about you."

"Yeah, apparently he heard about our little run-in on the road and wants me to dump this assignment."

"Could you actually do that if you wanted to?"

"Doubtful, and it wouldn't look good."

"Would you choose to dump it if you could?"

She looked at me a moment then smiled.

"No, this has turned out to be the most exciting case I've had in a long time, and besides, every minute I get to torture you is just icing on the cake."

"Lovely. Well I guess I should call the rental company and see if I can get a replacement—maybe something with a little more horsepower."

Five minutes later, Violet and I were going to the closest Hertz office to get me a new car. It turned out to be a white Chevy Suburban, or, in layman's terms, a Prius killer. Normally I preferred small cars in the islands because of the abundance of tiny backroads, but, after recent events, I was happy to get a little more steel around my body. Better still, it had a V8 engine and supposedly got around twenty-one miles to the gallon, which was something I doubted, though only time would tell. I grabbed the remainder of my things from the beleaguered Subaru, then gently patted its hood.

"What was all that?" Violet asked.

"I believe in what I like to call—Carma. And that's

Carma with a C, not a K."

"What?"

"I kind of assign feelings and a personality to my cars and therefore treat them as though they were family members, and they, in turn, provide me with loving transportation."

"Even rentals?"

"Even rentals. In fact, I once washed and detailed a rental car, because I felt as though it didn't receive adequate love in its sad existence as a veritable mechanical prostitute."

Violet looked perplexed.

"I'm not sure whether that's sweet or idiotic."

"Probably a little of both."

We mounted up in the goliath Suburban, and I took a moment to sinc my phone with its bluetooth system, then headed back to the resort to get Beeber and Rachel before going to pick up Doug. We swung in to the front of the hotel and found them waiting beside the valet, and Beeber had an annoying smile on his face as he looked at the vehicle.

"What are you—a fucking soccer mom now?" he asked.

"Would you rather be in this or the Subaru the next time some asshole tries to run us off the road?"

"This."

"Exactly, now sit the fuck down and put on your seat belt. Mom's had a long day and doesn't want to hear any more of your shit."

Beeber and Rachel piled in and took up residence in the

back seat while I pulled the goliath out of the resort and headed south until turning onto the H3, which would then take us west towards the airport. The ride was surprisingly smooth in the massive car, and it was kind of fun to drive something so different from my usual vehicles. As much of an inefficient spectacle as it might have been, there was something to be said for driving a battleship sized car. Other motorists made a point of getting out of the way, and the large V8 engine had plenty of power, which meant this might actually be fun.

We reached the airport about a half hour before Doug's plane was due in and decided to park and meet him in the terminal. The four of us took a seat just beyond the security checkpoint and waited for the second nerdiest man in the world to make his glorious appearance. The first nerdiest man was obviously Beeber, but their official ranking could change at any moment depending upon the circumstances. Bring up Star Wars or Lord of the Rings, and you would be hard pressed to discern the greater nerd. Ten minutes passed, and out walked Doug Griffith looking exactly as I remembered the fucker. He was about five eleven, lanky, and was sporting a reddish brown mop top hairdo, with the only visible change being that he had some very purposeful scruff that every two-bit hipster and reader of GQ seemed to have as of late. He had also stupidly worn his usual brown pants in spite of the fact I told him to wear shorts. Oh well, I suppose he would just have to learn his lesson when his balls overheated and dropped to his knees.

He saw us and smiled as he walked over and hugged Beeber then me before setting his eyes upon the women. He went to Rachel first, and he looked legitimately surprised.

"Holy shit!" he exclaimed.

"Nice to meet you too," Rachel said.

"Wait a minute. You're seriously dating Beeber?"

"Yeah, why do you sound so surprised?"

"Because you're totally out of his league."

"Fuck you," Beeber said.

"No, he's right, honey, but you make up for it with personality," Rachel said.

"Seriously? Personality?" I asked.

Before anyone responded, Doug turned to Violet and instantly fell in love. He had a thing for Asian women, and Violet being half Hawaiian was more than enough to capture Doug's heart.

"I'm Doug, nice to meet you."

"I'm Violet."

"Technically she's Special Agent Violet Kalili of the FBI," I said.

"Yes, and she's very special indeed," he said.

"Well, thank you, Doug. It's nice someone thinks so," Violet said, giving me a snarky little smile.

"Oh there's no doubt you're special, and especially cruel. Now, let's get Doug the fuck out of here, so he can lose those fucking awful city clothes."

We made our way out of the airport and back to the Suburban and loaded up and started driving east. This was

Doug's first trip to Hawaii, or anywhere tropical for that matter, so I decided that he should have his first cocktail down on the beach in Waikiki or, better still, at the Outrigger. I pulled out my phone, dialed Frank Williams, and heard his voice after two rings.

"What's up, Finn?" he asked.

"We just picked up my friend Doug at the airport, and we were hoping to take him somewhere special for his first drink on the island."

"How about the Outrigger? I'm headed there myself."

"That's what I was hoping you'd say."

"Well head on over, and I'll see you get the best table in the house."

"Thanks, we'll see you in a few," I said, before hitting the end button.

"Who was that?" Doug asked.

"Frank Williams."

"The Frank Williams?" Doug asked.

"Yeah, how many are there?"

"Only one that counts. He's probably the single most powerful person in Washington."

"Other than the president."

"Shit, presidents come and go, but Frank is there for eternity. So, how the hell do you know him?"

"He's an old family friend of John Matheson, and he's currently in charge of his campaign."

"What campaign? He hasn't said he's running yet."

"Exactly, and it's the main reason that I flew you over

here."

"Yeah, and speaking of that flight, what's the long story behind why I was in first class?"

"Fucking Finn basically won the lottery, and he has as much, if not more, money than me!"

"That's fucking bullshit. Guys like you get the looks, and guys like us get the money."

"But you don't have any money."

"Well, I have more than you, or at least I used to, and I would have as much as Beeber if I sold out and moved into the private sector."

"So, why don't you?"

"I have a soul."

"Working for the Agency? Doubtful."

"Whatever—just tell me how you acquired all this supposed money."

"Remember my Soft Taco Island job?"

"Yeah, the one you called me for help on."

"Well, the Agency ended up hiring me for a follow up job, and they paid me with more than a hundred million dollars worth of jewels left over from the arms deal I sabotaged on Soft Taco Island."

"So, it's blood money!"

"Technically, it kind of came from a secret society, but the jewels aren't even as valuable as my shares in cold fusion technology."

"Dude, all I can say is fuck you, and I will be expecting really awesome Christmas and birthday presents. We're talking Lamborghinis and Ferraris here."

"Fine, as long as you help make sure my friend doesn't get charged with murder."

"Deal, now explain what the fuck is going on."

I gave him a detailed briefing, and he listened intently, and his acute mind took in all the details and was probably already making connections mortal men could only dream about. He was a brilliant strategist and had graduated top of his class at MIT then remained at his alma mater to complete two doctorates—one in economics and the other in theoretical mathematics. He was soon recruited by the CIA, and that's when I met him and Beeber, and we formed the Three Amigos. Since Beeber and I left the Agency, however, we had scarcely seen each other and were more like *los tres extraños*, or, in English, the three strangers.

"And someone tried to kill all four of you earlier today?"

"That's why we're in a Suburban."

"Some vacation," Doug said.

"Come on, wouldn't you rather be killed in Hawaii than anywhere else?" I asked.

"I'll tell you after I've had a drink."

"Fine, a drink it is."

CHAPTER FOURTEEN
Beach Blanket Babylon

We drove another ten minutes and were soon pulling into the Outrigger parking lot, where I struggled to squeeze the Suburban into a normal sized parking, and the result was that the back end was sticking dangerously far out into the lane of traffic. Oh well, if anything happened, I had at least opted for the complete damage coverage. We walked down to the Outrigger entrance, and the hostess led us out to the Hau Terrace, where we found Williams sitting with a friend.

"Hello, Frank, this is Beeber, Rachel, and Doug."

Frank stood and smiled warmly at our entourage.

"Nice to meet you. This is my good friend and aide Rex Pearson."

Rex stood, and I saw that he was tall, probably about six one, and appeared to be in excellent shape, which, combined with his neatly trimmed hair and clean shaven appearance, did very little to hide his military past.

"I'm sorry to hear you were also in Afghanistan," I said, as we shook hands.

He chuckled.

"Yeah, feels like a lifetime ago now," he said.

"And not even a lifetime's enough to adequately forget everything you experienced over there."

Rex nodded his agreement, and I could see that far away look in his eyes that all men who've survived a combat tour shared.

"Please, everyone, take a seat and order some drinks. Rex and I have to leave soon, but we can at least stay for one," Frank said.

Everyone sat, and a moment later a waitress arrived and took our order before returning soon thereafter with a tray of sweet alcoholic sunshine. She handed out our cocktails, then I held my glass up to toast.

"To the Three Amigos triumphant return to service," I said.

Everyone clinked glasses and drank, and Doug, after looking out at the view, turned to me and smiled.

"You were right earlier. This would indeed be as good a place as any to die," he said.

"Well, let's hope no one else dies because of this fucked up situation," Frank said.

"I'll toast to that," I said, clinking Frank's glass.

We took a sip, then Frank smiled and regarded my new

arrivals.

"So, what kind of help can we expect now that you've reunited the Three Amigos?" Frank asked.

Beeber started to answer, but I cut him off, as I realized it was probably a good idea not to let Frank know that I would be employing some illegal means in trying to clear Jessica's name. As he was John's campaign manager, I wanted to make sure he maintained total deniability regarding my investigation shenanigans.

"Mainly technical stuff relating to the Honolulu Police Department's evidence chain," I said.

"Well, I'm glad to have you aboard," Frank said, tipping his glass to Beeber and Doug.

The table fell into conversation, and, with Rex in the next chair over, I ended up talking to him first.

"So, you were the PJ who rescued John. That was quite an ordeal."

"Yeah, but then so was every other day over there."

"Pretty much."

"What was your unit?" I asked.

"Delta, and I was attached as part of Joint Special Operations Command."

Delta was one of the Army's most elite units and comparable to SEAL Team Six. It had been formed by charging Charlie Beckworth after he spent some time in England with their world renowned SAS, and, upon returning to the States, he set about creating an American version—namely Delta Force. So, if Rex had been with Delta, then he had seen and done some serious shit.

"We may very well have crossed paths. When were you there?" I asked.

"Two tours between 2004 and 2006."

"I left in 2005."

"Good time to get out. It only got worse."

"I had no choice. Took a bullet in the hip rescuing John."

"That will happen."

"So, how is life as a civilian treating you?" I asked.

"Not bad. A lot fewer people trying to kill me. How about you?"

"It's a little boring, but sometimes boring isn't so bad. In fact, I wish today had been a little more boring."

"Oh, what happened?" Frank asked, looking concerned as he tuned into our conversation.

"A crazy asshole in a truck tried to run us all off a cliff today."

"Jesus."

"Yeah, I think things are heating up."

"Fucking Finn is a magnet for trouble," Beeber said.

"No shit. I don't get it. Life as a private investigator used to be pretty uneventful," I said.

"Private investigator? So, you're like *Magnum P.I.* now?" Rex asked.

Beeber and Doug started laughing.

"Not at all," I said.

"Bullshit. Finn is totally a shitty version of *Magnum P.I.*, and he wouldn't have solved any of his cases if it weren't for

Doug and me constantly saving his ass."

"Which means you two are like Rick and TC!" Frank said.

"Pretty much," Doug responded.

In the name of my personal dignity, I decided to try and change the direction of the conversation.

"Speaking of *Magnum P.I.*, Frank owns the house that was the fabled Robin Masters Estate in the show."

"Seriously?" Beeber asked.

"Yes indeed, and as I already told Finn, you're all welcome to come by and see it in person. Perhaps we'll do a barbecue tomorrow evening?"

"That would be awesome, though I have to ask—do you have a red Ferrari?" Beeber asked.

"I do, but it's a bit newer than the one in the show."

"Would Rex qualify as your majordomo—or Higgins in *Magnum P.I.* speak?" Beeber asked.

"I suppose he would," Frank said.

"Perfect! Now all you need is for Finn to move into the guest house and start leeching off you, and you'll have a proper reenactment," Beeber said.

Doug and Beeber giggled like idiots, but I decided not to chastise them, as their help was sorely needed, and, truth be told, it was nice being together again. I was also feeling all warm and fuzzy as I regarded my two old friends, for they were literally glowing in the warm light of the looming sunset. We continued to enjoy a lovely island evening until Frank gazed at his watch then nodded at Rex. The two stood, then Frank cleared his throat to get everyone's attention.

"I'm sorry—Rex and I have to get going, but please stay as long as you like and feel free to order dinner. It's all going on my club tab, so have a wonderful evening. It was nice meeting you all."

Frank and Rex said good night, and the two men exited and left the Three Amigos and their two hot tamales alone in the beautiful Hawaiian night.

"See, Frank is actually a big teddy bear," I said.

"Until you get on his bad side. Then I imagine he can be more like a grizzly bear," Doug responded.

"Then it's a good thing we're friends. Anyone hungry?"

"Hell yeah," Rachel said.

Our waitress came back around, and we all ordered dinner and another round of drinks, then the conversation turned to how Beeber, Doug, and I all ended up working together at the CIA. Apparently, the girls found it odd that the three of us would come together in a such a large agency when all of our skill sets were so removed from one another—and even more so in my case, as I was a field agent.

"Well, needless to say, what we're about to tell you cannot leave this table," I said.

"Cross my heart and hope to die," Rachel said.

"I believe I have the clearance," Violet added.

"Well, Finn, Doug, and I were all part of the CIA's elite Special Activities Division," Beeber said.

"The what?" Rachel asked.

"Special Activities Division or S.A.D. We did a lot of paramilitary missions—snatch and grabs, rescues, you name it. Anyway, a good operation relies on three critical areas. Step one, or intelligence gathering, is where I came in. I specifically used human intel, electronic surveillance, satellites, eavesdropping, spy software, and everything you can imagine to amass a great deal of data on critical targets. Then, Doug would utilize that data to form a plan, and Finn would be the action arm who went out and performed the mission. Thus, we were the Three Amigos."

"As in the movie with Steve Martin, Martin Short, and Chevy Chase?"

"Exactly."

"So, I still don't see how the three of you overlapped," Violet said.

Beeber, Doug, and I shared a smile.

"Well, in spite of working together, our true meeting was actually more about chance."

Eight years ago, Georgetown, Washington D.C..

I had a little downtime between assignments and was unfortunately spending it doing debriefings at the Agency, and, after a long day, I decided to get a beer at one of the trendy breweries in Georgetown. It was also near the University, so it was rife with college students drinking and desperately trying to make a love, or perhaps lust, connection. I strolled inside and, as usual, unconsciously scanned the crowd for threats and, more importantly, attractive women. There weren't any visible threats, but there were plenty of attractive women, and I ventured further into the chaos and took a seat at the bar and ordered a beer.

It arrived a short time later, and I took a sip, then had another look around and oddly spied two coworkers from the Agency sitting at a table a short distance away. I had seen them around but never spoken directly with them, because they were on the intelligence gathering and analysis side of the Special Activities Division. At the moment they appeared to be playing a game, and, as I looked closer, I saw that they were fucking playing Dungeons and Dragons right here in the middle of a crowded brewery. Worse still, they had all their various books, dice, and paper laid out on the table. Sweet Lord! What the fuck were those nerds thinking?

I turned my attention back to my beer and was soon joined by an attractive girl who had taken one of the open seats beside me. She was with some equally attractive friends, and I was guessing that they were probably graduate students, because they were in their middle twenties. She smiled and said hello, and I happily responded in kind, as it wasn't often that I had time to meet women. Being in my line of work meant that I was in a new country every couple weeks, so this was a rare pleasure. We continued to talk, and I learned that she was indeed a grad student and was finishing up a masters in political science at Georgetown. She asked me about my profession, and I told her I worked for the State Department, which earned me points, as it kind of related to her major. There seemed to be some hints of mutual attraction, at least I was hoping so, but a sudden commotion brought my attention away from my lovely new friend and back to my two nerd coworkers.

A group of four fit-looking frat guys were standing at their table and apparently wanted the nerds to move. The nerds weren't backing down, however, and told the frat guys that they were eating and drinking and therefore perfectly justified in continuing to occupy the table. The frat assholes weren't happy, and worse, they were starting to get agitated, as frat assholes often did when they were out drinking in groups. It was a typical pack mentality, and I'd seen plenty of it back during my college days at Stanford.

The unofficial leader of the frat assholes abruptly slammed this hand down on the table, and everyone in the vicinity grew quiet and turned to gaze at the commotion. Still, the gentle nerds didn't back down, and I was getting a bad feeling that they were seconds away from a frat asshole beatdown. To that end, I kindly excused myself from my lovely new female friend and walked over to make sure my coworkers avoided any unplanned trips to the emergency room.

"Hey, easy there, fratsters," I said, as I arrived at the table.

"Who the fuck are you?" the lead frat asshole asked, as he turned his penetrating gaze to me.

"I'm just a good samaritan."

"Oh—then are you here to tell these assholes that it's about time they gave up the fucking table?"

"No, I'm here to tell you that should leave these gentleman alone and walk away while you can."

"Oh, are you going to make me?"

"Well, it's better me than them," I said, gesturing at the nerds.

The frat asshole snickered and smiled.

"Dude, I assume you're joking?"

"Afraid not."

He sized me up for moment and saw that I was equal in height and perhaps a little ahead in terms of musculature, but, like all assholes, he figured the presence of his friends gave him the advantage.

"Look here, samaritan, these two fucks have been here for two hours already, and my friends and I would like their table."

"I understand that it seems kind of lame on their part, but, as long as they're eating and drinking, I'm afraid it's their fucking table."

"Well, not anymore," he said, as he reached down and grabbed the twenty sided die off the table and prepared to throw it.

"Dude, no!" one of the nerds called out.

The frat asshole hauled back his arm and began his

throw, but, as it came forward, I reached out and caught his forearm and stopped it cold. It made a loud smacking sound, and must have hurt a little because the asshole looked shocked.

"Now, I'm asking you nicely. Please put the die back on the table and leave," I said.

"Fuck you."

"Is that your final answer?"

"Yeah, so fuck you," he said, as he tried to wriggle his hand from my grasp.

I utilized a jujitsu technique that entailed twisting his arm back over his shoulder, and it drove him onto his knees. He gave out a pained grunt, and his friends all tensed and looked as though they were ready to fight.

"Easy there, assholes. If any of you move even a fraction of an inch closer, I'm going to dislocate your friend's shoulder, and, judging by your stupid matching T-shirts, you fucks, in addition to being frat brothers, are also on the lacrosse team. So, assuming your friend here is a halfway decent player, I suspect you're going to need him for your next game."

The guys all relaxed—mostly, anyway—so I had gained a little reprieve from an all out bar fight.

"Good, now if you would please follow me, we can go talk like civilized gentleman," I said, as I leveraged their friend back onto his feet and used a hold called a California come-along to guide him away from the nerds' table.

His friends followed, and, once we were well away, I

released my grip on the frat asshole leader.

"I know those two don't look like much, but the reality is that I just saved you from the biggest mistake of your young lives. Sure, they're sitting there playing Dungeons and Dragons, but that's the way they unwind after a tour."

"A tour of what?"

"A tour of duty. This two are Army Special Forces just back from Afghanistan."

"Bullshit."

"No, I'm deadly serious, and I shouldn't be telling you this, but between them they have more kills than Chris Kyle."

"The SEAL sniper?"

"Yeah.

"Bullshit. No fucking Special Forces play Dungeons and Dragons."

"It seems weird, but the Army therapist has them do it in order to help them revert back to their civilian lives — you know—a taste of childhood innocence to ease the heart and mind."

All of the frat asshole took a moment to look at the nerds to see they appeared to have completely forgotten the encounter and gone right back into playing their game. This actually added credibilty to my story, because rational people would have probably left the scene.

"I don't know," the lead asshole said, after a moment, so he appeared to need more convincing.

"Have you seen the movie The Three Amigos?" I asked.

"No."

"Well, in it, three idiots go into a bar and are mistaken for three badasses. Then, later, when the real badasses go in, they are mistaken for the idiots, and they kill everyone in the bar. Well, those two non-assuming guys over there are actually the badasses in this scenario."

"So, who are you?"

"The guy trying to keep them out of trouble until their next deployment," I said, as I pulled out a Department of Defense ID I occasionally used while in town.

The guys all looked at it and appeared to believe my story.

"So, in the spirit of détente, I'm going to give you a hundred dollars to go drink somewhere else."

"Dude, I'm not entirely believing your story, but I'm going to take your money, because it'll buy a shit-ton of beer."

"Exactly, now enjoy your evening, gentlemen."

The frat assholes went on their way, and I returned to the nerds' table, and they looked up at me curiously.

"Hello, nerds. The name's Finn, Tag Finn, and I believe we more or less work together."

"Yeah, I've seen you around the office. I'm Justin Beeber, and this is Doug Griffith," the one on the left said.

"Nice to meet you, boys."

"Dude, what did you say to those guys to get them to leave?" Beeber asked.

"Did you ever see the movie The Three Amigos?"

"Of course."

"Well, I told them you were like the three guys who went into the bar after the amigos."

"Had they even seen the movie?" Doug asked.

"No, but they got the point. Plus, I gave them a hundred bucks to go fuck off, and beer money goes a long way with frat assholes."

"Cool move."

"Yeah, but honestly now—what the hell made you guys come here to play D&D?" I asked.

"Dude, isn't it obvious?"

"No" I responded, legitimately curious.

"The chicks!" they both said, at the same time.

"But—you're playing D&D."

"Exactly!" Beeber said.

I shook my head, as I realized they really didn't understand that their D&D playing was the most effective form of birth control they would ever use—because no woman in this place would ever go near them. Oh well, I decided to forego any attempt at female companionship and instead decided I was going to get to know the kindly, though surprisingly oblivious, nerds."

"So, nerds, I have a sixteenth level Ranger I haven't been able to play in years."

"Where's your character sheet?" Doug asked.

"I have it in PDF form on my iPhone."

"Sweet, Beeber has a wizard, and I have a sorcerer, and we could totally use a better melee character in our team."

I sat down, and we managed to complete a fairly large

section of their dungeon and had a pretty darn fun evening of beer and battle. By midnight, however, it was about time to call it quits.

"Well, fuckers, we'll have to do this again," I said.

"Yeah, we worked well together as a team," Beeber said.

"Too bad it isn't like this at work," I responded.

I saw that Doug was thinking, and a moment later he looked at us with growing enthusiasm.

"You know, I've often thought that there was too much of a separation between intelligence gathering, analysis, and the action wing. If they were one unit, they could act more quickly on intel and be a hell of a lot more effective."

"Agreed," I said.

"So, let's become the Three Amigos in real life," Beeber said.

"I'm in," I said, as I held up my glass to toast.

"Me too," Doug said, holding up his glass.

"Me three," Beeber said, also holding up his glass..

"To the Three Amigos," I said, as we clinked glasses.

Everyone smiled and finished their beer, and, in the glowing aftermath of the moment, I had a rather sad revelation about my earlier actions in the evening.

"So, fellow Amigos, now that we're a team, is there any chance of you partially reimbursing for the hundred I gave to the frat boys?"

Back to the present, Outrigger Canoe Club, Oahu, Hawaii.

"So, Finn saving your asses at that bar is how the three amigos came to be?"

"Yeah, though we might have been able to take those frat assholes."

"I think Finn saved you from a night in the emergency room, so thanks, Finn for keeping my Beebs safe from harm," Rachel said.

"What about me?" Doug asked.

"And you too," she said.

"So, how long has it been since you've all gotten together?" Violet asked.

"Five years," Doug said.

"That's actually kind of sad," Rachel responded.

"Well, until now, Doug's been afraid to fly."

"Not any more. I have a new mistress, and her name is Lorazepam!"

"How do you know your drug is a she?"

"Because she's smart, sensitive, and highly effective."

"So, she's a typical woman," Rachel said.

"Yep, and thanks to her, the world is now my oyster."

Dinner arrived, and we enjoyed a lovely Hawaiian evening out on the Hau Terrace, where we were gently buffeted by the sea breeze that made the surrounding tiki torches cast a flickering ambience over the faces of the people at our table. I was eating the same chicken dish as before, but the others had all gone with fish, as we were in the middle of the ocean, and they thought it only made sense to eat locally. When we finished dinner, we left the Outrigger and headed up the H3 to reach the parking lot of our resort then spent a good five minutes searching for a space large enough to fit the Suburban. With the behemoth safely squeezed between two white Toyota Corollas, we checked Doug in to his room, so that he could change into some shorts and join the rest of us in my room. Once there, he went over the police report then asked about the other events—namely the death of Rudy and our little death race with the Toyota four by four earlier today. Satisfied that he had a decent picture of the situation, I made us a pitcher of dark and stormies, and we all adjourned to the beach, where I thought it was only proper that Doug at last dip his feet into the warm waters of the Pacific Ocean. With drinks in hand, we all walked down to the water and stood in the gentle surf, and Doug smiled from ear to ear as he held up his glass.

"I know this toast is probably getting old, but I have to say it. To the Three Amigos!" he said.

"Five Amigos," Rachel countered.

"Indeed, to the Five Amigos."

We all clinked glasses and sipped our drinks under a warm star filled night, and enjoyed the sound of the gentle waves rolling up onto the sand. Hawaii truly was a magical place, and it was amazing to think that we were all together in the middle of the Pacific Ocean on the most remote island in the world. We eventually finished our drinks and went to get refills before taking up residence on the nearby beach furniture, where Doug, after spending an inordinately long amount of time lost in thought, was the first to break the silence.

"So, I've been thinking about everything that's happened thus far, and, honestly, it has me a bit freaked out."

"Well yeah, because its fucking freaky."

"And terrifying. Who in the hell fucks with the current vice president and potential next president of the United States. The people or person who goes after someone like Matheson has to be extremely powerful and capable. The logistics of running an operation like this would take money, expertise, and, more importantly, experience, so we've got one hell of a job ahead of us if we're going to take these fuckers down."

"Yeah, which is why it's so nice to have the dream team back together."

"We always said that together we could move mountains," Beeber proclaimed proudly.

"Yeah, but we were usually drunk," I added.

"Like now," Violet said.

A noise came from behind us, and I turned around to see several figures walking down to the beach, and, considering my luck as of late, I started to wish I had packed some heat. That is, until I recognized the voices. It was Corn, Lux, Jessica, John, and of course his Secret Service detail.

"Ahoy, strangers," I said.

"Thanks for the invite, Finn," John said.

"Sorry, I figured someone of your stature only frequented beach parties in the Hamptons."

"No, I'm pretty much down with any beach where they have alcohol. Who are your friends?"

"How rude of me, Sasquatch—this is Doug Griffith, Justin Beeber, Rachel Stephenson, and you of course already know Violet."

"Nice to finally meet you all. This is my wife to be Jessica Thurman, and this hefty piece of man is Cornelius Wallace, or as we call him—Corn. Beside him is his better more beautiful half—Lux Vonde."

"And for the record, I dated her first but sadly humped her second," I said.

"Oh, Finn, seriously?" Lux said.

"I don't believe in secrets."

"Oh, then should I recount to our current company a certain event that took place in the ladies room at the luau?" she asked.

"OK, I officially apologize and have instated a gag order on any further revelations concerning me, Lux, or Corn."

"Wait, what happened at the luau?" Beeber asked.

"Nothing."

Thankfully, Doug, looking a bit shocked, interjected by stepping forward.

"Wait a minute! Your Corn is Cornelius Wallace? Deputy Director of the CIA and therefore, in a roundabout way, my boss?" Doug asked.

"Yep."

"Goddammit, Finn! Why the fuck didn't you ever tell me?"

"Don't worry, Doug, I won't hold it against you that you know Finn," Corn said.

"Thank you, sir."

"No calling me sir. Call me Corn. We're about the same age, and more importantly we're in Hawaii and over four thousand miles from Langley for fuck's sake."

"Corn it is."

"What are you drinking?" John asked.

"Dark and stormies. You?"

"Same."

"Great minds think alike."

"And drink alike, apparently."

A hotel employee materialized out of the darkness and spoke quietly with Sandra.

"What is it?" John asked.

"The hotel wants to know if you would like a beach bonfire."

"Yes, he does," I interrupted.

Ten minutes later, we were all sitting around a lovely fire, and Violet was beside me looking beautiful with her face aglow, and it felt like a proper beach party—something I hadn't experienced since college.

"What's the latest, Finn?" John asked.

"Not good. Today alone, our first lead was hit by a car and killed, then we were almost run off a cliff by a fucking Toyota four by four."

"Sounds like you should avoid cars for a while."

"Good thinking."

"I feel like this is all my fault," Jessica said.

"Definitely not. Whoever is doing this, clearly has Sasquatch in his sights."

"How do you know it's a he?" Rachel asked.

"I don't, but guys are almost always the problem."

"Isn't that the truth," Lux said.

"Amen, sister," Violet added.

"It's so nice to see you girls bonding," I said.

"It's a necessity when the world is full of so many man-whores," Lux said.

Violet laughed out loud. Wonderful—here it comes.

"I can't believe you just said that. I started calling Finn a man-whore this morning."

"I started calling him that about six months ago!"

"Can we request a guitar? I think there's way too much talking going on," I said.

Sandra got on her mic, and five minutes later a large man, likely of Hawaiian or Samoan decent, came walking down to the beach, and, under his enormous arm, he was carrying an acoustic guitar.

"Did somebody ask for music?" he asked in pidgin accented English.

"We sure did."

"Well here I am. Call me *Brudda* Abe."

"Cocktail, *Brudda* Abe?" John asked.

"I really shouldn't."

"I think you should."

"Wait a minute! You're da vice president!" he said, in total surprise as he looked at John.

"For the moment. Here, have a cocktail, Abe," John said, as he handed him a glass.

"If you run for president, you got my vote."

"Thanks, Abe."

"Any requests?" he asked, picking up his guitar.

"You know any Iz?" I responded.

I was of course referring to Israel "Iz" Ka'ano'i Kamakawiwo'ole, a Hawaiian singer who's golden voice brought joy to countless millions before his life and career were cut short by his premature demise in 1997.

"Of course. How about Somewhere Over the Rainbow?"

"Perfect," I said.

Abe started playing his guitar then set into the first verse, and, while not many people could sound as amazing as Iz, Abe came pretty damn close, and he brought the night alive with his magical voice. Violet even reached over and took hold of my hand, which was major progress. Soon, everyone was smiling, and it was strange to look around and see my closest friends from my adult life all in one place at one time. It was just too bad that it had to be under such shitty circumstances. After several songs and multiple cocktails, the girls needed a break to pee, and they trotted off to the beach baño and left us menfolk to ourselves.

"So, Agent Kalili is pretty fucking hot," Doug said.

"No shit," John added.

"Anything going on there?" Beeber asked.

"There was, but I kind of fucked it up."

"She looks very familiar, but I can't figure out why. I don't think we crossed paths in Washington, because I would have remembered her," John said.

"Can you keep a secret?" I asked.

"Of course, I'm a politician."

"No seriously, can you actually keep a secret?"

"Yeah."

"We both met Violet the night of your bachelor party. She was the blond stripper."

"Holy shit. The one you hooked up with?"

"Yeah."

"So, why is she stripping if she's an FBI agent?"

"Apparently, she did an undercover assignment at a strip club and made so much money that she continued doing it part-time to pay off her house."

"Good for her. Capitalism at work," John said.

"Finn, you are one lucky son of a bitch," Doug said.

"Not really. In this instance, she gave me a taste then closed the kitchen."

"How did you fuck it up?"

"Well, she told me in no uncertain terms that our working relationship meant nothing more was ever going to happen between us."

"Don't you know that's woman speak for something is definitely going to happen?" John asked.

"Apparently not, and I let alcohol compound my idiocy

enough that I got together with another woman the very next night."

"Sweet Jesus. You're putting my shenanigans to shame," John said.

"Yeah, sadly, and now she's spending all her free time making sure my balls retain their beautiful shade of dark blue."

"And you didn't even have to marry her," Corn said.

We all laughed, but, at that moment, the girls suddenly appeared, and we quickly quieted down.

"So, what were you boys all talking about?" Lux asked.

"Oh you know—the meaning of life and shit like that," I said.

"So, you were talking about us."

"Yeah, mostly," I muttered.

Brudda Abe, as if on cue, carried on singing more songs—some Hawaiian, some not, but all were familiar and crossed over into practically every music genre. The only hiccup of the night was when Beebs got overly excited and asked if *Brudda* Abe knew Eye of the Tiger. Apparently, Beeber was hoping for a duet, but saner heads prevailed, and he settled back down into just enjoying Abe's performance. The final song of the night ended with a singalong of the Beach Boys' Don't Worry Baby, which seemed oddly apropos of our situation and truly made it feel like a real beach party.

Midnight rolled around, and everyone was thoroughly buzzed, thoroughly tired, and ready to call it a night.

Brudda Abe again professed that he would vote for John if he did indeed run for president, which meant this was truly grass roots campaigning at its finest. Everyone said good night, thanked Abe again, and headed off to their respective rooms, leaving Violet and me alone as we set off for my suite.

"You are way too drunk to drive," I said.

"I am."

"So, I think you should stay here tonight."

"Nice try."

"It's not a ploy. It's for your own good."

She looked at me a moment with her thoughts obviously clouded by an abundance of dark and stormies.

"OK, but I'm sleeping with my gun under the pillow. Anything that pokes me in the night gets shot."

"Understood."

We entered the elevator then exited on my floor and headed to my room, where Violet immediately went to the bathroom, as she obviously needed to pee after having consumed so many cocktails. Two minutes later, I heard the water running and figured she was taking a shower to wash off the smoke smell from the bonfire. She emerged a minute later and smelled fresh as a daisy as she walked into the bedroom and stripped down directly in front of me.

"You didn't forget that I was here, did you?"

"Nope."

"So, you're doing it on purpose."

"Yep."

"Wonderful," I said, as I walked into the bathroom, peed, then stepped into the shower feeling happy to wash away the smell of smoke on my hair and skin.

A moment later, Violet walked in and proceeded to brush her teeth, during which she gazed at me for a brief second before turning her attention back to the sink.

"Can I help you with something?" I asked.

"No, I was just checking to see if you were jacking off."

"I'm just fine, thank you—in spite of your little show."

I finished up my shower, brushed my teeth, and came out to find Violet in my bed with the covers pulled up to her chin. I stripped down to my boxer briefs and a T-shirt then climbed into bed to find her completely naked.

"Seriously?" I asked.

"What? Do you have a problem with me sleeping in the nude?"

"No, as long as you don't mind waking up in a blizzard of jism."

She lifted her pillow and showed me that she had indeed brought her gun to bed.

"As you see, I've brought real protection, not the latex kind."

"All I'm saying is that anything that happens on this side of the bed, regardless of the lewdness of the act, is perfectly legal in this scenario."

"Fine, this is our personal Maginot Line," she said, running her hand down the center of the bed.

"You obviously know that it didn't stop the Germans in

World War II."

"Yeah, so keep your Panzer in your pants, Rommel."

I turned off the light and lay there listening to the nearby waves rolling up onto the shoreline. I was definitely tired, but sleep wouldn't come easily thanks to fucking Violet. Of course, the reality of the situation was that I had no one to blame but myself. I had acted like a man-whore, and now I could only wonder why in the hell I let myself end up in bed with Melissa Williams? Suddenly, Violet stirred and moved her legs over to my side of the bed and placed her feet against my calf.

"*Nein!*" I said.

"*Pardonnez-moi?*"

"*Unterlassungserklärung!*"

"*Quoi?*"

"I said cease and desist."

"My feet are cold."

"It's eighty degrees in here, and besides, isn't it a breach of our treaty?"

"Well, we didn't stipulate that I couldn't cross the Maginot Line."

"This treaty is unfair."

"All is fair in love and war."

"For women, apparently."

"We have to protect ourselves from man-whores."

"Fine, you can keep your feet over here."

She lay there with her cold feet against my calf, and she continued to gently wiggle her toes, so she apparently couldn't sleep either. She fussed a little and rolled onto her back and pulled the blanket down to reveal her lovely breasts, which were now glowing in the ambient light spilling in through the window.

"I thought you were cold."

"Only my feet."

I continued to stare in rapt attention as her breasts slowly rose and fell with each breath, and her nipples were starting to grow hard in spite of the fact that she was supposedly too warm to stay under the covers. Fuck. I needed to think about something else, so I rolled over and closed my eyes and tried to empty my mind of thoughts of Violet. After about two painful minutes, I couldn't take it any longer and rolled back over to see that Violet was now gently caressing her substantial nipples, and they were hard as all hell and fully elongated as they pointed skyward.

"Sweet Jesus, devil woman!" I said.

"What?"

"Do you really have to do that right now?"

"Sometimes it helps me sleep."

"Well it's certainly not helping me sleep."

"Are your nipples very sensitive?"

"Yeah, I suppose. Why?"

"Well, I can sometimes climax from nipple stimulation."

"Seriously?"

"Yep."

"So, how exactly is caressing your nipples helping you sleep?"

"I'm going to give myself a massive orgasm, then I'll sleep like a baby."

"I should have called you a cab."

"You don't want to see me have an orgasm?"

"Yeah, I do, but the problem is that I wish I could be a part of that orgasm."

"Too bad you blew it."

"Yeah, too bad."

"Maybe you should take off your underwear and that silly T-shirt."

My heart was starting to pound.

"Why?"

"Because you're about to start jacking off, and you wouldn't want to get them covered in filthy man-whore juice."

"What are you talking about?"

Violet pulled off the covers to reveal her lovely lady parts and immediately set to work by making slow circles as she flexed her pelvis. She started moaning and arched her back, and her breasts were now pressing skyward like two beautiful mountains of man-joy. After a moment, she sat up and moved onto her knees and continued her devious act of self pleasure—all the while watching me intently.

"I don't think you're going to want to miss this," she said.

Shit monkeys! I literally jumped up, slid off my underwear, and all but tore my shirt off my back before slipping back into bed. Violet was gazing lustfully at my manhood, and it was pushing my arousal level up to defcon one.

"Start whacking," she said.

This was officially now my third time engaging in what I called a mutual masturbation session. The first had been with a beautiful woman name Fiona, and the second had been with a beautiful pilot named Tatyana. Violet, however, would hold the distinction of being the first FBI Agent to engage in this act with me—something I hoped wasn't illegal. I took hold of Tag Junior and moved my hand fore and aft, and every second made me want Violet all the more. Of course, this was all part of her devious plan to continue making me pay for a night of poor judgement, and, with that painful thought firmly locked in my mind, I put my full attention on Violet. We were now face to face, with each of us perched on our respective side of the Maginot Line, and the show before me was a visual temptation of epic proportions. Her one hand was moving over her lady region while the other was caressing her nipples, whose obvious state of excitement was mirroring my own. Soft moans escaped her lips, and, soon, great thunderous cries were coming on in faster waves as she thrust her hips back and forth. Needless to say, I too was feeling release only seconds away.

"Do you want to be inside me?"

"Yes."

"How badly?"

"Really badly."

She leaned forward until her lips were only inches from my own.

"Kiss me," she said.

"Are you sure?"

"Kiss me!" she yelled.

I did as instructed, and the moment our lips touched, we both came with a mighty scream, whose volume was somewhat diminished by our entwined mouths. We continued on with our tongues completing the act that our bodies could not until finally coming to rest, whereupon we both relaxed and smiled.

"I feel better. I think I can sleep now. Good night, Finn," she said, slinking back under the covers as though nothing had happened.

I was feeling mildly dumbfounded as I sat there holding my manhood. It was still hard, as I suspect it too felt oddly unsatisfied in spite of having spilled its precious seed. I gazed down at the battlefield and was happy to see that at least my aim had sent my tiny soldiers over the Maginot Line and into what was technically now occupied France. I went to the bathroom, grabbed a towel, then came back and cleaned up my mess before dropping onto bed beside Violet, who now slept like an angel—or perhaps demon if I wanted to be more accurate. I closed my eyes, cleared my mind of the day's events, and let the soothing sounds of the Pacific take me off to the glorious abyss of sleep.

CHAPTER FIFTEEN
The Tip of the Spear

The sound of running water brought me awake, and I rolled over and looked at the clock to see that it was a little after nine. The curtains were open, and warm Hawaiian sunshine was filling the room. Suddenly, the bathroom door opened, and there stood Violet looking lovely and ready for the day. She had already showered, and, even better, was holding a cup of coffee in each hand—bless her heart. Perhaps there was still a chance at love after all. I sat up as she handed me the cup, then took a moment to hold it under my nose to let the aroma reach deep into my olfactory awareness. After a moment I brought the cup to my lips, took my first glorious sip, and felt the world around me transform into a place of sunshine, rainbows, sweet melodious bird song, and a cornucopia of unicorns humping each other in wild abandon in a fountain overflowing with my greatest hopes and dreams.

"You looked dreamy there for a moment. What were

you thinking about?" Violet asked.

"Sunshine, rainbows, sweet melodious bird song, and a cornucopia of unicorns humping each other in wild abandon in a fountain overflowing with my greatest hopes and dreams."

"Wow, someone apparently enjoys his morning coffee."

"I do, and to me this heaven in a cup," I muttered.

"So, how'd you sleep?" she asked.

"Like a baby. And you?"

"Same, now what's on the agenda today?"

"Three things. First, I want to call Steven's office in San Francisco and see if he had any kind of actual client meeting or reason to be here—other than blackmailing Jessica, of course. If he did, there's a chance that person or persons was part of the conspiracy, and his office might have a name or telephone number. Second, I want Doug to see if he can find our gunsmith, and, thirdly, I'd like to talk to the spear fisherman."

"You think Doug can find the gun smith's address? I already ran him through our system, but so far they haven't found anything."

"What? The FBI can't find someone?"

"Not our fault. He's a ghost."

"Well, hopefully the CIA will be more successful," I said, as I set my cup down and ventured into the bathroom to brush my teeth and take a massive morning horse piss.

I had just returned when there was a sudden knock at the door.

"Did you order room service?" I asked.

"No."

"Maybe the nerds are awake."

I quickly slid on my T-shirt and underwear as Violet walked to the door and looked through the little peephole.

"Oh for fuck's sake," she said, with a groan.

"Who is it?" I asked.

"Special Agent Dave Moore, and he looks especially grumpy."

"What the fuck is he doing here?"

"Probably checking up on me."

Violet opened the door, and there stood a very grumpy looking Dave, and he looked past her to cast his discerning gaze on me.

"Morning, special agent. Coffee?" I asked.

He walked in and looked around before speaking to Violet.

"I've been trying to reach you since last night. I even went by your place."

"Any special reason?" she asked.

"After I heard about what happened yesterday, I wanted to make sure you were all right."

"As you can see I'm just fine, Dave."

"So, where did you stay last night?" he asked, already knowing the answer to his question.

"None of your business."

"I think it is my business."

"No, it's not anymore. Move on."

"You sure you don't want any coffee?" I asked again as I refilled my cup.

"No, and why don't you stay out of this."

"I would, but you're in my room."

Dave abruptly turned and walked over to me.

"You might think you're hot shit because you work for the vice president, but I don't give a flying fuck. You're on my turf now, and you're going to play by my rules."

"What does that have to do with coffee?"

"Nothing, so listen up, glamour boy."

"Wait—Glamour boy? Should I take that as a compliment?"

"No, you shouldn't."

"Well, listen up, Dave. I'm sorry to say it, but Violet and I are working together—mind you, at the direct request of both the vice president of the United States and the director of the FBI, and that means you're going to have to man up, swallow your pride, and stay the fuck out of our way."

"Fuck you."

"No, fuck you. You came into my room acting like a complete asshole, and all I've done to offend you was offer you some coffee."

"After you slept with my girlfriend, asshole."

"Ex-girlfriend, and listen up, bigger asshole—we might have slept in the same bed, but we didn't sleep together in the biblical sense, so chill the fuck out," I said, leaving out the fact that two nights ago we had indeed slept together in the biblical sense.

"Don't tell me to chill the fuck out, you fucking asshole."

"Well, Special Agent Fuckface, I am going to tell you to chill out when you fucking need to chill out."

Dave had apparently reached his breaking point and shot out a pretty solid right punch straight for my jaw. It was hard to believe that I'd only been awake for ten minutes and was already involved in a fistfight with a special agent of the FBI. I had some pretty quick decisions to make—namely how I was going to handle the situation. First, I needed to diminish the power of the punch, and, to that end, I slipped back and sideways in order to get my face out of the way so that the punch would be nothing more than a glancing blow at best. It barely grazed the side of my chin, and, while it wasn't a complete miss, it was a lot better than getting knocked out. Now, I needed to respond in kind, but my options were fairly limited, as I was standing there with a cup of coffee in one of my hands. To that end, I followed my instincts and used the easiest weapon I had at my disposal—namely my beloved cup of coffee. I threw the remaining contents of the cup into his face, and while it wasn't exactly blazing hot, he still screamed.

"You fucking asshole! That was a bitch move," he said, as he took a step backward and used his hands to wipe his eyes.

"No, the bitch move was swinging on a guy who was still drinking his morning coffee," I said, as I set down the now empty mug.

Dave grew even angrier, and he stepped forward and

threw a solid right cross, so I moved left and parried the punch with my left hand then grabbed his wrist with my right and delivered a sharp left chop to his ribs that made him grunt and keel over. From there, I transitioned to an ulna press and rolled his shoulder down and drove him onto his knees. Dave was a pretty skilled fighter, however, and went with the move by going into a forward roll in order to take the pressure off his shoulder. He was now lying on his back on the ground in front of me, and he kicked his legs across and knocked me onto my back then climbed on top of me and threw a punch. I knocked it aside and trapped it then did a move I jokingly called the floor bump, which entailed thrusting up with my hips. It sent him rolling off to the side, and I went with the motion and ended up between his legs, where I delivered a solid knee to his groin. He winced in pain, and I used the moment to grab his right arm, rotate ninety degrees and trap him in place by barring his elbow across my groin. He squirmed and yelled a barrage of profanities, but I just kept applying more pressure until he finally relaxed and acquiesced. Suddenly, the door to my room opened, and in walked Doug, Beeber, and Rachel. Violet asked them to get help, and a minute or so later, a number of John's Secret Service contingent, which included Sandra, came running into my room and took hold of a very angry Dave.

"I'm an FBI special agent! Get your fucking hands off of me!" he yelled.

"You OK, Finn?" Sandra asked.

"Yeah, just starting the day with a little kitten play to get the blood flowing."

Sandra, with the help of her fellow agents, took Dave aside and managed to finally calm him down, at which point he walked back over and got in my face for some final words.

"This isn't over, asshole," he said, as he poked me in the chest with his right index finger.

"I wouldn't want it to be. This has been the most effective wake up call I've had in a long time. Can you be here tomorrow morning about the same time?"

He turned and strode out of the room, and the Secret Service followed close behind, probably to make sure he didn't get any more wild ideas. Sandra was last to leave, and she paused at the door and looked back at me.

"Never a dull moment, Finn."

"Afraid not. Thanks, Sandra."

"You're welcome," she said, closing the door.

Peace returned to my room, and the nerds just stood there frowning at me.

"Dude, what's with the macho gladiator shit?" Beeber asked.

"Yeah, isn't it a little early to be wrestling around in your underwear?" Doug added.

"I don't know. I'm kind of turned on," Rachel said.

"Thank you for your support, Rachel, and for the record, I didn't start that fight. Special agent fuckface did."

The three nerds proceeded to walk over and set their

laptops on my coffee table and quickly turned my living room into an operations center.

"You going to put some clothes on?" Beeber asked.

"Yeah, right after I shit, shower, and shave," I said

"Oh, Jesus—you haven't even shit yet?"

"Nope, and you know the rules. No intrusion once I enter my sanctuary."

I refilled my coffee cup and entered my sanctuary and took the time to make sure that the door was both fully closed and the lock properly seated. Next, I took a moment to admire the toilet's clean and simple lines before at last placing my backside in its loving embrace. I took a sip of coffee and relaxed my sphincter in order to signify the opening ceremonies of my personal olympic toilet games. The first event was obviously diving, though these fecal athletes mostly plummeted to complete the short though epic leap into bowl. With hardly a splash, the games came to a close in the cool waters of my commode, and the final ceremony, a shower of liquid gold, began to rain down on the winning athletes. There were no silver or bronze medals, as these competitors all deserved first place. Having completed my business, I entered the shower then emerged a few minutes later feeling clean and ready for the day ahead. I applied pleasantries such as deodorant, sunblock, and cologne then exited the bathroom to get dressed in my usual T-shirt and board shorts. Done, I headed out and refilled my coffee yet again before joining Violet and the nerds.

"Anything exciting happen while I was in the shower?"

"Yeah, Doug and I decided to follow your lead and stripped down to our underwear and wrestled."

"Who won?"

"The ladies, of course."

"Isn't it a little too early for you two to try and be funny? Now, what's the real news?"

"I was able to find an address for your gunsmith."

"Hot damn!"

"Yeah, he's an interesting guy, and get this—he used to work for us."

"The government?"

"Yeah, but, more specifically, the CIA."

"No wonder the FBI couldn't find him," I said, looking at Violet.

"Yeah, he lives pretty far off the grid on a nice big piece of land up on the North Shore. The address is 59-779 Pupukea Rd, and it sits across the street from Camp Pupukea," Doug said.

"It's a good start. Nice work, Doug. Any address for our spear fisherman?"

"I got that one. Danny Keahi lives down in Waimanalo," Violet said.

"Excellent. Any progress on the email yet, Beebs?"

"Not yet. Government email has a lot of firewalls to get through, but we'll get there eventually."

"Well then, I suppose we should go see Danny Keahi. Any of you nerds want to join us?" I asked.

"We were kind of hoping to get in a little D&D," Beeber

said.

"Seriously? You're in Hawaii—one of the most beautiful places on earth and you're going to stay inside and play D&D."

"Only for a few hours—until the barbecue at Robin's Nest."

"Well, we're off then. Hide away in your fantasy world of wizards and elves, and whatever you do, don't strain your little fingers rolling your twenty sided die."

Violet and I left the nerds and walked out to find my car, which was mildly tricky at first, as I had forgotten it was now a massive white Suburban. Wondering why the adjacent Subaru wouldn't unlock, I finally noticed the flashing lights of the white behemoth beside it. Violet and I mounted up and were soon were driving south towards Waimanolo. That part of the island also happened to be one of the areas where Hawaiian homesteading had taken place, which was an attempt by the government to make sure that native Hawaiians had access to their ancestral land. It was therefore a fairly local environment, and that meant plenty of large tan people. We drove through the main part of town and past a group of locals having a barbecue at a park, then turned left and headed for Laumilo Street, which skirted a beautiful section of beach. As we arrived at Danny's place, we saw a crowd and a number of emergency vehicles at the entrance to the beach, and I parked the Suburban. Violet and I continued the rest of the way on foot, and, as we neared the crowd, I spied a young woman on the fringe. She was wearing a wet bikini and had obviously been down on the beach.

"What's all the excitement about?" I asked her.

"A body washed up on the beach."

I was suddenly getting a bad feeling.

"Tourist or local?"

"Local."

"It wouldn't happen to be Danny Keahi would it?"

"Yeah, how'd you know? You psychic or something?" she asked.

"No, just very very unlucky."

"Here he comes now," she said, pointing at the stretcher.

I looked over and watched as the EMTs carried a young man of around twenty five on a stretcher. He wasn't moving, and his face looked oddly serene as the emergency workers transferred him into a body bag and zipped it up. Fuck! Another one down. I suddenly heard some rather ominously loud footsteps and turned to see a large Hawaiian looking man walking in our direction, and he didn't look all that happy at the moment.

"What you want with Danny?" he asked, in Pidgin accented English as he came to a stop well within the polite boundary of personal space.

He was one big imposing son of a bitch, and I felt the need to take a step back before responding.

"We just wanted to talk to him."

"About what?"

"About the gun he found when he was out spear fishing.

That same gun just happened to have been involved in a murder."

"Danny wouldn't hurt nobody."

"I know, and that's why I wanted to talk to him."

"It's too late now I guess."

"Do you mind if I ask you some questions."

"Depends on the questions."

"Do you think it's possible that Danny actually drowned?"

"Hell no. He spent his whole life in these waters. Swimming, surfing, fishing, you name it."

"Then it's pretty likely that your friend Danny was also murdered."

"Because of the gun he found?"

"Yeah."

The man thought a moment.

"So, you think it's possible that the same person who committed the other murder also killed Danny?"

"Most definitely, and I suspect they arranged for him to conveniently find that pistol, then they eliminated him once the job was done."

"Danny was young and had his whole life ahead of him. That's pretty fucked up," the man said, sadly.

"Yeah, it's as fucked up as it gets."

The guy took a moment to think, and I could see a real sadness overtake his features. He might have been big and intimidating, but he apparently also had a big heart and cared for his neighbors, so I gave him a moment to himself before asking another question.

"I'm sorry if this isn't the right time, but I have another question that might help me find Danny's killer."

"No problem. Ask away."

"Do you know if he might have been seen with any strangers recently? A *haole* perhaps?"

The man thought for a moment before answering.

"No idea—but I do know that Danny often hung out at the bar across from the Seven Eleven on the north end of town. Place is called the Blow Hole. You might learn something there. It's kind of a local's only place, so, if *dey* give you any trouble, tell them Johnny Kamoahoa sent you."

"Thanks, I appreciate your help."

"And if you find *da* guy who done this and need a little local help, just give me a call. Danny was like a *brudda*."

"How do I get in touch with you?"

"Same way you get in touch with your *haole* friends. Phone," he said, with a mildly condescending smile.

So, Johnny had heart and a sense of humor, which made him a good guy in my book. Of course, it never hurt to have a little local muscle, so I put Johnny's number in my phone then said goodbye and climbed back into the Suburban. We drove back to the main highway and headed north and soon found the Seven Eleven, and there across the street was the Blow Hole. It was indeed a locals only kind of place, as there were several large tan and tattooed dudes chilling and smoking off to the side of the front. We parked the car and ventured over to the entrance, and the men near the door gave us rather unfriendly stares, which wasn't exactly a warm welcome or good omen that we might learn anything useful.

Inside, we found a typical dive bar, with the overall design aesthetic being varying degrees of darkness. Places like this were always kept dimly lit, perhaps to provide respite from the harsh light of day or to make customers feel that timeless five o'clock desire to empty your troubles into a glass. I gave the place a quick three-sixty and saw that this effect was achieved by windows tinted to the point that almost no ambient light reached inside, and the only illumination was coming from fixtures mounted to the ceiling via chains. They were those classic bar lights, and their shades were adorned with beer logos, and all of them swayed in the subtle breeze supplied by the two ceiling fans. Of course, the moving air did nothing to cool the place, and instead swirled the stench of spilled beer and sweat, and I immediately felt at home.

Violet and I exchanged a nod then continued deeper into this alcoholic heart of darkness, where the only sounds filling the air were the quiet murmurings of the nearby patrons and the melodious notes of Hawaiian music coming from the jukebox. The place was obviously pretty popular to attract this many people so early in the day, and, as a consummate optimist, I'd describe it as being about half full. We approached the bar and took a seat on a couple of cracked vinyl covered stools, whose cushioning had become thin and lumpy from years of use and abuse. A heavyset man somewhere in his fifties or sixties, who kind of looked like an older version of Johnny Kamoahoa, came over and stood before us and glowered without uttering a single word.

"Aloha," I said.

"Very funny. What do you want, *haole*?" he asked.

"Information."

"You should try that thing they call the internet. I hear you can find out practically anything," he said, earning a laugh from the nearby patrons.

Violet stepped up to the bar.

"Look, we're investigating a murder here, so cut the locals only crap."

"Step off, girl. Don't think that you looking local means you can talk shit in my bar."

Two of the patrons, a couple of massive dudes, stood up from their stools and stared menacingly at us.

"Lou, Jimmy—do you mind escorting these nice *haoles* outside?"

Violet, looking frustrated, pulled out her ID and flashed it at the bartender.

"Look, asshole. I'm an FBI agent, and unless you feel like doing a little jailhouse bartending, you're going to answer our fucking questions."

"Lady, do you really think I give a fuck about de FBI?"

Lou and Jimmy walked over and stood directly beside us, and now, up close, I realized that they were both well over six feet tall and together weighed about as much as a

Volkswagen bus.

"Easy, everyone. Johnny Kamoahoa sent us."

"How the fuck do you know Johnny Kamoahoa?"

Just then, the door to the bar opened and light spilled in around a large, lone figure. The person walked closer, but the door closed behind him, leaving his face still obscured by shadows. As he reached the bar and stood directly beneath one of the lights, I finally recognized our latest visitor.

"Hey! Why you treating my friends like shit?" Johnny asked.

Apparently, our new friend Johnny had decided to come join us at the bar.

"Johnny, you know these two?"

"Of course, we belong to the same country club."

Everyone laughed, including me, and suddenly all was well in the bar. Lou and Jimmy returned to their seats, and I bought Johnny a pint of his favorite beer, which turned out to be Coors Light. He held up his glass, thanked me, and proceeded to drink it in one single gulp.

"Give him another," I said.

The bartender refilled Johnny's glass then came back and smiled like we were old friends.

"How can I help you?" he asked.

"Danny Keahi. You know him?"

"Yeah."

"You know he supposedly drowned today?"

"Yeah, I heard."

"Well, I believe he was murdered, which is why I need some information. I believe that the person or persons who killed Danny are also responsible for at least two other murders on Oahu."

"I take not that you're also FBI?" he asked.

"Fuck no, I'm just a independent investigator trying to help out a friend."

"OK, so, how can I help?"

"Did you ever see Danny meet anyone here that you didn't recognize? Possibly a *haole*?"

The man thought for a moment.

"Funny, but now that I think about it—he did. It was last week."

"Do you remember what the person looked like?"

"Not really."

"Height, weight, or hair color? Anything would help."

"They sat over on the other side of the bar, so I never really saw the guy's face."

"But he was a *haole*?"

"Yeah."

The bartender thought for a moment.

"Actually, he kind of reminded me of you."

Violet and I looked at each other, as we both remembered that those were Rudy's final words.

"Well, thank you for your time."

"You're welcome."

"Remember to call if you need any help," Johnny said.

"I will," I said, as Violet and I turned and left the bar.

We headed outside and climbed into the Suburban and continued north back up to the resort, where I wanted to check in with the nerds, as I was hoping that they had uncovered something—other than a raiding party of orcs. Fifteen minutes later, we were parking the behemoth, and five minutes after that we were in my room and watching as the nerds engaged in an epic battle against a twentieth level wizard. Beeber was looking anxious as he blew on his twenty sided die for good luck.

"Come on, let's get this done," he said, as he tossed it onto the table.

The die stopped on nineteen.

"Yes!" he screamed!

Doug rolled his dice to calculate damage then smiled.

"Killed him! Let me see your character sheets," he said.

"Are we interrupting anything important?" I asked.

"No, we just finished."

"The entire game?"

"No, just this last battle. What's up?"

"We have another murder."

"Holy shit. The spear fisherman?"

"Yeah, and he was only twenty-five. Supposedly he drowned, but I'm pretty sure they killed him."

"That's terrible. So, what now?" Rachel asked.

"Oh shit, I realize I still haven't done the first thing on my list."

I pulled out my iPhone and dialed Steven Green's office back in San Francisco. It was luckily still in my contacts, inspite of the fact that I hadn't dialed it since I had dropped his case six months previously. Three rings later, a woman answered on the other end.

"Steven Green's office," she said.

"Yeah, hello, I'm calling from Hawaii—um—sadly concerning Mr. Green's murder. Is Lucy available?"

"What do you want, Finn?"

"Excuse me?"

"We have caller ID. I know exactly who you are. What the hell do you want?"

Lucy was the law clerk with whom Steven had been having an affair when I had been working for him, so it would appear that they were still together, and she obviously held a grudge against me because I sided with his ex-wife.

"Oh, well might I say that I am deeply sorry for your loss."

"Yeah—sure," she said, coldly.

"No really, I mean it. Steven was an asshole, but he didn't deserve to get murdered."

"Well, thank you for such warm sentiments. Mind telling me why you called?"

"I'm trying to find Steven's murderer."

"The police told me they already found the murderer."

"The police have it all wrong and don't know shit at the moment."

Lucy was quiet, and all I could hear was her breathing until she spoke.

"What do you want from me?"

"I want to know if you have any information on what Steven was doing in Hawaii."

Again she was quiet.

"Look, I understand that you believe you're protecting him in some way, but the sad reality is that he's gone, and I need your help if I'm going to find the people who did this."

She sighed and took a moment to think before responding.

"Steven met with a new client about a month ago, but he didn't keep any written accounts. Every communication happened in person or on the phone."

"And this is the same person he supposedly met in Hawaii?"

"Yeah, he said this would be his retirement and that we were going to be set for life and live happily ever after."

"So, you don't have any names or anything?"

"No, but Steven and I talked the day he was murdered. He said he was going to go have lunch with his client and that he'd call me later that night."

"Did he tell you where he was going?"

"No, but he said it was near his hotel."

"OK, interesting. So, did he call later that night?"

"Yeah."

"Did he say anything interesting about the client?"

"No, he just wanted to say good night and tell me he loved me, and that was the last time I spoke to him."

"I'm really sorry, Lucy. I know it's not easy losing someone you love."

"Did you know we had gotten married?"

"No."

"We eloped to Vegas once his divorce was final."

"Out of the frying pan into the fire."

"Yeah, it seemed kind of impulsive, but it was his idea, not mine."

"Well, from what I saw, I think he really did love you."

"Thanks," she said, as her voice started to break up.

"Call me if you need anything. I mean it."

"Thanks, Finn."

She hung up, and I set down my phone and looked at the others in the room.

"Nerds, put down your dice. I'm going to need some credit card statements and phone records for Steven Green."

CHAPTER SIXTEEN
Pulled Pork and Other Sordid Tales

Doug regretfully put his dice on the coffee table and pulled out his laptop, which had been sitting beside him on the couch. He tapped a few keys then looked up at me with a slightly bored expression.

"OK, give me the name again."

"Steven Green."

He pressed several keys then paused before typing in what I assume was Steven Green's name. A moment later he looked up.

"OK, I have Visa, Mastercard, and Amex."

"Holy shit! That's all it took? There must be hundreds of Steven Greens out there," Violet said.

"There are—but only one who's recently deceased."

"Jesus, that was fast."

"You can thank all the new Homeland Security measures. We have access to everything these days. Which account do you want first?"

"Amex."

Doug pressed a few more keys then called me over and turned his laptop in my direction. I looked at the last entries and worked backwards and found a charge for dinner, gas, and, before that, one from a restaurant that went through a little after one p.m. on the afternoon in question.

"Bingo!"

Steven apparently had lunch at a place called Kimo's, and, according to the receipt, it was located just a short walk from the resort.

"Why do you think he only spent ten dollars?" Doug asked, as he gazed at the amount.

"He went there to meet someone and obviously ordered a drink while he waited."

"Oh yeah. That makes sense."

"Don't worry, it's all in my book."

"Yeah, Private Investigation for Dummies," he responded.

Beeber laughed and high-fived Doug.

"If you two are done, I'd love a peek at Steven's cell phone records."

Doug tapped some more keys, and, about forty-two seconds later, he had Steven's phone records, and he scrolled down to the week of the murder, and there were at least fifty calls that included several to Jessica. I looked down to the time of his lunch date and found a number with a

Hawaii area code.

"That's very likely our killer. Can you trace it?"

"Of course."

Doug hit a few more keys then looked up.

"Just as I figured. It was a burner."

"Yeah, no one who knows what they're doing would use their own phone. Alrighty then. Who's up for some lunch at Kimo's? My treat."

"Obviously, I'm in," Violet said.

"Nerds?" I asked.

"We're going to keep playing," Beeber said.

"Doug, are you in agreement with that statement?"

He looked at me then down at all of his D&D stuff on the table.

"Staying."

"Well, have fun with your recreational castration technique, and if you ever do manage to have the desire to use your penises again, you could just cast a level fifteen Viagra healing spell and get them back in working order."

"Dude, that's just stupid, because everyone knows a healing spell would be more than capable of getting our penises working properly again," Beeber said.

"Technically, he's correct," Doug added.

"The fact that you answered seriously and un-ironically means I need to get out of here before my balls stage a coup and jettison from my body."

The nerds ignored my final comment and happily returned to their game as Violet and I left the hotel and walked to the restaurant. It took a little over five minutes, and we found the place sat directly on the beach, which was usually a bad omen. Generally you were paying for the view, so the price of the food had an inverse correlation to quality. We bypassed the hostess stand and found a place at the bar, where we were sandwiched in between two groups of tourists. Both appeared to be doughy midwesterners, and their formerly white skin was now red from too much sun as well as the consumption of too many tropical cocktails. The bartender checked in on them then stopped in front of us and placed two cocktail napkins down on the bar.

"What can I get you?" she asked.

"Sparkling water and a little information," I said, slapping a twenty on the bar.

"What kind of information?" she asked, looking curious.

"Do you know who was working the lunch shift this last Saturday?"

"Me. Do I get to keep the twenty?"

"Maybe. Do you remember a good looking guy around fifty with a medium build and dark hair greying around the temples."

She thought for a moment.

"Yeah, he left me a five dollar tip on a five dollar vodka tonic."

That was definitely Steven, as the total amount of the bill and tip were ten dollars. Plus, I knew for a fact that he had a penchant for vodka tonics.

"Did he meet anyone?"

"Yeah, a guy joined him, but they left to go to a table."

"Do you remember any details on what either of them looked like?"

"Not really."

"Nothing?"

"Well, I would guess he was late thirties to middle forties and..."

She paused for a moment to think.

"What is it?" I asked.

"This might sound weird, but he kind of reminded me a little of you."

"Height or hair color—or are we talking straight up sex appeal?"

The bartender smiled.

"He definitely wasn't as sexy, but there was something about his posture and demeanor. Maybe it was the way he held himself—I don't know how to put it into words."

"Interesting—well, thank you for your time. If you think of anything else, please give me a call," I said, handing her a card.

"Will do," she said, with a wink and a smile.

As we stood up to leave, she abruptly came back.

"Oh, wait. You might want to talk to their server. He's right over there," she said, pointing at a tall, thin, and dark haired waiter."

"Great, thanks."

We walked over and found the waiter at a cash register,

where he was obviously preparing the check for one of his tables.

"Excuse me, do you have a minute?" I asked

"Sure, he said without taking his eyes off the screen."

"Do you remember a couple of male customers last Saturday afternoon. There were two of them, and they would have been here around one. One guy was good looking, around fifty, and had a medium build and dark hair greying around the temples. The other guy was—well—he apparently looked like me."

"Yeah, they left a good tip and paid with cash."

"So, you don't have a name or credit card for them?"

"No, sorry."

"Do you remember what they looked like?"

"Um, one had dark brown hair and the other had light brown hair."

"That's all?"

"Yeah, sorry I'm a guy. Had they been women, I could have told you height, weight, breast size, and whether one or both had a distinguishing birthmark."

"Indeed. Well, thanks anyway."

"Why did you want to know?"

"Just following up possible leads on a murder investigation."

"Oh, well I wish I could tell you more."

He finished up by printing a receipt and placing it in the little folder before walking back to the table in question.

"So, no lunch?" Violet asked.

"Too touristy for me. What say we head up to the North Shore and see if we can find our gunsmith and perhaps grab something on the way."

"Sounds good. I know a really good sandwich shop up there."

We climbed into the Suburban and headed west on H3 until it hit the H2 and eventually reached the North Shore. From there we angled east and followed the ocean until Violet told me to pull over and park in a spot that just happened to be directly across the street from Shark's Cove—my second favorite snorkeling spot on Ohau. Less than a block away, there was a Starbucks, and that was proof that one could find get a damn good cup of coffee—even in the middle of the fucking Pacific Ocean. We entered a small deli called Keiko's and stood in line with a large crowd of locals until eventually reaching the front of the line, where Violet ordered two pulled pork sandwiches. Five minutes later, we were sitting out front, and, true to Violet's word, were eating an exceptionally good sandwich.

"I'm really sorry about this morning. I had no idea that Dave was such a stalker."

"Don't worry. It wasn't your fault."

"Yeah, but it's still embarrassing."

"So, how long were you guys together?"

"Two years. We were even talking marriage, kids—the whole enchilada."

"Honestly, I think he blew it."

"We both blew it. Neither of us were willing to give up

our career."

"Well, it's also possible you both might have had some deeper underlying doubts about your relationship if neither of you were willing to give up your careers."

"Interesting—any more deep insights, Doctor Freud?"

"No, that's about it for the moment. Ready to roll?"

"Yeah, and roll is the right word. I'm feeling about as big as a house right now, and I'm thinking we probably should have just shared one sandwich. Sweet Lord, I forgot how big they were."

"Agreed. I might even have a second deuce in me when we get back to the resort."

We saddled up in the Suburban, did a U-turn, then drove back one block and turned left onto Pupukea Rd, which wound up through lush green countryside and past numerous beautiful homes. The number of dwellings diminished, and, after two long sweeping turns, we spotted Camp Pupukea, and just before it on the other side was the entrance to Walther Zeibt's ranch. It had a sign that said No Tresspassing-Violators will be shot on sight, which I took to be a bad omen.

The first couple hundred feet were gravel, but the remaining mile was all dirt, and I was thankful that we had a big all wheel drive vehicle to navigate the ruts and slippery spots. About a half mile in, the road dipped down into a little gully, and we crossed over a rickety old bridge that forded the stream that crisscrossed back and forth across the entire length of the valley. At last, we came over a final rise, and there stood an older looking ranch house with several outlying buildings—one of which was an old barn. There were three vehicles parked in front of the main house—an old tractor, a pickup truck, and an older dark green Toyota Land Cruiser. I suspect the Toyota was Walther's main ride because it was both functional and reliable. Anyone who's been to Africa or seen documentaries on television would recognize that it was one of the kind they used on Safaris—with the other being the British Land Rover. We pulled in and parked beside the Land Cruiser and left the relative safety of the Suburban, and, upon reaching the front door, I knocked, and, a second later, we heard a voice through an intercom.

"Please state your business," a gruff voice said.

"Hello, Mr. Zeibt, I'm Tag Finn, and I'm here with Special Agent Kalili of the FBI. Simon Wilson sent us."

"Just a second."

About four minutes later, the front door opened, and there stood Walther Zeibt. He was somewhere in his sixties and looked every bit the eccentric hermit with his matching khaki outfit and tussled mop of grey and blond hair that made him look like an African game guide. He also had a neatly trimmed goatee and piercing grey blue eyes, and he regarded me rather intently for a brief moment before turning his gaze to Violet, where, judging by the smile on his face, appeared to like what he saw.

"I don't get many visits from the FBI, least of all as lovely as you," he said.

Violet smiled.

"Thank you, Mr. Zeibt."

"Call me Walther. How can I help you?"

"We're investigating a murder, and we have an unusual weapon that we hope you might be able to help us with."

I pulled out the Beretta, handed it to him, and he held it up and looked at it through the plastic evidence bag.

"Well, do come in," he said.

We walked inside to what was obviously his living room to find it was sparsely furnished and looking a bit Germanic with its hard wood floors, white throw rug, and simple leather couch and chair. His last name was Zeibt, so he apparently he took his German heritage fairly seriously. The only things that even resembled clutter were the bookshelves that resided along three of the four walls, and every inch of shelf space was occupied by books that covered subjects from popular and classic fiction to mechanical engineering and metallurgy.

"Here, follow me," he said, as he led us across his house and into a hallway that connected to another building.

We were now obviously in his shop, which had workbenches on all four sides and was littered with all manner of tools including drills, lathes, and milling machines. Off in the corner he had a test-fire chamber as well as a pair of goggles and ear protectors. All in all, it looked a bit like Simon's gunsmith shop back in Honolulu, though it was a bit more rustic. Walther adjusted his glasses on his nose then took the Beretta out of the bag and held it under his desk mounted lamp and eyed its silencer appreciatively.

"This is very fine work," he said, with the subtlest hint of pride in his voice.

"Is it anything you might recognize?" I asked.

He turned and looked at us innocently.

"Definitely not, as you obviously already know that silencers are illegal."

Violet and I shared a brief glance before turning back to Walther, who quickly turned his attention back to the pistol.

"And you say this piece has been involved in a murder?" he asked.

"Yeah, I'm afraid so."

Walther's expression subtly changed, and a hint of sadness overtook his features.

"I think you should know that we're not really interested in who made it, but rather in the identity of the person it was made for."

Walther thought for a moment, and we could see a subtle conflict brewing behind his eyes.

"Yes, I understand, but people who do this kind of work generally deal with a very unusual clientele—one that prefers, or should I say demands, a great deal of discretion. It's therefore highly doubtful you'll ever find anyone willing to take the credit let alone divulge the identity of his client."

"I used to work with that particular clientele as well, so I understand your concern, but, in this case, I'm not exaggerating when I say the fate of the free world actually hangs in the balance."

That might have been a bit of an exaggeration, but with John potentially running for president, it did kind of concern the free world. Walther took a moment to think, and there was turmoil raging behind his eyes. Being a gunsmith was an unusual job, as the objects you created were designed to take life, human or otherwise, and that came with some ethical and moral turmoil. Of course, car makers also designed and built things that killed a whole lot more people, but their devices weren't supposed to, so they probably had no problem sleeping at night. We all sat quietly for a moment, as we all knew that we were at a stalemate of sorts until Walter got a distinctly nostalgic look in his eyes and started talking.

"I got into this business when I was knee high to a grasshopper. I'd help my dad on all kinds of projects, and it was only a matter of time before I was hooked. I loved the machinery, precision, and craftsmanship that went into every facet. Of course, it's easy to forget that these things kill, and, in most of my professional life, I believed that what I created was actually doing some good—helping us win wars and defeat our enemies. But, things are a bit different today, and it's a lot harder to know the good guys from the bad guys."

"It sure is."

Walther closed his eyes and rubbed his temples.

"I'm really sorry I can't be of more help."

I shrugged and nodded, as I understood his dilemma.

He was just a toolmaker, a man living his life doing what he loved, and his job and even his life really did depend on his utter discretion. I therefore decided to absolve Walther's conscience for the moment by leaving out the fact that two more murders had been committed in relation to this crime.

"So, are you much of a shooter?" he asked.

"I'm OK. Why?"

"I have a brand new rifle I've been working on. It's sort of a next generation of the M24."

The M24 was the Armed Force's main sniper rifle, and it was technically a military version of the Remington .30-06 changed to a Nato 7.62 x 51mm round due to the greater abundance of that kind of ammo. It employed a bolt action and could be fitted with all manner of scopes, so it was entirely customizable to the specific shooter.

Walther led us through a doorway and out into another room and pressed a button, and a garage door of sorts slid open to expose a long green field with a number of targets extending down the range. He grabbed a lone rifle off a rack on the wall and smiled like a proud parent as he brought it over.

"Here she is," he said, handing me his veritable mechanical baby.

"Beautiful," I said.

Walther had apparently taken the basic parts of the Remington, modified them, then married the assembly to a new custom stock, then painted it a green camo pattern.

Along with the various custom parts, it looked very futuristic, and, instead of the traditional bolt action, it had a lower magazine and was obviously semi-automatic—something a purest might not prefer. But, when your life was on the line and you had multiple targets closing in, having more rounds and being able to reload quickly could come in especially handy.

"As you can see it's semi-automatic, but I've re-tooled the entire lower receiver and loading system and there's practically zero possibility of a jam or misfire as long as the ammo is up to snuff."

"Really?"

"Oh yeah, she's my finest work. Want to give her a try?"

"Love to."

He grabbed eyes and ears for the three of us then handed me a fully loaded magazine and grabbed his spotter's scope. We all stepped outside and took up residence on a small patio covered in artificial grass. I assumed the prone firing position and sighted in the scope on the most distant target.

"I'm assuming the far target is about a thousand yards," I said.

"Good guess, though if you click the button on the right side of the scope, it will activate the laser range finder."

I reached up and clicked the button and saw that it was exactly one thousand yards. I checked the scope's settings and was happy to see it was already zeroed in for that distance. I glanced at the surrounding grass and figured the wind to be around five MPH from the east. I did a little mental math and adjusted my aim accordingly, so now it was about controlling my breathing and slowing my heart rate. When I could feel the space between each heartbeat, I gently slid my finger over the trigger and waited. Thump, thump, thump, then squeeze, and the rifle went off, and, a split second later, my shot impacted the very edge of the bullseye at the center of the target.

"Pretty nice first shot. Slightly right, and when I say slightly, I mean about a millimeter."

"Obviously, I'm just a rookie at this."

"Obviously, you're full of shit and have done this before."

I smiled.

"Once upon a time."

"I looked over and saw Violet staring at me.

"What?" I asked.

"I can't help but wonder what it is with me and sharp shooters."

"You're a hell of a target, obviously."

I settled back into firing mode, readjusted my aim, and squeezed off another shot, though this one went dead center."

"Bullseye!" Walther exclaimed excitedly.

I decided to test the semi-automatic action and fired off four more shots in quick succession, and the spread pattern was about an inch, as all landed within the bullseye.

"Sweet mother of God is this fucker smooth," I said.

"My crowning achievement."

"That was truly a pleasure."

We stood up, and I handed Walther his baby back, and we re-entered his main workshop, and he went over and lovingly placed the rifle in its cradle before turning his attention back to us.

"So, anyone thirsty?" he asked.

"Actually, yeah."

"How about a sparkling water?"

"Love one."

He went to a small refrigerator and looked inside to find it empty.

"I'll have to grab some from the kitchen."

Walther left us, and, as I looked around the room, my eyes fell upon the little test chamber over in the corner. I suddenly had an idea but wondered if I would have enough time. As luck would have it, Walther's voice came echoing down the hall.

"How about some cheese and crackers?"

"Love some," I yelled back.

"Are you crazy? We just ate like pigs!" Violet whispered.

"I know, but I'm trying to by us a little time."

I raced over to the test-fire chamber and opened its access door to see it was filled with ballistics gel that contained a number of rounds. I grabbed a screwdriver off the shelf and started digging, and Violet realized what I was trying to do and took up residence by the hallway and watched for our host. I managed to get all but one round out, and we could hear that Walther was about to leave the kitchen. Violet told me to get my hand out of the chamber, but I struggled to push the screwdriver deeper—all the while doing my best not to mar the bullet. I finally dug a deep enough channel and was struggling to reach it, when I heard Walther's footsteps coming closer. Violet again told me to get the hell away from the chamber, but I was so close that I decided to continue on, and beads of perspiration formed on my forehead. I finally managed to get my fingertips on the bullet, and I snatched it up and slipped it and the others into my pocket and quickly stood up beside Violet and tried my best to look as innocent as I could. At that very moment, Walther came walking in carrying a tray with cheese, crackers, and three mineral waters.

"You look a little parched," he said.

"It's this hot Hawaiian weather."

"Indeed, so what say we take our little picnic outside, so we can have a little fresh air and a nice view."

"Lovely," I said."

"We exited out a side door and stepped out onto a little lanai that looked over the range, and it fortunately had a table and chairs and several tall palm trees that provided plenty of shade. Everyone took a seat, then Walther passed us each a bottle of sparkling water, and I took a sip and turned my attention to the cheese platter. Fuck, the thought of eating was almost making me feel sick to my stomach.

"I don't get a lot of opportunity to entertain these days, so dig in! No need to be polite," Walther said.

I was as full as a tick, but I figured I should partake just to be polite. To that end, I grabbed a cracker and spread on what appeared to be some kind of chèvre goat cheese. It was pretty tasty in spite of the fact that I'd never felt less hungry, but I forced it down with a sip of mineral water. Sweet Lord, what in the hell had I gotten myself into? Fucking Violet and her pulled pork sandwiches.

"Oh, Violet, you have to try the cheese. It's delicious!" I said.

"Here, let me make you one," Walther said, as he piled a shitload of cheese on a cracker before handing it to Violet.

She took it and placed it in her mouth and smiled at Walther before giving me an icy glare. As a show of solidarity, I ate another one, and this cycle of tortuous eating continued, though, while Violet and I were forcing it all down, Walther was actually hungry and therefore happy to be eating. But, the more he ate, the more talkative he became, which was a very natural response, as digestion released chemicals in the brain that stimulated memory. That, in turn, stimulated conversation, and, Walther, after having consumed half a bowl of goat cheese and countless crackers, was literally chatting like a magpie and recounting endless stories from his past.

"Did you know I was in Vietnam?" he asked.

"Yeah, it was in your file, and it also said that you in were Special Forces."

"Yeah, I was in an A-Team."

"I'm guessing it wasn't anything like the television

show."

He smiled.

"No, it wasn't. We didn't have a tricked out van, and our plans rarely came together. It was just us, the jungle, and the Viet Cong."

"All combat tours suck, but I suspect Vietnam sucked even more."

"Yes it did. I take it you were also in the service."

"Yeah, once upon a time I was a Parajumper and served all over the world but finished up in Afghanistan."

"That probably would have sucked equally."

"Yeah, conflict is a motherfucker."

"Indeed, so when I got out, I returned to the only thing that made sense to me. Weapons."

"I believe it was the family business?"

"Yeah, it was taught to me by my father. He originally worked for SIG before emigrating to the States, where he opened up his own shop."

"SIG, or SIG Sauer as it came to be known, was a subsidiary of L&O Holding, and they had been around since the mid eighteen hundreds and were extremely capable at designing and building firearms. The odds were therefore pretty good that Walther's father was a master gunsmith, which in turn meant that Walther was also very likely a master gunsmith, though that was pretty obvious having just fired his magnificent rifle. It also stood to reason that Walther's extensive background and obvious skill meant there was very little doubt that he was also the person who built the silencer for Jessica's Beretta.

"And that's how you learned your craft?"

"Primarily, though I also have a masters degree in mechanical engineering and a PhD in metallurgy from Texas Tech that certainly helped."

"Yeah, both of those would certainly help."

"So, Tag, what did you do after you left the service."

"I worked with another branch for a bit."

Walther smiled knowingly.

"Yeah, I suspect we might have had the same boss."

Now it was my turn to smile.

"Yeah, and he can be a real asshole."

"Yes, indeed. So, have you managed to find a normal life after leaving government service?"

I thought for a moment and noticed Violet waiting for my answer.

"I'm still working on it. How about you?"

"I did—eventually—when I met a wonderful woman, married her, and moved to Hawaii. Unfortunately she passed away a few years ago."

"Oh, I'm sorry."

"Thanks, but we had a good life together while it lasted."

"Have you gotten back in the saddle and met any nice women since then?" I asked.

"I have actually, and she lives over that ridge and owns the second most remote ranch on the island."

"And only a mountain to keep you apart."

He laughed.

"Most days, I actually jog over to her place."

I looked at the mountain then back at Walther and realized that he did indeed have the physique of a runner. He was lean but had well defined sinewy muscles, and it made sense he had been in Special Forces, as they liked their people smart and fit.

"So, you're a private investigator now. How did that come about?" he asked me.

"Well, I decided that I wanted a quiet life, so I returned to Northern California and became a private investigator."

"Sounds interesting."

"It can be on occasion."

"Like now."

"Pretty much."

We sat and talked for a bit longer, then we told Walther we needed to get going, and he led us out to our car then stood at the window.

"I'm sorry I can't be of more help."

"I understand, but I think you should know that people connected with this investigation are dying at an alarming rate—and not by natural causes, so I suggest you be very careful."

"Thank you, I will. I've managed to survive this long, so I figure I can squeeze a few more years out of this life."

"I certainly hope so."

CHAPTER SEVENTEEN
Return to Nerd Island

We backed out, turned around, and began the trek out of Walther Zeibt's lovely ranch. Seven minutes later, we were back on the main road, and ten minutes after that, we were on the H2 heading south. My iPhone rang, and I looked down to see that Frank was calling, so I hit the hands-free answer button on the Suburban's steering wheel.

"Finn here," I said.

"How's it going?" he asked.

"Pretty good. No one's tried to kill us yet today."

"That's good news."

"Indeed."

"Well, we're on for the barbecue, and everyone who is anyone is coming. Do you have a pair of eighties jogging shorts and a Hawaiian shirt you can wear?"

"I do, and I've grown a hell of a mustache."

"Excellent, how does five o'clock sound?"

"Perfect, we'll see you then."

I hit the end button and looked at Violet.

"Finally, I get to see the fictitious home of my television alter ego."

"What should we do in the meantime?" she asked.

"We need to go to the Police lab to get these bullets examined."

"You know that they were acquired illegally and are therefore inadmissible as evidence?"

"I do, but I just want to find out if Walther is officially our guy. If so, he may very well be our last and only remaining lead."

"Yeah, but you heard what he said. His life depends upon his discretion."

"I know, but I think if it comes down to it, he'll eventually give up his client's name for the greater good."

"Maybe."

"He seems like a good guy in spite of his unusual profession."

"He does, but he probably works on a lot of guns, which means those bullets are a real long shot—so to speak."

"The silencer would have likely been fabricated within the last week, so I'm hoping he hasn't had a lot of projects in the meantime."

Twenty minutes later we pulled into a nice shady parking space in front of the Honolulu Police department, and we stepped out to see the entirety of the forensics department all carrying cups of Starbucks coffee as they arrived at the police station entrance. Obviously, they had all been on a break, and Velma, upon seeing us, smiled and stopped.

"Oh, hello, Finn and Agent Kalili," she said.

"Hello, sexy temptress of the Honolulu Police nerd contingent. How are things in the lab?" I asked.

"Good, how's your case coming along? Have you discredited us yet?"

"No, but I'm working on it."

"Wonderful, so, what brings you by?"

"I have some bullets I'd like Bert to check out."

Bert stepped forward and looked excited.

"Cool! Come on in, and I'll take a look!" he said.

We followed the herd of nerds inside and left the afternoon heat and headed down to the cool temperate recesses of the basement. The nerds fanned out to their various stations, and we followed Bert back to his desk, and I handed him the bullets.

"So, what have we got here?"

"Some bullets we've come across, and I'm hoping one of them will be a match to Jessica's gun."

"Oh, can you tell me where you found them?"

"Sorry, not yet. Unfortunately, due to recent events, we need to keep our investigation on the extreme down low."

"I see—well let's go ahead and have a look," he said, enthusiastically.

He placed each bullet in his microscope and took multiple pictures before transferring the images to his computer, at which point he started comparing the results and hit the jackpot on number three.

"We have a match!" he said.

"Hot fucking tamales!" I blurted out.

"Here, take a look," he said, pointing at his screen.

The two bullets were side by side, and the marks from the barrel lined up perfectly, which meant I had indeed found my gunsmith, and, in turn, a solid lead.

"So, you really can't tell me where you found these?"

"No, but I can say that they were in a gunsmith's test-fire chamber."

"Seriously?"

"Yeah, so now I know who built the silencer."

Just then, Alan Kamakana, the chief detective on the case, strolled in.

"I heard you were here, and I was hoping to talk," he said.

"What's on your mind?" I asked.

"I heard that two people related to this case have died."

"I believe the word killed would be more accurate."

"Meaning?"

"The first was run down and killed right in front of us."

"Yeah, but I hear the spear fisherman drowned."

"So it appears, but he spent his entire life in the ocean, so why would he drown now? It's not a stretch to think he was probably killed because of his part in this conspiracy."

"Yeah, and to that end—who, other than the vice president of the United States and his fiancée, would have the means to perpetrate something like this."

"Come on, detective, you know as well as I that a man about to run for president wouldn't have anything to do with all this."

"Or perhaps he would, as he obviously has a lot to gain."

"Maybe a typical sociopathic narcissistic politician, but not John Matheson or his bride to be."

"Well, you're still going to need to find something more conclusive to get your lady friend off the hook."

"Yeah, but it's getting harder with all my leads dying."

We stood there a moment, and Alan turned his gaze to the screen.

"You still going over the ballistics?" he asked.

Bert was about to answer, but I interrupted.

"Yeah, I had a few more questions for Bert."

Bert glanced at me, unsure what to say, but he thankfully remained quiet. Considering how things were going, I figured it was prudent not to give out any more information than necessary.

"So, the guy hit by the car. What was his story?" Alan asked.

"His name, as you probably already know was Rudy Rafael, and, interestingly, he was seen talking to Jessica Thurman in the bar on the night of the murder, and, according to the bartender at the resort, he is known as Roofie Rudy because of his proclivity for dosing women's cocktails."

"Hmmm—that is interesting."

"Yeah, but too bad he and my other lead are both dead."

"People around you have an odd habit of dying, so, do me a favor, Finn, and don't visit me unless it's absolutely necessary."

"No problem. I won't bug you until I have some really important news—such as the name of the real killer."

Alan Kamakana left, and we were again alone with Bert.

"Any reason that you didn't tell him about the gunsmith?" he asked.

"Yeah, I'm trying to keep my last lead alive."

Bert thought for a moment then looked a bit apprehensive.

"Shit, does this mean I might be next?" he asked.

"Don't worry, Bert. You're safe, as you're inadvertently working in the interests of the powers of evil at the moment."

"How reassuring."

"Well, thank you for your time. Now, we're off to see Velma."

He laughed as Violet and I exited his office and walked a short distance to find Velma at the water cooler.

"Large coffee and now water? You're going to be peeing like a racehorse."

"Caffeinate then rehydrate."

"The cycle of life."

"What's up?"

"I had another question about the GSR test on Jessica."

"Fire away."

"As I'm a hundred percent sure that she didn't kill her

ex-husband, I'd like to know how it's possible that she could have gun residue on her hand?"

"Well, she obviously fired a gun."

"Yeah, except that we have pretty convincing evidence that she had been roofied and was unconscious at the time of the murder."

"It's pretty hard to shoot a gun when you're out cold."

"No doubt, so how in the hell did she test positive?"

"Unfortunately, my tests are absolutely conclusive. The chemical reaction and subsequent discharge from a firearm can't be faked. It's not like you could sprinkle the chemicals on someone's hand. The spread and subsequent traces can only be created when the gunpowder is ignited and shoots out of the barrel of the gun."

"That's what I was afraid you were going to say."

"It is what it is."

"Is there anyway for me to get access to the crime scene?"

"What were you hoping to find?"

"I don't know yet. I suppose I'll find out when I get there."

"I assume you've already realized that you're running around with an FBI agent. She can get you access to just about anywhere you want to go."

"Except her pants, sadly."

"Very funny," Violet said, as she back handed me in the ribs.

"So, Agent Kalili, is her statement correct? Can you really get me access to the crime scene?" I asked.

"Of course."

"Well, why didn't you tell me?"

"You didn't ask."

"Velma, do you happen to have any extra fingerprint kits I could use?"

"Yeah, how many do you need," she asked, reaching into a drawer.

"Just a handfull."

She pulled out a number of kits, and each one contained an envelope, ink strips, and little information cards.

"Thanks," I said.

"I doubt you'll need them, as I swept the crime scene pretty thoroughly."

"Well, my reason for needing fingerprint kits is twofold, and the first part can be done right here."

"Oh really?" Velma asked, looking intrigued.

"Yeah, I want to have a look at Jessica Thurman's sweat-shirt."

"I assume you know that fabric doesn't really offer up much in the way of fingerprints?"

"I do, but I'm not interested in the fabric. I'm interested in the zipper."

"Interesting, but assuming you can find a print, won't it most certainly be Jessica's?"

"Maybe—maybe not."

"OK, come this way," she said.

We followed Velma to the official police evidence

storage room to find it was manned by a lone officer who resided at a desk behind a steel mesh wall. He was probably in his fifties and appeared particularly bored as he sat and stared at his computer screen.

"Howdy, Matt, do you mind buzzing us in?" Velma asked.

"Not at all. I could use some excitement," he said, hitting a buzzer that unlocked the nearby door.

Once inside, Velma led us over to the section of shelving dedicated to the Steven Green murder case, and she proceeded to remove the bag that contained the infamous blood stained sweatshirt.

"Should we be wearing rubber gloves?" I asked.

"No, all this stuff has already been cleared and catalogued."

She pulled the sweatshirt out of the bag and handed it over, and I could instantly smell the dried blood. It wasn't a pleasant experience, least of all to someone who'd survived combat and already smelled more than a lifetime's worth of the red stuff. I pulled out a fingerprint kit and proceeded to do the front of the tiny zipper handle. There was a print, but it was blurred and probably unreadable, so I did the back, and, sure enough, I found a readable though tiny partial print."

"Hot damn!" I said.

I wrote the details on the little note then placed it all in the plastic bag.

"Do you want me to process that?" Velma asked.

"Normally I'd say yes, but due to the minimal amount

of usable print, I want this one to go to the FBI's lab at Quantico," I said, handing it to Violet.

"Fine, go with the feds, but be sure to tell me if they find anything interesting."

"I will. Now come, Agent Kalili. Let's go inspect a gruesome crime scene and build up a healthy appetite for the barbecue."

"What barbecue?" Velma asked.

"We're going to a little party at the house where *Magnum P.I.* lived in the TV series."

"Robin's Nest?"

"Yeah, it belongs to a friend."

"Lucky you. Say hello to Higgins and the lads for me."

While Higgins was the majordomo in charge of the estate, the lads were two Doberman pinschers named Zeus and Apollo who had a habit of tormenting Magnum.

"I will, assuming they don't bite my ass, and that goes for Higgins as well," I said.

We left the lab and exited the police station to head out into the warmth of the Hawaiian sunshine. It was afternoon, and the temperature was at its usual eighty degrees. That was actually the joy of Hawaii—rain or shine, it was always the same temperature. Not too hot, not too cold—paradise. We took a seat in the Suburban and headed back to the resort, but, before going to my room, we made a point of stopping at the front desk. An attractive young woman, likely of Samoan or Hawaiian descent, was manning the counter, and she smiled as we approached.

"Hello, how can I help you?" she asked.

"Hi, we're doing a follow up investigation on the murder that took place here, and we'd like to get access to the room where it occurred."

The girl looked uncomfortable, which made sense, as no one liked talking about murder, least of all in the place they happened to work.

"I'll need to see some kind of identification if you don't mind."

"No problem."

"Violet stepped forward and flashed her ID at the girl."

Satisfied, the woman typed a command into the computer and, a moment later, handed us a key card.

"Oh, and one more thing. I was wondering who was working the night of the murder."

She went back to work typing on her keyboard then looked up at us.

"Ah, Scarlett was working that night."

"How can I get in touch with her?"

"Just a second."

The girl disappeared into the back office, and Violet looked at me.

"Why do you want to talk to Scarlett?"

"Oh it's probably nothing, but I was just curious about the call for an early maid service."

The girl returned a moment later with another woman.

"This is Scarlett," she said.

Scarlett was about thirty, pretty, and full figured, though

that description was only in comparison to the stick figures that inhabited most of the media and fashion magazines. In the fairly distant past she would have probably been called healthy or even rubenesque, which was a quality attributed to the Flemish Baroque painter Rubens, who had a propensity for painting women with lovely generous curves. Scarlett looked at us nervously, as she had obviously been told that a member of the FBI was waiting to speak with her.

"Hi, I'm Scarlett. How can I help you?" she asked timidly.

"Hi, I'm Finn, and this is Agent Kalili. I heard you were working the night of the murder."

"Yeah."

"So, the report says that the victim called down and requested an early maid service."

"Correct, but it wasn't Mr. Green. It was a woman who called."

Violet and I looked at each other, as that was interesting news, though the police would probably believe that it was Jessica who called.

"Really? Are you sure?"

"Absolutely, I took the call."

"And what time was that?"

"About twelve thirty."

That certainly fit within the time frame of the murder.

"Did the woman use the room phone?"

"Yeah, it came through the hotel switchboard."

Interesting. People were so attached to their cell phones these days that they often ignored landlines, unless they didn't want to have a particular call traced to their number.

"Thanks."

"That's it?"

"Yeah, you've been a big help."

We left the counter and went up to Steven's room, and I slid the key card through the slot and opened the door, all the while feeling a great deal of trepidation. I had been around death most of my life but had never really gotten used to it, and it was even worse at the moment, as it was becoming a regular occurrence of sorts. We stepped inside, and I looked around to see the room pretty much looked exactly as it had in the crime scene photographs, though the sheets had been taken as evidence. The mattress remained, and there was a large pool of dry blood staining the middle. It was hard to believe that this had been the place that Steven Green spent his final moments on earth, and deep down I felt mildly responsible for his death. I had introduced Jessica to John and therefore brought Steven unwittingly into this mess. Still, he was blackmailing them, and that fact seemed to nicely balance my guilt.

"So, what are you hoping to accomplish here?" Violet asked.

"A miracle, unfortunately."

I walked over to the phone, pulled out the fingerprint kit, and placed one of the ink strips over the "0" button.

"Good thinking. Whoever called the front desk would

have hit that button, though I doubt they were stupid enough to leave a print," Violet said.

"Yeah, but I have to check it just to be sure."

I sprinkled the powder, ever hopeful for an easy break, but found all the numbers clean.

"Oh well, it was worth a try."

I turned my attention away from the phone and took a little stroll around the room and tried to visualize how it all went down—specifically the location of both the victim and the shooter. This was clearly a cold blooded act as it was done point blank, and that was something beyond the morality of the average person. The technique of the shooting was also strange and hinted at someone with some serious wet work in their job description. Shooting up from the stomach and bypassing the rib cage to make sure that the bullet remained intact was not something the average person would think to do. It also hinted that the victim was lying down at the time and likely already unconscious. Something was clearly rotten in the sate of Denmark—or in this case, Hawaii.

Satisfied that I had gotten all I hoped to find, we left the room and ventured over to mine on the other side of the resort. The nerds were still there playing D&D and had apparently just killed a small party of Orcs. I realized that I had a second deuce in me and went over to the coffee machine and made a fresh pot, with the idea being that a little caffeine would help me power out a swift number two before the barbecue. Once it finished brewing, I filled a cup then proceeded to take a nice long swig, and it's warmth flowed down my throat and entered my bloodstream and made my heart race ever so slightly. Three more equally luxurious sips, and I left Violet with the nerds and made absolutely certain that I closed and locked the door. It had been a decent day thus far, so I wasn't taking any chances. I pulled out my iPhone, dropped my shorts, and hit the cool porcelain, where I hoped to glance at the local Hawaii news. Before I could even find a decent story, I was forced to listen to Beeber bitching about how much damage his Magic User had just taken.

"Just use one of your fucking healing spells and shut the fuck up!" I yelled from the bathroom.

"Blow it out your ass!" Beeber responded.

"I will, thank you very much."

I set back to work herding the pigs out of the pen and sipped my coffee and enjoyed some brief though meaningful alone time. Finished, I entered the shower and emerged five minutes later and put on deodorant, face cream, and cologne then dressed in some board shorts and a T-shirt. Now that I was properly ready for the evening, I rejoined the others to find that Violet had changed and was now wearing a rather form fitting full length tropical dress.

"Wow, you look amazing. Where have you been hiding that dress?" I asked.

"In my bag."

"Must be quite a bag."

"Well, I am going to a Barbecue at the Robin Masters

estate, so I figured I should dress up."

"Perhaps it's a magical bag of holding," Beeber said.

"Indeed, thoughtful nerd, and apparently it holds many fine linens."

I finished my coffee then retreated to the bathroom to brush my teeth before rejoining the others.

"You nerds ready to call it quits and head to the barbecue?" I asked.

Doug, who was the DM, or Dungeon Master in laymen's terms, looked at his players.

"This is a good place to stop. We can always play more later tonight."

Beeber, Doug, and Rachel regretfully put down their various pencils, dice, and character sheets and left to get ready, leaving Violet and me alone to sit and quietly ruminate about the day's events. I couldn't help wondering how I might unearth a kernel of evidence that could bring all we had learned into a concise story capable of influencing the police to accept that things were not as clear as they believed. Unfortunately, or fortunately, depending on your viewpoint, people rarely experienced conspiracy on this kind of scale, so the police ultimately saw what they wanted to see, which was a clear cut murder. I, on the other hand, saw the truth, which was far more complicated than anyone could have imagined, and Jessica and Steven were mere pawns, while the intended victim was John Matheson.

"What are you thinking about?" Violet asked.

"This fucking case. It's so obvious there's more going on

here, but how in the hell do we prove that to the police?"

"Well, at least this FBI agent here believes you. That's a good start."

"I suppose it is."

Just then, there was a knock at the door, and I opened it to find Doug, Beebs, and Rachel looking dressed and ready to party. Rachel in particular looked especially lovely, as she was now sporting a short floral patterned dress over a two piece bikini, that showed off her long shapely legs. I'd usually only seen her in her goth city clothes, so this was a rare treat.

"Rachel, might I say that you look lovely in your island attire."

"You may, and at least someone noticed," she said, as she gave Beeber an icy glare.

"Hey, I also noticed," Doug said.

"And so did I!" Beeber chimed in, with his voice suddenly going up about three octaves.

"Yeah, but the difference is that Finn noticed and bothered to say something."

"I'm still training him, Rachel. He'll get better."

"Hopefully."

"Everybody ready?" I asked.

"Yeah, Magnum," Doug said.

We strolled through the resort and out to the Suburban, where I started the engine and began humming my best rendition of the *Magnum P.I.* theme song, and it took three measures before Beeber finally realized what I was doing.

"I get it now," he said, as he joined in.

The rest soon followed his lead, and it became a *Magnum P.I.* chorus.

"Ne-ne-ne-ne, ne-ne ne ne ne neeee-ne. Ne-ne-ne-ne, ne-ne ne ne ne neeee neeee!" everyone belted out.

The car came alive with an absolutely terrible rendition of the *Magnum P.I.* theme song, as everyone's timing was a little off, but it showed a lot of car spirit and kept everyone happy as we headed out of the resort and south towards Robin's Nest.

CHAPTER EIGHTEEN
Robin's Nest

We drove along the eastern shore of Oahu, and, as we passed through Waimanolo, I could see a crowd of locals hanging out and smoking in front of the Blow Hole. A little farther down the road, we passed a beautiful stretch of beach and eventually came to the estate, which looked exactly as I remembered it in the show. I waited for a break in traffic, then I pulled across the road and up to the gate, where I saw that we were under video surveillance. I waved, and a moment later a voice came over the intercom welcoming us to Robin's Nest. The gate swung open, and in we drove along the very same winding dirt driveway that Magnum used to race Robin Master's Ferrari. Off to the left was the famous tennis court, and ahead was the main house. It must have been over twenty-five years since they filmed the last episode, and it was odd to see that the place looked pretty much the same.

We pulled up and parked in front of the open garage,

and inside was a red Ferrari, though it was not the original 308 GTS but rather a 458 Spyder. It was the convertible version of one of their latest and greatest models and could rocket from zero to sixty in the three second range—which was quick enough to make most people lose their lunch. We exited the Suburban, and our entire group walked over to check out the Ferrari, and no sooner had we arrived that we looked up to see Frank coming out of his garage, and he was dressed in shorts and a Polo shirt, which was the most casual outfit I had seen him in thus far.

"How do you like the car, Magnum?"

"Love it. Do you think Robin will let me take it for a spin?"

"He might—since I'm him."

He held out his hand to shake.

"Welcome to Robin's Nest."

I shook his hand, then he led us all around to the patio below the main house, where meat was already on the barbecue, and the tables had already been set.

"Get yourselves a drink, then I'll be back to give you the tour," he said, walking off to check on how the food was coming along.

We had a moment to ourselves to take in the estate, and, as I already knew from watching the show, saw that it was indeed a beautiful piece of property. It resided directly on the ocean on the eastern side of Oahu, and that meant gentle surf and ideal swimming conditions—even when you weren't in the fabled tidal pool. Once you left the beach, you came onto the highly maintained grounds of the estate where the grass was cut to perfection, and every tree and bush was neatly trimmed. Clearly, Frank liked order in his personal universe, and he took that penchant into his landscaping preferences as well. I ran my gaze past the shrubbery and along the beach towards the front of the house, where I was surprised to see that it now had a swimming pool—occupied by none other than Melissa Williams. She saw me then smiled and climbed out to come over and say hello. She was wearing a tiny red two piece bikini, and the wet, thin fabric was adhering to her skin and leaving very little to the imagination. She was truly a temptress, and a woman I now preferred to keep at a safe distance.

"Hello, Tag, how nice to see you again. Oh, and hello, Agent Kalili. We didn't get to officially meet the other morning," she said, turning her gaze to Violet.

"Yeah, nice to officially meet you," Violet said, without an ounce of sincerity.

Next, I introduced the nerd contingent, with the last being Doug, who I feared might have a panic attack when he laid eyes on Melissa. He generally had a thing for Asians, but a girl as hot as Melissa could quickly melt away any of his preconceived notions of attraction. With the introductions concluded, the lovely, though troublesome, Melissa turned and strutted back to the pool, thus presenting her backside as a taunting ornament of female curvature for all to see and enjoy.

"Sweet Jesus is she hot," Doug said.

"She is, but trust me when I say that it's not worth it. She's got some baggage."

"Yeah, and it's totally giving me a boner."

"Wait, how do you know so much about her?" Beeber asked.

"Um, well..."

I could suddenly sense Violet looking at me.

"He fucked her," she said.

"No way! When?"

"Two nights ago," Violet said.

"Dude, high-five," Doug said, holding up his hand.

I high-fived him out of courtesy but instantly regretted it when I saw Violet's scornful stare.

"Men," she said.

We continued over to the bar, and everyone got a drink, then Frank took us on a tour of the house, which had obviously been drastically remodeled since the show. First, was the living room, and it was lavishly adorned with modern Scandinavian style furniture, and the centerpiece was a massive beige leather multi sectional sofa that probably cost more than my houseboat, though that would make perfect sense—as the sofa was substantially larger than my houseboat. After that, came the kitchen, family, and dining rooms, and all were nicely appointed and equally austere. On the second floor was a sort of family room with a massive flat screen television as well as a number of bedrooms, and, as we ventured down the hall, I saw that one of them was occupied by a young man in his twenties, who was working on his laptop. I said hello, and he turned and smiled.

"Hello, youngster. You must be Frank's son."

"Correct, I'm Richard."

"My name's Finn, Tag Finn. Nice to meet you."

He stood and held out his hand.

"Nice to meet you too," he said.

"Don't tell me you're working when the rest of us are downstairs drinking," I said.

"I am. I got saddled with a last minute work project from the mainland, but I'm almost done."

I gazed at his screen and saw that he was outlining a car and removing it from a background.

"Ah, rotoscoping job."

Rotoscoping was the process of isolating something in film, often so that it could be altered or placed on a different background. I knew the term, because I had friends who worked for Industrial Light and Magic and performed the very same job.

"Yeah, you know about special effects?"

"A bit. I have several friends at ILM back in San Francisco. Where do you work? Los Angeles?"

"Yeah, but who knows for how long. A lot of my industry is moving overseas, as the labor is cheaper."

"Outsourcing—making America strong by giving away all of our jobs."

"No shit."

"Maybe your Dad could help by putting a little pressure

on the film industry. He is the most powerful man in Washington after all."

"Perhaps, but I suspect he's probably hoping this outsourcing might hasten my following him into the family business."

"Like every father, I suppose."

"Yeah, but my heart is in special effects."

"Well, follow your heart, padawan, and remember—it's your life, not his."

"Thanks, Mr. Finn."

"Finn is fine. No need to add a Mr."

"Finn it is."

"I'm going to catch up the tour. You keep going, you rotoscoping son of a bitch you."

Richard smiled and instantly returned his attention to his screen as I left the room and rejoined the tour. The second floor was officially over, so we were on our way downstairs to the famous wine cellar. Back on the main floor, our route segued through the kitchen and down another stairwell before at last coming to a large oak door. Frank lifted a little wrought iron latch, and in we went to find the room looking a lot like I remembered in the TV show.

"So, how do you keep Magnum out of here?" I asked.

Everyone laughed.

"A very advanced security system. As you can see, there are only two ways in—the door and the small window in the corner, and should anyone get through either of those, right up there on the wall is an infrared security sensor. No one will drink my wine before it's time."

Frank proceeded to show us a few rare wines, then he turned and led the group back upstairs, while I stayed back, because I noticed that the window latch wasn't closed all the way. There was nothing like having an obsessive compulsive personality to make me notice the most unnecessary and mundane of details. I moved closer and tried to close the latch, but the person who had painted the room had obviously gotten lazy and slopped some over the edge, so the window subsequently wouldn't close far enough to lock completely into place. I gave it one more try then gave up before turning and hurrying to catch up with the group.

Just beyond the wine cellar, I noticed another door slightly ajar, and I took a peek inside. It was a small security room, and a lone man was sitting behind a bank of flat screen monitors, which each showed a different area of the estate. Frank was obviously a careful guy and liked to know what was happening on his property. I left the man in peace and slithered away from the door and headed upstairs and managed to catch up with the tail end of the tour. We were done with the main house and therefore headed outside and made our way across the property and over to the guest house, which was Magnum's supposed domicile as part of Robin Master's security detail. Frank paused in front of the building, smiled, then proceeded to give us a little television insider knowledge. The building looked exactly as it had in the show, though the reality was that it was in fact, a boat house. They had used it as an exterior but obviously did their interior filming in a studio somewhere else on the island. We gave it a quick once over then left for the beach to get a close up view of the famous tide pool where Magnum swam every morning.

"Do you have two Doberman pinschers?" I asked.

"Sadly, no, but the wife does have three miniature dachshunds, though they are only aggressive when it comes to begging for treats."

I took a minute to look around and admire the view, and my gaze fell upon one of Frank's security men standing in the shadows. He saw me looking and waved, so I returned the gesture and waved back. It must be weird having armed guards around all the time, but people like Frank made a lot of enemies and therefore needed a lot of security. The tour was now complete, and we headed off back towards the barbecue to refill our drinks and relax by the pool. Along the way, I heard a horn and turned to see John and his entourage approaching the main house. His Limousine came to stop, and out came John, Jessica, Corn, Lux, Babs, Bridgette, and Matheson senior. Just behind them were two Secret Service Suburbans, and their occupants were stepping out and moving to the periphery while Sandra, as usual, stayed close to John.

"Don't tell me you're on time!" John said.

"Free food and alcohol. What would you expect?"

"Nothing less, of course."

"Enough talk, let's get you all to the bar," Frank said, jovially.

Everyone turned and walked to the small bar, and the young man behind it was suddenly inundated with drink orders. He knew his shit, however, and soon he had everyone properly loaded up with their favorite alcoholic beverage. With the rush having passed, I got a refill of my Mai Tai then joined the others.

"How goes the investigation?" Frank asked.

"Well, we have good news and bad news."

"The good being?" John asked.

"Well, it's incredibly clear that Jessica obviously isn't our killer."

"Wow, when did you figure that one out?" Jessica asked in an annoyed tone.

"I knew you were innocent from the start, but now we have a lot of circumstantial evidence to prove it. Even our FBI liaison would agree."

"True," Violet said.

"Such as?" Jessica asked.

"I'm pretty sure you were roofied and therefore out cold at the time of the murder."

"And when and how in the hell did that happen?"

"I believe a guy named Roofie Rudy slipped it into your drink during your bachelorette party."

"I did talk to someone at the bar. A young, good looking guy. Was that Rudy?"

"Yep, the bartender saw the entire exchange."

"Really?"

John suddenly looked bothered.

"Wait a minute. What the hell were you doing talking to a strange guy at the bar?" he asked.

"Trying to get lucky at my bachelorette party, obviously," she said.

"Very funny," John responded.

"Yeah, and be thankful I haven't asked for any details from your little bachelor party," Jessica said.

Violet and I shared an uncomfortable smile.

"So, that would explain the hangover," Jessica said.

"You got it."

"So, what exactly is the bad news here?" John asked.

"When we went to question Rudy, he did a runner and got hit by a car—and it wasn't an accident. Rudy was killed because he was a part of all this."

"A dead man tells no tales," John said.

"Exactly, and our next stop didn't go much better. We went to talk to the spear fisherman who found the gun and guess what?"

"Was he hit by a car?" Jessica asked.

"Not exactly. Any more guesses?"

"Was he hit by a boat?" John asked.

"Close—he drowned, which is a little too coincidental in my book. The guy spent his entire life in the ocean and suddenly drowns the day after Roofie Rudy was hit by a car."

"So, to recap. We have a very obvious conspiracy but still no way in hell to prove it."

"Yeah, but we also have a very good lead. I have absolutely irrefutable evidence that points to a local gunsmith who made the silencer."

"I suppose that is good news! Anything else you have that might cheer us up?" John asked.

"Well, we are pursuing some other avenues in this investigation."

"Sounds cryptic. Can you be more specific?" John asked.

Of course, my other good news was that Beeber was working his way into the governor of Hawaii's email system and would eventually be able to trace the chain of communiques that trickled down to the Honolulu Police Department. Once we knew specifically where it originated then we might just find a link to our conspirators. Unfortunately, as this entire part of the investigation was highly illegal, I decided it best to keep it as vague and non-specific as possible.

"I could, but it's best you not know too much. I can, however, tell you that we have some inquiries out concerning our police investigation timeline."

"Why do we care about that?" Frank asked.

"We have an interesting chain of events — timewise."

"Sounds, intriguing. Care to explain?" John asked.

"But, of course. You see — the Police Chief received an email from the Commissioner at seven fifty in the morning telling him to fast-track the investigation."

"So?"

"So, the commissioner did that after receiving a similar email from someone in the Governor's office at seven thirty."

"OK, but how is that significant?" Frank asked.

"The maid only reported the murder at seven forty, so the email from the Governor's office was sent out ten minutes before anyone even knew about the murder. Whoever initiated that chain of emails knew a hell of a lot more than he or she should."

"I see your point," John said.

"You're definitely onto something here, Finn, but how do you move forward?" Frank asked.

"That's the million dollar question, and one I don't yet know how to answer, so, for the moment we're focusing on the gunsmith."

Technically, I was lying my ass off, but I figured John and his people needed plausible deniability.

"So, that's it for now," I said.

Jessica looked at John and tried to smile, but I could tell that the emotional strain was starting to wear her down. Thankfully, Lux, who was sitting beside her, placed a reassuring hand on Jessica's shoulder.

"I'm really sorry you guys are having to deal with this shit," Lux said.

"Thanks, but I'm confident Tag will get us through this," Jessica said, trying to be stoic.

Everyone sat and quietly pondered the gravity of the latest developments until Frank suddenly held up his glass.

"Enough lamenting. Let's focus on the positive here, people. I say to hell with whoever is behind this. It's only a matter of time before Tag and Agent Kalili prove that Jessica is innocent, and then she and John are going to be the best Goddamn president and first lady this country has ever seen."

"Agreed," I said, holding up my glass.

Everyone toasted, and the mood improved for the moment as our attention was drawn to our drinks. Soon thereafter, platters of food started appearing on the nearby buffet table, and we had all the distraction we needed to enjoy the rest of the afternoon. Violet and I stood up and headed over for food and ended up just behind Lux and Corn.

"Save some for the rest of us," I said, to Corn as he piled up his plate with a king's ransom of barbecued pork ribs, potato, and macaroni salad.

"Don't tease Corn, or I might have to bring up your little indiscretion in the women's room the other night," Lux said.

"Wait, is this the same indiscretion you alluded to on the beach?" Violet asked.

"No, so let's drop it," I said, giving Lux an icy glare as I filled my plate with food.

"Yeah, and you'll be shocked to learn that this dipshit accidentally walked into the women's restroom at John and Jessica's engagement party," Lux said.

"Oh my God, I hope he didn't actually have to take a dump or anything. That scenario would have scarred him for life."

Before Lux could respond, I ushered Violet away and back to the table, where we ate and talked with the others, and I made sure she didn't hear about my embarrassing night at the luau. We finished dinner, and everyone moved to the pool, where the ladies all stripped down to their bikinis and entered via the shallow end. The guys, as guys often do, watched in rapt attention and stared stupidly at the bevy of scantily clad women. Lux, noticing the stupefied male audience, was the first to voice her disapproval.

"You idiots going to just stand there and stare or are you going to join us?"

"Join you," Corn said, as he slid off his shirt and did a cannonball that splashed everyone within twenty square feet.

It was incredibly childish, but the guys all laughed. The girls, however, thought he was acting like an idiot and proceeded to deliver a torrential onslaught of angry splashes the minute he surfaced. Inundated with a deluge of water, he dove down and resurfaced in the deep end, where he was safely out of reach of the agitated females. Seeing the reaction to Corn's performance, I did a rather low key dive into the deep end and then swam over to the shallow end to float and frolic amongst the females. I noticed Lux and Violet were talking, and I instantly feared that they were back on the subject of my diarrhea in the ladies room. As it turned out, they were talking about John and Jessica's predicament, and Lux was asking if the authorities had found the car that ran over Roofie Rudy.

"That's a good question. Any news on that yet?" I asked.

"Oh yeah. I forgot to tell you about it because it was a dead end. The police found the black suburban in a deserted parking lot up on the North Shore, and it was burned to a crisp and didn't have even the tiniest shred of evidence to be found."

"I'd have been surprised if it had been found in any other condition with the way things are going."

"No shit," Violet said.

The conversation continued, and we sipped our drinks until enough time passed that I realized the cocktails were having an impact on my bladder, and I desperately needed to pee. I exited the pool and walked over to the outdoor baño only to find it occupied. I therefore ventured into the house, where I was hoping to use the main one on the first floor. It lay between the living room and the kitchen and, like its pool counterpart, was fucking occupied. Lovely. Now, I was starting to panic and getting ever more aware of my impending need for release. I ran back across to the other side of the house and walked through the kitchen to what was likely originally intended as some kind of servants bathroom. As it turned out, it was full and therefore yet one more linchpin in the rapidly approaching flood of urine that was going to be flowing forth down my legs. Apparently, everyone at the party had suddenly chosen this exact moment to get busy on the porcelain.

I stood there wondering if I was going to be forced to piss in the kitchen sink, but thankfully Frank appeared, and I explained my dilemma. He told me to go ahead and use one of the upstairs bathrooms. Salvation at last! I thanked him and raced up to the second floor, where I was soon standing before an unoccupied toilet and giddily releasing a great torrent of urine. Three cocktails and a plate of barbecue was a lot to pack into my body, and I was now feeling the sweet relief of emptying my bladder. Having released what felt like the entire contents of Frank's bar into the bowl, I flushed, washed my hands, and was ready to rejoin the party. As I looked around the enormous bathroom, I realized there were actually three doors—the one I came in and two more that presumably went to bedrooms. Thank God I hadn't needed to drop a deuce, as there were far too many entry points to ever feel completely secure. As I was about to exit back through door number one, I decided to be adventurous and opened door number two, and there to my surprise stood Melissa Williams.

"Oh, hello, Tag! What brings you up here?"

"I had to pee, and this was the only available bathroom."

"That's what all the boys say when they're trying to get into my room," she said, raising an eyebrow.

Sweet Lord. What had I done? I was in Melissa's private bedroom, which, meant I was in the hellcat's lair.

"Sorry, I didn't mean to barge into your room. I was just trying a different exit and obviously took a wrong turn."

"I wouldn't say wrong just yet," she said, as she stepped closer.

I could now smell her perfume, and it brought on an

olfactory response that took me immediately back to our unfortunate night of passion. This, in turn, brought on some legitimate panic, and I found myself trying to make idle conversation as I took note of the exit and started trying to form an escape plan.

"So, this is your room?" I asked.

"Sure is, and it's where I spent every summer since fifth grade."

"Why would you even have a room at the resort when you can stay here?"

"I didn't want to worry about driving home after the party, so I figured a room would allow me to have a lot more fun."

"I see. That was probably good thinking."

I took a moment to look around the room in the hope that I might gain some insight into the crazy ass mind of Melissa Williams. Sometimes a person's bedroom could be like a snapshot of their inner psychological workings. A tidy room was thought to reflect a well-ordered mind while a messy one said exactly the opposite. Based upon our night of wild sex, I wouldn't have been surprised to find Melissa's room filled with whips, chains, and leather corsets, but the reality was rather mundane. On one wall, there were various pictures from her privileged childhood, with the majority being shots of her at exclusive functions—the focal point being her debutante ball. On the next wall over, there were the obligatory ribbons earned from childhood competitions, and the majority were, of course, from equestrian events. That wasn't very surprising, as it seemed that all girls, rich and poor, loved to ride horses, though the rich girls actually owned them. Interestingly, a certain Human Sexuality Professor I had back at Stanford had revealed that the shape of the saddle and subsequent movement of the steed provided a kind of stimulation to women's lady parts that was more or less comparable to masturbating—something guys achieved in much simpler way by using their hands. Girls road horses. Guys beat off. It was just one of the truths of the universe.

"I see that you're into horses," I said.

"Aren't all girls?"

"As far as I can tell."

I turned my gaze to the next wall and saw a picture of a teenage Melissa and an equally youthful John Matheson standing on the deck of a fancy yacht club. John was wearing top-siders, a Polo shirt, and preppy plaid shorts while Melissa was in some kind of flower print short summer dress, and to make it even more cutesy, she was kissing him on the cheek. Sweet Lord! It looked less like a family photo and more like a fucking print ad for Ralph Lauren. As I was about to ask Melissa when the picture was taken, she abruptly stepped closer.

"So, Tag, I haven't seen you since the other night, and I really had a lot of fun and was kind of hoping we might have a repeat performance," she said, as she reached out and ran her hand down my chest and over the front of my shorts.

"I did too, but…"

Before I could finish my sentence, she wrapped her arms around me and kissed me, and it was like being trapped by a gigantic preying mantis. She was strong and had a good grip, but I finally managed to pull my lips free. Unfortunately, she used this opening to yank down my shorts and take firm hold of my mantool. I tried to back away, but she followed me and ended up pinning me against the nearby dresser. With a wicked smile, she dropped to her knees and started into some unwanted, though oddly pleasurable oral sex. My mind reeled as I tried to stem the flow of blood, all the while knowing in my heart of hearts that it was wrong, and I needed to free myself from this hellcat's devilish mouth. Still, even as I tried to pry her from my loins, my member grew rock hard, and, having little success, I changed tactics and tried to sidestep my way to freedom. The result was that she remained stubbornly attached to my penis, and it felt as though I were using my manhood like a leash to try and pull a hundred and twenty pound pit bull.

"Wait, Melissa, I can't do this."

She suddenly stopped for a second and smiled up at me seductively.

"You don't have to do anything. I'll do all the work," she said, untying her bikini top and dropping it onto the floor.

That was my opening, and I used it to step out of her reach and try and pull up my shorts as I made a break for the hallway. Unfortunately, I couldn't get them past my boner, but I soldiered on and reached the hallway just in time to see Violet and Lux appear at the top of the stairs. Both froze, and their gazes instantly fell upon my raging hard-on, which was conspicuously pointing at them over my waistband. Lux began laughing, but Violet, however, wasn't amused, so, as usual, I was up to my neck in shit and fate was throwing a rock at my face.

"Any particular reason you're running around with a boner?" Violet asked, with a distinctively disapproving tone in her voice.

"Not a good one."

"Wow, Finn, talk about party fouls," Lux said.

Just then, Melissa came dashing out into the hall, and her bare breasts were bouncing about and very likely to make this situation even harder to explain.

"Oh, there you are, Tag," Melissa said, innocently.

"Yeah, there you are," Violet added.

"And there they are," Lux added, obviously referring to Melissa's breasts.

"Yeah—we're all here," I responded.

"It would appear there's a totally different dress code up here, so Violet and I will be going back downstairs to wait for one of those restrooms to open up," Lux said.

"Yeah, so have fun," Violet said, giving me an icy glare.

She and Lux turned around and walked back toward the stairs and disappeared from view, and, as inopportune as that chance meeting had just been, it at least afforded me a brief moment of de-escalation in which to attempt to thwart the unwanted advances of the hellcat Melissa Williams.

"Look, I'm sorry, Melissa. You're incredibly attractive, but I can't do this."

"Excuse me? You're going to pass on this?" she said, motioning at her glorious body.

"Well, yeah—sadly I must," I said, as I took a final look. Melissa seethed for a moment then appeared to calm down.

"Fine, but you'll regret it. They all do."

"You're probably right," I said, as I turned and headed downstairs still feeling oddly violated.

The awkward exchange with Violet and Lux had been just the right amount of discomfort to reduce Tag Junior's swelling, and I was finally able to wrestle him back into my shorts. Now that I was well below half-mast, I headed back out to the pool to join the others, and Violet, as expected, greeted me with a look of quiet disdain, but who could blame her after what she had just witnessed.

"Back so soon?" she asked.

"Yeah, and this time it really wasn't what it looked like."

"So, you weren't fucking Melissa again?"

"Not even close."

"So, your boner and her bare tits were perfectly innocent?"

"Well, this is going to sound worse before it sounds better, but you arrived at the exact moment I fled from an attempted blowjob. I'm not exaggerating when I say she tried to orally rape me."

"Wait, who raped you?" Doug asked, as he appeared at my side.

"Melissa Williams."

"Seriously? What happened? And don't leave out any sordid details," he said, with a little too much enthusiasm.

"She just fully forced herself on me."

"Dude, can you be more specific?"

"Let me put it this way. She just went full Dyson on Tag Junior, and I'm lucky it's still attached."

"A blowjob? That is fucking awesome!" he said, again offering me another high five.

This time I refrained and left Doug hanging, but I was hoping it might at least make Violet a little happier.

"Look, Doug, it wasn't exactly a blowjob, as I managed to break free and run for it long before anything serious happened."

"Like ejaculation?" he asked.

"Exactly."

"Dude, are you fucking serious?" Beeber asked.

"Yeah."

"Bullshit," Doug said.

"No, I'm serious, and when she reached down to take off her bikini top, I made a run for it—literally."

"Dude, is this you officially coming out of the closet," Beeber asked.

"Yeah, if that closet has that crazy ass woman in it, then yes—I just ran like fuck out of it."

Beeber and Doug stared at me with legitimate disapproval in their expressions, and Violet too wasn't pleased, and she walked away and sat on the pool's edge and dangled her feet in the water. I left the nerds behind and went over and sat down beside her in the hopes that I might try and make her believe me.

"Violet, I swear to you that everything I just said is true."

"So, what were you doing in her bedroom?"

"I took the wrong door when I left the upstairs bathroom."

"Bullshit."

"No, it's true, and I was only up there in the first place because every fucking bathroom on the lower floor was occupied."

She stared at me for a moment, and her expression softened.

"Well, I believe that part, because Lux and I came upstairs for the very same reason."

"And obviously the rest happened just as I said, because if I had actually wanted a blowjob, I wouldn't have gone scurrying into the hallway with my boner waving in the wind."

"Speaking of which—if you were indeed an unwilling participant, then what the hell was that massive boner all about?" she asked.

"The only answer I have is that fucking Tag Junior had a mind of his own and was a willing co-conspirator in that sexual assault. Honestly, I'm just thankful that you and Lux arrived when you did or that hellcat might have dragged me back into her fucking room."

We were quiet a moment, then Violet laughed out loud.

"Something funny?" I asked.

"I can't help imaging you trying to pull your boner free of her mouth and making a run for it."

"Yeah, it wasn't pretty."

"So, how long did it take to break free?" she asked.

"Maybe eight or ten seconds, but it's hard to be certain—time slows down during stressful moments like that."

"So, you were like a rodeo rider on a bucking bronco."

"Honestly, I felt more as though I were dragging a pit bull across the floor—with my dick as the leash."

"Jesus, how's your dick?"

"I'm lucky everything is still attached, though I'm thinking we should test it out to make it sure it still works properly."

"Nice try, but I think someone needs a shower first."

"That wasn't a no."

"True," she said, with a hint of a smile.

Just then, Melissa appeared, and her bathing suit top was now firmly back in place, and both of her breasts were properly concealed within its confines. Doug, of course, immediately went and sat with her, as he was obviously hoping to incur the same treatment I had experienced minutes earlier. To be honest, I wished him luck, as he didn't get out much, so scoring with the opposite sex was therefore kind of a statistical unlikelihood. It was a shame too, because he was a nice guy and decent looking, but ultimately it was his poor decision making process that was very likely the reason behind his having a hard time finding a date—case in point being that he was on a tropical island, rife with lovely females, and he chose to sit indoors and play D&D with Beeber and Rachel.

The barbecue continued on into the evening, and I looked out over the ocean to see the sun was getting close to dropping over the horizon, thus bringing to an end yet another day in paradise. People were beginning their official goodbyes, and I looked around to gather up my troops for the drive back to the resort but noticed that Doug was nowhere to be seen. A moment later, he appeared from the house, and he was walking taller than I had ever seen him in all the years we had known each other. Sweet mother of God. He must have gotten together with the hellcat Melissa Williams.

"Ready to adjourn to your D&D game, Doug?" I asked.

"Yeah, if there's time."

"What do you mean if there's time?" Beeber asked.

"Beebs, give Doug a break. He obviously just got laid—probably for the first time in a long time."

"Doubtful," Beeber responded.

"I'm afraid Finn's correct, Beebsy," Doug said.

"Wait a minute. Who did you hook up with?"

"Melissa Williams, of course."

"Dude, after she tried to give Finn a blowjob?"

"Well, technically yes but..."

"But nothing. Now you've basically had Finn's dick in your mouth."

"Don't be ridiculous."

"Did you kiss her?"

"Yeah, but…"

"But nothing. How's he taste?" Beeber asked with a scrutinizing gaze.

"Like you don't already know," Doug responded.

"Easy, Beebsy. Give Doug a break and let him enjoy his post coital bliss in peace."

"Yeah, and you're being incredibly gross," Rachel said.

"Oh, I'm just giving Doug shit. He knows that deep down I'm happy for him. I'd never be legitimately mean to my favorite Dungeon Master."

"There are just so many ways I could respond to that statement," I said.

The nerds quieted back down, then we walked over and thanked Frank for an excellent barbecue before saying goodbye and mounting up in the suburban. I had a quick nostalgic look around and lived out my last moments as the fabled *Magnum P.I.* before putting it in drive and heading out the winding dirt driveway of Robin's Nest. We reached the gate, and it opened automatically, and, as we headed north down the road, Violet's phone beeped, and she looked down to see that she had a text.

"Shit," she said, a second later.

"What is it?"

"I haven't seen my parents in a few days, and they want

me to come by for a visit."

"What's wrong with that?"

"Nothing, except my dad wants to meet you."

"Why?"

"Because we're working together. I told you how protective he can be."

"Well, I'd be happy to meet your parents."

"Seriously?"

"Yeah."

"Well, just so you know—my father can be a little intimidating."

"It's OK, I always get along with people's parents."

"All right, but remember that you willingly agreed to this. I didn't force you."

"I know."

"And we have three witnesses to back me up."

"True," Rachel, Doug, and Beeber said from the back seat.

"It's just a dinner. What could possibly happen?" I asked.

My words didn't appear to comfort Violet, and she had a pensive expression on her face as she turned to face the long and winding road ahead.

CHAPTER NINETEEN
Meet the Parents

I drove back to the resort to drop off the nerds as well as freshen up by taking a shower and brushing my teeth. Feeling a whole lot better, Violet and I headed south back towards Waikiki, where Violet's parents lived just east of Diamond Head on a lovely piece of ocean front property. Their place wasn't opulent or as big as some of the surrounding homes, but it was very homey and boasted a spectacular ocean view. I parked in the driveway in front of an open garage and peered inside to see a white Toyota Camry and, more interestingly, a silver Nissan GTR. The GTR was Nissan's entry into the world of super cars and one I had been thinking about buying after my recent financial windfall.

"Whose GTR?" I asked.

"My dad's, of course."

Regardless of what Violet had said to try and scare me, I was already thinking that her dad was a pretty cool customer. The GTR was an especially badass ride, because it was relatively affordable, yet was in the performance category of cars such as Ferraris and Lamborghinis. That meant its owners generally cared more about performance than prestige, and that, in turn, meant that I already respected Violet's father.

We exited the suburban and entered the tidy garage to find her father standing in front of his GTR. He smiled and came over to introduce himself, and I could now understand Violet's trepidation, as he was an imposing figure. He was about six foot two, muscular, and had the tan complexion and good looks of a full blooded Hawaiian, which was something of a rarity after so many years of new residents migrating to the islands and steadily diffusing the native population.

"I'm Edward Kalili. Nice to meet you," he said, holding out his rather large hand.

"Tag Finn. Nice to meet you too, sir," I said, taking his massive paw in my hand.

I was happy he had a normal secure handshake and didn't attempt to crush my digits.

"Call me Ed, as sir makes me feel old."

"I know the feeling."

"Hi, dad," Violet said, hugging her father.

"Hello, my little Pualani."

Little Pualani? What the hell did that mean? If I had to guess, I'd say it meant little stubborn one, but I'd have to verify that later when we were alone. Meanwhile, I turned my attention back to the GTR, and, as I admired its muscular lines, Ed noticed where I was looking and smiled.

"You know about the GTR?" he asked.

"Of course, I'm a man, and I've also been seriously thinking about buying one."

"You won't regret it."

"I know. It's a beauty, and I'm happy to see you're obviously taking excellent care of it."

"Yeah, I was just about to wax it."

"Need help?"

"Oh no, I've got it."

"I'm serious. I'd be happy to help, as I love working on cars, and, besides, I think properly maintaining an automobile is the hallmark of a real man."

"Well, in that case, grab yourself a beer and a microfiber cloth," he said.

There was a refrigerator against the far wall, and I walked over and found it loaded with a plentiful supply of beer along with a number of Costco overflow items that obviously didn't fit in the main unit in the kitchen. I grabbed a Corona and looked to Violet.

"You want one?" I asked.

"Sure," she said, still looking a bit shocked that I was getting along with her father.

I used the bottle opener that was magnetically attached to the fridge door and opened us both a beer and handed one to Violet before holding mine up to toast.

"To men and their cars," I said.

"I'm going to say hello to mom, then I'll be back out in a few minutes."

Violet stared at her dad and blinked her eyes strangely then, oddly, he blinked back in return.

"What the hell was all that?"

"Violet was just telling me to be nice to you."

"By blinking?"

"Morse Code. I taught it to her as a kid, and we've used it ever since to talk shit to each other when the wife dragged us to boring family events."

"Speaking of the wife—I should probably go introduce myself."

"Oh no you don't. You already signed on for this project."

"OK, but if she gives me shit for it later, I expect you two to back me up."

"Deal."

Violet headed inside, and I took a sip then set down my beer, grabbed a microfiber cloth, and set to work rubbing wax onto the left side of the car while Ed started on the right. Fifteen minutes later we met on the hood and took a minute to sip our beers and talk.

"So, I hear you're a special investigator for the vice president," he said.

"Correct."

"And from what Violet's told me, it sounds like you have a hell of a job at the moment."

"I do indeed, and I'm not sure how much you know, but we're up against some pretty serious people here."

I took a moment to outline the case, then told Ed all that happened in the meanwhile, and he looked a bit worried as he took another sip of his beer.

"You're not going to get my daughter hurt are you?"

"I'll do everything in my power to keep her safe."

"That's good to know. Now, if you don't mind me asking, how it is that you ended up working on this case?"

"Coincidence really. The vice president and I are old friends, and I was here to be the best man at his wedding, which is obviously on hold until I can get his bride cleared of potential murder charges."

"So, you currently work in some area of law enforcement?"

"No, I'm a private investigator at the moment, and I'm doing this for Matheson because we go way back."

"Oh, did you meet him working for the Secret Service?"

"No, I worked for a different government agency, but Matheson and I met before that when we were both in the military in Afghanistan," I said.

"Oh right—I saw that you had a Silver Star in your military record. Is that where you earned it?"

"Yeah," I said, with a small chuckle.

"What's so funny?"

"That you checked me out."

"Of course I did—you're working with my daughter."

"True, I would probably do the same."

"So, what made you leave the service?"

"Actually, I got shot in the hip rescuing the future vice

president of the United States from his downed helicopter."

"That couldn't have been fun."

"Definitely not, as he's a pretty big guy, and I had to carry him a really long way."

Now it was Ed who laughed.

"Now I see how you ended up as the best man at his wedding," he said.

I shrugged.

"Yeah, but, more importantly, he was a good guy, a fellow soldier, and already a friend."

"And you were in Air Force Pararescue. That's not a place for the lazy."

"Definitely not."

"So that others may live," he said, proudly.

"You've heard our creed?"

"Yeah, I was in the service myself after college, though I didn't experience anything as hairy as Afghanistan."

"It's all hairy when you're the one in it."

"I suppose."

We finished our beers, then Ed walked to the fridge, opened two more, and came back over and handed me mine, and, as we clinked bottles, he eyed me curiously.

"So, when you said you also worked for a different government agency, which one was it?"

"The one you can't talk about."

"Ah, you were a spook. That explains why there isn't any official record after you left the service."

"Yeah, I did five years in the Agency, then I got the hell

out and moved to the private sector."

"Quite an interesting career, my friend."

"I suppose."

"Well, as long as you keep my daughter safe, we'll get along just fine," he said.

We sipped our beers then went back to work on the car and rubbed off the remaining wax. Once we finished, we stood back to admire our work, and I had to admit that the GTR looked glorious and shined as though it were still sitting on the showroom floor. With our task finished, however, the conversation started anew, and the topic was Violet.

"I hope I'm not being too forward when I ask if you have any romantic intentions towards my daughter."

"What made you ask that?"

"The fact that you're here—in the Lion's den. Plus, I noticed the way you offered her a beer before taking one for yourself."

"Just being a gentleman."

"Maybe, but as a career officer in the FBI, I know how to read people, and I definitely saw a spark."

"From me or your daughter?"

"Both," he said.

"If only. The sad truth is that I really do like Violet, but our relationship is kind of complicated due to the fact that we're working together."

"I assume you know that she's recently gotten out of a long term relationship with someone she worked with?"

"Yeah, I met her ex Dave. He didn't seem to like me very much."

"He can be a little intense, but, under it all, he's a good guy."

"I'm sure he is, but I have yet to see that part of him."

"Well, you have to understand that they were very much in love, but it's tough to work for the Bureau and maintain any kind of reasonably normal relationship. Trust me, I know. I'm just lucky my wife had nothing to do with the FBI—aside from marrying me of course."

Just then, the door opened, and in walked Violet and her mother, and it was very clear where Violet got the other half of her excellent genetics. Violet's mother was very attractive and could have easily been a model with her strong bone structure, big blue eyes, and long beautiful blond hair. Now seeing Violet's parents standing side by side, I had the entire picture of where she got her good looks. Both parents were extremely attractive, but together had made for an even lovelier offspring, as her mother's European genes mixed wonderfully with her father's Hawaiian ancestry, and the combination created a uniquely exotic beauty. But, such was the wonder of the Islands, where people from all over the world met, fell in love, and made beautiful children.

"Nice to meet you, Tag, I'm Diora."

"Nice to meet you, Diora," I said.

"Are you two hungry?" she asked, in her warm motherly tone.

"Absolutely."

Violet looked at me, as she was probably wondering if I was being polite or was I sincerely hungry. I had eaten like a pig at the barbecue, but it had been several hours, and I had also done a little manual labor on the GTR, so I was actually ready to eat again.

"Well, come in when you guys are ready. I've made a lovely dinner."

Diora went back inside, but Violet stayed in the garage.

"You want to hang with the menfolk?" I asked.

"Yeah, to make sure you two aren't talking about me."

"We wouldn't do that—would we, Tag?"

"Of course not," I said.

Violet obviously didn't believe us and continued to quietly watch as we went around the car to make sure all the wax was properly rubbed into the finish. When we were finally done, Ed handed me a fresh beer then clinked his bottle to mine.

"Thanks for your help," he said.

"Um excuse me, dad. Where's my beer?"

"Still in the fridge. You didn't help wax the car."

"Dad, I'm your only daughter!"

"My only lazy daughter."

Violet let out a low groan then walked over to the refrigerator and grabbed herself a beer.

"Kids," I said, to Ed.

"No respect," he responded.

The three of us then left the garage and walked through the house and out to the back, where a table sat on a beautiful lanai only fifty feet from the ocean. We took a seat, and Diora held up her glass of wine.

"Here's to our guest," she said.

We clinked our bottles to her glass then settled in to eat dinner. It consisted of chicken breasts cooked in balsamic vinegar, turmeric, curry, and placed over a bed of lettuce. She called it Sunken Chicken, and it was particularly delicious and made for a perfect meal in the warm Hawaiian weather. We ate, talked, and enjoyed a lovely evening where I learned all about Violet's childhood, and it included numerous embarrassing stories that she would have preferred remain unspoken. But, it was a parent's prerogative to recount and humiliate their brood. How else could they retaliate for all the difficulties their little ones created throughout their childhood?

So, I learned that Violet had been tough as nails and stubborn as all hell during her formative years, which were two traits that clearly followed her into adulthood. If someone got on her bad side or threatened one of her friends, that person would receive some prompt two fisted justice. In fact, she was sent to the principle's office almost weekly, and, had her father not been an esteemed member of the FBI, she would have spent the entirety of eighth grade out on suspension. Fortunately, Violet mellowed during High School and turned her aggressive energies to sports and especially scholastics and managed to graduate as her school's valedictorian. She was accepted to all the most prestigious universities but chose to remain in her beloved

Hawaii, where she had a full ride all the way through grad school. She was by all accounts a hell of a woman, and, in truth, I didn't see her early childhood as embarrassing, but rather a sign that she was an upstanding and honorable person who wasn't going to take any shit. Of course, I wish her parents would have divulged something more horribly embarrassing such as an episode of explosive diarrhea at an amusement park, but such wouldn't be the case, so Violet's reputation, at least in my mind, remained intact. I finished the last bite of food on my plate and had a moment to relax and sip my beer, and Ed looked over and smiled.

"Glad you enjoyed dinner. I hate to see a good meal go to waste."

"I agree."

We talked a bit longer, but the evening eventually came to a close, and it was time to say good night to Violet's parents. Diora hugged me and Ed shook my hand, then we saddled up in the Suburban and headed out to the main highway, where I paused, as I wasn't sure which way to go.

"Do you want me to drop you off at your place?"

"Sure, and maybe this time, I'll let you come inside."

"Meow!"

"And that's come as in C O M E, not C U M."

"Obviously."

I drove west for about a half mile, then turned left and headed up to Violet's home. This time, she directed me into the driveway, and I navigated the suburban up through its narrow confines and stopped in front of her garage. I turned off the car and joined her on the front porch, where an automatic sensor turned on a number of flood lights. She pulled out her key then opened the door and quickly tapped in her alarm code before turning on the lights.

"Home sweet home," she said.

I walked across the living room and stood in front of a sliding glass door to see that it opened up onto a covered deck that offered a spectacular view.

"Drink on the deck? I make a mean Hurricane," Violet said.

"Sure, sounds good, though I don't think I've ever had one."

"You'll like it. Now go take a seat, and I'll be out there with the cocktails in a minute."

I opened the sliding glass doors and walked out onto her deck and saw that her view extended all the way from Coco Head in the east to Waikiki Beach in the west. At this hour it was all street lights and houses, but by day I imagine you could see the entire south eastern end of Oahu. I took a seat in one of deck chairs and listened as a rain squall blew in off the Pacific and enveloped the deck with the sound of millions of droplets hitting the roof above. Violet appeared a moment later, carrying two tall cocktails, and we clinked glasses and sipped our drinks safely out of reach of the deluge around us. She moved her chair closer then placed her feet up on my lap and wiggled her toes as a hint that she wanted a foot massage. I took hold of her delicate feet and rolled my thumb around the ball of her foot and worked my way back towards the heel before gently pulling on each of her toes. Next, I switched to her other foot and repeated the process until Violet actually moaned with pleasure.

"Oh my God that feels so good," she said.

"Want me to do your breasts next, Little Pualani?"

She smiled.

"I see you didn't forget my nickname."

"Nope, and I was guessing it means little stubborn one."

"No, it means heavenly flower, and to prove I'm not stubborn, why don't you start on my shoulders, and, in the meantime, I'll consider letting you do my breasts next."

"She slid over and sat in my lap, and I dug my thumbs into her shoulders and kneaded all the connective tissue like fine pastry dough then slowly worked my way down her back before pausing just above the soft curve of her buttocks. I moved my hands back up to her shoulders then ever so slowly around and down to the muscles just above her breasts.

"It might be more effective if you took off your shirt."

"Really?"

"Absolutely."

She abruptly slid off her shirt and bikini top, and I felt mildly dumbstruck as a healthy rush of blood began to flow to my man parts.

"Well?" she asked.

I placed my hands on her shoulders and began rubbing the tension out of her shoulder muscles.

"Lower," she said.

I moved my hands down her back and focused on the hard to reach rhomboid muscles than ran between the shoulder blades. She sighed, and her entire body began to relax in my arms.

"More to the front," she said.

I reached around to the front and worked the pectorals, though all I could think about was the enticing soft tissue residing mere inches below.

"Perhaps a bit lower."

I switched from massage to gentle caressing and ran my fingertips down her sides then back up, though this time I glided up the sides of her breasts and just barely skirted her areolas. As I brought them back down, I ran them directly over her nipples, and I felt both of them instantly harden and spring to life. My penis was experiencing a similar hardening, and, sensing its presence, Violet wiggled her backside against it. I took this as a likely sign that I was on the right track, and I brought each finger tip down and began circling her remarkably hard nipples, and it caused her to moan ever so softly and lean her head against me as she arched her back and pressed out her breasts. I kissed her neck and gave her ear a gentle little bite, then continued caressing her nipples until her entire body grew tense. Her breathing became shallower, and she suddenly turned around and sat across my lap and kissed me hard on the lips and began grinding her pelvis into mine. Her passion was now fully lit and burning out of control.

With the bonfire of our libidos ablaze, she brought her

tongue to mine, and we made sweet love with our mouths—our tongues slipping back and forth and side to side. Our hips too continued to grind together, and the only thing keeping us from progressing to intercourse was the thin fabric of our clothing. Suddenly, she pulled her lips free, leaned back, and pulled my head down to her breasts, thus forcing me to set to work on her nipples with my tongue—all the while acutely aware that she had said she could climax from nipple stimulation alone. Apparently, it wasn't an exaggeration, as she appeared to be nearing climax, and it was something I had only ever heard about but never actually witnessed first hand. This was pretty fucking exciting, and I made sure to use both my tongue and fingertips to stimulate both nipples equally, and her entire body started shaking as she set forth unto a violent climax. She began calling out and continued to do so until the waves of pleasure diminished, and she proceeded to lift my head and kiss me. We pressed our lips together and touched tongues, and, when we at last parted, she stared into my eyes and smiled.

"That was nice," she said.

"Yeah, and I got to see firsthand that you weren't exaggerating when you told me that you could climax from nipple stimulation."

"No, I wasn't, though that generally only happens on rare occasions."

"Such as?"

"Oh, you know—when the right guy gets me really turned on."

"So, at the moment, I'm Mr. Right."

"Yeah, at the moment, so don't fuck it up and become Mr. Wrong again."

"Deal."

"Good, now follow me, and I'll show you to the guest bedroom," she said, slipping on her shirt.

Shit. Foiled again. This was one cruel woman, and I was starting to get a taste of the stubborn resolve that her father had mentioned. She could hold a hell of a grudge, and I certainly wouldn't have wanted to have gotten on her bad side during childhood. We picked up our cocktails and headed to her room, where she was apparently getting some extra bedding. She grabbed a pillow from her closet then told me to check the top drawer for sheets. I opened it and did a double take. There were indeed sheets, but on the other side of the drawer there were a number of kinky sex toys—namely handcuffs, a vibrator, nipple clamps, and a ball-gag.

"Wow, I had no idea you were so kinky."

"What do you mean?"

"Um, excuse me?" I said, pulling out the nipple clamps.

"Oh."

Next, I pulled out the ball-gag and held it up for her to see.

"And this item?"

She laughed and walked over to peer in the drawer.

"Dave bought all this shit—well, except for the vibrator. That's one's all me."

"Did you ever use any of this shit?"

"Everything but the ball-gag, though I did make Dave wear it once."

"Ew," I said, as I instantly dropped it back into the drawer.

"Don't worry, I put it through the dishwasher after we broke up."

"Good to know. Well, this is a pretty interesting drawer full of goodies you've got here, though it does explain some things," I said.

"Are you referring to the fact that I handcuffed you to the bed on our first night?"

"I am."

"That had nothing to do with fetish and everything to do with being careful. You were a stranger after all."

"Careful? I'd say it was a little paranoid."

"I see a lot of shit in my job and therefore have a healthy amount of fear whilst engaging in new relationships."

"If you're that afraid of sex with a stranger, you might want to have just abstained from sex all together."

"Are you saying we shouldn't have had sex?"

"No, I'm just saying that if you needed to handcuff me to the bed for you to feel secure, then perhaps the prudent thing would have been to abstain until you got to know me better."

"No can do. I like sex too much."

She grabbed the extra sheets, closed the drawer, and led me to the guest bedroom across the hall. It was a little smaller, but it thankfully had its own bathroom.

"Are you going to help me make the bed?" I asked.

"Of course. What kind of hostess do you think I am?"

We placed the fitted sheet on first then did the top sheet, which she made a point of getting perfectly centered before employing hospital corners. She clearly knew her way around a bed, though I pretty much knew that the minute she handcuffed me to one. The final task was to pull a thin blanket out of the closet and throw it over the top.

"Voila!" she said.

"What about the pillow?"

"It goes back to my room."

"Seriously?"

"Yeah, you're going to need it to sleep after I fuck your brains out."

I took a moment to pick my jaw up off the floor then regarded the rather devious woman before my eyes.

"Excuse me?"

"I said that you're going to need it to sleep—after I fuck your brains out."

"That's what I thought you said, and if that's the case, then why in the fuck are we making this bed?"

"It was a test, and this time you passed."

"Sweet half Hawaiian Jesus! You're one crazy ass woman."

"Yeah, but you're still here, aren't you?"

"Yes, indeed I am."

"Exactly, now come with me, or I'll pull out my gun and the handcuffs."

She grabbed my hand and led me back across the hall to

her room, and she disrobed and called out over her shoulder as she walked into the bathroom.

"You coming?"

"Are you spelling that with a *U* or an *O*?"

"I guess you'll have to follow me to find out," she said, as she disappeared from view.

I took off my shorts and T-shirt and entered the bathroom to find that Violet was already in the shower, and the smell of her floral shampoo was particularly fragrant and inadvertently tugging at my olfactory receptors. I had smelled it in her hair on our very first wild night of passion, and now it was making those memories come alive—in my loins. I joined her in the large glass shower enclosure to see that it had three shower heads—two above and one below, and the lower one was positioned in such a way that it was spraying directly at my manhood and, combined with the olfactory response, was bringing on a serious boner that was now pressing against Violet's leg. She reached down and lathered it up with such enthusiasm that I had to stop her formidable efforts or end up covering her in pearlescent man-soap. At that point, I took her in my arms, and we kissed, and, with my mouth otherwise engaged, I felt the need to explore, and I ran my hands down her body and took hold of firm, round backside and gave it a healthy squeeze. From there, I brought my hands around to the front and at last came upon her precious lady region. It was hot, wet, and apparently expecting company, so I moved my fingers over its contours until happening upon her clitoris, which made Violet give my lower lip a teasing bite. Clearly, I had struck lady gold.

"I think it's time to get out of the shower," she said, turning off the water.

We dried off and headed to her bed, and she lay back against the pillows, with her expression welcoming and her eyes awash in lust.

"Get over here," she said.

"Just a second."

"Oh, did you need to warm up and perhaps stretch first?"

"I'm plenty warm, but I just had a thought," I said, as I stepped over to the dresser and grabbed the handcuffs out of the top drawer.

"Oh, do you want me to handcuff you to the bed again?" she asked.

"I'm afraid not, as it's time for a little quid pro quo m'lady. Now, put your hands over your head and spread your legs."

"You're definitely not going to need those tonight, Officer Finn, as your suspect is willing and able."

"Maybe, but I think this calls for a little bedroom justice."

She eyed me a moment as she pondered my words but soon relented and lifted her hands up to the top of the bed as she opened her legs. I cuffed her to the center vertical post of the headboard then took a minute to admire the view. She was everything I could want in a woman and more—smart, sexy, tough as nails, and utterly beautiful— and I mean beautiful. I was attracted to every inch, whether it be her eyes, the curve of her neck, her long muscular legs, firm round backside, or her rippled muscular abs that led from below her gloriously full breasts to her luscious valley of femininity.

"Anytime now, Officer Finn," she said.

"You don't just run through the Louvre, you stop and admire the art."

I reached down and ran my fingers up Violet's inner thighs then moved forward and kissed her stomach before making my way to her neck. From there, I nibbled her ear then at last reached her mouth. Her lips parted instantly, and her kiss bordered on frantic as she pressed her tongue to mine. I maneuvered my hips closer and inadvertently pressed Tag Junior against her lady essence, and it caused her to let out a moan of anticipation. That was my signal to move on, and so I retraced my steps down her body and paused only long enough to kiss each nipple before descending upon her golden valley of truth and justice. I made landfall with my tongue and pressed into her center before making my way north to her clitoris, where only the slightest touch caused her to arch her back and moan in pleasure. She was so reactive, in fact, that I was mildly startled and paused for a moment.

"Someone has a very sensitive clitoris," I said.

"No shit. You saw what happened with my nipples. Now, imagine that times ten."

"Ten? By the time I'm done, you'll be calling it twenty."

"Prove it."

"OK then—let God's work be done, Special Agent Kalili of the FBI," I said.

I set back upon Violet's lady fruit, though I was careful to vary the pressure and speed of my tongue movement, as getting there was half the fun. I therefore worked my way slowly and tauntingly up to a healthy pace then decided to up the ante by reaching around and taking hold of her buttocks and pulling her essence to me, so that I could bring to bear the full force of my mouth, lips, and tongue. Violet's hips started to rock violently, and she was propelled headlong into the throws of a powerful climax that made her entire body spasm with each wave of divine release. I eventually eased up and allowed her to catch her breath, and her beautiful lips parted into a big smile.

"Okay, fine. That was a twenty, and now I'd like to return the favor, so I'm going to need you to un-cuff me."

"I'm sorry, Agent Kalili, but I'm not quite done yet."

I leaned forward and kissed her on the lips then returned to her field of dreams and used my tongue to trace its outer dimensions before plunging back into its center. From there I made the short jaunt north to her lady trigger, and Violet again started moaning in pleasure. This time, however, I used my right hand and slid my ring, middle, and index fingers inside her so as to reach up and place a little extra pressure upon the fabled Gräfenberg spot as well as the lower, outer branches of her clitoris. Few people knew that this wonder of female sensitivity extended down like a wishbone along the outer sides of the vagina, and thus allowed for more areas of stimulation. Now, I had several powerful orgasmic forces at work, but I had to proceed cautiously if I hoped to prolong the inevitable. That meant applying pressure and speed gradually in order to keep her perched on the cusp of climax and reveling in pleasure for as long as possible. Outside the rain continued to come down, and lightening and thunder filled the sky, though nothing came close to the fury of Violet's violent screams of ecstasy.

"Oh God, oh God, oh fuck, we're definitely at twenty! Now please let me cum for fuck's sake, you fucker!" she screamed, as she writhed and pulled against the handcuffs.

I decided to add to the powerful orgasmic forces already in play by using my free hand to reach up and run my fingertips over her nipples. The mighty triumvirate of stimulation made her entire body begin to convulse, and sweet release came on so quickly that her cries of ecstasy were far louder than any thunder clap. She was lost in orgasmic purgatory, and her eyes were unfocused and her breathing heavy until I relented, and she went still and took a moment to catch her breath.

"Holy fuck," she said.

"Yeah, revenge is a dish best served with cunnilingus," I said, as I reached up and unlocked the handcuffs.

"Agreed. The prisoner has learned her lesson."

She immediately sat up and kissed me then reached down and directed Tag Junior into the loving embrace of her vagina, and I started to move in and out while adding a gentle clockwise hip motion at the apex of each thrust. It was meant to increase clitoral stimulation, though I wasn't exactly sure Violet required such extra care. The answer to that question was answered about a minute and a half later when she climaxed yet again, though, this time, the pleasure caused her to dig her nails into the soft flesh of my back. Fuck, the orgasm score was officially three to zero, but I was in the zone—the perfect balance between pleasure and release, and I could have stayed in that moment for eternity. In reality, it actually turned out to be about thirty seconds, as Violet had her own orgasmic itinerary in mind.

"OK, fucker, it's time to make good on my promise to fuck your brains out, so roll onto your back," she said.

I did as instructed, and Violet moved atop me and started grinding on my manhood and pounding my hips, and it sent her breasts bouncing about before my eyes like two tantalizing treats. I pulled her close and kissed her hard nipple until she moved and placed its neighbor in my mouth. With both breasts equally attended, she kissed me then leaned back and started to rock her hips even faster. I therefore took hold of her breasts and held them steady as I fondled her nipples. We picked up our pace and worked in perfect harmony, and soon were on the cusp of release, with Violet's cacophony of moans and movement the final impetus to push me over the edge. This was it. The reckoning. In only seconds we were both engaged in an earth shattering climax, and the world and our very existence were lost and forgotten to the selfishly divine pleasure of release. At last, Violet came to rest and leaned down to deliver a long, hot, final kiss before lying down beside me. Our bodies were now spent, our minds were at ease, and all was suddenly quiet except for the rain, which continued to pour from the sky and clatter against the roof.

"Have you ever considered transferring to San Francisco?" I asked.

"As of this moment—yes. Have you ever thought about moving to Hawaii?"

"As of this moment—yes."

Those were our final words as we drifted off to sleep, with our relationship finally re-consummated and my sins apparently forgiven for the moment.

CHAPTER TWENTY

A Plot so Thick You Could Eat It With a Fork

The rain was all but gone as I opened my eyes and looked out to see a beautiful blue sky. I sat up slowly and carefully to let my head adjust to the movement, as I was definitely feeling the effects of a night of far too much alcohol. I took a look around and saw that Violet was nowhere to be seen, so I stood upon wobbly legs to go use the bathroom before exploring the house to find my elusive hostess. I brushed my teeth, took a long well needed horse piss, then set off and soon found her out sitting on the deck, where she was holding a mug of steaming hot coffee and enjoying the view.

"Morning, sunshine," I said.

"Morning. I have coffee ready for you in the kitchen," she said, as she started to get up.

"Stay where you are. I'll get it."

I walked into the kitchen and grabbed my coffee before rejoining her on the deck, where I sat in the adjacent chair. I brought the mug to my lips and took a sip and instantly felt better the minute the warm brown liquid hit my palette. She reached over and placed her hand on my leg, and I placed my hand on hers, and the two of us enjoyed a nice quiet moment of morning-after epic sex intimacy. Sometimes people awoke after a night of passion feeling awkward, but such was not the case today. I felt as though I was in the right place, sitting with the right woman, and enjoying a beautiful morning in paradise. I might have even described it as the beginnings of love, but it was still a little early for such bold proclamations.

"What's on the agenda today?" she asked.

"The gunsmith again, though I'm a little afraid to visit anybody considering our luck."

"Yeah, no shit."

"Still, he's the only real lead we have at the moment."

We sat and sipped our coffee and watched as planes full of tourists flew by on their approach to Honolulu airport while, below them, numerous fishing and pleasure boats plied the calm morning waters. Eventually Violet stirred and set down her cup.

"Hungry?"

"Starving."

"Well, sit here and relax while I make us a quick breakfast."

"I can help."

"I got it. You just relax."

Violet took my coffee cup, refilled it, and returned a moment later and kissed me as she set it down.

"Sweet Lord, woman, between last night and this morning, I'm thinking I should propose."

"It's best to wait until you've tried my cooking."

"OK, fine, I'll wait until after breakfast."

She smiled and headed to the kitchen, and fifteen minutes later she appeared with two plates, and each was piled high with scrambled eggs, ham, potatoes, and freshly cut pineapple. Looking at the feast, I seriously wondered if I should indeed propose. Between last night and this morning, this really was heaven on earth—and that wasn't easy to find. We plunged headlong into breakfast then, after finishing and cleaning up the kitchen, decided it was at last time to get cracking on proving Jessica's innocence.

"You can use my shower if you want, but I imagine you'll probably want to take your coffee and go potty in the other bathroom."

"Do you have to say go potty? It kind of makes me feel like a three year old," I said.

"Would you prefer if I asked if you needed to take a shit?"

"Actually, yes."

"Well then, go take a shit like a big boy and make momma proud."

I left Violet and ventured into the guest room's bathroom, where I discovered, to my horror, that there was no lock. Fuck. This was not a good omen. I went back into the bedroom to look for a chair or anything that might serve to brace the door, but there was nothing of use except perhaps the bed. Clearly, it was too heavy to move in front of the door, and that meant I was going to have to dump fast and get the hell off the pot before Violet wandered in and inadvertently brought about some kind of catastrophic event. I hit the porcelain with my heart pounding, and I gave birth to my first intestinal child. So far so good. I finished off my coffee then set back to birthing the next and soon delivered yet another wonder unto the world. Fan-fucking-tastic! Apparently, I was the proud father of twins, though I would venture to say they looked less like their father and more like their mother, which I believe was a pulled pork sandwich. Either way, I was a proud and doting father until I reached over for toilet paper and instantly felt my insides turn to ice when I saw that the roll was empty. Somehow, I had been too stupid and impatient to check before I sat down. Oh heaven above have mercy. I suddenly heard footsteps approaching, so I reached around behind me and quickly flushed away the twins only an instant before Violet walked in holding an entire package of Costco toilet paper.

"Sorry, I forgot that I didn't have any in here."

Still in shock, I remained speechless with my eyes wide with terror.

"You OK?" she asked, looking concerned.

"Fine—it's just that…"

"Oh yeah, your bathroom thing. I'm sorry, I didn't mean to freak you out."

"It's more than that. You see, every time my morning dump get's interrupted, something terrible happens."

"Every time?"

"Pretty much."

"And you really believe this?"

"I do."

"They have drugs for this kind of thing."

"I'm serious. You've inadvertently just set some incredibly bad mojo in motion."

"Yeah, I guess we'll see," she said, as she threw me the toilet paper before turning and walking out of the bathroom.

Women—why was it so hard for them to understand how their actions could interact with the unseen forces of interconnectedness that existed between my dumps and fate. With a great deal of trepidation, I wiped and flushed yet again before heading back to Violet's bathroom, where I found her in the shower. I joined her and lathered up my hair, and I think she could see that I was still rattled by her intrusion, so she set about trying to mend my heart with a kiss before grabbing the soap and washing me from head to toe. It was a nice distraction and helped ease my feelings of foreboding, and even more so when she took special care to wash my favorite appendage particularly vigorously. We both entered the stream of water and were soon ready to towel off and get dressed.

I went with my same shorts, though Violet loaned me a clean T-shirt, which I feared belonged to her ex. It had an image of Princess Leia with her hand in Han Solo's pants, and the caption below the graphic read Han Job. Oh well, I was a Star Wars fan, and, least of all, I was in Hawaii, where clothing was all about simplicity. Anything more than shorts, T-shirt, and thongs and you were grossly overdressed. We brushed our teeth one last time and headed out to the Suburban, where I now had the difficult task of backing it out of her precariously thin driveway. We reached the street without losing so much as a side mirror, and I turned the hulking beast around and headed down the hill. We drove west, then turned north onto H2, where we reached the North Shore about thirty minutes later. The road wound along the ocean, and soon we were turning right onto Pupukea Rd until eventually reaching the entrance to Walther's Ranch.

All appeared quiet as we drove up and parked beside the same green Land Cruiser. The tractor and pickup truck were still there as well, so Walther was likely nearby. We knocked on the door and waited for some time but got no response. If he were working on a gun he might be wearing ear protection, but then he would also be firing it as well. Currently, the valley was as quiet as could be, and it caused Violet and me to exchange a nervous glance.

"Let's go around back and see if we can find him," I said.

"Yeah, good idea."

We walked around the house and found the back workshop was closed up tight, and there wasn't a soul in sight.

"Shit, I'm getting a bad feeling."

"Me too."

We walked back to the front and banged on the door but again got no response. I tried the doorknob and was surprised to find it unlocked, and I opened it, and Violet immediately drew her gun as we moved inside. We moved through the living room and passed through each area of the house before walking through the corridor and taking a quick glance in Walther's workshop to find it empty.

"Do you think they killed him too?" Violet asked.

"I sure hope not."

We headed back through the main house, then exited and walked out to the Suburban, where we paused and took a minute to look out at the farm and surrounding hills. I was hoping that Walther was somewhere out there tending to his animals or doing whatever farmers did, but it seemed doubtful. Suddenly, a shot rang out in the distance, and my immediate thought was that it was Walther testing a weapon. That is, until the bullet tore into the ground two feet from where Violet and I were standing. We dove for cover behind the Suburban as more shots rang out, and the entire area became engulfed by bullet impacts. I crawled to edge of the Suburban and tried to triangulate where our shooter was and soon realized that there was more than one and very likely at least three. Shooter one was directly across from us, high on the mountain, camouflaged in the lush greenery, and I made a mental note of his rough location by sighting in on a large palm tree before turning my attention to shooter two and three. They were spread out somewhere to the left and right, and both were equally well-hidden. Suddenly, a shot came from behind, and I realized that there was a forth sniper, and we were totally encircled and more or less completely fucked.

Violet had her pistol in her hand, and she was more than ready to return fire, but it would be mostly useless at this range. I therefore decided to pull out my phone and call for help, but, as luck would have it, I had no service. Violet also checked her phone but had the same provider and therefore the same lack of coverage. Wonderful. Now, we needed a landline or a miracle, and, as I didn't happen to notice Jesus lurking anywhere nearby, that left option one, which of course meant that we needed to go into Walther's house.

"Violet, I need you to fire a shot at each of our shooters, then we're going to run like hell for the house."

"Are you crazy? I can't hit shit at this range."

"I know, it's just a distraction to allow us a little time to get back inside the house."

Violet took a moment to gather her courage then leaned out and fired once in the general direction of each of our shooters. Right after the last shot, we ran like hell, and our covering fire was apparently ineffective, as bullets came raining down on us. Still, we made it into the house unscathed, and I went directly to Walther's landline to see if it had a dial tone. Of course, it was as dead as a doornail.

"Fuck! They obviously cut the line."

"How about his internet?" Violet asked.

"Good idea!"

We went to a computer that was nestled in a nearby hutch and tapped the keyboard. It came out of sleep mode, and I brought up Firefox and got the error message server not found. I looked under the desk and saw that he had DSL, which came in on the same line as the phone, so it was completely useless.

"Let me guess—he has DSL," Violet said.

"Yeah, so we need a new plan."

"I thought a moment and realized I was forgetting the obvious fact that we were in a gunsmith's house, and what did gunsmiths have in their houses? Fucking guns! If we were properly armed, we might stand a chance of making it out alive.

"Let's go to the workshop!" I said.

Violet obviously knew what I was thinking, as she followed me through the house to Walther's workshop, where I went to the wall that held all of his various gun projects. There, exactly where he'd placed it the day before, was Walther's baby—his beloved brand new sniper rifle. I pulled it out and smiled at Violet.

"The equalizer," I said.

"I suppose that Walther's probably dead isn't he," Violet said, sadly.

"Maybe," I said, as I checked the action and suddenly

smiled as I spied something unusual.

"Or maybe not. It seems he left a note folded up in the breach."

I unfolded it and read it aloud.

"Dear Tag and Violet. I really enjoyed our time together yesterday and decided to heed your warning after I spotted strangers moving around the periphery of my property early this morning. I therefore slipped out the back and went for a little jog to visit the friend I mentioned. Hopefully you won't need this rifle, but please enjoy it should the need arise. Merry Christmas, Walther."

"Finally a little good news," Violet said.

"Yeah, and if we can just stay alive, we'll have our first day without some kind of tragedy."

The sniper rifle had four clips, and each one held ten rounds. That meant we had forty chances to turn the tables on our attackers and get the fuck off the farm. Even if I could just get some shots close, they would likely change their firing positions, and it would give us the time we needed to drive the Suburban until we had enough cell signal to call in the Cavalry. I hit the switch for the garage door, and, after it was only a foot or so off the ground, I hit the stop button. I slid a clip into the rifle, chambered a round, and dropped onto the floor and slithered outside. There, I moved slowly and purposefully across the fifteen feet of open space then crawled under the table and began methodically searching the hill for the bad guys. Right now, they would be doing the same thing as me—looking for targets, so my goal was to beat them to the punch, or, more accurately, the shot. I started with shooter number two, the one on the far left, and began meticulously searching for any kind of anomaly. Unfortunately, modern camouflage was designed using computers to create disruption patterns that our brains couldn't recognize, and that meant I was looking for a veritable needle in a haystack.

I continued to scan in a grid pattern, looking for anything out of the ordinary, when luck gave me my first opportunity. The shooter moved. It was subtle, but through my sniper scope it was as plane as day, and now that I had a target, it was time for a little payback. I used the built-in laser range finder to determine the distance then adjusted the scope accordingly. Next, I tried to do a little wind calculation, which was my weakest link because my target was at a higher elevation and therefore, likely in a windier area than my own. I watched a tree sway in the breeze then estimated there to be about a ten mile per hour crosswind. Now, all I had to do was set my eyes on the target and adjust my aim accordingly. Close was all I needed.

I slowed my breathing until I could feel each individual heartbeat, and soon I could see the slow constant tremor of each one as it passed from my body to the weapon and into the scope. At last I found my rhythm and waited until I was between beats, then squeezed off my first shot. It impacted two feet left of my target, as it was indeed windier up on the mountain. The next shot would be better, and, as I adjusted my aim, the guy picked up his gear and scampered into the surrounding trees. I had one out of the way—at least temporarily.

I moved my aim right to search for the guy I had designated as shooter number one, or, unofficially, the middle man. Every second was critical, as I knew that the longer it took to find him, the higher the odds were that he or one of his friends might find me. When the fucker first fired at us, I had used a particularly tall palm tree on the far side of the ranch to mark shooter one's general location. I found the tree, then moved up the hill and scanned the mountainside but didn't get any movement. Obviously, this guy was better at holding tight to his position, so I therefore used landmarks to make a mental grid then started again but thought about where I would have chosen to hole up. There was a large lava rock outcrop with a dense thicket of trees, and I was pretty sure that's where I'd be, as it offered plenty of cover and a nice flat firing position. I visually scoured the area but still couldn't see the shooter, so I decided to wing it and put one in the center. Again, I slowed my breathing and waited until I was between heartbeats before squeezing off a shot. It impacted within six inches of where I was aiming, and suddenly a figure sprang up and ran into the cover of the nearby trees. Two down, or, more accurately, two on the run.

I scanned right and looked for lucky number three and didn't have to go very far before I saw a figure already running deeper into the trees. Apparently, they were in radio contact, and shooter two had just warned number three to bug out and reform in a new location. It was therefore safe to assume that shooter number four on the opposite side would be doing the same, which was both good and bad news. It was good because we had a small window of opportunity but bad because we'd have no idea where they would be until they started shooting at us again. Time to roll. I stood up and ran for the workshop, then Violet and I raced through the house and out to the Suburban. We reached it without incident, and I started it up and slammed it into reverse, and we accelerated backwards down the driveway, though I waited until I was doing at least twenty five miles per hour before I spun the wheel and hit the brakes. This brought the Suburban around a hundred and eighty degrees, and I put the pedal on the floor, and off we went, leaving behind a massive cloud of dust. Now, the race was on, and our goal was to reach cell phone coverage, call in the cavalry, and hopefully survive. Their goal was to reform, take up new firing positions, and kill us. It wasn't exactly encouraging, but at least it wouldn't be a boring afternoon.

"So, what do you think about my whole interrupted dump curse now?" I asked.

"I still think it's bullshit, and this is all a coincidence."

Violet pulled out her phone, gazed at the screen, and suddenly looked unhappy.

"Fuck!" she said.

"What is it?"

"My battery just died."

"It's the curse."

I looked at my screen and saw that I finally had a signal and was relieved that at least one of our phones was functioning. Just as I brought up my contacts menu, shots started ringing out from somewhere off to our right. Apparently shooter number four had found a new firing position. I varied our speed, and steered in a serpentine pattern, but it wasn't enough to keep a lucky shot from passing through the back right door and imbedding into the seat. They would have all of their fire teams triangulated and ready any second, so it was even more imperative to find cover and call for help.

"When we drive into that low section by the river, I'm going to stop, so we can continue on foot," I said.

"Isn't it better to keep going?"

"No, the rest of the road runs straight through the center of the valley, and we'll be too exposed."

Violet didn't look all that convinced, but she was apparently willing to trust my judgement for the moment. The road dipped down as it neared the river, and we were enveloped in a canopy of greenery that would serve as decent temporary cover. We crossed the bridge, and I stopped the Suburban and took out my phone and dialed Frank, who thankfully picked up on the second ring.

"What's going on, Finn?"

"We're in a shit ton of trouble and need the cavalry."

"Where are you?"

"Up at the gunsmith's ranch."

"Sweet Jesus. What are you doing back up there?"

"We were hoping to talk to our best lead."

"Did you find him?"

"No, but we do need help exfiltrating from a hot LZ."

"Who do you want? National guard, police, or FBI?"

"All of them—and as soon as possible."

"Got it. Keep your head down. Help is on the way."

"Thanks," I said, hitting the end button.

"So, what now?" Violet asked.

"We need to find a safe spot while we wait for the cavalry."

"Can I see your phone?" Violet asked.

"Sure. You calling the Bureau?

"Of course."

"OK, but I think Frank's already doing that."

"Then we'll both be calling."

Violet dialed a number and spoke with an FBI operator and relayed our current predicament. A moment later, her call was transferred to someone else, and her demeanor changed, which gave me the distinct feeling that she was getting chewed out—obviously by her ex.

"Dave, don't worry, I'm going to be fine, and no, do not come up here. Dave? Dave?"

Apparently he had hung up.

"All right, we need to find better cover. We're sitting ducks in this Suburban, and, more importantly, I can't remember if I got the extra insurance coverage, so we should draw their fire away from it," I said.

"Very funny, but isn't it safer to remain with the vehicle?"

"No, and instead, I'm going to use it as a decoy to buy us a little time. In the meanwhile, I'm going to need you to wait here for a minute."

"You're not going to take off and leave me here are you?"

"Hell no, I'll be back in two seconds."

"One-thousand-one—one-thousand-two," she counted.

"OK fine, ten seconds."

"And not a second longer."

Violet stepped out of the vehicle and watched anxiously as I drove up to edge where the greenery gave way to open pasture land. There, I hit the brake pedal, grabbed the sniper rifle, then released the brake and closed the door behind me to watch as it drove bravely forth unto its inevitable demise. I slipped back down to Violet and led her into a patch of ferns, which would allow us to remain hidden while we tracked the Suburban's progress. Less than a hundred yards down the road, the sound of bullets impacting steel filled the air, and I said a silent goodbye to yet another rental car. Damn, I was just getting used to that Suburban.

The frequency of shots dramatically increased, which meant that they had gotten their ranges correct, and all four shooters were currently pulverizing my beloved behemoth.

"You were saying?" I said.

"OK, you were right about us ditching the Suburban."

"Indeed, now let's get moving. Our lives, and, in turn,

our ability to fornicate lie in the balance."

CHAPTER TWENTY-ONE
A River Runs Through It

The river wound across then down through the valley and would hopefully provide decent cover while we trekked towards the main highway. We climbed down closer to the waters edge and made our way through the dense foliage until our only option to continue meant slipping into the water. It was about two feet deep in this part, and it made the going a little slow, and I was suddenly reminded of the Humphrey Bogart movie African Queen.

In it, he was a gin-swilling riverboat captain who was persuaded by a straight laced missionary to use his boat to attack an enemy warship. To perform this feat, he was forced at one point to literally drag his boat through a leach filled stream in order to reach the lake. Our stream didn't have any leeches, and our lake would likely be the FBI's local SWAT Team, so my task somehow felt a bit easier. Still,

I had a stream to traverse and two people to keep safe from a number of armed hostiles who had the advantage of the high ground. Fuck it—if those fuckers really wanted to kill us that badly, then they would have to come down here and fucking find us first.

We continued on, and the shooting stopped for the moment, which meant that our enemy was either closing in on our location or high tailing it out of here. Unfortunately, it turned out to be the latter, as, just as we came around a bend, I heard a feint noise a little ways off to our left.

"Did you hear that?" I asked.

"Yeah, it kind of sounded like a twig snapping."

"Shit, I was thinking the same thing."

I shimmied up to the edge of the stream and did a quick sweep with the rifle's scope, and, there, two hundred yards away, was a person in fatigues moving quickly along the tree line. He made an enticing target but shooting him meant giving away our position, and, right now, anonymity was more important than revenge. I continued to sweep the edge of the tree line and soon found another of the shooters moving in the same direction.

"It would appear that they're trying to head us off at the base of the valley," I said, to Violet.

"Seriously now, who in the hell would attempt to murder an FBI Agent and a special investigator for the fucking vice president of the United States?"

"Very good question, and the answer is someone with a serious grudge and a major league set of balls."

"Yeah, so what do we do now?"

"I could move up the valley and draw them back this way while you continue on and slip out. It would probably buy us enough time until help arrived."

"Fuck that. We're staying together."

"OK, but that means we need to cover some serious ground. You up for some running and gunning?"

"Do you think I got this body sitting at a desk?"

She had a point, and so we turned around and started moving up the stream, hoping to gain distance, and, therefore, precious time. As we came around a small bend in the river, a bullet suddenly ricocheted off a rock to our right, and it sent up a spray of fragments. Violet and I ducked down and crawled on our hands and knees for the opposite bank, where I slithered up the side and found a small opening between two rocks that I could use to look for the stray shooter. I scanned the horizon, desperately hoping that I could find him before he found me, and I was relieved when a small glint of light caught my eye. I looked more closely and found my shooter was lying down and apparently waiting to ambush us in the event that we doubled back. Fuck, these fuckers knew what the fuck they were doing.

Now that we were surrounded and they had a good idea of our position, there was also no sense in hiding any more, and that meant I finally got to shoot back. I relaxed my breathing, adjusted for distance and wind, then pulled the trigger. The shot was on target but I'd underestimated the distance, and the bullet dropped down and impacted into the ground and sprayed the shooter with a cloud of fragments. He stood and ran for cover, and I shot two more times, and, while both missed, they had at least made the fucker run a lot faster. Now, we had to be extremely careful, as their friends would be coming this way.

"Time to move downstream."

"Wait, won't they be waiting for us?"

"No, they'll be expecting us to run like hell upstream, so my goal is to slip through them."

I'm not sure Violet agreed with my strategy, but she followed me, and we began moving quickly downstream. The water made it a slow going at times and a little noisy, but we didn't have time to care, as our goal was to keep moving then go full stealth only when they got close. Ten long minutes passed, and I was sweating profusely and looked over to see how Violet was doing. She appeared to be just fine in spite of a nice patch of sweat that had formed on her chest and was making her breasts, or, more specifically, her nipples somewhat visible beneath her white shirt. She of course caught me looking and scowled.

"Seriously? We're on the run from a bunch of killers, and you're checking out my boobs?"

"Well, boobs and nipples, but I would think you'd see that as a compliment."

She thought for a moment then nodded.

"Annoyingly, I suppose you're right."

We continued on, and just ahead there was a waterfall, so we needed a detour. I stepped up onto a rock to see where we could climb around and froze when I heard the sound of footsteps coming up the river.

"They're making a lot of fucking noise, so, I'm thinking they're beating the bushes in order to try and flush us out like grouse."

"The birds?"

"Yeah, and in Scotland they have beaters that flush out the grouse, so that hunters can shoot them."

"I get it. We're the grouse, so we obviously need to hide—but where?"

"Did you see Rambo?"

"One, two, three, and four?"

"Two."

"Yeah, why?"

"I'm thinking about performing a reenactment of the part where Rambo is being chased through the jungle by the Viet Cong, and he hides, only to reappear when he opens his eyes to reveal he's encased in the muddy hillside?"

"Please don't tell me we're going to bury ourselves in the mud."

"We're not, but we are going to hide right here behind the waterfall, then let them go right past us."

"What about your phone? It is our only link to the outside world."

"It's waterproof."

"No, it's not. I have the same fucking one."

"No, you have a lowly eight while this is the ten."

"Oh, well hello, Mr. Fancy Pants."

"Hey, I live on the water. Do you know how many fucking iPhones I've accidentally dropped in the bay?"

"Plenty I'm sure, but what I'd like to know is if the ten can withstand being run over by a car. If so, then we're going to the Apple Store—assuming we survive, that is."

"We're going to survive all right, as long as we get our asses into the water."

We slipped into the cool water and started swimming towards the falls on the far end, as I figured that we could hold up in the relief behind it and slip under if anyone got too close. The moving water also meant that the bottom was constantly being churned up with sediment, and that would limit visibility beneath the surface and make for an even better hiding spot. We passed under the cascade of water and quietly waiting for our pursuers. A minute later, a guy carrying a sniper rifle appeared from down river, and he was fully decked out in combat gear that even included a balaclava to cover his face. More unsettling was that he moved with the practiced efficiency of a highly trained soldier, and that meant he had his weapon at the ready as he visually swept the countryside for signs of us. Thankfully, we'd been traveling via the river and therefore had left no trace of our passage.

Violet reached over and gently squeezed my arm, and I motioned for her to move even farther back behind the waterfall. Meanwhile, the guy stopped and spoke into his head mic then waited with his gaze unfaltering and his weapon at the ready. A moment later, three more men arrived, and they did a quick visual sweep of the area before one guy, the apparent leader, pointed in our direction. It was a smart move, as it was the first place I'd look. I squeezed Violet's hand and pointed down, and she understood and waited for my next signal. Two of the men started walking over, so I squeezed her hand again, and down we went. I looked up through the blurry haze of the water and watched as the men approached with their rifles at the ready. I glanced over at Violet, and she gave me a thumbs up, so I turned my gaze back to the men and watched as they continued to stand there. It felt like minutes passed, but it was probably no more than seconds, and I was starting to feel that burning in my lungs that occurred when your body's need for precious oxygen overruled your mind. Violet appeared to be feeling the same way, so I took hold of her hand and gave it a reassuring squeeze. Just a little longer and they would give up and leave. We locked eyes again, and I could see she was distressed, but she was able to use her mind to override her body's desire to surface. At long last, the two men turned and headed back to rejoin the others, and it allowed Violet and me to rise to the surface and take that glorious first breath. We had to be careful not to make too much noise, but, thankfully, the sound of the waterfall covered our labored breathing as we floated there and took in precious oxygen. The men exchanged some words then hightailed it down the valley.

"Good job," I whispered to Violet.

"That was getting a little tough at the end."

"No shit, and you were amazing."

"I was just trying to stay alive."

"Believe me, I've spent a lot of time with some very tough, very resilient people, and few to none of them could have handled themselves as well as you have today."

"You're only saying that because you like my tits."

"Well, of course I like your tits, but I also like your face, ass, shapely thighs, and of course your personality as well as your stubborn nature."

"You do realize you mentioned personality second to last."

"Yeah, but at least I mentioned it."

"Very funny," she said, as she gave me a friendly though strong punch in the arm.

"OK, fine, I find it all equally great—even the stubborn-ness."

"Good, now let's get the fuck out of here."

She moved closer and kissed me, and I could feel that her cheeks were cold from the water, but her lips were warm. Adrenaline was truly an effective aphrodisiac, and we were suddenly enjoying a very pleasant and impromptu meeting of the mouths. Sadly, I was pretty sure it was the first time I had kissed a girl beneath a waterfall, so, of course, the moment had to be overshadowed by the presence of a pack of ruthless killers. After parting lips, we heard a helicopter off in the distance, and I desperately hoped that it might be the cavalry. Violet and I climbed out of the river and up to where we had a better view and saw the helicopter coming in from the direction of Walther's house. As it grew closer, I could see it was the Air National Guard, and we began to wave our arms in the hope that they would see us. Annoyingly, it flew past and appeared to land lower in the valley. Shit—we were still on our own, so we set off down river towards our potential rescuers but took it slow and kept our movements stealthy. A short distance away, we heard numerous footfalls coming from lower in the valley, and we paused to listen.

"Do you think it's the good guys or the bad guys?" Violet asked.

"No idea, so we better hide just to be safe."

We moved away from the stream and slipped into a crevice behind a massive boulder that would give us a good observation point as well as an excellent field of fire should we end up in a shootout. I kept my finger resting on the trigger as we listened to the footsteps draw closer. We still didn't hear any talking, and I took it as a bad omen, because if they were the good guys then they should be calling out to us. We both therefore sat there as still as the earth beneath us until at last hearing a voice that we both thankfully recognized. It was Violet's ex-boyfriend Dave, and this time I was actually happy to see him.

"Violet!" he called out.

"I'm here," she responded.

Violet and I climbed out from behind the boulder and saw that we were surrounded by the FBI's local SWAT team as well as Dave, who was looking a bit harried.

"Why the hell didn't you say something sooner?" Violet asked angrily.

"We didn't want to give our position away until we were certain it was you."

"Well then how the hell did you know we were even here?"

"We've been tracking your phones, except yours went dead a little while ago," he said, to Violet.

Two thumbs up for the FBI. For once, I was extremely grateful for their diligence, expertise, and intrusive nature. As we stood there feeling relieved to have survived, Dave grew oddly quiet and looked puzzled as he stared at my chest. For some reason his puzzlement transformed into outright anger, and his face became flushed with blood.

"Is that my T-shirt?" he asked.

"Um—no."

"It is, isn't it?"

"Dude, with all that's just happened, you're curious about my fucking T-shirt?"

"Yeah—as how many Han Job T-shirts can there be on the island of Oahu?"

"I'm guessing at least two."

"Dave, who cares about a fucking T-shirt? The important thing is that we're alive," Violet interjected.

He continued to stare at the shirt for a moment, but fortunately he gave it a rest, and we began making our way south to where the FBI had set up a temporary base camp. We reached it about ten minutes later to find a swarm of agents and a number of local police.

"Where's the Air National Guard helicopter?" I asked.

"We told them we had the situation covered, so it left."

"Any sign of the bad guys that were trying to kill us?"

"Nope, they must have left in a real hurry when they saw us arrive."

"Figures. They were obviously professionals and knew when the hell it was time to exfiltrate the area."

"Speaking of which—mind telling me what the hell you two were doing up here?" Dave asked.

"We were hoping to meet with our last decent lead," Violet said.

"Did you find him?"

"No, we didn't."

"Well, could you at least give me a quick rundown of what the hell is going on here? I mean some people just tried to murder a federal agent for fuck's sake."

"And me," I added.

"Yeah, and you," Dave said, with a distinct lack of interest.

I realized that Dave obviously didn't know or understand the extent and importance of our investigation, so it was probably time to explain it all. Violet looked to me, and I nodded my approval, so she proceed to give him a quick accounting of the situation and all of the events that had transpired thus far. He listened without interrupting then took a long, quiet moment to think after she finished.

"Seriously now, Violet, do you know how extremely stupid it was to be this far off the grid without any backup?" he asked.

He was technically correct, though I would have never suspected that Violet and I would have been put in the crosshairs. I suppose it did, however, provide us with yet another clue as to the ruthlessness of our enemy. They would apparently go to all ends to achieve their goals and kill anyone who got in the way—even a federal officer.

"Yes, now chill out, Dave." Violet said.

Dave made a pained face and groaned as he turned to rejoin his fellow agents while Violet and I waited on the periphery. Fifteen minutes later, it was officially time to clear out and head back to the Bureau's headquarters to write up an incident report. With my Suburban out of commission, it was also time to get a new rental car, though there weren't any local offices on the north shore. That meant we would be riding with Dave all the way back to Honolulu. Lovely. We loaded up in Dave's car, which was a white government issued Ford Fusion identical to Violet's, then headed back towards the main highway. Violet inexplicably chose to sit in the backseat, and that put me next to Dave—something that I imagine made both of us uncomfortable. The first few minutes went by quietly, and no one spoke a word until Dave looked over and glanced at the T-shirt.

"So, where did you get the shirt?" he asked.

I looked at Violet then back to Dave before responding.

"Amazon."

"Good answer."

I thought so.

"How about we grab a coffee at the Starbucks. I'm suddenly feeling a little under caffeinated," I said.

"Coffee? Seriously?" Dave asked.

"Yeah, I could use a little pick me up after all that running and gunning, but don't worry your pretty little head, as it's my treat."

"Fine."

We reached the main highway, and Dave made a right and took us into the small shopping center that housed the Starbucks. The three of us exited the car and walked in to find it fairly busy with the midday lunch rush in effect. We eventually got to the front counter, and Violet and I ordered grande coffees with room for cream.

"You really buying?" Dave asked.

"Yeah, it's the least I can do."

"All right then. I'll take a caramel macchiato and a grilled ham and cheese panini."

"That's kind of a dick move," Violet said.

"What? He offered."

"Coffee—not lunch."

"It's OK," I said.

We walked over and joined the small crowd of people waiting for their drinks, and Dave again looked at my shirt.

"So, how much was it?"

"Twenty dollars."

"Does that include shipping?"

"No, I have Amazon Prime, so the two day shipping was

free."

"Good for you."

Jesus, Dave really wasn't giving up on the whole T-shirt thing. If he loved this fucking T-shirt so much, he should have taken it with him when they broke up. Our coffees arrived, but Dave had ordered a fancy drink and sandwich, so it would be another five minutes before he got his order. In the meanwhile, Violet and I added cream and stood there enjoying our coffees.

"Do you know how many calories there are in a caramel macchiato?" I asked Dave.

"I don't care. I like them."

"Two hundred and forty, and sixty of those are from fat."

"Not a problem. As you can see I stay in shape."

"Yeah, though not if you drink too many of those, but don't worry, because a chubby face will make you look younger."

Dave stewed for a moment then turned to me.

"Why don't you man up and tell me how the fuck it is that you came to be wearing my shirt?"

"Dave, enough with the fucking shirt!" Violet said.

"Yeah, Dave," I added.

"Honestly, it's time for you to shut the fuck up. It's just a shirt, Dave. Let it go," Violet said.

"Yeah Dave," I added.

"And you be quiet too. Stop provoking him. You're both acting like children."

"He is," I said.

"No, he is," Dave countered.

"No, he is."

"No, he is."

Violet turned and walked outside, as she was apparently done with both of us for the moment. Of course, I couldn't blame her, as it had been a particularly stressful morning, and now she had two fully grown adults arguing like children.

"See what you've done," I said.

"See what you've done," he responded.

"No, you."

"No, you times ten."

"No, you times infinity."

"You can't say that."

"I just did."

Thankfully, Dave's order came up at that moment, and we stopped arguing and walked outside to join Violet, who was sitting on the curb and looking out towards the ocean.

"You OK?" I asked.

"Yeah, I was just wondering what the hell we do now. All of the leads and potential witnesses are missing or dead, which means this case is sucking some serious dick at the moment."

"And not in the good handcuffed to the bed kind of way," I added.

Violet and I shared a little smile, and Dave groaned.

"Can we go now," he asked.

We loaded up in Dave's car, and Violet again relegated

me to the front seat, and we drove to the FBI's office. It took about twenty of the longest most quiet and uncomfortable minutes I had ever spent in a vehicle, and so I was relieved to at last open my door and step out into the warm afternoon sun. We walked inside and went upstairs, where Violet wrote out an after-action report of our encounter. The FBI, like every other law enforcement agency, took it very seriously when someone tried to kill one of their agents, and, two hours later, we were ready to go to the closest Hertz rental car agency. As we were about to leave, Violet's father walked in and immediately hugged her.

"Honey, I heard what happened. Are you OK?" he asked.

"I'm fine, thanks to Finn."

Violet's dad turned his attention to me and smiled.

"I'm glad to see you kept your promise, Tag. Now, How are you doing?" he asked.

"Fine, but I'm really sorry that Violet got dragged into this mess."

"She didn't join the FBI to play it safe, but, either way, you brought my little girl home safe and sound."

Dave, who was standing nearby, watched the exchange and looked particularly agitated as he walked over.

"I helped too," he said.

"Oh, hi, Dave."

"Hello, Ed. I didn't know that you knew Tag," Dave said.

"Yeah, we met last night."

"Over dinner at the Kalili home, where I also helped him wax the GTR."

"How nice of you," Dave said, as he covertly gave me the finger.

"Why don't we get some lunch, and you two tell me what happened," Ed suggested.

"Sounds good," I said.

"Where should we go?" Dave interjected.

"You already ate," I said.

"That was just a snack."

"Tag, I want to bring you to my favorite spot. I've been taking Violet there since she was a little girl, and I know that you're going to love it," Ed said.

I didn't even have to look at Dave to know that he was majorly annoyed at this rare privilege. Being taken to a favorite family restaurant hinted that I might be way more immersed in Violet's life than Dave would have ever guessed, but what can I say? I'm a people person. We left the FBI office and climbed into Violet's Dad's GTR, with Violet in one of the small back seats and me in the front. This time, I was happy about the seating, as it allowed me a hell of a lot more leg room and kept me from getting car sick. As it turned out, Ed drove rather aggressively, but then it wouldn't be very fun owning a GTR if you drove like a pussy. The best part was that Dave was following in his Fusion, and he was having to do his best to keep up.

We pulled into a small shopping center just below Diamond Head and parked in the outermost parking space—obviously as a deterrent to door dings. I knew the feeling and generally did my best to park well away from other motorists. Dave, however, parked directly in front of the restaurant, where he chose to be sandwiched between two beater cars that I wouldn't have gone near for fear of contracting a communicable disease. As we passed, Ed gave Dave a subtle, though disapproving, glance to relay this very feeling, and Dave, of course, completely misunderstood.

"Check it out! Right in front! How lucky is that?" Dave said, excitedly.

Ed ignored him and proceeded to hold the door for Violet and me, but I paused and smiled back at Dave, as I wasn't sure if he understood his faux pas. He apparently did, because he gave me the finger, so I proceeded to blow him a kiss before turning my attention back to the restaurant. The place was called Fat Momma's and was crowded with locals, which I always took as a good sign. It's easy to lure in a hungry tourist, but keeping the locals coming back for more meant delivering a good product.

The waitress came over and said hello to Ed and Violet, so it was obvious that they ate here fairly often. She then led us to a booth near the window and handed only Dave and me menus before leaving to get us water. I decided it was a moment to rely on my host, and I left mine closed and asked Ed what to order.

"If you're hungry, I'd go with the barbecue plate, as it comes with barbecued pork, rice, macaroni salad, and kimchee."

"Done," I said.

Dave, who was sitting and still going over the menu, looked up uncomfortably.

"I'll go with the that too," he said, closing his menu.

I could tell by the look in his eyes that he was as full as fuck from that Starbuck's sandwich and caramel macchiato, but he didn't want to look like an ass in front of Violet's father. This was going to be fun. Our waitress returned with our waters, then took our order, which consisted of four barbecue plates.

"I hope you're hungry," Ed said.

"Starving," I said, looking at Dave.

Less than ten minutes later, we had four steaming hot plates piled high with delicious looking food, and everyone dug in as though it were our last meal on earth. Well, everyone except Doug, who ate quite daintily or perhaps girlishly, though that would be an unfair description considering the fact that Violet, a female of the species, was devouring her food like a rabid coyote. Ed finished his last bite and leaned back in his chair then took a sip of his water before letting out a long sigh.

"How about you guys fill me in on today's exciting events," he said.

Violet proceeded to tell her father about the morning's dramatic encounter, and he spent a minute thinking and rubbing his temples before he spoke.

"Shit. You're really between a rock and hard place here. There's no doubt this is all part of a much larger, and highly sophisticated conspiracy, but it still doesn't take away from the basic fact that you have no definitive or tangible way to dispute the evidence that points to your friend as the killer. GSR, blood spatter, ballistics, surveillance footage—all that stuff looks pretty convincing to the police, and, more importantly, a jury."

"It's incredibly frustrating to have the truth be so obvious yet have no tangible way to prove it," I said.

"Well, you know the old Sherlock Holmes adage? Once you eliminate the impossible, whatever remains, no matter how improbable, must be the truth."

"Then there must be quite an improbable truth."

Ed asked for the check then turned his gaze to Dave, as he hadn't yet finished his plate.

"You're still not done?"

"Come on. Finish it up, rook," I added.

"I'm suddenly feeling a little full. Maybe I'll take the rest to go."

Ed regarded him and looked a bit displeased, and I had to laugh to myself now that I knew about Ed's predilection not to waste food. Classic. I almost felt bad for Dave—almost. Ed suddenly turned and read the front of my shirt and gazed at me with a disapproving look on his face.

"Han Job? Seriously now?"

I looked at Dave and noticed he was smiling smugly having just achieved a minor victory in the subtle, though hotly contested battle for Violet's affections—a key component being her father's approval.

"It's Dave's," I said.

Dave's face abruptly turned red, and he looked so angry that I feared his body might jettison his head before it exploded, but, before he could say a word, Ed turned to him and raised a disapproving eyebrow.

"Seriously, Dave. It's time to grow up."

Dave was about to say something but decided to remain stoically quiet, though I was pretty sure I would hear a lot more once we were away from Violet's father. Ed absolutely refused my offer to buy then paid the check, and we said goodbye to Dave and headed over to Hertz to get my third rental of the week. The pickings were slim, and my only options were a tiny Kia Rio or a large Dodge Grand Caravan minivan. I decided to go with the Caravan, as it afforded slightly more protection and seating for seven. It was white and loaded with every feature known to mankind, so it was a veritable party van and therefore needed a cool nickname. I decided the ultimate party guy was David Lee Roth and named my new vehicle the Rothster—regardless of the fact that it was nearly impossible to say a *th* sound directly before an *st* sound without feeling as though you had a major speech impediment. We said goodbye to Violet's dad then headed northeast towards the resort, and, about five minutes into the journey, my phone rang, and I looked down to see that it was frank calling, so I hit the answer button on the steering wheel. Modern life was way too convenient, and I couldn't help but wonder what the hell we did before bluetooth. I suppose we answered our phones, got distracted, and then rammed into other cars.

"Finn, you there?"

"I'm here, Frank. What's up?"

"We need to do another damage control meeting to-night. Can you make it?"

"Of course. Where and when?"

"Seven o' clock in John's suite."

"We'll be there."

"Great, thanks."

I hit the end button and looked at the road ahead, and was keenly aware that we would soon join in yet another damage control meeting, and it was therefore not likely to be a very fun evening.

CHAPTER TWENTY-TWO
Damage Control Part Deux

I pulled in and parked next to an identical minivan, only it was metallic red instead of white. I always liked red cars, especially sporty ones like Ferraris, but in a hot climate like Hawaii, I'd take plain old white any day of the week. Violet and I exited the Rothster and started walking towards my room, where we would get to take a little time to clean ourselves up. Running around in the country, fording streams, and dodging bullets all day took a toll on your wardrobe, and both of us looked forward to showering and changing into some fresh clothes.

We entered my room and found the nerds playing D&D, and they were currently in the middle of a tense battle and didn't even manage so much as a friendly greeting.

"Hello, nerds. How was your day? Oh, ours was fine, except for the part where we had to evade a team of deadly snipers and barely managed to escape with our lives—but thanks for asking."

"Isn't that basically an average day for you?" Beeber asked, as he rolled a twenty sided die, then followed it up by rolling a ten sided die.

His first roll was to determine if he scored a hit, while the second was the amount of damage. I obviously knew this because I had been a member of their little D&D club many years back, and, while I totally enjoyed the experience, I generally kept that fact mostly to myself, as it didn't seem to improve my image with the ladies.

"Yes! Killed that motherfucker! Now, if you two want to see some real action you'd be playing with us," he said.

Violet and I exchanged a knowing glance then retreated to my bedroom, and I hit the bathroom first, as I needed to take a second number two after having had such an active day and eaten a large lunch. Just as I reached down to hit the lock, Violet called out from the other side of the door.

"No need to lock it. I learned my lesson, and I'm not coming within a hundred miles of that fucking bathroom until you give me the official all-clear."

"Good to know."

I decided to test fate and left the door unlocked as I strolled over and dropped down onto my porcelain teddy bear. Its cool embrace was at once gentle and comforting, and no matter how crazy the world became, I at least had this time to myself. This was my constant, my rudder in the storm of my harried existence. I wiggled a little, found my sweet spot, then let lose a formidable fart, and its loud report became the signal to sound the charge. At that point, a small, though brave, army of fecal soldiers leapt from my anus and took the battle to the bowl to guarantee yet another brilliant victory. Finished, I wiped, flushed, and washed my hands before going over and opening the door.

"Bravery won the day, and victory is mine," I said.

"Sounds epic, so I'm guessing everything came out all right."

"It sure did."

"Good—my turn."

I left Violet alone in the bathroom and went to the living room bar and poured a splash of vodka in a glass and sipped it slowly as I took a moment to think about the day's events. There was something in the back of my mind that was making my *scrot-sense* tingle, but I just couldn't put my finger on it yet. Oh well, time would tell. Violet poked her head out of the bedroom and smiled.

"Done," she said.

"Done? I couldn't have even farted in that little amount of time."

"Girls are magical."

"Well, your buttholes are anyway."

"And are breasts too apparently—considering the way you men constantly stare at them," Rachel added.

"Sorry, I missed the last thing you said, as I was too busy looking at your boobs."

"Very funny, but you're probably not actually joking."

"Sorry, missed that too," I said.

I joined Violet in the bedroom, and we stripped down and entered the shower and stood there for a long time and just let the water pour over our bodies. Feeling a bit better, I grabbed the shampoo and rubbed it into Violet's hair, then did the same to my own. Now it was time for the soap, and I lathered up my hands then sudsed her up, making sure I didn't miss the critical areas such as her buttocks and boobs. When I finished, she took hold of the soap and did the same to me, though her extra attention to Tag Junior brought on a mild semi. We rinsed then dried off before applying the usual pleasantries, and, feeling human again, we exited to the bedroom to get dressed. I put on my usual shorts but decided to dress it up with a short sleeve button up shirt. Violet, who had fortunately left her overnight bag in my room, donned a lovely red summer dress that I hadn't seen before. She smiled, did a turn, and I could already feel my balls ramping up semen production because of how nicely the dress hung on her curvaceous figure. It had a low cut top and spaghetti straps that negated the accompaniment of a bra, and it made her nipples very obvious underneath the thin fabric.

"I like the dress, but I love the nipples."

"Thanks, now let's get this over with, so we can come back, get drunk, and make sweet love all night long."

"Last night you wanted me to fuck your brains out. Tonight it's all about making sweet love. What the hell will we do tomorrow?"

"I'll leave that up to your imagination."

We rejoined the nerds in the living room and almost had to physically force them from their precious game. D&D was like heroin with Doug and Beeber, and both were fully addicted. They begrudgingly put down their pencils and dice, and we left my suite and walked over to John's room, where we found everyone looking particularly tense as they sat in his lounge. Stuart, Dexter, and Jeremy took up one couch, and they all had their laptops open and ready while Frank and Rex occupied the next one over. Opposite them was John, Jessica, Lux, and Corn, and that left one final couch empty. We took a seat, and, as luck would have it, I was only an arms length away from Corn, who had a plate full of french fries on his lap. They looked and smelled too good to resist, so I reached over and grabbed a couple then gave one to Violet, and she gobbled it down hungrily. I reached over for more, but this time Corn smacked my hand away.

"Easy there. I need the carbs," he said.

"No, you don't. That's your second order," Lux said, pulling the plate out of his hands and handing it to me.

Corn gave Lux a scowl then sat back in his chair and looked more like a scolded child than the Deputy Director of the CIA. I glanced over at the end table behind him, and there was indeed an empty plate. I loved fries as much as the next person, but two plates was pushing it. Clearly, Corn needed some serious intervention if he hoped to trim some of the extra girth he'd acquired since our time together in Pararescue. With the plate of fries now in my hot little hands, all the nerds partook and quickly decimated the pile, leaving me with only one sad little end piece. I guess playing D&D burned more calories than I thought. I popped the fry in my mouth, and John, seeing everyone was settled in, brought the meeting to order.

"Finn, do you want to fill everyone in on the latest?" he asked.

"Sure."

I went on to recap the day's traumatic events, and Jessica appeared to take it the worst. She slowly moved her head from side to side as she reached up and wiped tears from her eyes. Obviously, she was upset that so much turmoil seemed to be occurring on her account.

"It's not your fault. Whoever is behind this, has a problem with John. You're just the patsy," I said.

"Thanks, Tag, but it's still hard not to feel responsible."

"Believe me, you're not."

"So, our last, best lead has disappeared?" John asked.

"Yeah, but at least he might still be alive, so there's hope."

"Not much," Stuart said.

"Look, it's obvious that we have a major conspiracy here, so it's only a matter of time before the police come around and drop their investigation of Jessica," I said, trying to be optimistic.

"Be that as it may, we're almost out of time. The day after tomorrow John either declares he's running or not."

"There's got to be something we can do," Jessica pleaded.

"Well, we still have some other avenues we're pursuing," I said.

"Anything you'd like to mention? I know I'm not alone here in that I'd like to have at least one piece of good news so I can sleep tonight," Frank said.

"I think it's probably best none of you know the particulars at the moment, but my hope is that it will lead to something tangible or, more specifically, someone tangible."

"Well, you better hope so if we're going to have any chance of salvaging John's bid for president," Jeremy said.

"I think we should start preparing an official statement in case the police decide to make a public announcement that Jessica is the primary suspect," Stuart, the public relations guy, said.

"We'll do nothing of the sort. We're giving Tag two more days to pull a miracle out of his ass. If anyone can do it, he can," John said.

I was thankful for the vote of confidence, but I hoped I could actually live up to his praise, as I didn't exactly feel any miracles occupying my anus.

"We do have something positive here," I said.

"Which is?" Brent asked.

"The fact that they tried to kill Violet and me today means they're afraid we're getting close. That means we're on the right track."

"Let's hope so," Frank said.

"All right then, I believe we're done here for the moment. There's no need to drag this on any longer tonight. I'm officially ready for a drink," John declared.

"I'll join you," I said.

"Me too," Corn added.

The three of us stood and headed for the private bar on the other side of the room, and John set about making a pitcher of martinis. Finished, he handed each of us a glass, and I realized that it felt like old times—except for the whole murder conspiracy thing. I sipped my martini and instantly felt a mild cathartic release, though it would probably only last as long as the buzz. Eventually, I would sober up, and, in that moment, feel a great deal of anxiety for my friend's predicament. I had already felt bad enough during the first damage control meeting, but now, three days later, I felt even worse having not been able to unearth any physical proof of Jessica's innocence. Yes, it was obvious she hadn't murdered her ex-husband, but how in the hell could I prove it to the police?

"Corn, any luck on your end coming up with a possible bad guy?" I asked.

"Not yet, and besides, most of our assets are focused outside the country if you know what I mean. Plus, it's a little tricky, as we don't want Sasquatch to appear as though he's using government assets for his personal problems, but, either way, we haven't found shit."

"It's like we're up against fucking Professor Moriarty here," John said.

"Yeah, and this one is not elementary, my dear Sasquatch."

We continued to drink, and my guilt subsided a bit as my buzz increased. I took a second to look around the room and saw Violet sitting with Jessica and Lux, and the three of them were engaged in an animated conversation and already looked like old friends. That was probably a good thing, as Jessica needed all the moral support she could get at the moment. Violet noticed the ladies were all needing a fresh cocktail, and she stood up and came over to the bar. I refilled their glasses, and, as she headed back over to the ladies, the three of us menfolk watched her go.

"That is the hottest FBI agent I've ever seen," John said.

"No shit," Corn added.

"So, how is your relationship coming along?" John asked.

"It's better now. She even introduced me to her parents."

"Uh oh. Have you picked out a ring?"

"No, but I should."

"Yeah you should. Join the club, and give up your sordid bachelor ways."

"Says the guy who's still technically single."

"Not for long. I'm going to marry that girl even if she goes to prison, and I end up as a high school shop teacher."

"Don't worry. That'll never happen. You're not handy enough to teach shop."

"Not true. I made a chopping block once."

"Declaring a two by four a chopping block doesn't count."

"Bullshit. You could totally cut the cheese on it."

"Yeah, but not without getting splinters in your butthole."

"True, but regardless, I'm going to marry that woman—splinters and all."

Suddenly, the girls glanced over in our direction and gave us a strange look that seemed to hint that they were talking about them. Fucking women had the most powerful radar on the planet. It could cover vast distances, penetrate the thickest lies, and uncover even the most minute details, and, with that in mind, all three of us did our best to clear our minds and stare back dumbly. It appeared to work, because they soon returned to talking.

"Phew, that was a close one," John said.

"Yeah."

A moment later, Rex came to the bar for a drink.

"Spare a martini?" he asked.

"Of course. Anything for a fellow soldier."

I handed Rex a glass and noticed he had a bandage on the back of his hand.

"Anything serious?" I asked, pointing at his hand.

"Not unless you call getting slammed into the coral serious."

"Surfing or body boarding?"

"Surfing."

"You any good?"

"Apparently not."

We all laughed, then I topped off Rex's glass.

"It'll help with the pain, and, if your hand gets infected,

you can always pour it over the wound."

"Well, thanks, medic," Rex said, as he turned and re-joined Frank.

Eventually, everyone decided that we desperately needed to go to the restaurant and eat something before all of us got completely trashed, and so we headed downstairs and managed to get an enormous table that was reserved for private parties. Even better, was that it was completely open on the side facing the beach, and it allowed us to enjoy the warm tropical breeze coming in off the sea. The weather in Hawaii was always changing, however, and by the time dinner arrived, a rain squall had blown in off the dark Pacific. Back home in Sausalito, that might have been a pain in the ass, as it meant getting soaked as I walked from my car to my houseboat. Here, however, it was warm and welcomed as a brief respite from the heat, and it made the tropical night that much more magical. We finished dinner, and everyone slowly excused themselves to retreat to their various rooms, and Violet and I were left standing alone at the patio's edge as we looked out into the rainstorm.

"You staying over at my place tonight?" I asked.

"Damn straight."

I started to turn to walk back inside, but Violet pulled me back.

"Let's go through the courtyard—it's faster."

"It's also pouring down rain."

"Yeah, and what do you think might happen to this dress if it gets wet."

She had a point. I therefore smiled and stepped out into the rain, and my clothes instantly started getting soaked in the deluge. She followed, and we made it as far as the pool, when I looked over to see that Violet's dress was now clinging to her skin and making quite a show of her dark hard nipples.

"What did I tell you?" she said.

"You were right. This was definitely the way to go."

I suddenly felt the very real urge to kiss her, and the rain poured down over us and made Violet feel like a port in a storm and her lips my refuge. We entwined our tongues, and with every second, my desire grew out of control until my heart was pounding and pumping ever more blood into my gentleman region. Violet could feel it pressing against her, and she ran her hands down and slid off my shorts and freed Tag Junior from his nylon prison, thus allowing his full length to fly free and proud in the stormy Hawaiian night. I, in turn, reached up and slid off her dress, and her body now lay bare and glistening in the soft ambient light of the nearby pool.

I kissed her lips then neck and soon felt her guiding my mouth down to her breasts, where I ran my tongue over each delectably hard nipple. Violet gasped in pleasure then took hold of my manhood and worked it fastidiously until it was as hard as carbon steel. I lifted her up and carried her to a nearby table, and she reached down and guided my member unto her glorious lady region. I pressed in and out with a slow, purposeful intensity, and the pace allowed us to entangle our tongues as I reached out with my hands and ran my fingertips over her nipples then reached down and took firm hold of her buttocks and pulled her hips into mine. The pleasure was steadily growing in intensity, and it caused me to quicken my pace, making each thrust a little faster and harder than the one before. We both started calling out, and the table was moving violently and scraping against the deck, but, thankfully, the rain was blanketing the sound of our coupling and enveloping us in a cocoon of privacy that felt as though it was providing refuge from the world at large.

Minutes that I wished would go on for hours passed, and I could feel we were both on the cusp of sweet release. I took hold of her breasts and cupped each nipple between a thumb and forefinger then kissed her and instantly felt her nails dig into my back, thus telling me in her own special way that it was time. I continued to thrust and grind with every ounce of remaining strength until we ran headlong into the most intense mutual orgasm I had ever experienced. My mind was lost to the moment, and our mighty screams of pleasure were carrying out over the Pacific and probably even reaching Japan. I never wanted the moment to end, but the eventuality of our mortal failings could not be postponed any longer, and I relaxed and looked into Violet's eyes as I delivered a long passionate kiss. We parted lips but remained biblically entwined, with the only sound being our pounding hearts and the falling rain. Oddly, I heard the slurping sound of a straw reaching the bottom of a drink and looked over to my left and saw that there was an older couple in the Jacuzzi a mere ten feet away. They were both slack jawed and staring as they sat there with their tropical cocktails in their hands.

"Oh, hello, folks, are you the couple that called the front desk and asked for a public sex act?"

"Um—no, but we did enjoy the show," the woman said.

"Great, because tips are always welcome."

"Can we bill it to our room."

"Absolutely, now if you don't mind we have to get cleaned up for an eleven p.m. show in the Wiki Wiki Room. Good evening," I said.

Violet and I left the pool and reached my room to find it was thankfully free of the D&D contingent. We went straight into the bathroom, showered, then got ready for bed, as it had been a hell of a day followed by a hell of a night. It was therefore nice to finally climb into bed and relax, and Violet snuggled up against me, and I gently ran my hand over her back as we lay there in the darkness. There was always something magical about the last few minutes before you fell asleep, as it was often a time of great clarity—and especially after coitus, but tonight I was troubled. My mind continued to process all the events of the last few days, and I couldn't shake the feeling that there was something I was missing. Regardless, exhaustion eventually managed to overcome unease, and I put it all to rest and fell asleep feeling ever hopeful that I might find answers in the day to come.

CHAPTER TWENTY-THREE
The Sand Man and the Boner

I was suddenly brought awake with a jolt, and I lay there with my heart racing as I tried to process what had just happened. I had been having an anxiety dream in which I had been back in Afghanistan, and, oddly, I was reliving the last five minutes of the time I rescued John. I was carrying him over my shoulder and was almost to the rescue helicopter's door when I was hit by the AK round. During the actual event, my adrenalin had been running so high that I hardly felt the impact, but in the dream it was so vivid and painful that it brought me awake. Interesting. I wonder what made me go back and live that particular moment? Perhaps it was the fact that now, like then, I was saving John's ass. Back in Afghanistan, I had been success-ful in spite of various setbacks—the bullet being the most obvious—and, this time, like then, I certainly had plenty of setbacks, though hopefully there wouldn't be another bullet.

I lay there and tried to go back to sleep, but my mind was restless with anxiety, and, oddly, my *scrot-sense* was tingling, though it wasn't because of any immediate or perceived danger. Instead, it seemed to be originating from this case, and somewhere deep in the recesses of my subconscious, there was something I was missing. I finally decided to get out of bed and throw on my shorts and a T-shirt then quietly slipped out of the bedroom to make myself a small cocktail to settle my nerves. There was a lot riding on me at the moment, so going back to sleep wouldn't be easy. I walked over to the little bar, poured myself a glass of rum, then went over to the lounge and sat on the couch. The nerd's D&D game was laid out before me, and I glanced down at their various character sheets and laughed to myself when I saw Rachel's. I was the person who brought her and Beebs together, and now I desperately hoped that my matchmaking skills would work out for John and Jessica as well. With nothing else to do, I opened my laptop and combed YouTube until eventually finding an episode of a long cancelled gun show on the Discovery Channel. In it, an all American family owned a gun business, though I, and most of their male audience, watched the show in order to see the particularly attractive busty mother and daughter as they fired their various weapons while wearing short shorts and tight shirts. These shots were usually done in slow motion, and the result was a rather lovely show of the effects of reverberation rippling through their ample bosoms.

I sipped my drink and waited in earnest for a slow motion shooting segment, and, in the interim, saw some sort of confrontation between two of their gunsmiths. The result entailed one of them firing an old Henry rifle into a small test chamber. The chamber was virtually identical to the one Walther had in his workshop, and the weapon, to the relief of the gunsmiths, fired without incident. The show moved on and at last came to an obligatory slow motion boob gun scene, then the credits rolled, and I closed my laptop and decided to take a little walk to clear my head and perhaps even do a little investigative work.

I slipped on my thongs, left my suite, and walked over to the room where Jessica had stayed on the night of the bachelorette party. I looked at my watch, turned, and started making my way towards Steven's room by following the exact path that Jessica had allegedly traveled the night of the murder. I entered the lobby, hit the button for the elevator, then looked up to see the clock directly beside the security camera and remembered that Jessica had done the same thing in the video. While I waited, I pulled out my iPhone and took a little video of myself looking up at the camera, and I finished it by saying Beeber massages my balls with his chin. I decided to play it back and laughed when I watched my wacky ending, and so I decided to play it again just for the hell of it, and something in the video made my *scrot-sense* tingle. I couldn't get my head around what was causing the sensation, so I stored it away and was hopeful that it might eventually make its way out of my subconscious.

The elevator doors opened, and I walked in and rode up to Steven's floor before exiting and heading to the other wing of the hotel. Upon reaching his room, I looked at my watch and saw that it had taken roughly four minutes and thirty five seconds. I walked back to the elevator and, while waiting, glanced out of the adjacent window and saw that the rain had stopped. The pool was now very visible in the courtyard below, and it made me think about Violet and our earlier adventure. It also made me think about something she said—namely that the shortest route from that side of the hotel to ours was to go straight across the middle. It was a very obvious point and something I should have already considered. The hotel was more or less horseshoe shaped with Steven's room at one end and Jessica's at the other. I therefore went back and decided to retrace a new route between their rooms. Starting at his front door, I went down the nearby stairs, walked across the courtyard, and entered the other side of the hotel to climb the two flights of stairs to reached Jessica's door. I looked at my watch and discovered that it was indeed faster—a full two minutes faster. I was suddenly very intrigued as I pondered something even more interesting—namely that the alternative route also bypassed all of the security cameras.

The killer, in walking through the hotel and using the elevator, was either incredibly stupid or very intent on being seen. Jessica Thurman was not stupid, nor did she want to end her future husband's political career, and so, if she had actually wanted to kill Steven, she would have done a hell of a lot better job. This was yet more annoyingly obvious evidence of a staged murder, and, filing away these new revelations, I started walking back towards my own suite then came around the corner of the main lobby to see the janitor and his cart full of cleaning supplies. He was just dipping his mop into the bucket as he was obviously about to clean the floor. He looked up and smiled, and I nodded and returned the gesture then moved on to stairs and ran up the final few to reach the next floor. I opened the door and saw a figure directly in front of me and was so startled that I screamed like a little girl. Recognition quickly set in, and I realized the stranger was Violet, and she was not amused.

"What the fuck are you doing out here?" Violet asked angrily.

"I had a nightmare and couldn't go back to sleep, because I kept thinking about all this shit, so I went out for a walk to try and clear my head and do a little work on the case."

"Anything good come of it?"

"Yeah, I learned some shit—some of which was based on something you said earlier."

"Do tell."

"Well, when we were heading back from dinner, you said that it's faster to cut through middle."

"Yeah, because it is."

"Exactly, so why didn't our killer do the same thing? Why take the long way there and back. It wasn't raining that night, so there was absolutely no reason not to cut through the middle—especially since the shorter route has absolutely no surveillance cameras."

"Apparently, our killer wanted to be seen."

"Yeah, it's just too bad that none of this really changes the situation."

"Maybe we'll get lucky tomorrow."

"Maybe."

"Ready to head back to the room?"

"Yeah, but what the hell brought you out here in the first place?" I asked.

"I was looking for you, obviously. I woke up and couldn't go back to sleep without you."

"Really?" I asked, with a smile.

"Yeah, but don't be getting all soft and sentimental on me."

"Me? I'm not the one who couldn't go back to sleep."

"Shut up and get moving," she said, as she prodded me along back towards the room.

"Careful, people will think we're in love," I said, quoting the famous line that Anthony Hopkins spoke to Jody Foster's character in The Silence of the Lambs.

We entered my suite and headed straight past the D&D lounge and into the bedroom, where we immediately stripped and slid back into bed. Violet threw her leg over mine and placed her hand on my chest, and a few quiet minutes passed before she looked at me with her big blue eyes.

"I've been an agent now for some time, and I've experienced some pretty scary shit, but today was definitely up there in the top spot for most crazy moment on the job."

"Being hunted by a group of trained killers is rarely fun."

"No shit, and I'm feeling pretty fucking alive at the moment."

"You can see how soldiers get addicted to the adrenaline rush."

"I can."

We both lay there in the quiet of the night as we continued to gently play our hands over each other.

"Do you think you'll be able to sleep now that you've had your little revelation?" she asked.

"I don't know. Why?"

"I thought I might be able to help."

She reached down and took hold of my manhood and began gently stroking it.

"I'm not sure I've got more in me," I said.

"That wouldn't appear to be the case."

I looked down to see she was indeed correct, as my penis was filling with bravado and starting to point north. She climbed atop me and slid down and looked up at me with a devious smile as she ran her tongue around the tip.

"I don't agree. In fact, I'm pretty sure you have one more in you," she said.

She set back to work on my penis until it was hard as all hell, and it was abundantly clear that she was correct, and I was more than ready to approach reentry. She lifted her hips and mounted me and started rocking ever so slowly up and down, and it was just enough movement to cause her breasts to dance about before my eyes. I reached up and gently ran my fingers over her nipples until they sprung to life, and Violet let out a soft moan. I was once again seeing the wonders of her sensitive nipples, for she increased her pace ever so slightly and proceeded to add a slow counter clockwise motion with her hips. The heat of our passion was rising, and a thin veil of lover's sweat was coating our bodies as we made sweet, hard love.

The sense of time and place diminished as we kept up a strong though luxurious pace that allowed us to prolong the pleasure and enjoy the moment. She leaned forward and slipped one nipple and then the other into my mouth, and I felt a bit as though I were bobbing for apples at a country fair. Soon, I had both nipples dangerously hard and dangerously delectable, as their generous tips were pointing proudly from atop her magnificent peaks. Violet cooed like a kitten until I moved on and kissed her neck, then ear, where I nibbled her soft lobes before returning to her lips yet again. In response, she gave my tongue a gentle nibble then sat up and placed her hands on my shoulders to brace herself as she started moving her hips ever faster. It was obvious that we were again approaching the point of no return, so I took hold of her breasts and gladly accepted responsibility for their safety and well being. Meanwhile, Violet plunged her hips violently fore and aft and made it abundantly clear that climax was inevitable. She abruptly leaned down and kissed me, and it became the final impetus to push both of us over the edge and into the orgasmic abyss. Our earlier lovemaking session down by the pool had been about bold uncontrollable passion, but this one was special, as it was about sharing a moment of complete intimacy for as long as possible, and, in that spirit, we continued our coital embrace through climax and well into the post orgasmic phase of resolution. Upon coming to rest, we parted lips but continued to stare into each other's eyes until Violet finally gave in and dropped her head to my chest and let out a long sad sigh.

"Fuck, I don't know what the hell I'm going to do when you head back to the mainland," she said.

"Well, I know what I'm going to do."

"What?"

"Get one of those little hula girl bobble heads then stick it on the dresser in front of my bed and think about you while I masturbate profusely every night until I fall asleep."

"That's the sweetest thing a man has ever said to me."

"I'm pretty romantic that way."

"You're like a special needs Shakespeare."

"Indeed m' lady—indeed."

Violet dismounted and moved beside me and took hold of my arm and pulled me into a spooning position. I kissed her neck and gave her a gentle squeeze and felt relieved that my earlier anxiety and inability to sleep were now replaced with feelings of contentment, optimism, and a tiny spark that I feared might be the beginning of love. Perhaps tomorrow would indeed bring a needed break in the case, and to that end, I closed my eyes and drifted off to sleep with thoughts of the beautiful Special Agent Violet Kalili filling my mind and warming my heart.

CHAPTER TWENTY-FOUR
The Last Breakfast

Morning came a little later than usual, which was just fine, because the night before had been particularly eventful. I had come up with some surprisingly good revelations and had not one but two epic sexual encounters. Violet was still in my arms, and I was mildly afraid to move for fear that all the previous night's alcohol might catch up with me this morning. I pulled my arm free, and the movement made Violet stir though not wake up. I sat up slowly and carefully and realized that I felt pretty damn good and had no trace of a headache. Miracles do happen.

I placed my feet on the floor and stood, then took a second to wait for my equilibrium to adjust before sauntering into the bathroom. I stood over the toilet, lifted the seat, and felt a bit wobbly, as my leg muscles were tired and sore from a day of running and a night of sex. Regardless, I managed to set forth unto a mighty horse piss, and a short time later I let loose a decent sized fart that I couldn't hold back without staunching the flow of urine. I therefore had to let it fly free and proud, and soon thereafter my body was empty in all ways, and I dropped the seat back down and brushed my teeth before ambling out to the coffee machine. In about five minutes, I had a pot ready to go, and I filled two cups, added cream, and returned to the bedroom to find Violet still sleeping. I placed the coffee on her bedside table, and the smell was enough to make her eyes flutter open. She sat up and picked up the coffee, and it brought her lovely breasts free of the covers, and allowed them to glow in the warm late morning sunshine.

We sat and sipped until our cups were empty, at which point Violet stood up and headed to the bathroom for her obligatory morning pee. Soon thereafter, I heard the toilet flush, then after that she brushed her teeth before returning and throwing on some clothes. Together, we sauntered out into the living room and picked up a menu then called room service. I was hungry as all hell and therefore ordered a man sized breakfast that included an omelet with ham, green pepper, onions, avocados, and cheese. On the side I went with hash browns and two pieces of wheat toast. Violet ordered the same, though she chose fruit instead of potatoes, as she thought she could eliminate the extra calories by only having a couple bites of my hash browns. Fucking women. If I had a nickel for every time one of them ordered the healthy meal only to scavenge my plate, I would have been a millionaire a hell of a lot sooner.

Breakfast arrived twenty minutes later, and, again, the

same waiter appeared at the door. He rolled in his cart and placed breakfast on the table then filled our cups with fresh coffee from a large carafe. I signed the bill and gave him another formidable tip, and he left the carafe and the tray with our food on the table then turned and started rolling his cart out of the room. As he passed the little D&D station he paused and looked intrigued.

"Is this yours?" he asked.

"Not exactly. It belongs to my friends. Why? Do you play?"

"I do, but sadly I haven't yet been able to find other players here on the island."

"Yeah, sunshine, a warm blue ocean, and beautiful weather do tend to draw people outdoors."

"Yeah," he said, sounding a little sad, obviously missing the irony of my statement.

"Well, I can ask the nerds if they want another player."

"Seriously? I'd be incredibly grateful. It's been a long time."

"No problem. Leave your name and number on the table, and I'll pass it along."

The young man leaned down and wrote Jerasian along with his number, and I had to look at his name tag to see that his name was indeed Jerasian.

"Unusual name," I said.

"Yeah, my parents couldn't decide between Jeremy, Jason, and Ian, so I ended up with the compromise—Jerasian."

"Still better than Cricket, Apple, Knute, or North."

"True, well thank you. I'll leave you to your breakfast now."

Jerasian left, and we dug into breakfast, and the calories felt as though they were being instantly processed by my body—with my testicles perhaps needing most of the re-plenishment after last night's double hump session. Every few bites, however, Violet would shoot her fork across the table and grab a clump of hash browns, and, while at first I saw this as a sign of intimacy, I was now starting to wonder if I'd get enough food for breakfast.

"You know you could have just ordered hash browns," I said.

"Too greasy. Fruit is healthier."

"Yeah, but hash browns are not any healthier on my plate."

"I only wanted a bite."

"Or two. Or three. Or four."

"Oh quit your bitching. You can have half of my fruit."

I reached over and started to spear the chunk of pine-apple, but Violet swiftly parried me away with her fork.

"Sorry, not the pineapple. That's my favorite."

"Of course it is."

I left her fruit alone, as I realized that the war for breakfast was already lost. Instead, I focused on my plate by seizing as many bites of my omelet and diminishing pile of hash browns as quickly as possible, and, in seconds, my plate was empty. Violet's was nearly empty as well, though it still contained the nearly untouched fruit bowl, whose only missing occupant was the pineapple. Done eating, it was time to shit, shower, shave, and get on with the day, and I grabbed more coffee and entered the main bathroom feeling utterly confident that Violet now understood the code. I therefore didn't even bother to lock it or close the door all the way. I knew I was taking a big chance, but trust was important in a new relationship, and now I trusted Violet. We'd shared a life and death encounter after all.

I pulled out my trusty iPhone and brought up my email, took a sip of coffee, then opened the damn and brought forth a great flow of humanly waste. Meanwhile, I went line by line through my email and deleted spam while reading the others. Interestingly, I had exactly forty-two emails, which was the answer to life, the universe, and everything in Douglass Adams's Hitchhiker's Trilogy. What did that little coincidence mean for me at the moment? No idea, but at least my dump had been interruption free thus far.

I reached over and took another sip of coffee then brought up my browser in hopes of searching the local news. I clicked on the top story, which was a piece about the large number of recent car thefts on the island of Oahu, and I had only read the first line when Violet walked in and froze in place with a legitimate look of fear in her eyes.

"Oh my God! I'm so sorry! I saw the door was open a crack and figured you were done."

"Goddammit!"

"Don't blame me. This time, it's your fault, you idiot!

You left the door open!"

"It was a test."

"A stupid test."

Of course my test was stupid.

"Whatever, just leave me in peace to finish up. You now understand what you've unleashed after what happened yesterday."

"I do, and I'm really sorry."

"What's done is done."

She left and closed the door behind her, and I took a moment to try and relax. Two dumps in a row. What did that mean? Double the trouble, and, if so, what could possibly be worse than yesterday? Fuck. I flushed and entered the shower, and, a moment later, Violet joined me, and she was looking apologetic.

"You still mad?" she asked.

"No, just scared."

She started lathering me up from head to toe and spent a lot of extra time in the groinal region, where Tag Junior, in spite of the omen of doom, was seemingly impervious to fear, as he was standing up tall. Trading tit for tat or, more accurately, tat for tit, I decided the proper thing to do was lather up my shower buddy, and, to that end, I took a lot of care to get her boobs, buttocks, and thighs particularly clean. Now that we were both mutually sudsed from head to toe, we moved under the torrent of water and rinsed off, and Violet looked at me with a deviously predatory look in her eyes.

"If something terrible really is going to happen today, then maybe we should have sex again—in case it's our last time," she said.

"Right here?"

"Right now. Maybe it can break the curse."

She kissed me, and our tongues mingled while she reached down and steered my man-sword unto her lady-sheath. I took her in my arms and lifted her onto the small ledge of the shower, and I proceeded to bring my hips to hers, knowing full well that it may be our last moment of sexual abandon on God's green earth. My head was spinning as I tried to focus, but my attention was diverted equally between the physical pleasure and the visual spectacle of watching her writhe before my eyes. Within minutes, we were both calling out loudly, and the tiny room was echoing with our lustful cries.

"Oh God, yes!" she yelled.

"Oh fuck yeah," I responded.

"Oh, fucking fuck me!"

"Fuck yeah! I'm going to keep fucking you until I pass out, my fucking balls explode, or I start crying!"

"Oh shit, I'm going to cum!" she screamed.

"Me too! Here come the tears!" I said

I held her tightly in my arms as we pounded our way headlong into climax with an ear crushing crescendo of cries of passion serving as the unlikely swan song of our sweet lovemaking session. We stopped moving and shared a long kiss before finally parting to rinse and leave the shower. We dried off then got dressed before exiting the bedroom to find the entirety of the nerd army already engaged in their D&D game. Annoyingly, they all turned and started clapping and cheering. Fuckers.

"Finn, from the sound of things in there, I'm thinking that maybe you could give Beebs a few pointers," Rachel said.

"Rachel!" Beebs said, plaintively.

"Oh, you know I'm just kidding," she said, before mouthing to me that she wasn't.

"So, what's the big plan today?" Doug asked.

"That depends on you fuckers. How's the email trace coming?"

"Should have it any minute," Beeber said.

"Good, so for the moment, we wait."

There was a knock at the door, and I opened it to find Lux, Jessica, and Bridgette.

"What's up?" I asked.

"We're going out for some lady time and wondered if Violet and Rachel wanted to join us."

"What the hell is lady time?" Beeber asked.

"Manicures, pedicures, and shopping. I thought it would be a nice stress reliever."

Rachel, who was sitting at the table a few steps away and holding a twenty sided die, immediately dropped it and stood up.

"I'm in," she said.

"Wait—what about our game?"

"I could use a little break."

"Don't worry, guys. I have an alternate, and he works here at the hotel. His name and number are on that piece of paper."

Beeber looked at the paper and thought for a moment.

"OK, you go and have fun. We'll fight the Orc king with this Jerasian guy."

"What kind of name is Jerasian?" Rachel asked.

"Parents couldn't make up their minds—Jeremy, Jason or Ian, so he ended up as Jerasian."

"Cruel."

"No doubt."

"So, what do you say, Violet? You in?" Jessica asked.

Violet looked at me questioningly.

"We don't have anything to do except wait around for Beeber's software to finish up, so you should go have some fun. I'll hang around here and hit the beach, get a massage, and, I don't know, maybe even meet a nice girl."

"The hell you are. You're staying right here with the nerds while I'm off with the girls."

Violet kissed me goodbye then joined the hen party as they left the room, and Beeber immediately picked up his phone and dialed Jerasian, and, five minutes later, there was a knock at the door. I went over and opened it, and our unlikely third player came in carrying a satchel.

"What's in the bag?" I asked.

"My D&D stuff."

"You carry it around with you?"

"Totally."

"But you said that no one around here even plays."

"Which is why I have it with me at all times. I have to be ready when the opportunity arises."

"Will you get in trouble for this?" Beeber asked.

"Not if you guys don't tell anyone, but, honestly, it wouldn't be the worst job to lose. I mean, shit—I have a PhD in Computer science from University of Hawaii, but this was all I could swing after grad school."

"Dude? Seriously?" Beeber asked.

"Yeah, I know. It's probably time to move to the mainland."

"No doubt. I could get you a job in the Bay Area in about three seconds."

"Really?"

"Yeah, I have my own security software company called Helm's Deep."

"Holy fuck! You're Justin Beeber?"

"In the flesh."

"He's not the Justin Beeber you're probably thinking of," I said.

"No shit. He's the talented one. I studied some of your code in school. It was amazing," Jerasian said, his face instantly lighting up.

"Thanks. It's nice to be appreciated."

I was watching real life nerds fall in love and decided that it was time to get the hell out of the hotel room and experience a little sunshine.

"Knock yourselves out, brave knights, I'm going to the beach."

"Um, hello, I'm playing a Ranger, who, while being in the fighter class, is hardly a knight," Beeber whined.

"And I'm playing a Wizard," Doug said.

"And I'm playing a Rogue," Jerasian added.

"And I'm going to be playing with myself for the rest of my life if I don't get the fuck out of here," I said.

I left the nerds to their nerding and walked down to the beach, where I passed a large party that was just being set up. The hotel staff were setting tables and laying out silverware and napkins while servers brought out large trays of food. I thought back to my incident at John's party and my bad time with the poi and decided I should have a little talk with the chef. There was a cute young woman nearby, likely of Filippino descent, and she was busy lighting little Sterno canisters, so I went to her first.

"Excuse me. Are you the chef?"

"No, that would be Bianca. She's right over there," she said, pointing to a woman on the other side of the courtyard.

I walked over and saw that she did indeed look like a chef and wore the obligatory checkered pants, white shirt, hat, and, of course, clogs. She was probably around forty and appeared to be some kind of Pacific Islander with her lovely tanned skin and Polynesian features.

"Excuse me, chef," I said.

"How can I help you, sir?"

"Well, I'm not sure how to say this because I really make it a habit never to complain to restaurant staff, but a few days ago I got some bad poi at a dinner here."

"Are you talking about the vice president's pre-wedding dinner?"

"Yeah, that's the one. I got a terrible case of diarrhea—as did a number of other guests."

The woman looked skeptical.

"I'm sorry, but I personally tasted every item that went out, and I can say without a doubt, that the poi was perfectly fine."

"How do you explain the diarrhea? Could the poi have sat out too long and gone bad?

"No, obviously you don't know poi. Even if it had sat out for a long time—hours or even overnight, it would become sour poi, which is also one of the ways we prepare and serve it."

"Interesting. It doesn't actually go bad."

"Not in a way that would make you sick, but I'm still very sorry for your discomfort. I honestly can't believe your food poisoning came from my kitchen. Cooking for me is a family experience, and I take it very seriously. If you are at one of my tables, then I cook for you like I do for my family. Only the best."

I believed that the chef was sincere, and I hated that I even brought up the topic, except that more than one person getting sick was considered an epidemic and not something to be taken lightly. Still, her explanation of poi was hard to contradict.

"Well, thanks for taking the time to talk to me," I said, now feeling even more confused.

"You're welcome."

I was about to walk away when I remembered something the bartender had said.

"Oh sorry. I have one more question. Was Rudy Rafael working that party?"

She thought a moment then nodded.

"Yeah, he helped with food setup that night. Sad what happened to him—even if he was kind of an idiot."

"Yeah, I suppose. Well, thanks again, I'll get out of your hair now."

"No problem, and sometime I would like to cook for you again and show you that I stand behind my work."

"That would be nice."

I left chef Bianca and moved down to the beach then kicked off my thongs and walked to the water's edge and paused to gaze out at the clear blue Pacific Ocean. It was kind of frustrating that I was at the mercy of technology and therefore didn't have a lot to do today except relax and reflect. I needed a break in this case more than ever, but all I could do was wait. I moved out into the water and played in the small waves and did a little body surfing before coming out to walk along the beach and do a little people watching.

The sun was directly overhead, and the sand was hot, thus forcing me to stick close to the water so that I didn't burn my feet. There was a crowd of youngsters building sand castles just ahead, so I segued inland to the grass that bordered the sand and continued my northwesterly journey along the shore. Up ahead, I saw a man going for drinks, and he had apparently opted to wear his wife's pink frilly sandals in order to make the painful journey over the burning hot sand that loomed between their reclining chairs and the bar. I had deduced this fact because the sandals were at least three sizes too small and had large yellow decorative flowers over the toes, which made them look completely hilarious on his large manly feet. As if that weren't enough, their small size made for an even better show when he tried to walk, as his toes spilled over the edge and looked a bit like shrimp cocktail, which made his steps short and awkward and his progress painfully slow. He noticed me watching and smiled as he approached.

"Anything for a drink," he said.

"Don't worry. It takes balls to wear pink sandals."

"And even bigger ones if they happen to have yellow flowers."

"No doubt," I said, before the two of us shared a small laugh.

I continued on and eventually left the resort's grounds and continued for another hour and enjoyed the time and used it to clear my head and think about things. My *scrotsense* had been tingling on and off for the last few days, so something was brewing in my subconscious. I eventually turned around and headed back to the resort to find his majesty the vice president sitting on a lounge chair on the beach. Sandra and a bevy of other agents were also nearby, and they were ever watchful as I sat down and took up residence beside Sasquatch.

"What gives, miracle worker?" he asked.

"Not much. Just waiting."

"Well, at least the girls are having fun."

"Want to go snorkeling?"

"Sure, but Sandra won't be happy. She's a little afraid of the ocean."

"She can't swim?"

"She can swim like a fish, but she's afraid of sharks."

"Aren't we all."

John signaled for Sandra to come over, and when he explained his plan, he received a decidedly unhappy look in return.

"You'll love it out there. I promise," I said.

"We'll see," she responded.

I headed off to grab my snorkel gear from my room, and, ten minutes later, I came back just in time to see Sandra slip off her cover up dress and reveal a spectacular figure. I already knew she was extremely attractive, but I had no idea she was hiding the body of a fucking fitness model all this time.

"Sweet Lord, Sandra, you are stunning! How is it that someone hasn't locked you into holy matrimony yet?"

"I haven't found the right guy—or girl, for that matter," she said, a little sadly.

"Well, being open minded to either improves your odds by at least fifty-percent, and if you continue to wear that bikini, he or she will surely find you."

The three of us headed down to the water and began swimming along the hotel's reef, and the other Secret Service agents watched from the beach as a small Coast Guard ribbed inflatable idled just offshore, where it thankfully kept its distance so as not to scare the fish. It was a good day on the water with excellent visibility due to the minimal amount of wind or wave action, and we managed to see a turtle and just about every other major fish. Sandra was actually starting to relax and enjoy herself—that is, until a school of young tunas encircled us, and she panicked and climbed up onto my back. The crisis was soon averted, and we continued on until eventually returning to shore about two hours later, at which point John and I decided to spend another hour watching girls in bikinis as they frolicked on the beach. One girl, a drop dead gorgeous twentysomething, recognized John and looked enamored as she approached him. He was polite and talked with her for some time and finished up by autographing a cocktail napkin. She thanked him, and, as she was walking away, she suddenly stopped and turned back towards us.

"If you run for president, I will totally vote for you," she said.

"Thanks," he responded.

The girl turned and continued on, and both John and I watched her lovely tan backside as it moved down the beach.

"I'm impressed," I said.

"Why?"

"You didn't flirt at all. The john I knew would have had that woman in his room in about six seconds flat."

"This is the new John, and he's desperately in love."

"I can see that, and it makes me happy, because, believe it or not, I really want you two to get married, so you can be the next president, and it's not because I think it'll make me cool because I know you. It's because I sincerely think you'll do a good job."

John regarded me for a long time, and I was starting to wonder if he was about to cry. We usually only gave each other insults, so compliments could get pretty emotional. Before either of us could say another word, we heard a loud wet fart and turned to see Corn was soaking wet from head to toe, as he had obviously just come from the ocean.

"Am I interrupting something? You two look like you were about to kiss," he said.

"Look, John, it's a talking whale, and the fucker came up on to land to empty its lower blowhole."

"Fuck you, this is all muscle," Corn responded, as he patted his belly.

"Apparently, it's a talking whale that is very sensitive about its weight," John added.

"Perhaps we should we get some kind of gurney and carry him back into the ocean."

"Dude, we're going to need a fucking flatbed."

"Ha ha ha—making fun of the married guy. Well, you two assholes will see what happens after you walk down the aisle."

"We're going to get fat?"

"Oh yeah, now enough about me—what are you two lovebirds up to?" Corn asked.

"Snorkeling and moping, mostly."

"And Finn was espousing his undying love to me until you interrupted us with that fucking fart."

"I was just setting the proper mood. So, any good news yet?" Corn asked.

"No, but we should have something soon. In fact, I should probably head back to my room, get cleaned up, and check in. Do you fuckers want to meet in my suite for a drink in a half hour or so?"

"Sounds pretty romantic," Corn said.

"It will be, once you two get there."

"I'm in," John said.

"Will there be hors d'oeuvres?" Corn asked.

"*Oui.*"

"Well then I'm in too," Corn added.

I walked to my room and was surprised to find that the nerds were working rather than playing D&D, and all three were in front of Beeber's laptop talking animatedly about root access and a bunch of other shit. Apparently, Jerasian really did know a thing or two about software.

"What's up, nerds?"

"We've had a breakthrough."

"Really?"

"Yeah, thanks to Jerasian."

"Do tell."

Beeber went on to explain that he was having a hard time focusing on the D&D game because his software hadn't cracked the Governor's firewall. He and Jerasian started discussing the problem and rewrote a piece of Beeber's code that apparently allowed it to detect and bypass unnecessary information and drastically reduce the anti-encryption time—whatever the fuck that meant.

"We're in," Beeber said.

"Sweet fucking titties. Start searching, gentle nerd!"

Beeber sifted through the various sent emails and soon isolated the one in question—namely the one sent from the Governor's office to the Police Commissioner. I'd glanced at it briefly in the commissioner's office, but it had obviously been a dead end, as its sender came with a generic title. Any one of the Governor's staff could have sent it, including the Governor himself, so I'd never know the answer to my question without questioning each and every person in his employ. Of course, if that person were a part of the conspiracy, then they obviously wouldn't tell me shit, so we had to use the nerds. Beeber, meanwhile, continued his search, and, upon finding the sender of the email, he looked up at me with legitimate surprise.

"Shit, it was sent by the governor himself," he said.

"Are you sure?"

"Pretty much, as it came from his actual computer."

"Someone else in his office could have accessed it."

"This came via his official email account—from his home computer."

"Fuck, that means our conspirators have the help of a pretty powerful person, but the upside is that we finally have something. Nice job, my brilliant amigos! Now, I'm going to celebrate with a shower."

I left the guys and proceeded to take a lovely hot shower then dressed and returned to find them all still engrossed in their snooping activity. It was nice to see them hard at work, and it gave me faith that we'd soon bust this fucker wide open. I looked at my watch and saw that it was almost five, and my company would be arriving soon. No sooner had I stepped up to the bar that there was a knock at the door, and in walked John and Corn, though Sandra remained outside.

"Hello, boys. The nerds here have been busy, so I have some good news," I said.

John and Corn came over and joined me at the bar, and Jerasian looked up for a moment to see who had arrived and practically shit his pants.

"Holy shit!" he said, loudly.

Everyone turned to look at him.

"What did you find?" Beeber asked.

"Um, the vice president of the United States."

"Yeah, that's who all this is for," Beeber said.

"Oh my God. I'm sorry about the profanity, sir."

"Not a fucking problem," John said.

"Don't worry, youngster, the vice president is more than comfortable with all manner of profanity—and depravity, for that matter."

"Speaking of which—where's my fucking cocktail, Finn?"

"Coming, your majesty."

The nerds returned to their work, and I set about mixing up a pitcher of Mai Tai's. Finished, I gave john and Corn a glass then offered one to the nerds, and they all accepted gratefully, except for Jerasian, as he was worried he might get fired. Beeber explained that he already had a far better job waiting for him in San Francisco, so it was time to live a little. Jerasian accepted a cocktail, and, drinks in hand, our merry band of men and nerds toasted and set to work on the first cocktail of the evening.

Now that the liquor was flowing, I explained our latest news, and John's mood immediately improved, and he pulled out his phone and called Frank. Frank was equally happy, and he would, in turn, make some calls in his old boy's network to get things rolling for a meeting with the Governor. It was a decent break in the case and would hopefully lead to something concrete, though we were approaching treacherous ground. If the governor was actually complicit in the conspiracy, then things were going to get very complicated—very quickly. Hopefully, he was just a man passing on a favor for a friend—a friend who would be our next link in uncovering the bad guys behind this conspiracy. Frank called back about a half a cocktail later and said that the Governor was in the middle of a formal dinner and would call as soon as he was free.

"Shit, we need a name right now if we're going to figure this out in time," I said.

"I know, but what choice do we have. Frank's doing his best," John said.

I made another pitcher then filled everyone's glasses before taking a sip, and, as I sat there thinking about the situation, I suddenly felt a little bothered that we had managed to uncover so much yet still hadn't salvaged John's political career.

"I can't believe you were finally about to make it to the alter when all this shit went down," I said.

"Yeah, though I got pretty close once before."

"Bullshit."

"It's true."

"Really? When?"

"Right after Afghanistan."

"Who was the unlucky girl?"

"Melissa Williams."

"Wait a minute. You were going to marry Melissa Williams?" I asked.

"Yeah."

"What happened? Why did she dump you?" Corn asked.

"She didn't me. I dumped her."

"No fucking way!" Corn said.

"It was a difficult time, as I had just returned home, and I realized marrying her wasn't the right decision. Plus she was bat-shit crazy."

"No doubt," I said.

"You sound as though you're speaking from experience," John said.

"Well, we had a little thing a couple nights ago and having experienced that hellcat I would totally agree with your whole bat-shit crazy summation."

"Yeah, so would I, but I kind of liked it," Doug added.

"Wait a minute. Is that how you fucked up with Violet? By sleeping with Melissa?" Corn asked.

"Yeah."

"Gross, that means that you and John basically touched dicks."

"Exactly!" Beeber blurted out.

Jesus. More man logic. First it was Beebs giving Doug and me shit about Melissa, and now it was Corn giving John and me shit about Melissa. Fucking Melissa was a magnet for trouble and had the inexplicable ability to bridge the metaphorical gap between men's dicks.

"Not so fast, Corn. It doesn't count if it's been more than five years. Dick particles have a limited lifespan—kind of like the Nexus Six robots in Blade Runner, so John and I are free and clear of the dick to dick conundrum," I said.

Of course, John and I had almost shared yet another girl more recently, namely his wife to be, but thankfully Jessica and I only had a night of harmless fun, and it didn't involve any kind of intercourse.

"Well, you might get off on a technicality with John, but

you definitely connected dicks with Doug," Beeber said.

"Easy, Beebsy, it was just a little harmless cock play between a couple of cocksmen," I countered.

Suddenly, Corn stood up and slapped his hand on the table.

"Wow, Corn—are you issuing an official objection, or is there some other reason for your oddly timed hand slap," I asked.

He didn't answer and instead grabbed the television remote control and turned it on and started going through the channels—probably hoping to check on the score of a Notre Dame game, as it was his beloved alma mater. He furiously passed one channel after another until happening upon a local news station, where I saw a familiar face, and I felt my *scrot-sense* begin to rumble in my undercarriage.

"Holy shit! Can you go back?" I asked.

"Dude, seriously? I'm dying to find out the score of the Notre Dame game," he complained.

"I know, but I just need you to go back for a second then you can continue on to your precious game."

He hit the back button, and there was the face, and I immediately recognized the man, though it was his name and title below him in bold white letters that was triggering the *scrot-sense* reflex. It turned out that the man on the screen was the Governor of Hawaii, and I remembered exactly where I'd seen him recently, and this, in turn, became the impetus for me to suddenly connect the dots and achieve enlightenment in our current situation.

"I know who's behind all this," I said, which made the entire room instantly go quiet.

CHAPTER TWENTY-FIVE
Resident Evil

I had to take a moment to steady myself, for my head was spinning as all the pieces of the puzzle started to fall into place. My heart was also racing, and I decided to pour myself another drink to steady my nerves. With my drink in my hand, I sat down and took a large sip before speaking.

"Fuck," I said, before letting out a long pained sigh.

"Do you mind sharing with the rest of the class?" John asked.

"Yeah, but you're not going to like it."

"Why, is it really that bad?"

"Yeah, because I think Melissa and Frank Williams are behind this entire thing."

"Are you insane? They are some of my oldest, dearest friends and my main political supporters."

"Yeah, and you left Melissa hanging at the alter. You know the old adage that hell hath no fury like a woman scorned?"

"Yeah, but trust me. You're wrong."

"No, I'm afraid not. It all fits perfectly, and now I know how it all went down."

"I'm telling you right now—it's going to take a hell of a lot to convince me."

"The motive alone is enough. Think about it. You left the most powerful man in Washington DC's little girl on the alter. What would have happened if the Mathesons and Williams came together through marriage? You would have been the most powerful family in United States history, but you fucked it up my friend—at least in their eyes I imagine."

"Bullshit. Frank has been behind me throughout my entire political career."

"Until you decided to marry Jessica. I imagine that was the last straw."

"Dude, seriously—it can't be the case. Trust me. I've known these people my entire life."

"OK, I'll prove it. Beeber, can you bring up the security footage?"

Beeber, who had been listening intently, brought his laptop over to the bar and set it in front of us, and everyone else gathered around and watched as he opened the folder that contained all the security footage.

"OK, Beebs, can you bring up the clip of Jessica leaving her room."

He double clicked on an icon, and we saw Jessica appear and walk from her room. Next, it cut to the elevators, where she glanced up at the camera before entering, at which point, it cut to the next floor and showed her walking down the hall towards Steven's room.

"Alrighty, play that back and watch her closely," I said.

Beeber backed it up, hit play, and everyone watched.

"I don't see anything," Beeber said.

"Me neither," John added.

"Beeber, play it again, and this time, everyone watch her very closely."

He played the clip again, but this time Jerasian spoke up.

"She's walking funny," he said.

"Exactly, but why?" I asked.

"No idea," John said.

"Well, I'll tell you why. Her shoes are too tight!" I said excitedly.

"Care to elaborate?" John asked.

"Yeah, you see, earlier today on the beach, I saw a guy wearing his wife's sandals and..."

"Why was he wearing his wife's sandals?"

"The sand was too hot for bare feet, so he borrowed his wife's sandals and looked, more or less, similar to our mystery woman in the video. It's funny, but now that I think about it—the first time I watched the footage, I saw something odd, but it didn't really sink in until I saw that guy today. So, based on the police evidence, we know for a fact they're Jessica's shoes, but they obviously don't fit, which means it's not Jessica."

"So, why did the person in the footage wear them?"

"It created more items for the evidence chain," I said.

"And if the shoes don't fit, you must acquit," Doug said.

"In a manner of speaking."

"That still doesn't mean it's Melissa," John said.

"Just wait, as there's more. On the night of your engagement party, I walked up and accidentally slapped Melissa's ass at the bar, because I thought she was Jessica."

"So, you thought you were slapping my bride-to-be's ass. Is that supposed to make me feel better?"

"It will, because I learned at that moment that Melissa and Jessica are very similar looking. They have the same height, build, hair color, and sensational backsides, with the only major difference, excluding their faces, being their feet."

"And how would you know that little fact? Do you happen to have a foot fetish amongst all your other neuroses?" John asked.

"No, but I did go swimming with Melissa and noticed that she could swim like a fish, and can you guess why?"

"Because of her large feet?" John replied.

"Yep, and having seen both Melissa and Jessica's feet, I can safely say that Melissa is at least a size or two larger—especially judging by her discomfort in that video."

"Be that as it may, it still isn't enough proof."

"So, how do you explain the fact that my software came up with an absolutely positive ID on Jessica?" Beeber asked, sounding a bit defensive.

"Because it was working perfectly. The face on the footage is Jessica's."

"I'm getting confused. You just said it was Melissa," John said.

"No, I said the woman is Melissa, but the face is Jessica's."

"So, you think someone Photoshopped it?"

"In a manner of speaking, but in film they call it rotoscoping. They isolate the actual person's face, then they go frame by frame and replace it with a new one. They did it in the movie Blue Crush when they needed a close up of Kate Bosworth surfing a big wave. They could have used a green screen, but instead they placed her face over a professional surfer's body."

"Yeah, but you can still tell it's a special effect," Doug said.

"Yeah, but remember that was a moving shot. A static one like the security footage would be a hell of a lot easier."

"And just who in the hell did they get to do that on such short notice?"

"Frank's son Richard Williams. He does special effects for a living and just happens to be visiting from the mainland."

"Wouldn't it take too much time to get it done?"

"Unlikely, as the footage is already digital, so all they'd have to do is alter the few seconds where she looks into the camera. That would be a piece of cake for someone who knows what their doing."

"True, but they'd also need to gain access to the security office," Beeber said.

"Which probably isn't an obstacle for people who have already managed to draw the vice president's soon to be wife into a murder investigation."

Everyone quietly pondered that, until John spoke up.

"How can you prove the footage was altered?" he asked.

"Beebs, can you bring up the still frame from the security footage."

He brought up the picture of Jessica, and everyone scrutinized it closely.

"It looks legit to me," Beeber said.

"It does. In fact, it looks a lot better than the shot in Blue Crush, but there's one problem. The lighting is wrong. It's off by a hundred and eighty degrees, which I know because I took a video of myself in the same spot. When I played it back, there was something about it that made my *scrot-sense* tingle, and now I finally understand the reason."

"*Scrot-sense?*" John asked.

"His little voice," Beeber said.

"Oh, I get it. Like *Magnum P.I.*."

"Can you fuckers focus?" I asked.

"Yeah, but it'd be a lot easier if you didn't call your intuition *scrot-sense*."

"Fine, let's forget about my *scrot-sense* for the moment, because I'm going to grab my iPhone and show you fuckers what I'm talking about."

I went to my room and grabbed my iPhone, and, as I

hadn't checked it since I went to the beach, I saw that I had a missed call, a voicemail message, three emails, and two apps to update. That would have to wait, however, as I was on a roll and about to break this case wide open. I returned to the bar and brought up the video I had taken by the elevator. It showed me looking at the camera and then speaking my short quip at the end where I said Beeber massages my balls with his chin. Everyone laughed except Beeber, who looked confused.

"What's the point of saying I'm massaging your balls with my chin?" he asked.

"It means his dick is in your mouth," Doug responded.

"Oh, I get it now," Beeber said, finally laughing.

"Um, you probably shouldn't be laughing, as this is usually the part where a better man would have made a witty comeback," Doug said.

"Oh, then how about this—I'm only laughing because..."

"You just love sucking my dick. Now, it's obviously too late for a comeback, so enough talk about sucking my dick! Come, children, let's focus on the problem at hand," I said.

I scrolled back on my video and paused it where the lighting was most prominent.

"See, my face and body are lit from the right. In the still frame of Jessica, the light on her face is coming from the left, but here you can clearly see the light on her body is coming from the right."

"Holy shit! You're totally right!" Beeber said.

Beebs, you said you used Jessica's Facebook profile pic

for comparison. Can you bring it up?"

Beeber tapped a few keys, and brought up her profile pic. He then placed it side by side with the security frame grab, and the pics were absolutely identical and very likely one and the same.

"Your software got a perfect match, because it was looking at the same picture. Young Richard must have used the same pic when he did the work, as it would have been more than good enough resolution to blend into a grainy security camera shot."

"OK, I'll admit that the video is very likely doctored, but what about all the other evidence. How did they fake the gun powder residue and blood spatter report?"

"Good point, and it's elementary, my dear Sasquatch. Violet's father said something interesting the yesterday. He quoted that old Sherlock Holmes adage that said once you eliminate the impossible, whatever remains, no matter how improbable, must be the truth. So, let's assume Jessica actually did fire the gun—or at least was manipulated to have fired it."

"You can't just fire a gun at a crowded resort—even if it is silenced. The bullet would make a lot of noise on impact, and you can't go firing it out the window without the possibility of somebody seeing or hearing it," Doug said.

"Exactly, so I asked myself how that feat could have been accomplished? Well, last night I couldn't sleep and went on YouTube and watched an episode of that show about the family that owned a gun store."

"Oh yeah, the one with the hot mother and daughter with the big tits! I loved that show!" Beeber blurted out.

"That's the one."

"Fuck, it's too bad it's not on the air anymore."

"Yeah, now part of last night's rerun had the gunsmiths test firing a rifle into a little chamber, and I believe our killers could have used a similar contraption. All they'd have to do is roll it in to Jessica's room, hold the gun in her hand, pull the trigger, and voila! Perfect gun splatter residue."

"And with the roofies, she'd never even know what happened," Beeber said.

"Correct."

The evidence against Jessica was beginning to pile up around Melissa, and John was starting to look particularly uncomfortable. He downed the remainder of his drink, refilled it immediately, then took another sip before letting out a long pained sigh. I couldn't blame him, as he had spent a lifetime with the Williams Family, so all this would be extremely hard to process.

"So, how did they get the test-fire chamber into her room?" John asked.

"Beeber, can you go back farther in the security footage?"

"Yeah, which camera and how far?"

"Eleven thirty—main lobby."

At ten minutes to twelve, a woman appeared with a large house keeping cart. It had the usual bin for laundry in the middle, and was piled high with various sheets and towels.

She had short dark curly hair and wore the hotel's standard maid's uniform. After a minute, she entered an elevator and disappeared from sight.

"Can you bring up the footage from the camera on Jessica's floor?" I asked Beebs.

A second later, the same maid was moving down the hall and out of view.

"That's it. That's how they brought the firing chamber in, and I'd bet a hundred pounds of poi that it's in the cart, and that's Melissa pushing it."

"I'm sure a maid on Jessica's floor is by no means an unusual occurrence," John said.

"Actually it is. Maids don't come to work until six a.m.," Jerasian said.

John thought for a moment.

"OK, suppose it's Melissa. It still doesn't explain where Frank comes into all this," John said.

"I understand this can't be easy to hear, but I'm sorry to say that I have even more to tell you. The nerds tracked the email from the Governor's office right to the Governor himself. That wasn't as meaningful, however, until I saw the Governor on the television tonight and realized I'd seen him before—at the Outrigger Canoe Club. Frank was leading us into the first damage control meeting when he excused himself to talk to some dude. I now realize that the dude was the Governor. In fact, Frank even thanked him for some favor—probably the email he sent to the police commissioner that informed him that he wanted the investigation fast-tracked."

"But what about all the people that have been murdered? There's no way in hell the governor of Hawaii or Frank would have been a party to that."

"I don't know about the Governor, but I'm afraid your good buddy Frank is clearly the mastermind. Of course, he didn't personally kill Steven Green, Roofie Rudy, or Danny the spear fisherman, but he did order Rex to do the job for him."

"Rex? Seriously?"

"Yeah—along with the other members of Frank's personal security team—a team that I'm betting are all ex Delta and likely served together."

"Rex seems like such a nice guy."

"I agree, but the last thing I asked Rudy before he died was what the man who hired him looked like. Oddly, he looked up at my face and said *you*. It got even weirder when I talked to the bartender at the restaurant where Steven had his official last meal. She said the guy with him reminded her of me, though it wasn't necessarily a physical thing. It was his bearing and posture, and what do all people who have been in the armed services share?"

"Posture and the military bearing that is hammered into you from the first day of basic training all the way through OCS. Try as I might, I've never been able to lose mine either," John said.

"Indeed, so our bad guys were in the service and clearly not average soldiers, and these fuckers have been using their formidable skills to conduct a highly sophisticated operation without leaving any clues or traces behind."

"Which is the kind of thing that Delta Force does on a daily basis. Those fuckers know their shit backwards and forwards," Corn said, chiming in.

"Oh sweet fucking Jesus! Maybe it's about time we brought my father in on all this, though he's going to be equally surprised and may very well have a heart attack," John said, pulling out his phone.

He called his father, gave him a brief recap, then hung up and said that the senior Matheson would be coming down to join us momentarily.

"Fuck, why didn't I put this together before now?" I said.

"You can't really control inspiration," John said.

"No shit, and after watching that show, I still couldn't sleep and went for a walk."

"Really? I usually jacked off after watching that show," Beeber said.

"Why not during?"

"Living room was too exposed."

"You should have installed blinds. Anyway, I did something I should have done in the first place, which was retrace the murderer's steps. Using the security camera footage as my guide I walked from Jessica to Steven's room. Then, I did it again, only the second time, I followed a faster, more direct route and shaved more than two minutes off my time. That means the killer, or should I say Melissa, walked the longest possible distance between Jessica and Steven's rooms, which made no sense until I realized something."

"What?" Corn, John, Beeber, Doug, and Jerasian asked at the same time.

"The security cameras of course! Our killer obviously wanted to be seen, otherwise she would have taken the other route. If I shared this and the other revelations with the lead detective, I'm pretty sure he would consider dropping the charges."

"At least we now have something to tell the police."

There was a knock at the door, and in walked John's father—the esteemed Senator Matheson. He immediately came over to the bar and asked for a drink, and I filled his glass then proceeded to tell him all that we had uncovered. When I was done, he lowered his head and rubbed his temples, as the news appeared to be both physically and emotionally painful.

"Frank is my best friend. I'm the godfather to his children for God's sake. How could he do this?" he asked.

"Blood is thicker than water, and the man's ambition and ruthlessness apparently knows no bounds."

I finally had a moment and looked at my phone and saw that the missed call was from Violet, and she had fortunately left a message. I hit the play button and listened as she relayed that the girls were all having a lot of fun, but she had received a call concerning the partial print we had gotten off of Jessica's sweatshirt zipper. The FBI had found a match, and the answer was, of course, Melissa

Williams. Initially, there hadn't been any matches in any of the criminal databases, but they finally cross checked the public ones—namely those used for vetting teachers and various government employees. Melissa's short stint as a teacher would inadvertently be the vehicle of her undoing, though it was surprising she had managed to make this one little mistake. Of course, it was always alluded to in murder mysteries that the culprit, no matter how clever, always overlooked one tiny detail and eventually got caught. In this case, I was guessing it was simply a matter of convenience. The sweatshirt had gathered sleeves, so she probably removed her gloves first figuring it would be easier to get her hands free of the garment. Either way, we had her by the short hairs.

"Hot damn! We finally have physical evidence!" I called out excitedly.

Everyone became quiet and looked over at me, as they were obviously curious to hear my news, but I continued to listen, as Violet's message was still going. Suddenly, my heart skipped a beat, and I looked down at the time of the message and immediately hit the call button, hoping to God that I might reach Violet in time. The phone rang three times, then I heard a familiar voice say hello. It was Frank Williams.

CHAPTER TWENTY-SIX
The Orc Lord

I stood there utterly transfixed in thought with my heart pounding in my ears as I waited for Frank's next words. I couldn't believe that I had not checked my phone sooner and warned Violet, but fate, as usual, had its own cruel agenda. While she had been out with the girls, she received the news about the fingerprint, and, not having been able to reach me, took it upon herself to tell Frank the terrible news that his daughter was very likely the real killer. Unfortunately, she didn't yet know that he too was a part of the conspiracy, and she had unknowingly dragged herself and all the women into the Lion's den. Things had just taken a major turn for the worse.

"You might want to put your phone on speaker, as I imagine the others will want to hear this," Frank said.

I hit the speaker button and placed the phone on the bar.

"Hello, friends, I suspect that it's about time we had

another damage control meeting, though this one is about t
of five very lovely ladies who are currently at my house."

"Frank, we've been best friends for forty years. You're
godfather for fuck's sake! How can you have done this?" D
asked.

"I imagine you must be a little shocked, but so was I whe
called off his marriage to Melissa ten years ago. It didn't
who he was. He broke my little girl's heart and, worse still,
what would have been the single greatest consolation of
and influence this country has ever seen. The Mathesons a
Williams officially entwined in holy matrimony would hav
the next Camelot."

"I'm sorry, Frank, but what can I say? Melissa and I just
meant to be," John said.

"Your loss, young man. Now, to our current problem. In a
world, I would have been satisfied just destroying your p
career, but seeing as Finn and his friends have proved to b
capable than we thought, we've reached a different outcome

"What do you want, Frank?" the senior Matheson asked.

"A meeting, as I suppose we might still be able to come t
kind of resolution."

Douglass looked around the room for a consensus, and ev
nodded, as there really weren't any other options at the mo

"Where and when?" Douglass asked.

"Tonight. My place around eight, and I expect all of yo
there."

"All—meaning?"

"Meaning everyone—John, Douglass, Corn, Finn, and o

his team of nerds, and I want all of you in one vehicle. When you get to the gate, my guards will do a headcount and search your vehicle for weapons. If you're all not here or they find anything, all your ladies get a very unceremonious bullet to the brain, so please don't do anything stupid, and, just to be clear, make sure you don't involve the Secret Service or FBI in this matter."

"You know as well as I that John can't take a piss without the secret Service knowing," Douglass said.

"I'm sure you'll figure something out, and remember that I have eyes and ears everywhere. If you alert anyone— I'll know. If even a whisper of this travels beyond out little group here, all the women are dead."

"Speaking of the women. We're going to need some kind of proof of life. How do we know they're not already dead?" I asked.

Frank was quiet a moment, then Jessica came on the line.

"John?"

"I'm here."

"John, don't trust him. I'm pretty sure he's going to..."

Her voice trailed off, but John called out to her anyway.

"Don't worry. We're coming for you!" he said, frantically.

"All right then, gentleman. I believe we're done talking for now," Frank said.

"Yeah, fuck you very much, Frank. We'll see you at eight," I said.

Frank clicked off, and all of us stared silently at each

other.

"What now?" Douglass asked.

"Well, I think it's hardly a stretch that he plans to kill all of us the minute he get's us to his estate," I said.

"Maybe he just wants to arrange something. Perhaps force the wedding that never happened."

"Highly doubtful. What's to keep us from calling it all off the minute the women are safe? No, he wants us all there so he can kill us and be done with it in one fell swoop," I said.

"True, but how in the hell could he think that he's going to get away with killing all of us, let alone the vice president of the United States?"

"You know the saying about absolute power corrupting absolutely. Well, think about it—Frank's lived with a whole lot of power for a whole lot of time. It can warp a person's mind, as he clearly has no compunction about murder. He killed Steven Green, Roofie Rudy, and the spear fisherman, so why not kill a few more, and it certainly makes it easier when he's got a personal hit squad at his beck and call."

"It's just so hard to believe this is the same man I've known all these years," Douglass said.

"Indeed, and I suppose we should call Babs and tell him his fiancée is being held hostage by the godfather of the groom."

I picked up my phone and rang Babs, who just happened to be only a short distance away lounging on the resort's beach. Five minutes later, he was at my door wearing a red and white striped Speedo and a T-shirt, and his feet were still covered in sand.

"Nice outfit," I said.

"I was at the beach."

"In America."

"I'm still French."

"Obviously, now hurry your ass in here before you catch a cold in that thing."

He walked inside, and I explained all that happened, and he immediately poured himself a drink then took a seat.

"*Merde*," he said, which was French for shit.

"*Merde* indeed," I responded.

"So, what the fuck do we do?" Babs asked.

"Yeah, what?" John added.

"Seems pretty straightforward to me. We go rescue our fucking women," I said.

"So says the low rent James Bond, but you're forgetting that Frank holds all the cards here. One false move and they're dead."

"He's going to kill them anyway. We have to do something."

"That'll be hard with all of us driving into his estate in the same car and without any weapons. You heard him— any shenanigans and the women are dead, then, once we're all inside, I imagine we'll also be killed soon thereafter."

"He's not going to do anything too rash. He has neighbors, so he'll need to at least be a little subtle and probably take us all somewhere nice and remote before he kills us."

"That's not very reassuring," John said.

"Trust me, it doesn't matter—it'll never get that far. Now, enough nay saying. Let's look at the logistics here. How many security men does Frank actually have?"

"Including Rex, I'm guessing between eight to ten, and they're all ex-Delta Force," Douglass said.

"Well, let me tell you—eight isn't enough. Not this time and not against this group."

"I like your enthusiasm, Finn, but do you honestly believe what you're saying has any merit?" Douglass asked.

"I do, and not to sound harsh, but you pussies are all forgetting that we have a veritable platoon of ex-special operations soldiers and trained intelligence agents in our very midst," I said.

"I think you're forgetting that most of us have been out of the game for quite a while," Corn said.

"And some of us were never really in the game. At least not in the field anyway," Beeber said.

"Don't be so defeatist. We can do this. Think about it," I said.

"We're talking about going up against a trained cohesive group of killers on their own turf, and these men have seen combat and have no problem pulling the trigger."

"I know, but don't forget that we're also trained—and more importantly, smarter."

"Well, Doug and I are anyway," Beeber said.

"You're more than smart—you were a gun toting badass on the Pickles case and took out a dangerous Chinese agent all on your own."

"That's an exaggeration," Beeber said, as he smiled impishly.

"It's still too dangerous. We're going to need help," Douglass said.

"You heard Frank, he has too many connections. We alert the Secret Service or FBI, and he'll know it before we even hang up the phone. We are lone wolves on this one, but buck up, little campers, we have a few wild cards up our sleeve."

"Such as?" Douglass asked.

"He didn't mention Babs," I said.

"*Excusez-moi?*" Babs asked.

"*Oui, vous.* Are you forgetting that you're an ex naval commando, third world president, and maker of fine rum?"

"Are you suggesting I get them drunk?"

"No, I wouldn't waste an ounce of your rum on those pricks, but I do remember how you helped take down a group of ornery terrorists back in Tunisia."

"That was different."

"Not really. It was about rescuing a damsel in distress from a bunch of assholes, so it's exactly the same, except we have several damsels and approximately eight to ten assholes."

"I suppose we must do what we must do," he said, resolutely.

"So, what are our other wild cards?" John asked.

"Jerasian, for one."

"Yeah, speaking of me—I'm really sorry to interrupt

and all, but I can't imagine I'll really be of any help here, so it's probably about time for me to leave," Jerasian said.

"No chance, you're on the team now, kid. Your country needs you, and we need you, so start thinking how you can help," I said, patting him on the back.

He looked nervous, but soon his quiet demeanor changed into a nerdish form of resolve. The other people in the room, however, still appeared to be a bit apprehensive.

"Finn, honestly I think your balls are writing checks your dick can't cash," John said.

"Look here, people, we don't have any other choice. We need to pull together and form our very own dream team. Fuck Frank and his evil minions, they don't know who they're messing with."

"I think they do, and that's the problem," John said.

"Bullshit—everyone in this room has more than enough balls and ability to pull this off. Corn, do I even need to remind you of what we faced everyday in Afghanistan?"

He shrugged.

"And, John, sure you were a pilot, but you were also the pilot who spooned with me on a fucking riverbank in the Shah-i-Kot valley while we fought off an entire contingent of Taliban and Al Qaeda militants."

"You two spooned on a riverbank?" Beeber asked.

"It's a long story," John said.

"You guys were in combat, but what the hell can I do to help?" Doug asked.

"Doug, seriously? You were one-third of the elite Three

Amigos? The Agency's best and brightest team in the Special Activities Division."

"Wait, you guys were the Three Amigos?" Corn asked.

"The one and only," I said.

"Your operations were legendary. I heard the stories, but your identities were always a highly guarded secret, even to senior staff."

Beeber, Doug, and I smiled at each other and shared a brief, though knowing, exchange. We had done some legendary stuff together at the Agency but never dreamed anyone had the slightest inkling of our noble deeds—least of all Corn. The two of us had lost touch after leaving the service, and I had no idea he was working his way up the CIA's management ladder. The Agency was obviously a big place, and because of compartmentalization and secrecy, it was easy for people to never cross paths.

"Come on, fuckers, let's do this. It's time to pool our brains and form a plan. Nerds, this is where you come in. Think of it like your D&D game. Now, what was the last thing you were trying to accomplish?"

"We were trying to sneak into an orc lord's castle and steal his treasure."

"Well, there you go, only Frank is the Orc Lord, and our women are the treasure."

"And the Orc Lord's men are ex Delta Force soldiers, which makes them like twentieth level fighters," Beeber said, grimly.

"Exactly, they don't have a wizard, a thief, or a Frenchman in a Speedo."

I went over to the coffee table and looked at their dungeon map and figurines and suddenly had an idea.

"OK, nerds, let's construct a D&D style mock up of Robin's Nest. Doug, any chance you could quietly tap into any of the CIA's spy satellites? Some real time intel would certainly help."

"Oh gosh, I don't know. Do you think anyone back at Langley might notice if someone suddenly repositioned a satellite?"

"Have you forgotten that you're in the company of the deputy director of the CIA and the vice president of the United States?"

"I had, actually," he said, smiling as his interest suddenly piqued.

Doug walked over to his laptop and started tapping keys, and Corn followed and watched over his shoulder as Doug started entering various passwords in order to work his way through the many firewalls that protected the Agency's computer system. Minutes passed, and the two men were bonding like a couple of frat boys, which made sense as the CIA liked to instill a sense of fraternity in its employees.

"Perfect!" Corn suddenly blurted out.

"What?" I asked.

"Good news. Doug found us a satellite currently offline over the Pacific, as it's in transition to a new target location."

"I could easily divert its course for a few hours," Doug said.

"Can you do it so none of Frank's Agency contacts have any idea what we're up to?" I asked.

"Yeah, no problem. As long as it's in transition and not on any active target, no one will notice a thing," he said.

"Leave it to the Agency guys to get us our first break," Corn said, as he held up his hand to high five Doug.

The two slapped hands, then Doug reached down and pressed a number of keys before looking up and smiling.

"We'll have eyes on sight in five minutes. No big deal."

"Excellent! Now, gentle nerds, let's use your graph paper and google maps and construct a mock up of Robin's Nest."

Beeber, Jerasian, Doug, and I started taking pieces of paper and laying it out on the table before taking pencils and accurately drawing Frank's estate using a zoomed in view from Google Maps for reference. It also was a major bonus that we'd just been there, so it only took a matter of minutes before we had a pretty accurate representation. I grabbed several of their little figurines and set them on top of the layout.

"These will represent the bad guys," I said.

"You're really going to use the Paladin? Technically he's lawful good," Beeber said.

"Yes, even the fucking Paladin."

Fifteen minutes later, Doug was patching us in to our rogue CIA satellite and bringing up a live feed of the compound. He pressed a few more keys, and our view switched to infrared so that we could now differentiate the bad guys from the background. A minutes later, we had seven people officially laid out on our little mock up. There were two guys by the gatehouse at the main entrance, and one more in the opposite corner along the front fence line that bordered the street. Two more were located on each side bordering the northern and southern neighbors, and one was covering the beach.

"Clearly, Frank has his security on high alert in the event that we tried any kind of monkey business."

"Wonderful! We finally have some good news," John said, sarcastically.

"Actually, it is good news," I said.

"And how's that?" he asked.

"As you can see, he's placed most of his people to defend against a land based assault, while only leaving one guy to guard the beach. That's where they're vulnerable."

"Too bad we don't have a SEAL team."

"We don't need one. We have me."

"Oh—well aren't we feeling awfully good about ourselves," Doug said.

"It's not like it sounds. I just happen to have a really good plan, and it only requires two people to initially breach the estate."

"Let me guess. You and this unnamed partner are going to parachute in utilizing a high altitude low opening jump, land on the tennis court, and then casually make your way through the estate as you take down Frank and all of his men all by yourselves," Beeber said.

"Well, that would be the case if this were a cheesy movie or book plot, but this is the real world, so I have a better plan. Namely to swim in, neutralize the beach guy, then gain access to the main house via the wine cellar. Once there, we'll make our way to the security room and neutralize guard number two, who monitors the cameras. Without him, they'll effectively be def, dumb, and blind."

"Wait a minute. How do you even know where in the hell the security room is located?" Beeber asked.

"I saw it on the tour. It was downstairs next to the wine cellar."

"I never saw any security room."

"That's because you're a desk jockey, and I'm a trained field agent."

"Well la-de-da, Mr. Bond."

"Everyone has their place, Beebs. It's nothing to be ashamed of."

"Frank expects you to be in the car, so unless you can teleport, your plan already has a big fat hole in it."

"Babs will play my part."

"Lovely! I get to be a decoy."

"Don't you think they'll notice?" John asked.

"No, I've never been that close to any of them except Rex, so I'm confident Babs will pass muster—even though he's French. We're about the same height and hair color, and, as long as he can go ten minutes without consuming brie cheese and wine, it should work."

"Assuming we make it that far, what then?" Corn asked.

After you've passed through the gate and been given the all clear by Frank's security, I want you to drive in as though you're going straight to the main house. Fifty yards before you reach the garage, cut off the driveway and hightail it over the lawn and towards the house. Park just to the right of the tennis court, exit the vehicle, and take up defensive positions behind the stone wall that borders the pool."

"Are you fucking crazy? We won't have weapons to defend anything!" Corn said.

"Yes you will, because me or one of my team are going to place them there. They'll be directly beneath the lounger in the southeast corner. Once armed and situated, you'll have an excellent position with clear unobstructed views of the entire estate."

"Yeah, until Rex and his men converge and kill us. Honestly, Finn, this sounds a little sketchy," Corn said.

"I'm sorry, but I kind of have to agree with Corn," John said.

"Don't worry, there's more to the plan. I'm going to leave my number two man in the security room to monitor their communications and keep track of the bad guys' movements through the Estate's excellent camera system. That leaves me free to join you and cover your left flank while Secret Team Three takes up position in the boathouse, which will ultimately leave Rex and his men exposed in a classic pincer move in the center of the estate."

"And just who in the fuck is part of this right flank in the boathouse?" Corn asked.

"Another wildcard—Johnny Kamoahoa."

"Johhny who?"

"A local *moke*, and a guy who already offered his help."

"And who's your number two man for your beach insertion?" John asked.

"Jerasian, assuming, of course, that he knows how to scuba dive."

"Wait, what?" Jerasian asked.

"Do you know how to scuba dive? I assumed you did since you live in Hawaii."

"I do—in fact I'm a certified open water diver, but what you're talking about seems a little beyond my skill set."

"Rubbish. Did you ever dream of becoming a Navy SEAL?"

"Well yeah, as has every other guy in the world, but…"

"But nothing, here's your chance, and, better still, you get to utilize the traits of your D&D character."

"I think you lost me somewhere between Navy SEAL and D&D."

"Dude, you said your character is a rogue, and everyone knows the rogue is a sneaky fucker with a wicked sneak attack. That's the guy I want with me when we infiltrate the estate."

That talk seemed to bolster Jaserian's courage, and he nodded his approval.

"What's to keep Rex and his men from regrouping back along the opposite side of the estate?" Corn asked.

"Secret Team 4, our final wild card and ultimate ace in the hole, or, more accurately, our ace on the hill. Violet's ex-boyfriend was a sniper in the Army Rangers."

"Ex-boyfriend to the woman you're currently boning?" John asked.

"One and the same."

"If I were you, I'm not so sure I'd want that guy covering my ass."

"Trust me, it's not a problem," I said.

I considered his words of warning and couldn't help but think back to the Han Job T-shirt affair and seriously wondered if John might have a valid point. Agent Moore and I weren't exactly the best of friends, but I was guessing that he would do anything and everything in his power to help Violet.

"Then, after we take down Frank and his men, Voila! Our mission is accomplished, so we grab the girls and go back to the resort for a massive celebratory party. Any questions?"

"Yeah, what's the plan again?" John asked, looking confused.

"Don't worry, Sasquatch, I've made a digital copy, and it's embedded on a microchip right here under my fingernail," I said, as I held up my middle finger.

"Wait, I have a real question," Doug said.

"Fire away."

"When you say neutralize, do you actually mean kill?"

"I'm afraid so. We can't afford any kind of long and prolonged assault. We need to hit them fast and hard so they don't have time to use the hostages as leverage against us."

"With use as leverage being a nicer way to say they might kill them?" Beeber asked.

"Yeah, in the worst case scenario."

"Fuck, I finally got the perfect girl, and now she's being held by a madman and his private army."

"I know how you feel, but channel those emotions. Use them to help you get the job done. These assholes are highly trained and more than willing to kill, so we need to be totally committed."

"Not to be a downer here, but where in the hell are we supposed to get weapons on such short notice?" Corn asked.

"You raise a good point. At the moment, all I have is a sniper rifle and Jessica's Beretta, but I'll make some calls and see what I can scrounge up. After that, we need to go on a little shopping trip."

"Who are you calling? Don't we have to be careful about who we contact?" John asked.

"Don't worry. The rest of our rescue team aren't anywhere even close to Frank's watchlist, but, just to be safe, I won't use my own phone. Jerasian, can I borrow yours for a second?"

"Sure," he said, pulling it out of his pocket and handing it over.

I dialed the FBI's local office, reached an operator, and immediately asked to be transferred to Special Agent Dave Moore, and he came on the line a moment later.

"This is Special Agent Moore. How can I help you?"

"It's Finn. We need to meet."

"No, you need to fuck off."

"I'm serious. Violet is in real trouble, as are several others, and I need your help to rescue them."

He was quiet for a moment, and all I could hear was his breathing, which sounded oddly angry—something I'd never experienced from listening to air moving out of a person's lungs.

"Are you fucking serious?" he finally said.

"Dead serious."

"Fuck—where do we meet?"

"Helena's in one hour."

"I'll be there."

"Thanks, and one more thing—can you scrounge up as many firearms as you can find."

"What?"

"We need weapons, but you can't file any official releases for them. This op is completely off any kind of official radar."

"I knew you were an asshole the first moment we met."

"Believe me, I feel like an asshole for dragging Violet into this, but, right now, I'm the asshole who's trying to rescue her as well as several other innocent victims."

"I'll do what I can," he said, before hanging up.

I only had one more call, though this one would likely be a little less awkward, and I could use my own phone. I brought up the number for Johnny Kamoahoa and hit send, and he thankfully answered on the fourth ring.

"What up? This is Johnny," he said.

"It's Finn."

"Who?"

"We met a couple of days ago. I'm the *haole* investigating Danny's death."

"Oh yeah, what up? You find *da* guy yet?"

"I did, and it's several guys, and I'm actually going to need a little local help to take them down."

"Whatever you need, *brudda*."

"Can you meet me at Helena's in about an hour?"

"You buying?"

"You bet."

"I'll be der," he said, before hanging up.

"So, seriously now—who the fuck is this Johnny Kamoahoa?" John asked.

"As I already said, he's a local *moke*."

"And we can trust him?"

"Yeah, he's a good guy, and he was friends with Danny Keahi—the spear fisherman who Frank's people killed."

"I suppose avenging a friend's murder is a good motivator," John said.

"All right, now we have to figure out how to get John out of here without the Secret Service finding out."

"Good luck," he said.

"Jerasian, can you get a room service cart?"

He smiled, as he instantly understood where I was going with the question.

"Totally, I'll be right back."

Jerasian left and returned about five minutes later and brought in a cart that had a food tray on top and, more importantly, a table cloth covering the lower section.

"That was fast," I said, lifting one of the lids and finding it occupied by a half eaten turkey sandwich.

John stared at me and shook his head.

"Have you figured out the plan yet?" I asked.

"Yeah, but I was just thinking that this may very well be the first time in history that the acting vice president of the United States was smuggled out of a hotel room beneath a half eaten turkey sandwich."

"At least you'll finally be number one in something."

We pulled back the cloth sheet that covered the cart, then John squeezed onto its lower shelf and looked particularly uncomfortable. It was too funny not to immortalize with a picture, so I quickly pulled out my iPhone to snap a picture and managed to capture him just as he gave me the finger. Classic. If all went well, maybe it could end up as next year's White House Christmas card. Now that we had John situated, Jerasian took hold of the cart.

"So, where do I take him?" he asked.

"Good question. How about you go to the back of the kitchen, and we'll get the minivan and meet you there. Oh, and do you have any shorts in your satchel?"

"Yeah, why?"

"The S in SEALs stands for sea, and that's where you and I are going to be."

"No problem, I've got it," he said, as he set off and pushed John slowly out the door and past Sandra, who was quietly standing guard.

"What doesn't that kid keep in that fucking Satchel?" Corn asked.

"Condoms, obviously," I responded.

Now, I needed to dress Babs so he'd look more like me, and the first critical detail was to replace his fucking Speedos with a pair of my shorts. He followed me into my room, and I found a pair nearly identical to the ones I was wearing. They were black board shorts with blue trim, and Babs went from swishy Frenchman to American beach stud in a little under six and a half seconds.

"Nice!" I said.

He didn't look amused.

"Maybe I should carry a hotdog around and fart every few minutes in order to truly complete the image," he said.

"Excellent idea, and maybe even drip a little mustard on your shirt for good measure."

"Yes, though I'd use Grey Poupon, as having even a little bit of France would make it more bearable."

"Whatever it takes, Babs. Alrighty then, I believe we're done here."

I grabbed a baseball hat from the dresser and handed it to Babs as we exited my room and joined the others in the lounge.

"It's go time!" I said.

We gathered up everything we would need for our

rescue mission, then Matheson senior, Babs, Beeber, and Doug left. I, however, remained behind in my room, as I needed it to appear as though John and I were still here. If I'd walked past Sandra without John, she would have been immediately suspicious about why he stayed behind by himself, and our rescue plan would have been over before it began. That meant I needed another way out, and I walked out onto the deck and looked over the edge to figure out how I was going to get to the ground. I was on the third floor, and while that wasn't exactly like being on the top of a skyscraper, it was high enough that I could fall and do some serious bodily harm. I therefore needed to be extremely careful.

I took a breath to steady my nerves then stepped over the rail and lowered myself down until my feet touched the lower deck's railing. From there, I carefully climbed down and performed the same exact series of moves then dropped down onto the ground level to find it was occupied by a lovely topless brown haired female sunbather. She heard the noise and looked over her shoulder, and I was actually more startled than she was, for it was none other than the attractive brunette from the luau—the one who had called me shitter after my embarrassing bathroom incident.

"Hello, shitter," she said, with a smile.

"Hello, witness to my most demoralizing moment on earth, I hope you don't mind me dropping in on you like this," I said, pun intended.

She smiled and inexplicably rolled over and sat up, thus exposing her very lovely and very large tan breasts. As if that weren't already unexpected enough, she opened her legs in a very suggestive manner then placed her feet on the ground on each side of her lounge chair.

"Not at all. Do you have time for a drink?"

"Maybe later," I said, as I exited the small gate that led to the resort's grassy center courtyard.

"And don't worry, I have plenty of toilet paper!" she called out.

"Good, because I'm bringing poi," I said.

I walked around and through the lobby then out to the parking lot, where I joined the others as they waited beside the Rothster. Everyone loaded in, and I drove us around the hotel to the back of the kitchen, where we found John and Jerasian standing beside the garbage dumpsters. Jerasian looked excited, but John appeared ill humored at having been sequestered in such humble circumstances. Oh how the mighty had fallen. They piled in, and off we went on our little scavenger hunt, with my minivan occupied by the oddest rescue team ever to have been assembled in the history of the world. Next stop, Walmart.

CHAPTER TWENTY-SEVEN
Scavenger Hunt

We headed south towards Honolulu on the Pali Highway until it became Bishop Street, and then we made a right and parked at Walmart. Babs and Matheson senior stayed in the van, while John, Beebs, Doug, Corn, and I headed inside and were greeted by the door person, who did a double take when she saw John. We continued on to our section, and a twenty or so year old male employee asked if we needed any help. I said yes, and he approached us looking rather happy to have a customer.

"So, what do you need?" he asked.

"We're running security for an adult video shoot and need hand held radios with headsets, and if any of them are waterproof it would be even better," I said.

The guy raised an eyebrow.

"Um, waterproof?"

"Adult movies can get messy if you know what I mean."

"Interesting, do you happen to need more security? I'm

a film major, so, I'm always up for working on any kind of shoot," he said.

"Sadly, we're already maxed out budget-wise."

"Oh well."

He turned and led us over to the shelf that held all the various models, and they fortunately had two of the waterproof kind available as well as eight more of the standard. All of them would work with the headsets, so we had settled our communication problem. I also grabbed a bag of extra long cable ties, and we went to the front, and the clerk told us it would be two hundred and forty two dollars and fifty two cents. We all looked at each other, as none of us were sure who was going to pay.

"You're the man in charge," I finally said, to John.

"Yeah, but this is all your idea."

"True, but I came up with this plan, so that you can get married and become the most powerful man on earth."

"Fine, you cheap asshole. I've got it," he said, pulling out his wallet.

He ran his card, then we all waited for the transaction to clear. The machine beeped, and the clerk asked if he could see John's card.

"Is there a problem?" John asked.

"No, it's just standard policy to verify the identity of the cardholder."

Apparently, our clerk didn't recognize the vice president of the United States. Classic. I couldn't help but smile, and John looked at me and scowled before returning his attention to the clerk.

"Do you need to see my license to verify my identity?" John asked.

"No, it's cool. Your credit card has a picture, so we're good," he said, handing it back.

John signed his name, then the clerk pressed a button, and we all waited for the transaction to finish. When it was done, the clerk glanced at John, except this time I could see a little recognition in his expression.

"Dude, you look really familiar. Are you famous?"

John turned and smiled smugly at me before returning his gaze to the clerk.

"A little," John responded.

"You're the guy from the Viagra commercial, aren't you!" the clerk blurted out.

John's smile faded, and he quietly grabbed the receipt, turned, and headed for the exit, leaving the clerk looking confused.

"He's not?" he asked.

"Him? No, he's just the vice president of the United States," I said.

"Oh well," the clerk said, sadly.

As we turned to leave the clerk spoke up.

"Wait, why's he buying a bunch of radios?"

"We're doing security on a porn shoot."

"But, he's the vice president."

"Dude, exactly, so what the hell else is there for him to do?"

"I suppose you're right."

We left Walmart and reentered the Rothster and headed to Helena's to meet Dave and Johnny. They were already there and coincidentally were sitting one chair away from each other in the waiting area. I told the hostess that we'd need a large table, and she suggested we take the banquet room, which sat just off the main dining area. Our ever growing procession of people walked over and settled in, and I made introductions. Needless to say, Johnny was more than a little surprised when I introduced John. It wasn't every day that you met the vice president of the United States in an impromptu hostage rescue strategy meeting at a Hawaiian barbecue restaurant.

The waitress soon came in to take our order, and everyone looked perplexed as to whether or not they should eat. I suggested that it might be our last meal, and that inspired everyone to go with the daily special, and the waitress exited and left us to begin our unusual meeting.

"Shit, *brudda*, I had no idea I would be meeting *da* vice president."

"Sorry, I didn't want to say too much on the phone."

"Finn, would you please just tell me what the hell is going on!" Dave said.

"Yeah, and I'd like to know too," Johnny said.

"Alrighty then."

I told Dave and Johnny the entire situation and what we were planning, and both listened intently, but Dave was the first to speak—though speak was perhaps too gentle of a term.

"You fucking asshole! I can't believe you dragged Violet into more shit," he said.

"I totally agree with you there, Dave."

"And now you need my help yet again. Man are you an asshole."

"Yes, you've said that at least twice, and I agree with you, but, Dave, this isn't about you and me or even your fucking precious Han Job T-shirt."

Beeber suddenly butted into the conversation.

"Hey, I have that same shirt!"

"Lucky you, as somebody stole mine," Dave said, gesturing at me.

"Borrowed, and, either way, Beeber's statement proves that my earlier claim that I'd bought it on Amazon could have been true, and it also proves that there is indeed another one out there."

"Which still doesn't really change the fact that you were wearing mine."

"Dave, seriously. Please forget about the T-Shirt for now. Believe me, I understand that it probably represents something more important—namely your breakup with Violet, and I completely empathize with your feelings, but, right now, it's time to focus all that angst into rescuing her and the others."

He was obviously stressed and using the T-shirt to redirect his anxiety, so I gave him a moment to consider my words, and he appeared placated, which allowed Johnny to enter the conversation.

"Wait a minute bra. How the hell can I help?" he asked, looking a little confused.

"I need some diving gear and a boat, but the boat has to look local. It's important that we blend in. If we go anywhere near that place in something looking too shiny or rented, it'll be over before it begins."

"No problem. My cousin Greg has a boat and dive gear, and he'll take you."

"Well, sweet monkey tits. That's pretty much most of what we need—aside from some additional firepower."

"Actual firepower?"

"Yeah, and people to pull the triggers, assuming you have any friends who might be willing to join this crazy rescue mission."

"No problem der. You bring beer and I could get half de island to help."

"Cool, I'll buy as much beer as you all can drink."

"That's a whole lotta beer," Johnny said, with a smile.

"And we'll need a creative way to get you and your friends onto the estate—preferably by sea, so you can reach the corner boathouse."

Johnny smiled.

"Don't worry, I got a way—and it's old school. Real old school."

"So, what exactly do you want from me?" Dave asked.

"Violet said you were a sniper in the Army Rangers, so I was hoping you could take up a position on the ridge above the estate and be our eyes in the sky. From up there, you could cover the entire place and more importantly our asses."

"Don't you think it would be a hell of a lot smarter to just call in the FBI SWAT Team?"

"It would, but we can't. Our bad guy knows a lot of people, so we have to keep this operation closer to home. Besides, almost everyone at this table has been to the house and knows the layout. First hand knowledge of your target location is pretty useful."

Dave thought a moment and nodded.

"OK, but just so you know. I don't have a sniper rifle, nor can I get one on short notice from the Bureau."

"No problem, I've got one for you, and you're going to love it."

Dave reached up and ran his fingers through his hair and looked troubled, as he was obviously used to doing stuff by the book, and being a part of a rogue rescue operation to free five hostages, one of whom was his ex girlfriend, was a little daunting.

"Fine, I'm in," he said.

"Good, did you scrounge weapons?"

"Yeah, and you're fucking lucky as hell. We just got a load from a drug bust, and they haven't been checked into evidence yet. I've got four Glock pistols, an AR-15, and an AU Aug assault rifle."

"Not bad. Not bad at all."

The food arrived, and everyone ate with little or no

conversation, as it was time to take in precious calories, reflect, and think about what lay ahead. When we finished, the waitress cleared our plates, then Johnny made a few calls, and it was time to head for Waimanalo. We decided to give Frank's Estate a wide berth and take the long way, and that meant following Johnny in his Toyota four wheel drive truck all the way along the Pali Highway before turning south and heading down the coast. He pulled over in front of the Blow Hole Bar and walked inside then returned a moment later with Lou and Jimmy, who Violet and I had met on our first visit to the bar. While the three talked, I went into the Seven Eleven and bought four twelve packs of beer and loaded it into Johnny's truck. At that point, Lou and Jimmy jumped in his vehicle, and I took a seat in the Rothster, and off we went to the beach, where we parked near an old boat ramp. The area was fairly crowded with people all enjoying this scenic piece of Oahu, and several hundred feet off shore was a weathered looking fishing boat. It was about thirty feet long and had a small cabin as well as the usual assortment of nets, poles, and fishing tackle. Johnny waved, and a man on the boat waved back then dropped an inflatable raft over the side and came ashore and joined us.

"This is my cousin Greg," Johnny said.

"Nice to meet you all. I hear someone needs a ride."

"That would be me and my squire. We need to get onto the old Robin Masters estate."

The guy laughed.

"The old *Magnum P.I.* set. Yeah, I know that place. I've

fished down there before. Lots of sharks."

"Big ones or little ones?"

"Both," he said, with a smile.

"Do you have enough diving gear for two?" I asked.

"Yeah, I also do scuba diving tours, so I have plenty of gear on the boat."

"Perfect."

We took a seat on the beach, and I explained our part of the plan to Greg, Lou, and Jimmy. Johnny also used the time to reveal his unusual water born insertion plan. It turned out that three of our helpers belonged to an outrigger club, and they would be using one of the smaller outrigger canoes to breach the beach.

"Old School. I totally get it now. That's fucking awesome," I said.

Johnny laughed, but then his demeanor changed, and he looked a little concerned as he spoke.

"So, dis guy has the wife of the deputy director of the CIA, the fiancée of the vice president, an FBI agent, a CIA officer, and her sister all held as hostages—and all you got for help is us?"

"Yeah, I know, and I also feel a little sorry for the bad guys."

Everyone laughed, and we were officially ready to get the party started, though I noticed that Jerasian had a perplexed look on his face.

"What is it, junior?" I asked him.

"Shouldn't we all have cool codenames?"

"Sure, any ideas?"

"I was thinking I could be Rogue."

"Not bad, and I'll be Santa Claus."

"Wait, why Santa Claus?" Beeber asked.

"Because I'll be bringing my presence to the estate. Get it? Presence spelled with a CE instead an NTS."

"That's stupid."

"You're stupid."

"You're both stupid, and in order to be less stupid and more cool, the team in the van shall be Trojan Horse," John said, obviously in honor of Homer's Odyssey.

"Cool, and I'll be Frodo, and Lou and Jimmy can be Peregrin and Took," Johnny said.

"I'll be Captain Ron," Greg chimed in.

"Why Captain Ron?" Bieber asked.

"Hello? The movie starring Kurt Russel and Martin Short?" I responded.

"Oh, that Captain Ron," he responded.

"As if there's another."

I had to admit that Greg just earned style points by choosing a codename that referenced one of my many guilty pleasure movies.

"Do you have a red Speedo?" I asked, referring to Captain Ron's outfit of choice in the movie.

"I do, though I only wear it when I have French tourists out for a diving expedition. It seems to put them at ease."

I looked at Babs and smiled, but he returned the gesture by giving me the finger. Apparently, Frenchmen, while having the gall to wear them, still didn't like being teased about their swimwear. I suppose it was one of the great ironies of being French. Now, everyone had a codename except Dave, so we all looked at him and quietly waited until he relented.

"OK, fuck it! Call me Zeus."

"Zeus? That's all you could come up with?" I asked.

"Fuck you, Santa Claus. Are you forgetting we have Trojan Horse, Rogue, and three of the biggest fucking hobbits I've ever seen?"

"Fine, Zeus it is, but why?"

"Lightening bolts, and I'll be residing upon my veritable Mount Olympus."

I thought a moment and smiled.

"I take it all back, Dave. It's a good codename."

Done picking codenames, first and foremost, we did a radio check, as communication and timing would be the key to our success. With our radios working and our plans in order, we each left to our assigned posts. John, Corn, Beebs, Babs, and Doug would drive south towards Robin's Nest then park a short distance away and wait for the signal to go while Johnny and his unusual threesome would leave to pick up some rifles and hit the canoe club just up the beach from Robin's Nest. Dave would drive south of Frank's place, park, and then hump it up the hill to find a good sniper spot, and, as usual, I had the toughest job at the moment, but at least I had an assistant, and I was feeling fit and ready for the job.

Jerasian and I got in the raft with Greg and paddled out

to his vessel, and we were soon weighing anchor and heading south. The sun was now hanging low over the western horizon, and the water was fairly smooth and the wind light and coming in from the east as we passed by Bellows Field, whose beaches were mostly empty during the week, as it was reserved for military personnel use only. Next came Waimanalo Beach, and soon I could see Robin's nest and its tide pool off in the distance. It was time to get ready.

We put on all our dive gear then lay down on the deck on the outbound side of the boat. We were pretty far out, but we still had to be particularly careful to stay hidden from view on the off chance that they might be using binoculars to watch the boat traffic. Of course, that also meant that Greg had to set up some equipment to make sure he looked like a proper fisherman. To that end, he put out some poles and tackle then sat back and manned the helm while keeping his attention on his equipment rather than us. With everything ready, I relaxed on the deck and took the time to visualize the plan and mentally walk through all the steps. Finished, I reached back and double checked the zipper on my watertight dive bag to make sure that it was properly sealed, but I wouldn't know for sure until I reached the tide pool.

Greg told me we were on target, and Jerasian and I gave him a thumbs up then rolled off the side of the boat and submerged as quickly as possible, hopeful that the wake from the boat covered any evidence of our presence. Greg continued on, and the quiet thrumming of his boat's engine slowly trailed off as we dove ever deeper under water. I reached the bottom at about twenty five feet down, got my bearings, then signaled Jerasian, and we started swimming towards Robin's Nest. It was always strange to be in the ocean when the light of day was rapidly diminishing, and I wondered if I might have been wiser to have chosen Corn or perhaps even Babs as my swim buddy. Corn had been a Parajumper before becoming Deputy Director of the Agency, but those days were many years and many meals in the past. Babs, to his credit, had been a French naval Commando, but, like Corn, had done a lot of wining and dining since his time in the service, so, ultimately, this all left me here with a rookie in the big, dark blue Pacific Ocean.

I swam along the bottom and performed regular checks of the surrounding waters, desperately hoping we didn't run into any Tiger Sharks. Unlike Great Whites, which usually bit people by mistake, Tiger sharks were aggressive and territorial and even more so late in the day when they began hunting for their next meal. Of course, it was getting darker by the moment and our visibility was rapidly diminishing, so, if one decided to attack me, it would strike with such speed that I'd never actually see him coming. I proceeded to try and put those thoughts in the back of my head as I soldiered on and followed the coral, feeling ever grateful that the water was getting shallower. Ten minutes passed, and the setting sun was making it even harder to find my way, but I at last reached a large open sandy expanse on the ocean floor. I had seen it on the satellite picture, so I knew I was perfectly on course, and, up ahead, I spied the breakwater that surrounded the tide pool. I altered my course ever so slightly left of the large opening, and, upon reaching the rocks, discarded my dive gear then unzipped the waterproof bag and pulled out the contents. Thankfully, everything was dry as a bone, so I pulled out the pistol, checked the action, and chambered a round. So far so good.

I grabbed the duct tape and some cable ties then zipped up the bag and handed it to Jerasian, who would wait here until I took down the first guard and gave him the all clear. I set off and swam along the breakwater to my right and paused at the opening to scan the beach. On the satellite feed, the beach guard was just this side of the tennis court, but at the moment he was nowhere to be seen. Shit, the sun was now officially below the horizon, and it was creating great swaths of shadow, and any one of them could be inhabited by my target. I waited with my body perfectly still as I meticulously swept my eyes across the beach and used my peripheral vision to search the line of trees and shrubbery. Few people knew that our peripheral vision was actually more sensitive in low light than our main vision, because it hadn't been burned out by a lifetime of looking into bright lights. On my second pass, I found him crouched under the eve of a tall tree, and he had a pair of binoculars in front of his eyes as he looked out to sea—probably at Greg and his boat. Perfect. We still had the element of surprise.

I moved ever closer, and my heartbeat became more pronounced as I approached the point of no return. Things were about to get very serious, and fellow humans might die by my hand. I never enjoyed killing, nor did it ever get any easier, but the irony was that I was good at it. When the time came that I needed to pull the trigger to save the lives of the innocent, I did it without hesitation. Bad people came to bad ends, and I had lived with that truth from the time I was a PJ up until my years in the CIA's Special Activities Division. Of course, I had been removed from that life for some time, but Frank and his men were bad people and therefore deserved a little old school justice.

I swam the last few yards to the beach but was careful to keep the Beretta above the surface in order to keep the water from fouling its action. As my left hand touched sand, I realized it was time. The guy was thirty feet away and very likely wearing body armor, which brought me to a major moral dilemma. Do I go for a head shot or center mass. The head shot would take him instantly out of the game but was a lot harder. People always did them in the movies, but in real life it took serious practice and skill. At about twenty feet, a barrel movement of an eighth of an inch left or right would move the shot off target by more than a foot, and those numbers only increased with distance. If he heard the cough of the silencer and I missed, he would be on the radio to his friends, and everything would over before it even started. The other option was center mass, and it would be a guaranteed hit, but if he were wearing body armor, it would do little more than temporarily incapacitate him. To kill or not to kill? That was the question. Did the guy have a family, or was a he a troubled soul still trying to acclimate to civilian life? Those thoughts were weighing heavily on my conscious, but it was time to get my head in the game. Just as I decided to go with the headshot, I saw the wedding ring. Fuck, center mass it is.

I raised up and kept my right arm extended and left bent at the elbow in order to brace the pistol in my usual firing posture. It was called the cheek weld, and it allowed me to look straight down my arm as though it were the stock of a rifle. Whatever you saw, you killed. Now, I was staring at my first adversary, and it took him a second to register my presence before he lowered the binoculars and reached for his pistol, but it was too late. I fired twice, and both impacted his chest and sent him falling backward onto the ground. I quickly closed the distance, but kept the gun still aimed at him until we were face to face, and I could see his pained expression as he lay there mostly incapacitated. He had the wind knocked out of him by the impact of the bullets, but he had been wearing a vest, so he was therefore still very much alive. He stared up at me with fear in his eyes, and it was odd to think that we had once been on the same team and perhaps even played in the same game, but life had somehow brought us together on a collision course as enemies. I reached down, zip tied his arms and legs, then duct taped his mouth before removing his radio, body armor, and very sweet silenced HK 94 submachine gun. I put on the armor then attached his radio to my free ear and felt good to finally have a little good luck. Now, I had a way to hear the bad guys, but, at the moment, all was quiet, and that meant everything was going to plan. It was therefore time to bring in the Rogue and take over their security room, so I cued my waterproof mic.

"Rogue, Santa is on the beach, bring in the bag of toys, over," I said.

Jerasian swam in then climbed out of the surf and joined me beside guard one.

"Holy shit, this is really happening," he said, looking down at the man.

"It is, and so far you're doing a great job. Now, hold tight here until I give you the next all clear. At that point, you're going to fulfill your D&D character's traits—but in real life. Are you clear on your next objective?"

"Yeah, make my way to the pool and leave the extra weapons and the radio under the lounger in the southeast corner. When I've completed that mission, I check in and then hall ass to the security room."

"You've got it, now wait here until I give you the signal."

I slipped back to the beach but kept below the line of ocean front greenery as I made my way to the main house. Fortunately, they didn't have any direct camera coverage on the beach, but the house was a different story. Just above the wine cellar window was a camera that turned through a hundred and eighty degree arc, and I waited for it to cycle all the way to one side then ran over and crouched directly below it where I was safely out of its view. At that point, I knelt down at the wine cellar window and smiled to myself as I thought back to the tour of the estate. For once, my obsessive compulsive personality had come in handy, as I had seen that the locking latch on the wine cellar window wouldn't fully engage. Now, I had a nice easy place to breach the estate, and I reached down and slid the diving knife out of the sheath on my leg then wedged the blade under the window edge and easily moved the latch until the little locking arm was completely clear. Next, I opened the window and peered in to find my next obstacle—an infra red motion sensor located on the wall to my right.

Five days ago, I had defeated a very similar sensor, though it had been part of a toilet, and its function was to automatically flush when the occupant disembarked. This little unit detected the same kind of heat source and would entail a similar principle, but I'd use duct tape instead of toilet paper. I tore off a piece of duct tape and lowered it down and stuck it over the sensor, thereby temporarily blinding it's ability to detect heat signatures—namely my own. The security system was temporarily defeated, and I slid through the window legs first and dropped to the floor, where I quickly moved to the wine cellar door. I put my ear to its old wooden planks and listened carefully for the sound of any people out in the hallway. All appeared quiet for the moment, so I lifted the latch and eased open the door and saw that all was thankfully clear.

I left the wine cellar and made my way to the security room to find that the door was closed this time, so I reached down and slowly turned the knob, ever hopeful it was unlocked. It continued to turn, so I cautiously opened the door and discovered that the chair in front of the monitors was empty. The only thing occupying the desk was a radio headset, and that meant that the guy who had been wearing it couldn't be far away. I looked around the room and spied another door, but as I moved closer, it suddenly opened, and there stood the man I had seen the day before. He had obviously just used the bathroom, which was the reason he had discarded his radio. No one liked to accidentally broadcast a bathroom stop—especially if it was a number two. He looked stunned but reacted quickly by retreating back inside and slamming the door. Fuck, this was an unexpected bump in the road, but the good news was that his headset was still out here, and his bathroom radio etiquette just earned him five gentleman points in my book.

Gentleman or not, I still had to go in and get him. Just as I moved towards the door, two muted shots came right through the center and both hit me in the chest and knocked me onto my back. He might have forgotten the radio, but he obviously remembered to bring his gun—a wise move considering the circumstances. Lying on the floor with an aching in my chest, I realized that life was always about setbacks and lessons learned the hard way. Thankfully, this lesson had worked in my favor, as I had been wise and donned his friend's vest, thereby freeing myself from a traumatic and premature demise.

I was still flat on my back and recovering when the door opened and my adversary emerged. I fired up into his chest to return the favor, and it knocked him off his feet. He, like his peers, was wearing a vest and therefore experienced the very same wrenching pain and knockdown. I struggled to my feet and closed the distance and arrived just in time to kick his gun out of his hand. I tried to follow it up with a stomp kick to his wrist, but he dodged my effort then wrapped his arm around my ankle and rolled to his right, thereby forcing me to the ground. Just as I landed, he slammed his left elbow into my inner thigh, and it caused a massive jolt of pain. Disregarding it, I rolled to my right to create enough space to send a kick with my free foot square up into his jaw. It knocked him backward, and he hit his head on the hard tiled floor and released my other foot. I shifted slightly and threw another kick, though this one was to his groin, and it brought his head back up and into range for the last kick. This time I put a bit more gusto into it, and the blow split his nose and knocked him unconscious. I got up and quickly zip tied his hand and feet then applied duct taped to his mouth and dragged him into the bathtub. The score was good guys two, bad guys zero. I went over to the security monitors and saw that all of the bad guys were still in their same positions, so I cued my radio.

"Rogue, step two completed. Deliver the presents and come join Santa in the Jacuzzi—clothing optional."

I monitored the security cameras and watched as Jerasian made his way to the pool, and I had to give the guy credit. He was indeed sneaky and did an excellent job of using the available cover to make the journey without being seen by Rex and his men. After delivering the package, he did a radio check.

"The presents are under three," he said.

"Roger. The Jacuzzi is nice and hot, if not a little lonely. Get your Rogue ass in here."

Jerasian left the pool area and once again kept to the shadows and maintained a low crouch as he moved swiftly across the estate. I lost visual when he reached the wine cellar, then I heard a noise and turned my gun towards the door but lowered it when I saw that it was Jerasian right on schedule.

"Everyone check in, over," I said.

"Trojan Horse is on station," Corn said.

"Zeus is in place, over," Dave said.

"Frodo, Pergegrin, and Took are ready to leave the Shire, over," Johnny said.

"Roger that. Secondary teams, move into place. Trojan Horse, wait for final approval."

I brought up the camera closest to the beach then turned its view until I could see the edge of the tidal pool. Three minutes later, a small outrigger canoe landed on the beach, and Johnny, Lou, and Jimmy, with their rifles in hand, stepped out and moved towards the boathouse before checking in a second later.

"The Hobbits have reached Magnum's place, over," Johnny said.

"All right you are officially our eyes, Rogue. Lock that door after I leave and keep an eye on these fuckers."

I left Jerasian and walked back to the wine cellar and slithered out the window and moved to a position on the western side of the property. I had an excellent view of the estate, and my back was to a wall, so now it was time to call in the diversion.

"Trojan Horse, you are clear to go. Good luck and godspeed."

"Roger and out."

They would discard the radio and head for Robin's Nest, so now it was time to wait, watch, and pray that everyone and everything went according to plan.

CHAPTER TWENTY-EIGHT
Did You See the Sun Rise Part III

Every job in the world had downtime, but none of them had the stress that existed when that job was related to combat. I'd spent countless hours in planes, boats, submarines, and Humvees simply waiting—waiting to deploy, and every second of that time was spent trying my best to focus on the success of the mission rather than the failure, as failure often meant death. This was one of those moments, only now it wasn't just my life or the lives of my fellow soldiers on the line. Most of the people here were civilians—innocents, who didn't ask for this kind of danger. The stress level was therefore about tenfold to anything I'd ever experienced, but I was a professional, and more importantly, deep down, I was a pathological optimist, and so, when life offered up lemons, it was time to man up and make a lovely lemon tart. Still, I was a bit on edge and looked at my watch to see that two minutes had passed without any word.

"Fuck, " I said, aloud.

A second later, Jerasian finally came over the radio.

"Trojan Horse is at the gate, over," he said.

"How's it looking?" I responded.

"OK, but the Trojans have the Greeks out of the horse and have searched every orifice except for their buttholes."

I felt my heart pounding in my chest as I desperately hoped that we made it through this stage of the plan. If they suspected anything, things would get very ugly—very quickly.

"Trojan Horse has passed muster! Greeks are back inside and on the move."

"OK, teams, this is where Santa, the Hobbits, and Zeus earn their keep. Everyone be careful and keep watch, as these fuckers are damn good at killing people."

Halfway across the estate, the Rothster veered off the main driveway and raced across the lawn and slid to a stop just past the tennis courts. Corn, John, Babs, and the nerds piled out and ran for cover behind the stone wall, and, a second later, Corn's voice came over the radio.

"Trojan Horse has landed, the Greeks are armed and in place."

I watched as one, then another of Rex's men began heading towards the Rothster. At the moment, they were spread out around the estate, but, as trained military personnel, they were used to operating as a cohesive unit. That meant they would coverage on one position in order to be ready to mount some kind of counter attack. Perfect. Their radio chatter was harried, but they moved swiftly and efficiently until they were all on sight and staring at the empty vehicle. Rex, looking confused, cued his mic.

"Eyes, can you tell us where they are?" he asked.

I was pretty sure they were referring to the guy I had left tied up in the bathtub.

"Negative," I responded.

"Repeat over."

"Negative. All clear."

It appeared that Rex didn't recognize my voice as being that of Eyes, and he looked around nervously then ordered his men to move and take up defensive positions. They formed up so that each faced a different direction, but it was too late. Our people were already in superior firing positions.

"Rex, it's Finn here. You're surrounded. Lay down your weapons and place your hands on your heads. There's no need to die for Frank Williams."

"You really think I'm the least bit worried about you?"

"Probably not, but you should be. You're completely surrounded by a team of well armed and trained operatives in superior firing positions."

"Believe me, it's not a problem."

Rex and his team started moving towards the opposite fence line.

"I wouldn't go that way," I said.

I signaled Johnny, and he and his threesome of locals

popped their heads over the sills of the windows in the boathouse and brandished their large caliber hunting rifles. Rex and his team paused, and he cued his mic.

"Seriously, Finn? You think a band of local *mokes* is going to make any difference?"

"Yeah, I do—as long as we also have you pinned down by a decorated Army Sniper."

"Bullshit."

I had no idea if Dave was actually a decorated Army sniper, but war was also waged on a psychological level, and we needed every advantage. I cued my other radio and told Dave that we needed a show of force. A second later, I heard the sound of a rifle, then a bullet impacted six inches from Rex's foot. Startled, he jumped sideways then tried to better his position, but it was pointless with Dave high overhead on the ridge. I watched as Rex looked around then whispered something to his men. Clearly, he wasn't ready to give up, and, without warning, he and his entire team made a break for it and fired in multiple directions with their silenced HK submachine guns as they tried to carve themselves an avenue of escape. I should have known that former Delta Force soldiers wouldn't go down without a hell of a fight, so this was probably going to get worse before it got better.

Bullets started flying in all directions, and it was hard to tell which were from friend and which were from foe. I aimed the HK I had taken off the beach guard and fired a three round burst at the group, and, while my shots missed, they landed close enough to make Rex and his men scatter and separate into two fire teams as they turned and began working their way towards the garage. I decided to cut around the back of the house, as I was hoping to cut off their retreat, and, as I moved along the fence line, sporadic gunfire continued out on the main property. It was time for a SITREP or, in civilian terms, a situation report.

"Rogue, what's going on? Over!"

"They've split up but appear to be heading towards the garage. It appears that at least one of them is wounded, over."

"Roger. All teams, I'm moving around the back of the house to intercept," I said.

It was always a good idea to check in and report your position to your team, so they wouldn't get you confused with the enemy. I moved past the house, but between me and the garage lay a large hedgerow, and beyond that was mostly open ground dotted by the occasional palm tree. I slowed my progress and kept close to the hedge and soon spied Rex and his team moving methodically, with one man always covering their retreat. I pulled up the HK and was about to fire when I heard Dave's rifle go off, and, an instant later, was startled by the sickening thud of a bullet impacting flesh just behind me. I turned to see that one of Rex's men had doubled back as an extra measure of security and was now splayed out on the ground. I should have known an ex Delta soldier would do something like that, but I was still a little rusty from having been out of the game, and I was suddenly feeling incredibly lucky as I cued my mic.

"Thanks, Dave. I owe you one."

"What makes you think I wasn't aiming for you and missed?"

"Because I still have your T-shirt, and you wouldn't be able to get it back if you killed me."

"True, over."

Jerasian came over the radio sounding worried.

"They're in the garage now," he said.

"Thanks, I'm on it."

Looking over to the east, I saw Corn, John, Babs, and the nerds moving up the far side of the property, while over at the boathouse were Johnny and his merry band of *mokes*. I was thinking we had a bit of a turkey shoot on our hands, until I heard an engine rev in the garage then watched as the door opened, and out came a white Range Rover. The driver gunned the engine and raced up the dirt driveway towards the front gate while the occupants fired from its open windows. We all returned fire and peppered the Range Rover with bullets, and fifty yards up the road it veered off the dirt path and came to an unceremonious halt when it rolled into a large palm tree. I called a cease fire over the radio then switched to the pistol as I walked up to the vehicle. With my weapon at the ready, I visually inspected the interior of the car and found two men splayed out, bleeding, and covered in glass shards. I pulled open the passenger door and realized they might still be alive, so I started pulling them out and laying them on the ground in an improvised triage.

They were still breathing and might live, but, as I was about to dial 911, I realized something very important. We were at least a man or two short, and Rex was nowhere to be found. Worried that this was a planned distraction, I cued my mic.

"Rogue, you see any other hostiles sneaking around? Over."

All was quiet, so I repeated myself.

"Rogue, any sign of the remaining hostiles?"

"Only me," a man said.

I turned around and saw one of Rex's men emerging from the direction of the main house, and he had his arm around Jerasian's throat and a gun to the young man's head, which unfortunately meant that I had found one of our missing bad guys. Now we had another hostage situation and still didn't know where in the hell Rex was hiding, so I cued my mic.

"Zeus, do you have a clear shot?" I asked.

"Negative, Santa."

"Well, take it if you get it."

"Roger."

The man continued to use Jerasian as a human shield as he walked closer, but he came to a stop about twenty feet away.

"Well played, Finn. We underestimated you."

"Yeah, you and my high school guidance counselor."

He laughed.

"You OK, Rogue?" I asked Jerasian.

"Yeah, but I forgot to lock the door."

"It happens, so, what now?" I asked the man.

He looked at his phone then back at me.

"Good question," he said.

"Most of your team are captured, dead, or dying. The best chance you have of saving them is putting down the gun and releasing the kid so that we can call for some medical help."

"They knew what they were facing when they took this job. Every soldier that steps out onto the field of battle knows that he or she might never come home."

"They don't have to die this time."

"We have a mission to accomplish."

"What the hell are you talking about? You're working for a God damn lunatic!"

He looked at his phone again then smiled.

"Mission accomplished," he said, pushing the kid away and bringing his pistol up to his mouth and firing.

A swath of pink mist shot out the back of his head as he crumpled and dropped to the ground. I raced to his side and saw that he was already well into the afterlife and likely looking at a two bedroom condo in one of the quieter neighborhoods in hell. At least, in his final moments, he did the noble thing and spared Jerasian. I cued my mic and signaled an all clear but suddenly had a bad feeling. Why did the guy keep looking at his phone, and what the hell did he mean by mission accomplished? Nobody called losing most of his team and killing himself an accomplishment unless it somehow achieved something else. I raced over and picked up his phone, and on it was a text from Rex that simply said all clear-everything in place.

"Jesus, why in the hell would that guy sacrifice himself like that?" Beeber asked.

"War changes people, and sometimes they can't leave it behind. They need a mission and orders, and it doesn't even matter what they are or who they come from."

"Tragic."

"Indeed, but enough lamenting. We need to get into that house and free our women," I said.

We raced up to the front door, found it open, and entered the house to discover it empty.

"I'm getting a very bad feeling," I said.

"No shit," John added.

"Do you think this was all planned?" Corn asked.

"Not sure, but these men wouldn't have sacrificed themselves for nothing. There is definitely something we're missing, so we better find the girls and figure out what the hell is actually going on here."

We moved through the dark house, room by room, and the anticipation and anxiety grew with each empty space we encountered. At last we saw a light at the end of the hall on the third floor and moved forward cautiously in case there were any more of Frank's security men still entrenched in the house. Only feet from the door, I heard a quiet murmur then silence.

"I think I might have heard one of the girls," I whispered.

"Just one?" John responded.

"I'm not actually sure, but, so far, this is way too easy, and my *scrot-sense* is tingling like a motherfucker. I'm thinking everyone better hold up while I check this out."

Rex and his team were ex Delta Force, and that meant that they, like me, were versed in many skills of combat—two of them being explosives and traps. A dark house with one lit room seemed like a giant trap, and I was feeling like a big fat rat, and the lit room was the cheese. I took out my iPhone and turned on the flashlight app and worked my way very slowly down the rest of the hallway, and there, just above the floor and extending between two ornamental statues, was a laser tripwire. Cross it and something happened—likely something very bad. I stepped over the beam and traced the wires to a small electronic unit wired to some C4 explosives. Lovely, there was enough to take out the immediate area and us with it. Clearly, Frank and Rex weren't fucking around, and so I disconnected the device from the explosives and switched off the beam.

"Fucking Frank and Rex are bigger assholes than I previously thought. They had a nice big bomb wired up to take us out if we got this far."

"Remind me to kiss your scrot and give it a big ol' thank you," John said.

"I will, but I better check for more shit before we start celebrating."

As there might still be more traps, I dropped down into a crouch and slipped my head past the doorframe and hazarded a brief glance around the room. Oddly, it was empty, and the only light was coming from a large wall mounted computer monitor. I slithered in until I could see the entire screen, and there before my eyes, in all their digital magnificence, were our women. They were sitting in chairs with their hands and feet zip tied to the arms and legs, and their mouths were covered in tape. They appeared to be in some kind of concrete structure, and Jessica was in the center while the others were on either side of her spread out in a neat line. Rachel and Violet were to her right while Bridgette and Lux were to her left, and all of them looked terrified and vulnerable, but at least Violet and Lux were trained field agents and therefore had the potential to hopefully aid us in some way—though it seemed unlikely given their situation. I continued to stare, unsure if it was picture or video, when I suddenly saw movement.

"Holy shit! Get in here!" I said, which brought all the guys rushing in to join me.

The girls all suddenly looked directly towards the camera, which meant that it was a live feed, and they could hear me.

"Violet! It's Finn."

Violet tried to speak, frantically moving her head, but the duct tape kept her from making any sense.

"Where are you? In the house?"

She moved her head left and right, signifying the answer was no.

"Then where?" I asked, knowing full well it was a stupid question, as she obviously couldn't answer.

Meanwhile, Beeber pulled out his iPhone.

"I better record all this in case there is some kind of clue we're not seeing," he said.

"Good idea. Violet, can you give me any kind of signal or clue? Anything?"

Suddenly, Frank walked in from the left and stood in the center and looked like a smug asshole.

"Hello, everyone. I assume that if you're alive then the remainder of my security team are dead or captured, and we have officially moved on to the contingency plan."

"What the hell are you talking about, Frank?" John asked.

"Come now, John. Do you think a man gets to my position in life without having a contingency plan? Speaking of which, I must offer my congratulations on getting past the tripwire. Rex and I both figured that one would do the trick."

"Do you mind getting to the point, Frank?" John asked.

"No problem. So, I assume you've realized the idea was to kill all of you, but, if by some off chance that didn't happen, we put in place some counter measures, the first being the bomb, the second being that we relocated all the women to a more secure location."

"To what end?" I asked.

"To John's end, or at least the end of his political career."

"Not going to happen, Frankie. We have proof that Jessica is innocent."

"Perhaps, but you don't have Jessica, nor any of the other ladies for that matter."

"So, what are you going to do? Hold them indefinitely?" John asked.

"No, just until tomorrow when you announce that you're not running for president."

"After that, I'll give you their location."

"That doesn't make any sense, Frank. Why would you do that when you know that you're going to prison?"

"Prison? Hardly. I'll be long gone, enjoying my retirement and living like a king in a country without extradition."

"You've been in the game too long to give it up so easily."

"I've had a good run, and I'm ready for retirement, but it doesn't really matter what you believe, because I hold all the cards. So, I expect you to do exactly as I wish, then we'll come to some kind of arrangement for your precious loved ones."

Some movement caught my attention, and I glanced over and saw that Violet looked particularly uncomfortable, though I couldn't tell if she was crying or perhaps had something in her eye. God only knew what horrible shit Frank had already subjected them to in the pursuit of his evil agenda. My attention was abruptly drawn back to Frank when he cleared his throat and continued speaking.

"Just so you know. The girls are all wired up to about four pounds of C4 explosive, which I can remotely detonate with my phone here," Frank said, holding up his hand.

On his phone's screen we could clearly see a digital display which had two large buttons, one red and one green. Above it was a digital timer, so the fucker had some kind of app on his fucking phone that could remotely detonate a bomb. What the hell was the world coming to when some asshole actually created an app for such a twisted purpose?

"I hit button number one and a thirty second countdown sequence begins. If I don't hit the second button before it reaches zero, boom! All of these lovely ladies will be very dead, and the best part of it is that I can activate it from pretty much anywhere in the world. As I said, I hold all the cards, so don't be getting any more ridiculous ideas about attempting another rescue."

Frank walked over and stood closer to the camera so that his face was now huge and looming over us.

"Well, I can't say it hasn't been a little fun, but I look forward to seeing you on television tomorrow morning, John, as you wrap this all up to a nice, tidy end. Oh, and make sure you get plenty of sleep. I wouldn't want you looking bad during your last official day in office."

"Fuck you very much, Frank," John said.

"Until tomorrow, ta-ta," Frank responded.

The video window suddenly went black as the connection was terminated, and all of us stood in utter silence unsure what to say or do.

"Now what?" John asked.

"Nothing's changed. We get our fucking women back."

"Yeah, but how do we accomplish that? We don't even know where they are."

"I'm still working on that part of the plan."

Shit, I seemed to have a real gift for believing I was at the glorious conclusion of a difficult affair, only to be thwarted by some unforeseen element. If I had a dollar for every time it happened in recent memory, I'd have enough money to buy Dave a whole drawer full of Han Job T-shirts. Oh well, it was time to put our thinking caps back on and get our shit together, as lives were literally in the balance.

CHAPTER TWENTY-NINE
Arousal Release Resolution

John called Sandra and reported his location, and, after about five solid minutes of profanity, she calmed down enough to hear the rest of the story. It didn't absolve our sins of smuggling the vice president out from under her watchful gaze, but she seemed to at least be a little more understanding. Within minutes, the Secret Service as well as the local police, emergency medical workers, and, last but not least, Special Agent Dave Moore descended upon the estate. Frank's security men were ushered into custody or ambulances, and I was hoping that at least one of them could tell us where they took the women. As fate would have it, most were in critical condition, and those able to speak were remaining quiet.

We thanked Johnny and his friends then left Robin's Nest and headed back to the resort to convene in my room to discuss our options. The mood was somber, but Beeber, Doug, and Jerasian were adamant that they might be able to decipher something from the video or perhaps even trace Frank's conference call. All three nerds set to work and continued on for a good fifteen straight minutes before Jerasian suddenly spoke up.

"Hey, do you remember what Frank said?" he asked.

"Yeah, what about it?" I responded.

"He said he could detonate the explosive device from anywhere in the world."

"So?"

"So, how would he achieve that?"

"Good question. I imagine he could use a long range radio signal or perhaps a cell phone."

"Perhaps, but what entity unites the entire world at the moment?"

"According to Doug, it's Porn."

"Very funny," Doug said.

"Yeah, but where do we get our porn?" Jerasian asked.

"The internet—the source of Doug's porn," I said, starting to understand where Jerasian was going with his reasoning.

"Exactly, and I'm guessing he's accessing the bomb via an internet connection, which means we might be able to find the bomb's IP address, and, if so, we could override his access and possibly deactivate it remotely."

"You are officially my new CIO when we get you back to San Francisco," Beeber said.

I was suddenly feeling optimistic, as we were starting to climb out of the depressing helplessness of ignorance.

"Wait a minute! Beeber, can you play that footage from your phone for me?"

"Yeah, I've already downloaded it to my laptop."

I walked around and looked over his shoulder, and, this time, I focused on Violet. Earlier, I had stupidly thought Violet had something in her eye, but now as I watched more closely, I realized that her eye movements were deliberate.

"Can you rewind it and play it again?"

Beeber dragged the progress bar back and hit play, and it suddenly made sense.

"How could I be so stupid?" I blurted out.

"Right now or in general?" John asked.

"Right now, asshole, because I just realized Violet is fucking doing Morse Code with her eyes!"

"Seriously?"

"Yeah, its something her dad taught her as a kid, so that they could use it to secretly communicate at boring social events."

"Wait, you know about the whole Morse Code thing?" Dave asked, sounding irritated.

"Yeah, Violet and her dad told me about it at dinner."

Dave groaned.

"So, when are you heading back to the mainland?" he asked.

"Violet didn't tell you I put in an offer on a place in Hawaii Kai?"

"No, did she tell you that's within rifle range of my place?"

"I hate to interrupt your lovefest, but are you serious about this Morse Code thing?" John asked.

"Yeah."

"Well then let's figure out what the fuck she's trying to tell us."

Everyone suddenly jumped up and moved over to the computer to look at Violet. I had learned Morse Code in the military but hadn't done it in years and could only make out a few letters. The first was dash-dot-dot, which stood for D. The next letter was dot dot, which I remembered was either S or I, but, luckily for us, Doug still remembered his Morse.

"We have D and I," Doug said.

Next was dot-dash then dash-dash.

"And A and M," Doug added.

We had D, I, A, and M. Holy shit! I knew where they had the girls.

"Diamond Head!" I said, excitedly.

"How can you be sure?"

"Keep watching."

When she was finished, Doug looked over at me and smiled.

"You should have been on Wheel of Fortune," he said.

"Beebs, bring up everything you can on Diamond Head, namely what it's used for at the moment."

He tapped a few keys then looked up.

"It's mostly a tourist attraction, but it also has a National

Guard base."

"Holy shit! It all makes perfect fucking sense now."

"What does?" John asked.

"Everything—and especially the location. When Violet and I were in trouble up on that farm, an Air National Guard helicopter arrived on scene but was gone by the time we rendezvoused with the FBI. I bet they exfiltrated the hit team. It's the only way they could have disappeared so quickly, and you of course know who has authority over the national guard?"

"Frank's good friend—the fucking Governor," John said.

"Exactly!"

"Well, it makes sense that they're not out in the middle of nowhere, as they have reasonably fast internet based on that Skype call," Beeber said.

"Does having the location hasten your ability to hack into the explosive device?" I asked.

"Absolutely."

"Good, now, you guys work on the bomb, and I'll work out the details on finding out their specific location within Diamond Head."

I took out my laptop and opened Google Earth and zoomed in to the famous crater to get a feeling for its basic layout.

"Doug, do you still have access to that Satellite?"

"Let me check."

A minute later he looked over and smiled.

"Yep, got it right here."

He proceeded to zoom in until the entire crater and all of its buildings filled the screen.

"Shit, it's a pretty big place, and thermal imaging won't penetrate the buildings."

"I know, but I'm assuming that they had to have a pretty big vehicle to move all the women, and I'm thinking a minivan at the very least. If we can find the vehicle, we can determine the actual building."

"Good thinking."

Doug zoomed in even more then meticulously scrolled over each building until he found a white passenger van parked beside an outlying structure.

"That's likely it," he said.

"OK, now we have to figure out the best way to do this."

I brought up Google street view and did a visual walk-through of the grounds. It was standard government issue with chain link fences and barbed wire, and, annoyingly, there was a lot of open ground between the fence and the building, and the entire area was likely well-lit considering the abundance of lamp posts. A stealthy incursion was therefore going to be difficult to say the least.

"Any thoughts?" I asked.

"They have a three hundred and sixty degree view with no obstructions," Corn said.

"I was thinking the same thing. No wonder he chose that place."

"Of course, we can't even be sure that Frank or any of his people will be there," John said.

"I suspect Frank will stick around," I said.

"Yeah, but you heard him. He could detonate the bomb from anywhere in the world. Why not take off?"

"He's an egomaniac. I think he'll hang around a bit to glower and gloat," I said.

"OK, so, assuming he stays on site. What's our best way to get in there without him seeing us and pushing the button on his phone?"

Doug smiled.

"I think Beebs already nailed it earlier. Do a high altitude low opening jump, but this time drop right in on their blind spot by landing on the roof."

"How in the hell could we put that together on such short notice?" I asked.

"Well, we are currently sitting here with the vice president of the United States and the deputy director of the CIA."

"OK, suppose we somehow arrange a plane and a fucking parachute—who's going with me?"

Everyone suddenly got quiet.

"Corn?"

"Jesus, I haven't jumped out of an airplane since that last mission in Afghanistan when my chute fouled."

"Have you done any jumps lately?" Doug asked me.

"Not in the traditional sense."

"Meaning?"

"I used a parasailing rig to infiltrate Soft Taco Island, and I also escaped out of the back of an old cargo plane on a pallet being used to air drop supplies to a remote village in Jordan."

"Good enough, let's arrange a ride," John said.

"Fuck it. Why not. You only live once."

"And only die once as well," Beeber added.

"So who do I call?" John asked.

"I've got this one," Dave said.

"Seriously?"

"Yeah, hello! I was an airborne Ranger, so believe me—I know who we can go to for help with parachuting on this island."

Dave got on the phone, made a call, and five minutes later had me booked on a private charter with a local parachute company. The owner was a retired Navy SEAL and former member of the elite Leap Frogs parachute team, and he was more than happy to do a favor for his friend Dave as well as the vice president of the United States. Now, we had the beginnings of a plan, but it was time to set it in motion. First and foremost, Beeber, Doug, and Jerasian would continue trying to hack into Frank's bomb and hopefully deactivate it long before I even touched down on the ground. In the meantime, the rest of us and a team of Secret Service would immediately head to the airport, where I'd leave the group and get on the plane. The others would continue on to Diamond Head and hang back on the periphery, except for Dave, who would hike up to a good observation spot and serve as my forward air control of sorts. With all the teams in place, I would parachute in and make a quiet incursion so as not to alert Frank or Rex if they were indeed on site and keeping watch over our women. When I had secured the location, I would signal for everyone to come in and clean up the scene. We all had a task to perform, but mine, as usual, was the most dangerous.

We left the resort, and twenty five minutes later we were meeting Captain Carl Binder USN retired. He was a genuinely nice guy with movie star looks, perfect teeth, and the obvious physique of a SEAL — meaning lots of upper body development. He was around six foot and didn't crush my hand when he shook it, which I always saw as a good sign of a secure well adjusted person. The others left to get in place while I went inside with Carl, and he gave me a brief refresher course before allowing me to personally pack my chute. It was a habit from the good old days of Pararescue and always gave me a little more confidence when I was stepping off into the great blue yonder.

With everything ready to go, we walked out onto the tarmac and met the pilot. His name was Dennis, and he was also former Navy, which gave me yet another boost of confidence that he wouldn't accidentally drop me off somewhere over the Pacific Ocean. The engines fired up, and we belted in and prepared for takeoff. Four minutes later we had clearance, and the PAC P-750 XL airplane was soon lifting off and taking us skyward. This particular aircraft could fit more than fifteen people, but tonight, including the pilot, there were only three of us, and the emptiness of the plane only made the journey that much more foreboding.

"So, how long since your last jump?"

"Five or so years."

"And last night jump?"

"Five or so years."

"Well, don't worry. It's as easy as falling off a horse."

"Yeah, a twelve thousand foot horse."

"Don't worry. We won't be that high. This is actually going to be more of a LALO," he said, with a smile.

"Low altitude low opening. Funny."

Low altitude meant having less room for error. If my chute fouled, I would have very little or no time to cut it away and deploy the reserve, which made the possibility of dying a horrific and premature death a much greater possibility. I looked out the window and saw the lights of Honolulu glimmering not so far below and started to wonder what kind of idiotic adventure I had gotten myself into. Then, I thought about Violet and the others and realized that my task, no matter how difficult or treacherous, needed to be done. So that others may live. That was my credo in the old days, and I was again living up to its noble standards.

"Approaching Diamond Head. Time to get ready."

We stood and walked towards the rear of the plane, and Carl clicked into a safety harness then opened the door. Soon thereafter, the pilot called out from the cockpit.

"Ten second warning."

Carl counted down.

"Ten, nine, eight, seven, six, five, four, three—good luck, PJ," he said, patting me on the back.

Out I went into the dark Hawaiian night, where the drone of the plane was instantly eclipsed by the roaring howl of the wind. I threw out my arms and legs to stabilize my descent, then took a moment to get my bearings and sight in on my target. The Diamond Head crater lay just below, and its well lit interior and buildings stood out in stark contrast to the dark outer rim. I maneuvered a little to my right and adjusted my course and soon could discern my landing zone. Six more seconds passed, and I checked my altimeter and saw that I was at my target altitude, and it was time to pull the ripcord. I said a silent prayer for my testicles then yanked. The drag shoot trailed out, then shortly thereafter the main shoot popped open, and my balls slammed deep into the parachute harness, which made their cries of angst almost audible over the rushing wind. Still, their temporary discomfort meant that I had again avoided a premature demise—at least for the moment, anyway.

"Chute successfully deployed. How's the LZ look? Over."

"All clear. No one in sight, over," Dave responded.

"Roger that, I'm heading in, over."

With the chute open, my course was more subject to the wind and, therefore, more difficult to control as I tried to steer towards the target building. I'd done hundreds of jumps, and the coordination and muscle memory came back quickly, but this was still the most brutally short refresher course I could have ever imagined. I was about two hundred and fifty feet from my target and reaching the most critical part of the jump. If I missed the building's roof, then I would land out in the open and forfeit any possibility of surprise. I needed this to be perfect. So far, I was right on course, and, better still, the wind was now mostly non existent with my descent now shielded by the crater's high walls. The roof drew ever closer, and when it was only about fifteen feet below me, I pulled back on the straps, and the chute flared, and I landed in the very center of the roof as softly as a butterfly's kiss. Safely on target, I cued my mic and spoke.

"The eagle has landed," I said.

"Roger that, I have visual," Dave responded.

"As do we," John said.

Somewhere up on the ridge above me was Dave, and somewhere off in the crater around me were John, Corn, Babs, Douglass, and Sandra. The nerds were of course back in the hotel room, where they had plenty of wifi that they would hopefully utilize to deactivate the bomb.

"Any word, nerds?" I asked.

Beeber's voice suddenly came on the radio.

"We're close. Already hacked into their local area network, but we're still working on getting into the actual explosive device, over."

"Roger and out."

I rolled up my parachute, stowed it beside an air conditioning unit, and took a minute to survey the roof and gather my courage. I'd done plenty of rescue operations but very few where the majority of the hostages were close friends let alone lovers. This one was therefore especially difficult on many levels, with the first and foremost being that it was entirely personal. I pulled out the Beretta, chambered a round, and then moved along the roof to look for a way down into the building. For once, luck was on my side, as up ahead lay a roof access hatch. I tried it and found it open, which wasn't too surprising, as practicality often won out in large bureaucratic systems like the National Guard. People had to access the roof on occasion and having a locked hatch called for a key—something easily lost in a large building with an ever changing and semi-transient population. Therefore, it made more sense to leave it open, especially when you took into account the obvious question as to who in the hell would possibly try, let alone be able, to gain access to the building via the roof—without a parachute and a death wish that is.

The building was two stories tall and about the size of a small gymnasium, which meant I had a lot of ground to cover. I quietly descended a white steel ladder to find myself in some kind of janitorial maintenance room. I slipped past the mops, buckets, and cleaning supplies, and moved out into a large and dimly lit hallway. All was clear as I walked along and checked each room I passed until finally coming to a closed door. I turned the knob and opened it to discover the entrance to the stairwell. That was it for this floor, so it was time to go downstairs.

"Nerds, any news, over?" I asked.

"We're still working on the device. Any minute now, over."

"Good, I'm getting closer to the lion's den, over."

I moved into the stairwell and down past the middle landing to the main floor. The stairs continued lower to some kind of basement level, but I needed to clear the main floor first to make sure someone didn't sneak up behind me—most likely that fucker Rex. I turned the knob and opened the door a crack and saw another empty hallway, and I slipped outside and moved along and checked each room before rounding a corner and seeing a light on at the end of the hall. I eased silently forward with my gun at the ready until reaching the edge of the doorframe, whereupon I peered inside and, judging by the bank of security monitors, had discovered some kind of security room. I stepped inside and took a quick look around the room before turning my attention to the monitors. The entire building and outside were completely covered by cameras, which at least justified my extreme means of infiltration. I turned my attention to the center monitor and saw that it had a wide angle view of the women, and they looked as they had earlier, except, from this vantage point, I could see that Frank was working on a computer off to the side. Clearly, I had the right building, but I still needed to find the right room.

Just as I turned to leave, Rex appeared in the doorway, and he was holding a silenced SIG Sauer. He reacted quickly and fired off several rounds, but I dove behind the desk then rolled to the other side before popping up and returning fire. My shots impacted the doorway only inches from his head, and it sent him diving for cover. With Rex temporarily out of view in the hallway, I immediately got up and moved, as close quarters gun battles were all about sighting your enemy, shooting, then changing positions as soon as possible. People who camped in one place generally got killed, so, if I wanted to live, I needed to move.

I took up residence behind the door and was precariously perched on top of a small filing cabinet. It was a ridiculous location, but the idea was to be in an unlikely a place as possible in order to add a little surprise to our next exchange. Rex wasn't your average bear, so I needed to get creative if I hoped to stay alive. A second later he came through the door, and he stayed low as he quickly swept the room. He obviously wasn't expecting me to be up on the cabinet to his right, and I used that moment of confusion to fire off two rounds, and they impacted him center chest. He gasped in pain as he fell backwards onto the floor, and I hopped down, closed the distance, and kicked his pistol out of his hand before realizing he, like his fellow security men on the estate, was wearing a bullet proof vest. The impact had stunned him, but he was quick to react, and he spun and kicked out my legs from under me. I was knocked to the floor beside him and now had to contend with a very dangerous adversary in extremely close quarters.

Our first point of contention became my gun, which Rex was trying his best to twist free from my grip. It wasn't a bad idea on his part, as it was generally a good strategy to focus on the item most likely to kill you. But, it also made you vulnerable, because you could become overly focused and forget about other avenues of attack—point in fact being my next move. I used my leg to deliver an awkward but reasonably powerful kick to Rex's knee, and it hurt enough to make him release the pistol. It seemed like a really excellent move on my part until the fucker responded by slamming his elbow into my chest. It was a solid hit, and it knocked a fair amount of air from my lungs, so I needed to come up with a decent plan of action if I hoped to avoid another one. I therefore tossed my pistol across the room, where it skidded to a halt about fifteen feet away. Apparently, Rex thought this was a mistake on my part, because he smiled cruelly before he spoke.

"That was a bad move," he said.

"We'll see."

He tried to scramble across the floor for the gun, but I managed to get ahold of his ankle and lock it under my armpit in a figure four hold. Obviously, Rex thought that going for the gun was the correct strategic move, but I saw it as a direct insight into his skill set and potential weaknesses—namely hand to hand combat. All special operations guys learned unarmed techniques, but their primary goal on a mission was to get the job done, then get the hell out of Dodge. That meant going in with heavy firepower, shooting first, and asking questions later. There generally wasn't time or reason for fisticuffs. I, on the other hand, just happened to have been a bit of an oddity, as I'd loved and done martial arts from an early age and was just as happy to lose the gun in this instance and settle it empty handed—mano a mano.

With his leg locked up, I kicked out and caught him in the groin and doubled him over. Fighting through the pain, he rolled onto his back and returned the favor by using his other leg to land a kick to my chest that sent me backwards. This freed his ankle, and he scrambled onto his feet and made another break for my gun, but I managed to twist my legs around in time to catch him at the knees. With one leg in front and one in back, I rolled over and performed a take-down that put him face first onto the hard linoleum floor. From there, I kept my right leg in the crook of his knee and moved forward and trapped his foot against my waist. He tried to raise up and squirm free, but it was too late. I had him pinned and used that moment to land a hard punch to the base of his skull that sent his forehead smashing into the floor yet again. I repeated the punch two more times for good measure then released his leg and moved in to apply a proper blood choke. To his credit, Rex still had some fight in him and managed to roll away and struggle back up onto his feet, where he now had blood dribbling from his nose and flowing down his chin.

I got to my feet as well, and we stood toe to toe and squared off like a couple of fighters in a ring. He threw a feint with his left then followed with a nice right jab that just caught the edge of my jaw. He might not have been the best at hand to hand combat, but he could throw a decent punch. Happy to have landed a blow, he got reckless, however, and threw another, though this one was a big sweeping haymaker. I parried it with my left hand and caught it with my right with a move called a block-check-counter—only the counter was still to come. Continuing with the motion of his punch, I pulled him forward and into a low left hammer fist straight into his solar plexus. He doubled over, and I took hold of his head and delivered a brutal knee to his face in the hope that it would at last finish him off. Against all odds, he broke free and fired off a quick undercut straight into my solar plexus, and it nearly knocked all the wind from my lungs. I stepped back to catch my breath but kept my eyes on Rex, and I had to admit that I was more than a little surprised at his ability and drive to continue the fight. It was now abundantly clear how he had gotten into Delta Force—sheer inimitable force of will.

He decided to take advantage of the success of his last strike, and he stepped forward and threw another uppercut. This time, I brought both hands down to block, and the moment I had stopped its energy, I threw a right vertical fist into his solar plexus then immediately followed it up with a right side palm to the same target—the double blow being a purposeful attempt to knock the wind out of him. He was stunned and unable to respond, so I used that moment to throw an elbow up under the chin, and his head rolled back and was now clear for a back fist square on the nose. It impacted right on target and compounded his nose injury and clouded his vision. He wobbled on his feet with his eyes unable to focus, and I realized this goose was just about cooked.

I had one final move as the icing on the cake of his undoing, and, as he wavered ever so slightly back and forth, I stepped forward, rotated, and delivered a full power right spinning back kick to his solar plexus that sent him flying violently backward and onto the floor. It likely cracked his sternum and, more importantly, put him officially down for the count. Now, as placated and docile as a sleeping baby lamb, I zip tied his hands and feet and left him lying on his side in order to make sure that he didn't choke and die on his own bloody vomit, as Frank would surely need a roommate in prison. One down, hopefully one to go.

I performed a quick sweep of Rex and the room to make sure I didn't leave behind anything useful or dangerous that Rex might utilize if he woke up, and, with everything officially clear, I moved back to the stairs and began my final descent. Upon reaching the bottom level, I slowly opened the door and discovered a large dimly lit basement. In the middle there were a number of large steel shelves and occupying them were file boxes. Just beyond them I could see light emanating from the other side, and so I continued on past to a large open space. On one side, Frank was sitting at a desk behind a large computer screen while in the middle were the women, and all of them looked exactly as they had on the monitor. I waved, and all their eyes slowly turned to me, and I held a lone finger up to my lips to make sure they didn't stir. As long as Frank held on to that phone, we were all in extreme danger. I slipped closer to the ladies and pondered cutting all their zip ties so that they could get up and quietly leave but unfortunately discovered that all of their feet were shackled to a long line of chain that was bolted into the floor. Apparently, Frank and Rex had thought of everything.

I therefore needed to take care of Frank first, but that would entail crossing the room as silently as possible, so that he didn't see me before I could get ahold of that fucking phone. I crept forward on the balls of my feet and controlled my breathing and beating heart, and while the distance was only feet it felt like miles. Thankfully, Frank was engrossed in his computer and oblivious to my presence, as he typed away and looked at the various screens, spreadsheets, and websites. To the right of the keyboard, and only inches from his hand, was the phone he had brandished earlier. There it was. My Holy Grail and the key to the end of this entire mess. With my eye on the prize, I continued on, but when I was only twenty feet away, Frank clicked on an icon, and up came a window that showed one of the security cameras views. It was from one of the outside cameras and looked over the main entrance, which was, of course, deserted at the moment. He clicked his mouse yet again, and a new camera view replaced it. I moved ever closer and watched as he continued clicking and cycling through all the views. When I was within a few feet and about to reach for the phone, he clicked once more, and there I was on the screen. Frank instantly grabbed the phone and backed away from the desk, with his expression looking harried and manic.

"Finn! How in the hell did you find us?" he bellowed angrily.

"I have a built in asshole detector, and it led me right to you."

He looked at the pistol in my hand nervously then held up the phone and smiled as he played his thumb over the green button that activated the bomb.

"Nothing's changed. I click this, and they die."

"And so will you."

"Maybe."

"I'll make sure of it."

"Then you too would ultimately die trying to save them."

"Of course—so that others may live. That's my credo."

"I must say, Finn, you really have surprised me. I'd heard the story of how you saved John in Afghanistan, but people tend to exaggerate their old war stories. I know I did."

"For better or worse, I never needed to, but let's stay focused on the present, Frank. No one has to die. Let's be sensible and talk about this and see if we can come to some kind of peaceful resolution."

He thought for a moment.

"Maybe, but first you have to drop the gun, or I swear to god I'll press the button."

"OK, fine just relax, and I'll set it on the floor."

"No tricks!"

"No tricks," I responded.

I set the Beretta down and looked calmly at Frank.

"Happy?" I asked.

"Yeah, but I'll be even happier when you kick it out of reach."

I kicked it across the floor, and Frank relaxed and smiled.

"Wow, you are far too trusting. That was extremely stupid for someone of your supposed intelligence and abilities," he said, as he suddenly pulled a pistol out of his jacket.

He walked over and picked up my gun then started moving towards the door on the opposite side of the room, all the while keeping the pistol and his eyes trained on me.

"Where do you think you're going, Frank?"

"Retirement," he said, smiling.

"I don't think so."

"Who's going to stop me. I hold all the cards."

"I always keep an ace in the hole," I said, as I slid Rex's SIG out of my waistband and pointed it right between Frank's eyes.

He looked terrified, but he still managed to lift the phone and hold his thumb directly over the button.

"Don't do it, Frank!" I yelled.

"Goodbye, Finn. It certainly wasn't a pleasure."

He pressed the button, and the digital display showed thirty seconds then began counting down. Sweet mother of God. Why can't it ever be easy? Frank suddenly turned and started running, so I fired a warning shot in the hope that it would slow him down. It more or less worked, because he ducked in behind some metal filing cabinets then managed to fire back. I dove for cover but popped back up and fired yet another warning shot, and it sent him back behind the filing cabinets. A second later, he leaned out and fired his gun repeatedly, and, while his shots were wild, I still took cover behind the shelves. When he ran out of ammo, he took off running, but this time I aimed carefully and winged him in his left leg and sent him sprawling onto his stomach. He struggled onto his feet and continuing hobbling towards the door.

"Frank, hit the stop button!" I yelled, as I ran over to him.

He continued on, somehow believing he was still going to get away.

"Goddammit, Frank!"

Just as I caught up to him, he turned around to face me, brandishing his phone.

"I still have this!" he said.

"It's over! Stop the countdown."

"Fuck you."

I reached for the phone, but he turned and struggled like a child trying to keep hold of his favorite toy. I suppose he had a different plan now and had decided that if he couldn't get away, then he would die killing us all. Fed up with his ridiculous tantrum, I punched him in the stomach, and he released his grip and finally allowed me to take hold of the phone. I hit the cancel button, but the timer kept counting down. Ten, nine, eight...

"Frank! Why isn't it stopping!"

"I—I don't know."

"Come on, Frank. You need to help me here! Why isn't it stopping!" I said, slapping him across the face.

"I don't know. I swear!" he cried out.

The countdown continued as I furiously hit the button. Five, four, three…

"I'll see you in hell, you son of a bitch," I said, accepting my fate and preparing to die with my greatest failure being that I had let the others down.

Two, one…

In a last moment of rage, I smashed the phone into the floor, and the timer screen cracked and froze on the number zero. I turned my gaze to Violet and the others, and my heart was breaking as I waited for the explosion and, in turn, the great beyond. Nothing happened, and I waited some more, imagining the countdown sequence was somehow like a car's fuel tank and perhaps held a small amount of time in reserve. Still, nothing happened, and, after a full minute, I stood up gingerly and wondered if perhaps the bomb had suffered a glitch and might still explode at any moment. My radio suddenly chirped, and the noise sent a jolt of fear through my entire body, then, a second later, I heard Beeber.

"What's the situation over?" he asked.

"Roger, what's the situation?" John chimed in a second later.

"Yeah, what's the situation?" Dave also asked.

"I'm not sure. I recovered the phone and hit the cancel button, but the countdown still continued to zero, so I'm afraid it might still go off at any second," I said.

"Oh yeah," Beeber said.

"Oh yeah what?" I asked.

"Oh yeah that makes sense—because we already overrode his phone's connection and deactivated the bomb, which is why the counter continued to zero."

"And just when the fuck did you do that?" I asked with my ire rising.

"I don't know—about five minutes ago?"

"Did you know that I have been fighting for my life and the lives of all your loved ones for the last five minutes and could have desperately used that little piece of information?"

"Well excuse us for diffusing the bomb."

"Wait a minute—what the fuck have you been doing for the last five minutes?"

There was no response.

"Well?" I asked.

"Um—discussing our D&D game."

"Remind me to slap both of you across the face right before I kiss you and buy you assholes a drink."

"Will do," Beeber said.

"OK, all clear. Send in the cavalry," I said.

I picked up the Beretta then checked on Frank's leg wound. It wasn't serious, so he'd live until he was placed in a nice prison cell, where he would spend his retirement without the luxury he was expecting. I then set about freeing the ladies and fortunately found the key to the leg cuffs in Frank's desk. I released their ankles, snipped the cable ties holding their hands, then removed the duct tape from their mouths, and the girls, happy to be free, immediately jumped up and encircled me in a massive group hug. John, Corn, and the others walked in at exactly that moment, and, a second later, Beeber's squeaky voice came over the radio.

"What's going on?" he asked excitedly.

"Well, Finn is being showered with affection from all of our ladies," Corn responded into his radio.

"Goddammit! He always gets the girl," Beeber whined.

"You mean girls," John corrected.

"Fucking Finn," Beeber said.

"Excuse me, ladies, but this was a team effort," John said, in his commanding politician's voice.

The group hug broke up, and each girl moved to their respective man, except Rachel, who borrowed my radio in order to talk to Beeber.

"Don't worry, I know you helped, Beebsy Deebsy Do," she said.

"What did you call him?" I asked.

"Nothing," I heard Beeber say over the radio.

"Oh, I wouldn't call that little pet name nothing," I said.

"Thanks a lot, Rachel," Beebs said, with legitimate dread in his voice.

Sandra and her contingent of Secret Service came in and took over the scene, and her first action was to come over and talk to us.

"Well, folks, we can clean up here while you get back to the resort. You have a wedding to plan after all."

"Thanks, Sandra," John said.

Everyone walked upstairs to the main level and headed

outside to where there was a temporary command station set up by the Secret Service. Frank and Rex were just being loaded into an ambulance, and Frank looked over at us with his eyes seething with rage.

"Get well soon," I yelled.

He raised his hand and gave us the finger and held it aloft until the paramedics closed the two back doors. At that moment, Dave came walking up and hugged Violet before turning his attention to me.

"Dude, I'm still not happy about my Han Job shirt or you dating Violet, but you fucking came through and did a good job—in spite of having been Air Force."

"Thanks, Dave, and you also did OK in spite of the fact that you were a pussy-ass Army Ranger."

He smiled and we shook hands, though this time no one tried to crush the other's digits, and that was some serious progress. We all loaded up into the Rothster and headed off towards the resort. A little ways down the road, I looked over at John and smiled.

"Well, Sasquatch, I guess you're just going to have to get married and become the president after all."

"I guess so," he said, as he took hold of Jessica's hand, and the two shared a smile as they gazed into each other's eyes.

Violet, meanwhile, reached over and took hold of my hand.

"I guess you got my signal," she said.

"Yeah, and we can all thank you for this happy ending."

"No problem, and I'll be sure to give you one hell of a

happy ending when we get back to the resort."

"What could be happier than this?"

"Oh, you'll see."

"In case you've forgotten, I'm still here," Dave said.

Everyone enjoyed a little laugh, and we continued along in the Rothster, with everyone, except perhaps Dave, feeling pretty damn good about how the night turned out.

CHAPTER THIRTY
Holy Fucking Matrimony

It was yet another beautiful day in Paradise with the sun just overhead and a warm breeze blowing in off of the beautiful blue Pacific Ocean. We were down beside the resort's private beach beneath a great canopy of tropical flowers, and Corn was to my right, and John was to my left, and all those in attendance were awaiting the arrival of the blushing bride. I pulled out the flask I had prepared for just this occasion and offered John his final drink as a single man. It was Soft Taco Island's Premium Reserve Rum, and Babineux had brought it all the way from his island distillery just for the occasion. John took a sip, then me, then Corn, and the three of us stood there smiling like schoolboys.

It was hard to believe we were finally here, considering all the events of this past week. Seven days ago Jessica was accused of murdering her ex-husband, and only two days ago we were finally able to prove her innocence and thwart Frank Williams's evil plan. Yesterday, John had officially announced that he was running for president, and today Frank, Melissa, Rex, and his men were all officially indicted on charges of murder, extortion, as well as conspiracy and several others. Frank's son was apparently an unknowing accomplice, as he believed that his special effects work was merely part of an elaborate prank. If that turned out to be true, he would likely survive the legal storm with a simple slap on the wrist.

Interestingly, it was only now that we could at last put together all the pieces of this veritable poi predicament. Technically, it all started ten years ago when John cancelled his marriage plans with Melissa, but the real catalyst that would set everything in motion was his announcement that he was engaged to Jessica. Realizing his political dynasty was officially never going to happen, Frank and his daughter put into action their plan for ultimate revenge.

It began with Frank's knowledge of Jessica's abortion. As the head of John's campaign, it was his job to know about any and all skeletons that might creep out of the closet at an inopportune moment, and he used the information to put together a secret blackmail plot. It was easy to lure in Jessica's douche of an ex-husband Steven Green with promises of a great deal of money, and Steven, at Frank's insistence, then sent the extortion letter and traveled to Hawaii, thus setting in place the first stone of the pyramid of lies that they would build to undue John's upcoming marriage and, in turn, his run for the presidency.

Step two of the plot then took a rather unceremonious turn when Roofie Rudy poisoned the poi. Frank and his team had a very tight timeline to follow and this was an attempt to make sure that all the post wedding festivities ended in a timely manner. No one stayed up late partying when they were metaphorically chained to a toilet by diarrhea. The second part of step two occurred when Rudy dosed Jessica's drink with Ruphinol, and, with Jessica down for the count, the conspirators had all the time they needed for step three, which consisted of constructing an airtight chain of evidence. It started with Melissa dressing as a maid and delivering the cart that was carrying the test-fire chamber. Once in the room, she proceeded to hold a very drugged Jessica's hand and fire her Beretta into the test chamber in order to ensure a positive gunpowder residue test. Then, Melissa, wearing Jessica's shoes and sweatshirt, walked through the hotel to Steven's room, where she stood by as Rex expertly shot a sedated Steven with Jessica's Beretta—which, incidentally, had been smuggled to Hawaii in a diplomatic pouch carried by Rex himself. So, due to Rex's expert gun handling, the perfectly placed shot allowed for the bullet to remain intact and create yet another piece of damning evidence.

With Steven dead, they doused the incriminating sweatshirt in his blood, and Melissa donned it and returned to Jessica's room, which also explained why none of Jessica's other clothes had blood spatter. The conspirators then departed, and Rex went out and placed the gun in the designated spot on the reef where Danny Keahi would find it in the coming hours. Lastly, Frank made a call to the Governor, who, as it turned out, had no idea he was actually helping to facilitate murder and extortion. With everything in place, the conspirators sat back and watched as their evil plot unfolded perfectly to plan, but, unfortunately for Frank and his team, humans were imperfect creatures, and their failings, however subtle, made their plot unravel piece by piece.

Of course, certain mistakes were only now obvious in hindsight, and the first and most obvious one was Frank's call to the governor. Apparently caught up in the excitement of his evil plot, he mistakenly called in his favor to the governor before the crime had even been reported. It was a silly rookie error, but it was often the little details that unraveled complex conspiracies. There was also another less obvious mistake, and it occurred when I had called Frank from Walther's ranch to ask for help. The problem was that, in the confusion and stress of the moment, I never actually gave Frank the address, nor did he ask for it—because he obviously knew exactly where we were, because his people were currently there trying to kill us. Additionally, that Air National guard helicopter that supposedly flew up to rescue us was nothing more than a pickup for Rex and his men.

All in all, they had a good plan, but they never imagined that my unusual team and I would somehow sift through their lies, and, in the course of a week, thwart their dastardly plans. Now, the villains were in jail, and the victors were free to celebrate, and what better way than an oceanside wedding.

Standing here at this moment, I felt that I was a part of something great—something that might change the world for the better. This was the first potential president that I truly knew to be a good and just man, and I was proud that I helped him get this far. It was funny to think that it all started back in Afghanistan ten plus years ago and led all the way here to Hawaii—to this very alter. At that moment, the same guitar player who joined us on the beach four nights ago, began doing yet another lovely rendition of Iz's Somewhere over the Rainbow, and, shortly thereafter, Jessica came walking down the aisle, and she looked absolutely beautiful in her wedding dress as her father proudly led her to the alter. She came to a stop beside John, who was glowing with happiness as he looked at his bride to be. Jessica glanced over at me and smiled then silently mouthed the words thank you, and I returned the gesture by mouthing the words your welcome. The reverend officially began the ceremony, and, soon thereafter, I was handing John the rings. They each slid one onto the other's finger, and they were officially declared man and wife then exchanged a long loving kiss while the audience cheered enthusiastically.

I gazed out over the wedding guests and had to smile. It was quite an interesting group, and probably the most unique of any potential president in the history of the United States. There were, of course, fellow politicians, colleagues, family, and friends, but there were also a number of unusual guests—namely Violet, Beeber, Doug, Rachel, Special Agent Dave Moore, and Johnny Kamoahoa, Lou, and Jimmy—the three locals who were more than willing to put their lives on the line for a bunch of crazy *haoles* trying to thwart a diabolical murder and extortion conspiracy. It was in this special moment, surrounded by all these special people, that I had an epiphany. I had always seen life as a great chain of chaos in which all of us were just variables traveling through the universe and bouncing in and out of each other's lives with our paths random and our futures constantly changing. But, now, seeing how all of us came together to unite these two, I truly understood that the sum was indeed greater than its parts, and perhaps we all did have a greater purpose in this life and that our existence was meaningful, and we were at some level facilitating a better future and, in turn, a better world.

John and Jessica began their ceremonial walk back up the aisle, and everyone clapped, and suddenly I felt a surge of emotion that made tears form in the corners of my eyes. Corn looked over at me then gave me a soft elbow.

"Are you crying?" he asked.

"No, are you?"

"Maybe a little."

"Yeah, me too."

"They grow up so fast," he said.

"They do indeed."

He put his arm around me, and we stood there gazing in

wonder as our friends walked up the aisle and likely into the history books of our great nation as the next president and first lady of the United States.

TAG FINN WILL BE CONTINUING HIS ADVENTURES IN

CHALUPA CONUNDRUM

Private investigator Tag Finn, a former special operations soldier and member of the CIA's elite Special Activities Division, is having a nice quiet evening at home until his phone rings, and he answers it to hear the voice of his beloved ex-girlfriend Estelle pleading for his help. She abruptly screams, the line goes dead, and the next morning Finn learns that Estelle and her entire group of UCLA archeologists have gone missing from their dig site at the mysterious Chalupa Ruins in Costa Rica. Due to Finn's current occupation and unusual background, UCLA's dean of archeology hires him to oversee the search for the missing team, and he heads down to Central America, where he is joined by beautiful local archeologist Dr. Alessandra Hitzig. Together, they will venture into the primeval jungle to the Chalupa ruins and be caught between myth and reality when they unwittingly face off against a thousand year old ghost king and his army of undead warriors as well as a ruthless billionaire businessman intent on acquiring the land around the site.

Thrills, chills, spills, and indeed some sexual frills await, so come along with Finn and his beautiful new colleague on this incredible adventure where they must use every ounce of their cunning if they hope to solve the ever deepening mystery that is the Chalupa Conundrum.

THE MANTASY SERIES:

SOFT TACO ISLAND

TOPLESS AGENDA

GORDITA CONSPIRACY

MR PICKLES

STRIPPER BOAT

POI PREDICAMENT

CHALUPA CONUNDRUM

PROMETHEUS PROTOCOL

ACKNOWLEDGEMENTS

I suspect every writer has a large list of people who make their work possible, and mine begins with my wife, who hears every one of my idiotic ideas and gives her opinion freely and without fear that I might get offended and stop helping with the housework. Next, would be my editors, Ruth A. Bright, Chris Cooper, and Aria Pearson who have generously given their time to comb the book for mistakes and keep me grammatically, if not politically or morally correct. After editors, comes my army of proof-readers, namely Matt Zeeman, Chris Imlay, Bob Horton, Katherine Gundling, and Jason Bright. Following them is my family, especially my father Fred Christie, who has always believed in my artistic endeavors and supported them both figuratively and literally. Next would be my mother Jane Christie (Posthumously), who definitely played a roll in my odd sense of humor. Also in the family category, is my pushy sister Sheree Wilson who helped get me into a posh New York Literary Agency, as well as my less pushy sister, Shelly Hall. From there, it continues on to two special friends who helped in a very unusual way, namely securing the Macbook Pro laptop that I would use to write while incarcerated at Stanford Hospital. Those two generous souls, inadvertently responsible for the proliferation of the Mantasy Genre, are Michele and Dan Scanlon. Next is my oldest friend and layout expert Chris Imlay followed by Dianna Woods, Jimmy and Jodie Woods, Robert O'Brien, all of whom have been willing to suffer through early drafts, mistakes, inaccuracies, and a vast number of unusual sexual metaphors.

Another special thank you goes out to Greg Owens, good friend and international man of business acumen, who passed on the following advice from his mentor George Leonard—take the hit. Which means: should you ever be sidelined with something such as five years of cancer treatment, do something positive with the time—in my case writing a bunch of escapist, erotic, adventure novels.

I'd also like to thank Mike Rowe and his Dirty Jobs show, as well as Jeremy Clarkson, James May, and Richard Hammond and their show Top Gear (which is now more or less the Grand Tour on Amazon), as they helped make many, many—many hours in isolation bearable. After leaving the hospital, I had a new immune system and more or less was the equivalent of an adult toddler and therefore had to avoid the public and all of the requisite germs. To that end, I was home all day every day, and the only way to keep from going totally bonzo when I was writing was to have a show on in the background. My two favorites were Dirty Jobs on the Discovery Channel and Top Gear online, and both shows provided the prefect inspiration for me to create a wacky escapist book series. So, to both entities and all those involved—you have my gratitude!

My final word of thanks goes out to my vast martial arts community, all of whom helped keep me alive and well throughout the dark days of cancer treatment. At the top of that group, and requiring special thanks, are Matt Thomas, Rick Alemany, and Margaret Alemany whose wisdom and teaching helped inspire many of the techniques in the book. Beyond them and within our own karate community is Lauren and Rob Sandusky, Thandi Guile, Aria and Daniel Pearson, Tom Jacoby and Jennifer Solow, John Hedlund, Michele & Dan Scanlon, Katherine Gundling, Bob Horton, Sue Fox and J.T. Meade, Mark, Matt, Brad, and Jade Zeeman, Ted Hatch, James Parks, Jeremy Holt and the Holt Family, Sabrina Haechler, Jonathan Johnson, Brannon Beliso, Catherine and Eric Engelbrecht, Catherine and Ian Moore, Tamera Blake, the families and students of Christie Kenpo Karate, Michael Mason MD, Natalya Greyz MD, Sally Arai MD, and the Stanford University BMT Unit & ITA. If you don't see your name here, don't worry—there is a more comprehensive list of the karate community on the Thank You page of my website.

To all of you, I say be well—and more importantly—dump well.

ORIGIN OF THE MANTASY GENRE

In 2010, I was diagnosed with Stage 4 Non-Hodgkins T-Cell Lymphoma Cancer, and, with only weeks before my imminent demise, began rigorous dose dense chemotherapy. With an extremely low survival rate, about one in five, I was particularly lucky to achieve a full remission in just over two months. I went on to receive a stem cell, and eventual bone marrow transplant at Stanford University, the last procedure being the most effective treatment for a lifelong cure.

So, what exactly does a person do when faced with extreme isolation and the fear of a potentially premature demise? Well, I started reading Harry Potter and filled many long hours hooked up to a chemo drip, spending my time with the life and adventures of the boy who lived—hoping, in my case, to be the man who survived. There aren't many books more removed from the doldrums of cancer, so it became the perfect escape. The problem, however, was that I tore through them so quickly that I was soon on my own again—desperately in need of something to fill my long, anxiety filled days.

I tried several popular novels and authors I liked but couldn't find anything to adequately fill the endless hours of isolation. Of course, I could have wallowed in self pity, but I really didn't want the months of downtime to be meaningless. If I was forced to sit around like a piece of shit, then I wanted to do something with the time. I immediately decided that I should turn my screenplay writing skills into the ultimate, tell-all cancer book, but, five pages in, I realized the topic was too depressing and decided to instead write a novel. It was going to be the book I desperately wanted to read and would include all the things I lacked at that moment—namely sex, alcohol, adventure, travel, and privacy in the bathroom—the key elements for a truly rewarding existence.

I finished chemo at Kaiser then headed south to the Stanford University Hospital and quickly realized that I would have nothing but a window and the internet for a companion in the coming months. Worse still were the medical horrors that would soon become a part of my daily existence. My morning nurse, concerned about the debilitating physical effects of intense chemo, entered my room each day with the following words:

"What would you like me to check first? Your balls or your butt hole?"

"Um—neither?" I responded.

At that point, all I desired went into my writing, first and foremost being a little privacy in the ol' baño. The nurses had an annoying habit of always wanting to weigh my stools—something to do with keeping track of fluid and food intake and the subsequent amount of release. My bathroom contained what I called the cowboy hat, a plastic insert to catch waste entering the toilet. Peeing in the little urinal was enough indignity, so whenever possible, I woke up early and dumped before they could make their rounds. Every day that I sent a number two un-accosted down the drain was a small, though cherished victory. I felt like a prisoner—a veritable Count of Monte Cristo, though my prison was a hospital and my battles were waged over porcelain.

Continuing with the theme of writing about all I lacked meant that the book would sizzle with sex, adventure, and humor. Three months later, I would complete book one and within the year, finish two more—completing what I called at the time, The Mantasy Trilogy—the word Mantasy, being the combination of Male and Fantasy. The following year, I managed to write five more follow ups, all with the same character and eccentricities but with new and exciting storylines and locations. Now, I had a Mantasy Series. Or, if I wanted to follow in Douglas Adam's footsteps, I would say—books four, five, six, seven, and eight in the Mantasy Trilogy. I'm currently finishing books nine, ten, and eleven.

Writing has always been one of my great loves but sadly, it took a life threatening illness to bring us back together full-time. I have written a number of screenplays and had two optioned for motion pictures, but traditional writing is more complicated and requires a hell of a lot more work. It is, however, more rewarding because you have the ability to deliver your story directly to an audience, whether it's your friends, the woman at the Post Office, or the thousands of potential readers trolling the online eBooks. It doesn't need a fifty million dollar budget, a production team, distribution, and funding for it to reach an audience—and that is pretty awesome.

ABOUT THE AUTHOR

Lyle Christie was born in San Francisco, raised in Marin County, and attended the University of Kentfield, San Francisco State University, the Academy of Art College, and Dominican University, where he majored in film and social psychology, and minored in Philosophy, Anthropology, and Human Sexuality—all of which gave him the diverse educational background to become a writer and director. In addition, he holds a fifth degree black belt and teaches Kenpo Karate, Jujitsu, Arnis, and Wing Chun. During his lifetime in the martial arts, he has taught civilians as well as police and military personnel and has the unique pleasure of training with elite members of the United States and international defense and intelligence community.

He also teaches firearms, swords, sticks, and knives, though he is equally deadly with the nunchaku, machete, goat, tether ball, and skin flute—the last perhaps being his greatest skill set. Above all else, he maintains excellent, if not grey, hair and lives aboard a yacht in Sausalito with his wife, French Bulldog, and Miniature Dachshund. When he's not writing, directing, teaching martial arts, or training with the real life James Bonds of the world, you'll find him fighting injustice, cherishing a number two, working out, or riding his mountain bike through the scenic hills of Marin County.

You can learn more at www.lylechristie.com.